The Reunion

BETH REEKLES

SPHERE

SPHERE

First published in Great Britain in 2024 by Sphere

1 3 5 7 9 10 8 6 4 2

Copyright © Beth Reekles 2024

The moral right of the author has been asserted.

*All characters and events in this publication, other than those
clearly in the public domain, are fictitious and any resemblance
to real persons, living or dead, is purely coincidental.*

A CIP catalogue record for this book is available from the British Library.

ISBN 978-1-4087-3023-2

Typeset in Caslon 540 LT Std by Palimpsest Book Production Limited,
Falkirk, Stirlingshire

Printed and bound in Great Britain by Clays Ltd, Elcograf S.p.A.

Papers used by Sphere are from well-managed
forests and other responsible sources.

Sphere
An imprint of
Little, Brown Book Group
Carmelite House
50 Victoria Embankment
London EC4Y 0DZ

An Hachette UK Company
www.hachette.co.uk

www.littlebrown.co.uk

Also by Beth Reekles

The Kissing Booth YA series
The Kissing Booth
The Beach House
Going the Distance
Road Trip!
One Last Time

Other YA novels
The Summer Switch-Off
Sincerely Yours, Anna Sherwood

Adult novels
It Won't Be Christmas Without You
Love, Locked Down
Faking It

For my friends. Most likely to . . . have GREAT taste in books.

Tisdale Leavers 2014

Stephanie O'Connell

Posted Wednesday 17th April 2024

Hi everybody! Long time no speak! Hope everybody's doing well – just wanted to share this ol' thing I found on an old USB stick. It's our leavers' assembly presentation! All our 'most likely to' lists and fun memories – and tons of photos of us ten years ago! How cute is that?! Anyway, just thought I'd share as I got a real kick out of it ☺☺☺ xx

Attachment: LEAVERS ASSEMBLY DIGITAL YEARBOOK_ CLASS OF 14

Shaun Michaels *Wow! What a throwback! This is so fab, thanks for sharing, Steph! LOL, look how young we all were!*

Bryony A *omg, love this*

Ashleigh Easton *shut tf up, Steph, this is hilarious. @Hayden Vaughn, you seen this?*

  Hayden Vaughn *I have now!!*

1

Hayden Vaughn *Awesome find, S! Those old pics of you and Shaun are adorable. I've been back in town a bit helping my mum clear out the house, so weird driving past the school all these years later.*

Bryony A *omg bet, I totally thought the same last time I passed by. If you're in town @Hayden Vaughn, we should hang! I'm around for a while, my next movie doesn't start filming for a couple of weeks*

Stephanie O'Connell *Ooh let me know if you do, I can come visit my parents and see you guys at the same time! It'll be like a cute little reunion!*

Bryony A *WAIT NO WE SHOULD TOTALLY HAVE SOME KIND OF REUNION*

> **Shaun Michaels** *@Bryony A, don't even get her started – you know what Steph's like, she'll have a big party organised for the entire year group before you know it!*
> **Stephanie O'Connell** *Ugh, I would if I had the time! Between work and getting my degree part time – not to mention a wedding to plan!!!*
> **Shaun Michaels** *You don't have to tell me twice* ☺

Ryan Lawal *yoooo, somebody say reunion? I'm down.*

Hayden Vaughn *Pls nobody let Ryan organise a reunion. If prom was anything to go by, we'll all be legless after the first glass of spiked punch, idk if I have that kind of alcohol tolerance these days*

Ashleigh Easton *buddy you didn't have that kind of alcohol tolerance in *those* days either.*

Ryan Lawal *pfft like you're one to talk, Easton. regular party animal over here*

Ashleigh Easton *Not all of us needed booze to compensate for a distinct lack of personality.*

Ryan Lawal *hey those are my friends you're insulting. don't listen to her, lads* 😬

Ashleigh Easton *Piss off, Ryan.*

Ryan Lawal *such a way with words still . . . can totally see why you won that essay competition in Year 12 you never let anyone forget about.*

Ashleigh Easton *File under things *I* never forgot about: that I need to use only small words to communicate with you.*

Hayden Vaughn *Guys, please. I haven't had this many Facebook notifications in years. Stop.*

Bryony A *Yeah, take it to the DMs you two* ☺

Ryan Lawal *she started it*

Ashleigh Easton *He started it.*

Ryan Lawal *HA! beat ya to it!*

Ashleigh Easton *@Bryony A, didn't you do some drama workshops at the school last year or something? Think they'd let us use the hall for a get-together?*

Bryony A *I know some people. I'm sure I can make it happen xo*

Stephanie O'Connell *Yayyyy! Bryony, you're a lifesaver! This is going to be so cute!* ☺☺☺

Ryan Lawal *star of stage and screen to the rescue! yes, Bryony! see you tossers there* ☺

108 more comments . . .

Chapter One

Bryony

'Most Likely to Become Famous'

There are few people I truly loathe in this world, but Steph O'Connell and her sparking the idea for this school reunion is one of them. I'm a close second on the list, right now, for going along with it all.

The balloon-arch delivery guy is competing to take my second-place spot, though, after shrugging his shoulders and saying that the assembly 'isn't part of his job' and meaning that I'm spending my free period at the end of the day wrestling with hundreds of blue and silver and white balloons, tying them to the framework of an arch per the YouTube tutorial I've just found.

'You know,' says Yaz, one of the history teachers, who started here around the same time as I did, 'considering you're seeing all your old schoolmates and hosting an epic party tonight, you don't look very excited about it.'

'Oh, no. What gave you that impression? I'm super excited.'

The words slip out with a growl – an actual, honest-to-God growl – as I wrangle a bunch of balloons into place on the wire frame. Yaz just laughs. She must put my stress down to the last-minute change in schedule to deal with the decorations because she just says, 'B, relax, it's gonna be fine. Everybody's going to love it. Plus, you know – it's in the school hall. They're hardly expecting the Oscars, are they?'

That's exactly the problem though, and I can't bear to explain it to Yaz. I have a sneaking suspicion she has her *own* sneaking suspicions about me, but admitting it out loud is . . . Ugh. A full-on shiver rolls down my spine. It's unthinkable. Unconscionable.

I didn't intend to be the one organising the entire reunion, but somehow it ended up like that after I mentioned I could help out and then suddenly half the damn year group were jumping on the bandwagon, thanking me for arranging it . . . Steph was always in charge of stuff like that when we were in school. Even bloody Ashleigh used to organise talent shows and fundraisers and things. I just showed up, the life and soul of the party.

But I guess that was a long time ago, and we're all different people now.

For example, Steph is not the defacto organiser extraordinaire anymore. The rugby lads have proper jobs now. Trendy Elise from my A-level English lit class spent three years living on a farm in New Zealand. And I am a liar.

Something surges up from my stomach to sting the back of my throat, hot and acidic and violent. I think it might be shame, but the thought spooks me so much I decide to call it plain old 'panic' instead.

It's okay, though. It's just one night. I've been – well, not

6

lying, exactly, but . . . vaguely untruthful, for years on my social media. That's *way* more difficult to maintain than breezing through a few face-to-face interactions, especially when everybody will show up with such a solid preconceived notion of who Bryony Adams is these days.

They'll show up expecting glamour, and glitz, exactly as would be befitting of a starlet like myself. Fun stories of times I bumped into hotshot actors and rubbed shoulders with household names, tales of parties and places they can only imagine. It's – just another role to act. That's all.

And I can do that.

No, you can't, and that's why you're scrambling to save face.

I shove the nasty little thought aside and take a deep breath. I can't let intrusive thoughts like that win. Not today. I have to get into character. I have to *become* the Bryony they're all expecting me to be. The one I've been touting online for the last ten years.

Yaz and I finish up the balloon arch, swapping gossip about the maths teachers who are shagging and think they're being subtle about it, whinging about our Year Nines who have totally checked out now they're dropping our subjects come September, and gloating about the Year Eleven prank to hide dead fish in the staffroom that got scuppered thanks to Yaz overhearing some boys plotting by the bike shed when she was on duty the other lunchtime. It's enough to take my mind off anything except my mental checklist of party preparations, and I'm glad she was free to help me out so I'm not left alone with my own thoughts and guilt.

(Panic. *Panic*, not guilt.)

Between the two of us, the hall is transformed. The

caretakers cleared away the rows of chairs for school assemblies earlier and, without them, the space is bigger than I ever realised. A cheap, synthetic roll of red carpet runs from the double doors to the centre of the stage. The balloon arch, finally complete but ever so slightly wonky, is set against a stretch of blank wall with a box of photo-booth supplies next to it – cardboard glasses, feather boas, moustaches on sticks, the lot. There's a long trestle table set up, with packs of paper cups and plates ready to go. I'll bring the snacks and soft drinks in later, and the dinner ladies are generously making a vat of fruit punch they'll leave out for the party. Yaz and I arrange a few chairs I asked the caretakers to leave behind into small groups, rather than the strict interlinked rows they'd usually form. There's a guest book, and a box of felt-tips and markers I borrowed from the geography department – although how many of them actually *work* is anyone's guess.

As a finishing touch, I Blu-Tack posters up around the hall, covering some of the displays and the windows with them. I've printed out all the 'Most Likely To's from our old digital yearbook. I've got a slideshow to put up, but this will be fun too.

And, most importantly, it means that right now, I get to stick a piece of paper over the big *MEET OUR STAFF!* board, where there is a passport-sized photo of my face smiling out from the position of Head of Drama.

I cover an entire section of the board with a large print-out of eighteen-year-old me striding across the stage in this very hall dressed up in gingham for my role as Dorothy in the school play that summer. For a second, I let my fingers trail over the edge of the photo. The memory of that performance is so visceral I can feel the chafe of cheap tulle against my legs, hear the cheers of the standing ovation I got. It felt like the beginning of the rest of my life.

My eyes drift from the photo to the words above it. My name, my predicted future.

Most likely to become famous.

Yeah, right.

Chapter Two

Steph

'Most Likely to End Up Together'

'Sweetie, are you almost ready? We're meant to be leaving in fifteen minutes!'

'Uh-huh!' he yells back from the bathroom, and I hear the shower start up.

I can't help but huff a laugh and roll my eyes, and my reflection in my childhood vanity unit is grinning back at me. She looks giddy and lovestruck, because *of course* he knows how much time he has to get ready – based not on when we're supposed to leave, but on how far through *my* routine I am.

In fairness, I've only just started my eye makeup. He's got time.

As I blend in some sparkly bronze eyeshadow and catch sight of the dress laid out on the bed behind me, excitement fizzes through me. I feel like I've just necked an entire glass of Prosecco in one go. There's something oddly familiar about this whole thing: shutting myself up in my room while the noise of Mum and Dad watching telly downstairs drifts through the thin walls of the house; a new party dress just waiting to be worn while I paint my face for the evening and think of all the things I want to tell my friends.

It's been *years* since I saw most of the girls from school. There are a couple I stay in touch with sporadically, but considering I haven't thought much about these people in the last ten years beyond liking their Instagrams or commenting *congratulations!* on the big life updates they share on Facebook, I suddenly can't wait to hug them and hear every detail of their lives. I wonder if Thea ever got over Josh cheating on her *for a whole year*, or if it wrecked her trust in men and that's why she doesn't seem to have settled down now; why Priya got a dog with her partner even though she always said she was allergic; if Morgan came around to like being a doctor when we all know her parents pushed her into doing a medicine degree.

I wonder what they'll think of me. If they miss me, like I realise I've missed them.

There's a photo tucked into the frame of my mirror, faded from the sunlight that's been at it in the last ten years, of me and the girls on holiday. Seven of us stand in a tight group in front of some random club, arms wound around each other's waists and shoulders, all of us in skimpy outfits and sky-high heels, glitter and neon paint covering our skin ready for the rave we plan to go to later in the night.

I smile, looking at it, and it's easy to envisage us all now as more mature adults, sitting around with bottomless mimosas over brunch – every bit as raucous and vibrant as we were back then. Maybe I'll suggest it. I *do* love a Sunday brunch with the girlies, to be fair, and unless their personalities have taken a complete one-eighty in the last decade, I think the old gang would like it, too.

There are other photos around my room, remnants of a former life. There's a string of Polaroids strung above my bed, most of which are more pictures from that group holiday after we finished school. Tickets from bands that everyone went to see, or cinema tickets kept special from dates with Shaun – memories that teenage me felt it was so important to preserve – are pinned to a corkboard that would occasionally host a revision timetable; there are a couple of photos from my time at uni and a giant poster of Edward Cullen on the wardrobe door I never could quite bring myself to take down.

There's something surreal about the familiarity of my old bedroom. I know that pink duvet so well – remember picking it out of the Argos catalogue one time – and I could feel my way around in the dark no problem. One of the plugs by the bedside table doesn't work and if you don't close the curtains just so, they'll slip open, let the light in and wake you up too early. I know every inch of this room – but it's like a well-preserved relic. Something out of a museum that I'm experiencing as a bystander, not quite able to marry it against the idea of *my bedroom*, the one where I sleep on the left side and he has one of those gentle-wake-up sunrise lamps, with potted plants and an expensive rug over the original parquet flooring – a room that's functional and comfortable, and doesn't need to be the sole expression of my personality in the home.

Oh, if teenage me could see me now . . .

Applying a meticulous streak of eyeliner, I do a quick audit of my life. The misguided year studying French at university before realising I wasn't cut out for it and actually, quite honestly, could not stomach the idea of a year abroad all by myself, and the abrupt change to studying a business degree – useful, yet broad enough that I could grant myself time to decide on my future. The time bouncing between jobs every eight months, trying to discover what was right for me, and finally settling into the role of paralegal three years ago while getting my qualifications part time.

Then, of course, there's the 'fun' side of the highlight reel: the holidays and monthly Sunday brunches, the horse-riding classes that turned into show-jumping competitions. The swish apartment, and the glittering diamond on my left hand.

I'd give my life full marks, if it were up to me. Glossy and shiny on the outside looking in – and utterly lovely in reality, too. I'm doing a job I love, have a beautiful home and vibrant social life, and I'm planning the wedding of my dreams to the man I love. It's exactly where I pictured myself being.

I set aside the eyeliner, finish my mascara, and dig through my makeup bag for my lipstick before realising I forgot to pack lipliner. Damn it.

That's alright, though – teenage Steph to the rescue! I'm sure I must have left *something* behind during the summers home from uni . . .

I open the left-hand drawer on the dressing table and, lo and behold – makeup stash of old. The Benefit mascara there is so ancient that half the writing has worn off the tube, and the nail varnishes left behind are probably dried up and useless now, but there's also a stumpy MAC lipliner pencil – one I bought to match the Ruby Woo lipstick I got for my sixteenth birthday off the girls.

13

There's something so *right*, I think, about using this now. How many parties did I wear this to, back when? That Ruby Woo was my pride and joy. It's a very full-circle moment.

Curious, I root around in the drawer to see what else I might have left behind in here. There's a tiny pink pencil case that I used to carry around in my schoolbag to keep my tampons in (it's still got some in it, and I think I should probably throw them away but just push them further to the back of the drawer for now), a tangled-up and tarnished necklace, half a pack of long-dried-out makeup wipes . . .

My fingers brush the glossy paper of a photograph, and I push the tat aside to get a better look, finding a small pile of them.

Oh, I think. *I remember this.*

It was the school orchestra trip to Italy, in Year Twelve, just after Easter. The photo on top is the entire group, with the teachers who chaperoned the trip and all, at some old church where we played a concert for the locals. We're all holding our instruments, beaming at the cameras. I pick out familiar faces of friends from my year group. Bryony is front and centre, hip jutting out and flute held high and proud above her head while she smoulders at the camera, which makes me laugh. I spot Shaun and Hayden in the back of the group with the rest of the percussion section, Hayden's bright orange hair and awkward grimace a sweet contrast to the funny face Shaun is pulling, undoubtedly because he knew Hayden wouldn't smile for the camera properly. He was always sweet like that.

There's a photo of me and the girls in some pizzeria, one of all of us in the wind section at another concert, one of a bunch of us in the hotel playing card games. I crack up laughing at one showing a crowd of random people in a square gathered around while Ryan stands on the ledge of a fountain and plays his trumpet, and Ashleigh stands facing the camera, glowering as if to say, 'Are you seeing this prick too?' She looks ten thousand per cent done with him even as everybody else cheers him on, and I suddenly remember all their bickering on the bus – and in class, and in the hallways. The petty rivalry to end all petty rivalries. I can see why I hung onto the photo.

The last one in the pile gives me pause, and my fingers trace over it gently.

Teenage me looks up with a broad smile and glittering eyes, cheeks flushed and tanned from the Italian sun, face pressed against Shaun's. He looks so young there, with that softness to his face, the barely defined jaw hinting at the man he was growing into. His skinny legs stick out of his shorts in the photo, his toned arms are wrapped snugly around my waist to anchor me in close, and – he's not looking at the camera. Of course he's not.

He's looking at me. Like I'm the only thing in the world worth looking at. I do a double take at how tangible it is, to see the adoration pouring off him in that photograph. I don't remember taking it – but I remember how it used to feel, with Shaun. How he was the very centre of my world right from the very first kiss we shared. It's no wonder everybody thought we'd be the most likely to end up together; we were always destined to be the childhood sweethearts who rode off into the sunset. We were forever, we used to say.

My traitorous heart gives a little somersault, seeing the two of us so completely in love.

15

Quickly, I shove the entire stack of photographs into my handbag for the night. I bet the others will love to see them too, and we'll all get a kick out of that one of Ashleigh. I'm sure she'll have a good laugh over how much she used to argue with Ryan over every little thing, and how silly the whole thing used to be. And, if nothing else, it'll be a nice little memory to pull out if ever the conversation gets a bit stilted – we can reminisce over the shared memories of the trip.

I ignore how dry my mouth is, and how hard my heart is beating.

The shower shuts off in the next room. He comes back, dropping a kiss onto my cheek before getting ready, the jeans and shirt laid out next to my dress waiting for him.

'You look gorgeous.'

'It's not too much?'

'Never.' That grin and those dimples make me swoon every dang time. Except, right now, it feels like an uneasy swoop of my stomach, tying it into knots.

Instead of trying to smile back, I double-check my bag, making sure to pop my lipstick and old lipliner in there, and a tissue to blot, and then slip into my dress and shoes.

He's ready to leave by the time I ask, 'Zip me up?' – because of course he is. He knows me so well. Beat for beat. A synchronisation that's existed since the very first time we said 'hello' in the hallway.

The fingers tracing up the bare skin of my back are sure and gentle. The hands that settle on my waist so he can hold me there for a moment while he brushes a kiss on the back of my neck are familiar and natural. The scent of his cologne teases my nostrils, and it smells like home.

16

I think about the photograph of me and Shaun in my handbag, and the fact that tonight I'll be seeing him in person for the first time since the break-up, then turn to Curtis to slip my hand in his, hoping he doesn't feel it shake. The cold metal of my engagement ring presses into my finger.

'Come on. Time to go.'

Chapter Three

Shaun

'Most Likely to End Up Together'

'Darling, I'm *really* not sure about this . . . Don't you think I'll just be a bit superfluous the entire night?'

I laugh, not because Aisha uses words like 'superfluous', but because she thinks even for a second that I might feel like she's getting in the way tonight. As if I wouldn't enjoy a night out with my gorgeous, brilliant fiancée. I step aside from the steady stream of people making their way from the car park up the slope to the main building. My arms slip around her waist and I drop a kiss on the tip of her nose, so I don't mess up the pretty pink lipstick she's applied.

'Not in the least,' I tell her. She bites her lip, which makes me want to laugh again, because now *she'll* be the one ruining her lipstick. 'Lots of people are bringing their partners and spouses tonight. And Bryony was very clear on the invitation – the more the merrier.'

'I know, but I just think . . .'

'And you know some of the guys already. I've introduced you.'

'I know, Shaun, but . . .'

Uncertainty flickers in her brown eyes and I feel a pang of sympathy for her. It's not that Aisha hates parties or is uncomfortable meeting new people, but – I get it. This isn't a few old mates from my schooldays. This is *everyone*. Around eighty or ninety people, plus whatever significant others show up. Admittedly, I haven't seen the vast majority of them for ten years so they'll be as good as strangers to me, too, but we'll still have shared experiences and fond memories to reminisce over. I'll still know who they are.

If I had to show up with about a hundred and fifty people that Aisha had some connection to while I knew nobody, I'd probably feel a bit of a third (or, hundred and fifty-first) wheel, too.

Then she checks the time on her phone and says, 'I suppose even if I did get a train now, I'd be too late to catch the others anyway,' and I remember I convinced her to sack off plans with some of her work friends to come here with me tonight. She's not *anxious* – she just thinks she had a better offer for Friday-night plans.

Which I also get, in fairness. If I had the choice of a night at the pub with the guys or mingling with Aisha's old schoolmates, I know what I'd prefer.

I give her a smile and tell her, 'Come on, it's going to be great. I promise. And besides, I can't wait to show you off to everybody.'

That puts a gleam back in her eyes. Aisha sways slightly, her body brushing against mine, and then her shoulders give that little wriggle before she straightens up to her full height (which is not inconsiderable in those heels – she might even put some of the rugby lads to shame) and says, 'Okay.'

I squeeze her waist once more before we join the current of people moving towards the school.

'Huh,' I say.

'What?'

'Oh, nothing. Just – that little building there, with the blue guttering around the roof? That used to be these rickety old demountables. The languages department was out here.'

Aisha laughs, her arm looping through mine as she relaxes a bit more. 'The kind with asbestos, that they probably should've torn down even before you were in school, you mean?'

'That's exactly the kind.'

It's weird to see the change. Weirder still that it *feels* weird. It's been ten years – of course things wouldn't have stayed the same here. As much as I hated trudging across to German class in the pouring rain, and how freezing it was in winter, and the musty smell that clung to the place no matter what Frau Jones did with Febreze plug-ins . . . I feel kind of sad, to know that it's gone.

Which is stupid, obviously, but the nostalgia hits me so hard that I barely even pay attention to what Aisha is saying about something someone's just posted on their Instagram Story.

Time slows down as we make our way up the stone steps and through the main reception, past the rows of lockers that lead to the cloakrooms and toilets. My head swivels towards each thing I used to know so well – like the wall where they still have a big board tallying house points. (My old house, Dickens, is currently lagging behind in last place, which seems about right – not *everything* around here changes, I guess.) I look off to the right, to the cloakrooms, my mind following the path to where I used to hang up my coat and bag for PE or sports clubs, and that time I snuck into the girls' to snog Steph, and the overwhelming stench of Impulse sprays that coated the air in there. We pass a corridor on the left that I know leads straight to the maths and geography rooms, with a staircase at the end of it coming out at the back of the school to the art and DT block.

It's like I'm sixteen again, mucking around in the hallways between classes with my mates or claiming a radiator by the window at lunchtime in winter, ready for when Steph and her friends arrived and she'd give me a kiss and thank me for saving them from frozen bottoms. I smile at the memory – I'm looking forward to seeing Steph again. Congratulating her on everything she's achieved, and even her new man. I hope she's doing as well as she makes out on social media; she deserves that.

A phantom school bell peals through the halls and, for a moment, the people around me are in itchy black jumpers and blue ties, hair gelled up and school bags swinging from their shoulders.

I blink, and the only sound is the pulse of pop music coming from the hall and the quiet chatter of my fellow ex-students and their partners, who are dressed in varying degrees of casual- and partywear.

I suddenly feel underdressed in my jeans. Like I should've worn a suit, or something. Like Mr Grantham is going to leap out from a corner with those wiry glasses perched on his bulbous red nose and scold me for not having my top button done up or my shirt tucked in per the school rules, and if he catches me looking like such a layabout again, that'll be detention.

I shake it off when Aisha squeezes my hand.

She's grinning at me. 'This looks so cool! Why didn't you say? I thought it was going to be some sad, boring old thing in a gym!'

There are strobe lights flashing inside the hall, and laughter pouring out from it. More like a party than a get-together.

I manage a smile. 'Bryony was organising – and she never did anything by halves. She did promise us a spectacle. An *event*.' I try to say it with enough of an air of grandeur to mimic the girl – woman – herself, but I don't think Aisha will truly understand unless she meets her.

I realise that a bit of a queue has formed and, craning her neck to look, Aisha tells me that everyone seems to be getting greeted one by one on their way in, which makes me snort, because yeah, that sounds about right. Sounds very Bryony.

The queue moves forward steadily, not forming too much of a bottleneck. I'm not expecting to find Bryony herself manning the door, checking people in. Her chestnut-brown hair is dyed so dark it shines purple. She's in a rainbow-striped sequin jumpsuit that shows off her cleavage and makes her look like she belongs in a nightclub, not a school hall. The lights bounce off her outfit, turning her into a human disco ball.

Her eyes slide to mine and I watch the question in them gutter out as recognition takes its place. She clicks her tongue and flips her long ponytail over her shoulder. 'Ah, I know you! Shaun! You haven't changed at all, have you?'

A laugh slips out of me and I move to hug her. Bryony squeezes me tight. 'Speak for yourself! Hey, this looks amazing. How'd you pull it all off?'

'Oh, you know.' She flicks her head, ponytail swishing,

and winks at me. 'I know some people who know some people. It wasn't so hard.'

I introduce her to Aisha, and Bryony dazzles her with that same smile that used to bag her orchestra solos and leading roles in the school plays and saved her from ever getting in trouble for being kind of bitchy – like that time she told Ryan his new haircut made him look like an army reject and called him the 'colonel' of the rugby team until it grew out. I imagine it's the same smile that has her sailing through auditions now, too.

'I'm so glad you guys could make it,' she tells us, and for all I know about Bryony being a great actress, I can see that she's sincere. 'There's a guestbook just inside, and help yourself to food and drinks.'

'Thanks,' I say, but Bryony catches my arm as Aisha wanders on ahead of me into the hall.

She arches an eyebrow at me. 'Steph's here, you know.'

'Uh, yeah. I figured.'

She grins and lets me go. I don't have to look to know she's watching me like this is her new favourite soap opera; she always used to love stirring up shit and then seeing how it played out, like that whole mess with Josh and Thea.

Walking into the hall, I don't pay attention to the lighting or the décor or even stop to laugh at the fact that she's rolled out a *literal* red carpet for us – I'm just thinking, *Did Steph say something about seeing me? Is she nervous? Why would she be nervous? It's been forever.*

But then, as Aisha and I collect some drinks, I see her. Blonde hair in soft, delicate waves down her back, her body rounder, cheeks fuller than they used to be, and looking drop-dead gorgeous in a strappy, bright purple dress. It flares out from her waist and teases along her mid-thigh, the fabric swishing gently as she moves, gesturing animatedly as she talks. There's a man at her side I've seen on Facebook and she's surrounded by a gaggle of girls that I recognise just from the back of their heads – as a group, they're unforgettable, and it's like no time has passed, seeing them all together like this.

As she's talking, Steph's eyes move around the room, and her gaze lights on me.

My heart stops beating, and I swear even the world stops turning. Is she going to ignore me? Run over to hug me? Do that awkward wave when you're not sure what else to do and go back to her conversation? Make a point of touching that guy on the arm or chest as if to drive home that she's not mine anymore?

I'm all too aware of Aisha standing beside me, and wonder if I should be sliding an arm around her waist, wonder what Steph thinks of her – of me and her, *together*. I want her to know how well I've done for myself and how happy I am and – I also do not want her to be noticing Aisha at all in this moment.

I don't know why her reaction suddenly matters so much to me. I was okay about seeing Steph. Looking forward to it, even; we shared a lot of the same friends at school, moved in the same circles. We'd been friendly even before we were an item, and the break-up was hardly some big, vicious bust-up where we both said and did unforgivable things. It was pretty amicable, all things considered.

But seeing her across the school hall . . .

It brings back a lot of memories. A lot of feelings I thought were left well and truly in the past.

Until finally, she smiles at me.

It's that smile she always used to give me. The one that felt specially reserved for *me*. A little bit cheeky around the edges, and entirely kissable. Blue eyes warm and open, like she has nothing to hide from me, is willing to lay every emotion that might flicker through them bare for me to see.

Like she's so completely and utterly happy to see me.

I can't help but grin back at her, and I know I'm done for.

Chapter Four

Hayden

'*Most Likely to Succeed*'

The school feels so . . . *plain*. When did it get like that?

These halls used to hold so many memories – good and bad. This place was the epicentre of years of my life. The most ordinary things used to feel so important, like the fact that my locker was right in the middle of the bottom row and I'd practically get trampled by everyone else in between classes just trying to swap out my books, or that one seat in the library that I favoured because it had good natural lighting *and* the librarian couldn't see if I was eating lunch there, and the supply cupboard down by the English rooms that I avoided for an entire year, taking the long way around to class, because I heard some of the rugby lads were shutting unsuspecting people inside it for a laugh.

I don't know what I expected to feel, coming back here, but I do know it wasn't this sense of . . . complete *underwhelm*.

It's just a building. Just walls with too many layers of paint on, and scratchy carpets and creaking radiators and fluorescent strip lighting. It's so unextraordinary that I pinch myself, wondering if my sense of detachment is because this is all a weird dream.

Nope. Real.

I rub my arm and fall into step behind a couple I don't recognise, joining a small queue for the party. Bryony is ushering people in, greeting them like a hostess, which makes me scoff. I bet she's loving having the limelight, despite the fact she called this whole idea 'kitsch'.

(I did wonder if she thought it meant 'cute' rather than 'tacky', but I don't think Bryony's the kind of person to get that wrong. She strikes me as someone who is – who always has been – very deliberate in everything she does.)

Still, I manage a smile for her when it's my turn to enter the party, and I see the blank look on her face before she does a double take, her whole body physically reeling backwards as she blinks up at me in shock. '*Hayden?*'

I give a stilted chuckle. 'That's my name, don't wear it out. How's it going, B?'

She just blinks at me for several seconds longer, her green eyes wide and her mouth hanging open. Finally, she gets a grip, and draws me down for a hug. Once upon a time, I probably would've baulked at that sort of unnecessary affection. Once upon a time, I would've assumed that the only reason Bryony Adams would have to hug me was to stick a *kick me* sign on my back – 'You know, to be *ironic*!'

'God, sorry,' she's saying as she draws back. 'You're just – you don't look anything like I thought you would. Did you dye your hair? I swear, it used to be bright red. Like, properly *Weasley*, you know?'

I scrub a hand through it. It's already a mess, so I can't make it much worse. Her own hair is bright purple in the

27

harsh lighting. 'Nope. Just, uh, faded with age, I guess. Few premature greys.'

She pouts. 'Well, now you're just an ordinary ginger. That's boring, isn't it?' She laughs, and I don't get the joke but smile back anyway. Her gaze snags on my hands, and she pulls a face. 'You know you've got pen *all* over you.'

I look down at the colourful felt-tip streaks over my fingers and palms as if seeing it for the first time – which I sort of am. I'm so used to getting in such a mess after a colouring session with Skye who, at four years old, enjoys turning her dear old dad into artwork as much as she does her colouring book, I hardly notice things like this anymore.

'Er . . .' is all I manage, and stuff my hands into my pockets instead. There's a snotty tissue from Margot in there I forgot to put in the bin earlier. I panic for a moment that Bryony can sense that, too. 'Right. Occupational hazard.'

She laughs, and does a much better job of pretending to get the joke than I just did. Then Bryony adds, mostly to herself, 'Jesus, and you got so *tall*, too,' before telling me, 'Guest book's just inside on the right, help yourself to food and drink.'

'Thanks, B.'

I can't escape the conversation quickly enough, but once inside, I'm stunned.

I had pretty high expectations that Bryony would do something outlandish since she was organising this – I almost expected some cheesy theme and to walk into a scene from a prom in a high-school romcom – but she's *really* outdone herself.

The place looks fantastic. Sure, there are some of those awful plastic chairs dotted around (they're really still using those? They must be donkey's old by now) and the table of party food and cheap bottles of pop looks a bit sad, but she's

28

got a *red carpet*, for crying out loud. Loose balloons scatter the floor and a massive banner declaring *CLASS OF 2014* hangs across the stage. There's a balloon arch in the school colours, currently a focal point with about twenty people gathered around, rooting through a box of dress-up supplies to take photos with, and little box-lights in different colours set around the room, flashing pink and blue and green and white like a nightclub, which does a great job of distracting from the fact that, you know, it's a party in the school hall, like a crap Year Seven disco. The playlist – currently Arctic Monkeys – and the presentation scrolling automatically up on the projector add to the atmosphere. Even I'm not immune to the sense of nostalgia this time.

For a minute, I stand in the middle of the hall and watch the slideshow play out. It's the same one that Steph shared with us a couple of months back, but, I quickly realise, Bryony must have updated it.

I watch as eighteen-year-old me, with his violently red hair cut short and school tie only *slightly* askew, all the rebellion I would allow myself back then, stands in front of a robot, looking a bit awkward but also a bit excited, showing off my creation for a national competition. I remember that robot. ADA – Automatic Dynamic Android, named for Ada Lovelace. She took home second place, but I still maintain that the winning robot only won because it had voice recognition. (ADA's morse-code operation was a selfish indulgence because I was really into World War II spy stories at the time. I was my own worst enemy.)

'Most Likely to Succeed – Hayden Vaughn' the slide declares, and I feel a pang in my stomach for that kid on the screen. He was busy tinkering with robots and reading up on neurological

science breakthroughs or trawling *Game of Thrones* fan-theory forums, with no idea of what was waiting just around the corner. (And I don't mean the turn the writing and plot took in Season 8.)

Not that I think I would've done anything differently. I would've still been a shy, geeky kid.

I'm still a shy, geeky person now, and I'm twenty-eight years old. I guess not *that* much changes, really.

But even as I think it, the slide cartwheels with a corny animation into a new one. It still has the same title, but the picture is replaced by one I recognise from my Instagram, and how Bryony tracked down my Instagram, I have no idea. Either she's a master sleuth when it comes to social media, or Ashleigh, the traitor, provided it to her without asking me first.

Still, it's a nice photo. My favourite, actually. I have it printed and framed in the kitchen at home. It's of me crouched down with an arm around each of my girls on a snow day, Skye on one side and Margot on the other, all of us beaming at the camera and hugging close together, our cheeks pink with the cold.

Smiling, I turn away and scan the sea of not-so-familiar faces throughout the room. I know partners are welcome, but even people I went to school with suddenly seem to have changed beyond all recognition, and most of the ones I do recognise, I can't remember their names anyway.

Steph is easy to pick out, because she still looks like the ray of sunshine she always was. It helps that she also looks exactly like she does on social media, and that she's standing with the same group of girls she always used to hang out with at school. I almost expect to see Shaun with her, but the guy standing next to her, talking to some other men I don't know, is definitely not Shaun. Good-looking in that conventional, cookie-cutter way, taller than Steph (though that's not hard) and with a friendly face – but not Shaun.

No, Shaun is standing at the drinks tables, chatting to two of his best mates, Josh and Hassan. The tall, slim lady next to him is decidedly not Steph.

I don't know why it's hard to process seeing them both with other people, but they were always such a *pair* around school, it's hard to consider them as separate entities now. Hard to consider them as true individuals ever existing outside of one another at all, really.

There must be about a hundred people here already, and it's barely ten past seven. We must be getting old, I think, if almost everybody is here so on time for a party that started at seven. What happened to being fashionably late? Weren't they all supposed to be pre-drinking somewhere before getting a lift in an hour after they said they'd show up?

I sort of wish I'd had a beer before coming, but settle for getting myself some of the punch. I don't think the worst of the 'lads' are here just yet, so it should be safe. I joked about Ryan spiking it and I know we're all adults now, but ... I still wouldn't put it past them.

'Hey, Hayden! I thought that was you!'

I finish pouring myself a glass and hold it out to one side as I return Shaun's one-armed embrace. He pats my back roughly, grinning when he pulls away.

'How's it going, mate? It's been forever! You remember Josh and Hassan, right? And this is my girlfriend – fiancée, sorry – Aisha.' He gives a cheeky wink that's classic Shaun Michaels, and says, 'Still getting used to saying that.'

Aisha blushes, and I give her a friendly smile before

31

shaking the boys' hands. The guys' – the *men's*. A processing error flashes up in my brain, not quite computing that we're no longer teenagers.

'Didn't recognise you for a minute there,' Hassan tells me, peering up at me in that same way Bryony did. Like his brain is struggling to reconcile these two images of me, too. 'Were you always this tall?'

Josh grins and digs an elbow in Hassan's ribs. 'Nah, but you were always this short.'

He's laughing as Hassan shoves him off, then Josh hooks an arm around his neck in a playful headlock, mussing his hair before Hassan wriggles free.

Yep. Some things just don't change.

Shaun catches my eye, like he knows exactly what I'm thinking, and I relax a bit. I always liked Shaun. Everybody did. He and Steph were some of the most likeable people ever; the kind that you wanted to hate just for being so damn perfect, but they were so *nice*, you were incapable of doing anything but enjoying their company. I never heard anybody badmouth them, not once – not even Bryony.

'Did you bring anybody with you?' he asks, glancing around like someone might pop out from behind me.

'Nah. Just me. The girls are with their mum tonight.'

'Oh, man, that's right! I straight up forgot you had kids.' Josh claps me on the shoulder, brow furrowed. 'Was real sorry to hear what happened, mate. It must've been rough.'

The only semblance of answer I can form is, 'Uh.'

Hassan is busy explaining to Aisha, 'Hayden was going to be *it*, you know? The next Steve Jobs. Honestly, when I heard about that guy who created Wordle, you remember that? When I first opened that article, I thought, hand on heart, that was gonna be Hayden. He was a total genius. Gutting, though – he had to drop out of uni after he got some girl pregnant.'

'I didn't *have* to,' I say, bristling at how tawdry he makes it sound.

Aisha looks at me with a softer smile, head cocked slightly to one side. It's curious, and there's not the same sort of pity in it as in the guys' faces. 'You've got daughters, then?'

'Um.' I clear my throat. 'Yeah. Margot – she's nine, now. And Skye, she's four.'

'I didn't realise you had *two*,' Hassan says, aghast.

Josh gives a melodramatic shudder. 'And both girls.'

Shaun rolls his eyes, but says to me, 'Are you still with Margot's mum, then? I didn't know that.'

'Oh, um, no. No, we just . . . Uh, she—'

'Have you got any pictures of the girls, Hayden?' Aisha asks. She must be able to sense I'm out of my depth and I breathe a sigh of relief as I get my phone out, showing her the background. The girls are squished into a toy car that Margot's definitely too big for, so they're both half spilling out of it, the photo capturing them both mid-laugh – and moments before Skye fell on her bum and started crying, and then Margot had a tantrum.

'Oh, my gosh, they're precious! They look like you.'

'Poor them,' I joke, and everybody laughs now. As Aisha takes control of the conversation, asking me polite and non-invasive questions and teasing Shaun about how they're hoping to start trying soon, after the wedding is out of the way next year, I feel some of the tension ease out of my shoulders.

By the time I move on to chat to another group, and receive another round of sympathy and one audible 'Ouch!'

33

for the fact that I became a dad instead of a graduate, I'm starting to wish the punch *was* spiked. When they exchange uncertain looks over the fact that I work from home part time as a software developer so I can look after the kids, because the girls' mum is a nurse, and someone tells me they're *sorry* about it, I'm starting to wish that *I* spiked it.

'You were meant to be the next big thing,' someone tells me.

'I thought you said you were going to invent the next Facebook,' Chris from my GCSE French class says.

'You were always so bright. You could've been buying up Twitter and building rockets, if you'd wanted.'

'I always thought you were gonna, like, win a Nobel Prize or something.'

'I swear I still think I'm going to see you on one of those 'thirty under thirty' lists – LOL!'

'You used to win all those awards and stuff, didn't you?' a girl called Elise says, face twisted in a sad frown. I think she was in my English class at some point. She used to wear non-regulation hoop earrings and blue eyeliner. 'That must be so hard, Hayden.'

'I don't know,' I say, feeling everyone's eyes on me, and not quite sure when so many people clustered around to hear about the 'sorry' state of my life and express their sympathies for the death of my would-be success. 'The girls got me a mug for Father's Day last weekend, and apparently I'm the World's Best Dad.'

They erupt into laughter, and hands clap my back affably and affectionately. I muster up a smile, and wonder if it's too early to call it a night.

Chapter Five

Ashleigh

'Most Likely to Kill Each Other'

I'm not hiding out in the school toilets.

I'm *not*, obviously, because I'm not fifteen years old.

I'm just . . . taking my time. Checking my hair, making sure my lipstick hasn't smudged from the liquid courage I downed in the taxi on the way here.

Yeah, that's all.

I lean into the mirror above the sinks in the girls' toilets; it has that dark, dappled look around the edges and I'm sure it's some original fixture from the seventies nobody has ever bothered to update, like the sinks and cubicles. My lipstick, at least, is flawless, and I don't let myself second-guess the deep red shade, dark and stark against my pale, freckled skin. I try not to fidget with my hair either – the wispy fringe, and loose tendrils that frame my face where they weren't quite caught in my bun. It's held in place by about a dozen hairpins and sheer dumb luck, so I dare not disturb it.

Trying to occupy my hands, I smooth them over my flared trousers, pull my skintight top with its puffy, off-the shoulder sleeves back into place. Considering it's my go-to outfit for a night out because it makes me feel so confident, all I can see now is how big my thighs look and how silly that tiny strip of stomach on show looks and how ridiculous the sleeves are, making me look wide and bulky instead of sexy and feminine.

I haven't even said hello to anybody yet, and I'm already sweating like I have to get changed for PE and am paranoid that everyone will notice I forgot to shave my legs.

Spoiler alert: nobody ever noticed.

Okay. I can do this. This is *fine*. It's just a party. I like parties now.

And I liked school, too, for the most part. I liked plenty of the people, and I'm still friendly with some of them. I was looking forward to tonight.

If only because there are plenty of people whose faces I'd like to rub my life in, and put them in their place. I'd *really* love it if some of them aren't doing so great, too – maybe their partner left them or they were fired or, even better, they're stuck in a job they hate with their dreams all turned to ash, while I'm out here doing so well for myself. What a shame that would be.

I grip the cold porcelain sink tightly, teeth clenched.

This is *ridiculous*.

But this reaction, however much it's taken me by surprise, isn't wholly unexpected. I'm returning to the place I spent my formative years of pre-adulthood to face a lot of people who tried their best to make my life miserable. The worst part of hiding out in the toilets and wanting to run home is that I was usually so much *better* than that, at school. It was a reaction I learnt to temper and control, so the comments about being a square and a try-hard and (my favourite, the most bizarre and inexplicable of all) a slut, would roll off my back. I stopped batting an eye when people snickered at me in the hallways. I trained myself to stop caring.

So why do I care now?

Why do I want them to like me?

I don't. I don't care about that. I don't need to be the belle of the ball and centre of attention. I'm not vying for prom queen. I just . . .

Is it really so bad, that I want to prove to those kids who *did* look down on me, that I'm someone worth looking up to, now? It doesn't make me a bad person to want that sort of vindication, does it? Just – human.

My phone buzzes somewhere inside my bag and I know it's probably Hayden, following up on the SOS text he sent a few minutes ago. I promised I was almost here; he'll be wondering where I've got to.

With a deep breath, I snatch up my bag, roll my shoulders back, and tell my reflection to get it together.

Bryony squeals when she sees me, even doing an excited little dance. 'Bitch, look at you! You came to *play*! Um, hello!'

Equal parts embarrassed and gratified, I strike a little pose and give her a spin before walking the rest of the way to give her a quick hug. Bryony was always a hugger, so I imagine that's why she's stood at the door accosting people on their way in. That, and the glory of playing hostess tonight.

I've barely spoken to Bryony in ten years beyond a few civil exchanges on social media, but between her 'bitch' greeting and the warmth of her embrace, it feels like no time at all has passed – and like we're closer friends than we actually were at school. Not that we ever *were* friends at school – merely classmates, peers. Maybe, I think, we'd actually have a good relationship these days, if we met now.

'What about you? Look at you! You look fabulous. This is gorgeous,' I tell her, admiring her sparkling jumpsuit.

'This old thing?' She tosses her ponytail over her shoulder like it's all no big deal, but glows under the praise. She sniffs, a party bloodhound, and arches an eyebrow. 'Someone snuck a cheeky pre-drink in, I see.'

I cover my mouth, trying to smell the tequila on my own breath. I'd had a mint afterwards, but I guess nothing escapes Bryony. She did used to know everything about everyone, so.

But she giggles and stage-whispers, 'You're not the only one. Freddie Loughton and all that lot, they went to the pub beforehand. Raising hell over a pint of Guinness, I don't doubt. *Classic* rugby lads – they never change.'

My smile falters a bit and my eyes dart past her, into the hall.

But I say, 'Are most people here, then?'

'Looks like it! I'm going to give it five more minutes then come join the party. I'll come find you and we can catch up properly, yeah?'

'Sounds good,' I say, because it really does. Bryony already seems so much more approachable and laidback than I remember from school. Her life looks so glamorous online, with all the travelling and acting jobs and volunteer work she does. I'm pleased it all worked out for her, but I'd also love it if I could stick by her side until some of that easy confidence rubs off on me. Or, at least until I remember that *I'm* a confident person – usually.

I weave through the crowd in the school hall with my head held high. Aside from the cloying layer of bleach that clings to the air and the scuffed flooring, the place is transformed. Trust Bryony to strike just the right level of cheesy nostalgia and unironic fun.

I make a beeline for Hayden. He's easy to spot since he stands a good few inches above most of the men in the room, with his lanky body and ginger hair. I catch sight of his expression before I reach him – the terse smile on his face that doesn't reach his eyes, the way he's mentally counting down like he does when the girls are being naughty and kicking up a fuss, and he's trying to decide between letting them get it out of their system or stepping in and putting a stop to it.

He must sense me looking, because his eyes start to rove around the room, away from the conversation that's so clearly not holding his attention, and light up when he sees me. He pulls a pained face, eyes crossing as he rolls them in a cartoonish show of melodrama that sets me giggling. I half debate going to mingle first, and make a gesture to him to convey that.

'I will end you,' he mouths at me.

Yeah, it's probably time to put the poor guy out of his misery.

I step into the group – a random assortment of people I wouldn't normally have seen together in our school days – and say hi to everyone, and do my best to end their conversation by crossing the space to hug Hayden. He wraps an arm around me in a firm, familiar squeeze. I like how affectionate he's gotten in the last few years; it's sweet.

'So much for *five minutes*,' he hisses in my ear, and I nudge an elbow into his ribs. Hayden gestures towards me with his paper cup. 'Um, everybody, you remember Ashleigh, right?'

One girl jokes, 'How could we forget?'

The others all join in laughing, and I don't know if she was trying to be nasty or if I'm reading too much into it in my newfound paranoia, but I give them all a beaming smile, like even if it was an insult, I don't give a shit. I drop my weight onto my back leg and readjust the strap of my clutch bag more comfortably on my shoulder, relieved that I opted to dress up as I do a quick survey of the group.

I know it doesn't make me better than Elise Chambers that I'm dressed like I'm on my way to an expensive, exclusive bar and she's got a frumpy handbag resting by her foot and her skinny jeans are a bit faded, but it feels *good*. She laughed at me for still wearing one of those plain pink Angel bras from the M&S teen collection when we were in Year Ten, like my underwear was any concern of hers, so I don't deny myself the satisfaction now of seeing her swallow her awe at my outfit, or how her body language shifts just a bit into something put-out and defensive.

A little of my usual confidence starts to trickle back in.

It helps when Hayden shoots me a grateful smile and takes the opportunity to make his escape. He hands me his drink on his way, mumbling something nobody else especially listens to about how he'll get himself another and be back.

We both know he won't be back.

'So,' I say, and give my best boardroom-shark grin to the group. 'What's everybody up to these days?'

The first half-hour of the party is a blur of old familiar faces and violent panic when someone greets me super-enthusiastically only for me to realise that I cannot, for the life of me, *remember their damn name.*

There are hugs and cheek-kisses and handshakes. Some people, I greet more genuinely than others. It's nice to see Steph and Shaun again, for instance, and every so often I swing by whatever little group Hayden is talking to in case he needs rescuing again. And I quite like it when Bryony calls time on her hostess duties and joins the rest of us mere mortals, but hooks her elbow through mine like we're lifelong besties, like we're a set. Like I am, and always have been, every bit as deserving of the spotlight as she is. Like it's an impossible idea that people would ever have *considered* putting me down instead of worshipping the ground I walk on – or like she ever did that herself, from time to time.

It's pathetic, how much I enjoy it.

I know it's only for a night, but there's something exciting and exonerating about being one of the popular girls at school for a change.

I like it when people do a double take at my outfit, and I relish it when they congratulate me on my career, especially when I don't have to explain that I work in research development for the pharmaceutical industry trying to fight degenerative diseases, because for whatever reason, they already know. I don't pretend that I'm not immensely proud of myself, or that I don't love that my work is making a real difference in the world. I don't bother to hide the smugness from my voice when I tell them things like, 'Yes, my team just made a really exciting breakthrough,' and, 'I got to spearhead a new drug to treat that, you know. It's actually going through its next stage of trials soon before it can be formally approved, but things are looking good so far.'

Now, I slip away from Bryony, who's telling a story about when she went to a premiere party with Olivia Coleman that has everyone hanging off her every word, aware that I've left Hayden unattended a little too long. I know he's a big boy and he can look after himself, but he's my best friend and I know he was nervous about coming tonight.

Based on the number of times I've heard people murmur, 'Isn't it a shame about Hayden?' his concerns weren't unfounded.

But when I find him chatting to a group of girls I recognise from A-level maths, he's animated, flushed, telling them, 'I swear, some days, that big blue dog is my *nemesis*. Bandit, you know, the dad? He's always playing these great games with Bluey and Bingo, and then of course *my* kids expect me to do the same because I'm at home with them most of the time, and I don't know how to explain that I *cannot keep up with this damned cartoon dog.*'

Bloody *Bluey*, I think, and swallow a laugh. Even I've watched the episodes multiple times over when I swing by to hang out, or when I've looked after Margot and Skye; I reckon Hayden must know some of them word for word by now.

But our old classmates are laughing, and one of them starts up saying how the 'Grannies' game from the show is her son's favourite thing and she can never play it for laughing too hard because he's too good at pretending to be like his nan, and then someone mentions the name 'Peppa Pig' and a collective groan sounds from the group.

I leave Hayden to it, glad he's found some safe ground in fellow parents for a while, and circle back around the room.

Bryony has moved on to a new group, but flags me down when she spots me.

'Ashleigh! Ash, over here! We were just talking about that Red Nose Day talent show we did, d'you remember? The one you organised in Year Twelve?'

A few heads turn at the sound of Bryony's voice. It's always carried, like her natural state is to project, and I don't hate when the eyes shift to me.

So I call back to her, 'D'you mean the one where you coloured your hair red with cheap hair dye that ran everywhere? By the end of the day, you looked like one of the Angry Birds.'

Bryony laughs, hand reaching for me to pull me into the group. There's a buzz as the topic ripples through the party and people start reminiscing about that particular talent show. The teachers that sang ABBA or got up to ballroom dance, Shaun and his mates who formed a little band to sing 'Wonderwall' (unironically), when Roisin and Noodles Greg (why did we ever call him that? Why can't I stop thinking of him as 'Noodles Greg'?) tried to do a sort of circus double-act and he knocked himself out with the juggling clubs . . .

'That was mint, to be fair, Ashleigh,' someone is saying to me now. 'You got us the whole afternoon off lessons for it, remember?'

It takes all my willpower not to roll my eyes. Of course *that's* what they remember now – not how peeved people were with me after making the grand announcement in the common room and how much they grumbled about having to waste their afternoon on some stupid fundraiser rubbish.

But I smile and say, 'I know. It wasn't easy.'

Bryony catches my eye, the tip of her tongue bitten between her teeth like she *knows* what I'm not saying is that

I had to fight tooth and nail with our Head of Sixth Form for it and prepared a kickass presentation for the occasion, and got no thanks from anybody for it – even after they had such a great time. It was one of the rare times I found a true ally in her, taking my side against the rest of the year group; she was all for an excuse to show off, and the first to sign up.

What she says to the others, though, is, 'Well, we all had to make sure we put on a good show after that. Ash never skipped lessons for just anything, did she! You swot!'

The group falls to dissecting their favourite memories of the talent show, and I listen with only mild interest.

The hairs on the back of my neck prickle and I don't notice at first, not until my hand clenches so tightly around my paper cup that it crumples in on itself.

And I don't know what's wrong, until I do.

It's an hour into the party. Everybody's here.

Almost everybody, anyway.

There are heavy footsteps approaching, a confident stride that nobody else seems to notice, not until the double doors are thrown open by a broad man in an expensive suit, who stands there while heads throughout the hall swivel towards him and conversations hush, as if his very arrival deserves that particular mark of respect.

It doesn't.

Ryan Lawal gives us all that smug, shit-eating grin that hasn't changed a bit in ten years, and stands there like he's God's fucking gift. The prat is even wearing his *school tie*, for Christ's sake – bright cobalt that would be unremarkable but for the silver imprint of the school badge on it.

I always remember him as a big guy, and while he's not

as tall as Hayden, he seems to take up the entire doorway, his ego filling the space his body doesn't. His dark hair is short, not like the long, floppy style he preferred at school, and he's still annoyingly good-looking.

Worse, actually.

He's devastatingly good-looking now. He must have worked out what length to grow that particular scruff of stubble on his jaw to make him look just the *right* amount of rugged in order to balance out the polished look his suit grants him. The top button of his shirt is undone and his suit jacket is slung over one shoulder; one of his hands is tucked into his trouser pocket in a stance that is both casual and commanding all at once.

Still every inch the arrogant arsehole I remember, by the looks of it.

The only changes I can truly remark on are that his shirt is tucked in and his tie is done up properly. Pulled ever so slightly loose around his collar, but not the ridiculous chunky knot and three-inch tie slung halfway down his chest I recall him and a bunch of the other boys wearing around school.

He swaggers into the room with all eyes on him, and declares, '*Now* it's a party!'

Chapter Six

Ryan

'Most Likely to Kill Each Other'

I walk into the party to a chorus of cheers, and the crowd presses in around the red carpet to get a piece of me. Slapping my back, pecking my cheek.

I know the second I enter the room she sees me, but I don't give her the satisfaction of acknowledging that I've noticed her there. That I even remember she exists, and might be here tonight.

Instead, I'm busy getting not-so-mock tackled by some of the lads from rugby and almost go sprawling on my arse. Freddie is telling me with a wink that he's brought a bottle of gin to spike the punch with – 'Just like old times, eh, Ry?' – and RJ, Hiro and Tommy pepper me with commentary. That they didn't think I'd actually make it, that I need to meet their missus, that it's been too long, that did I hear about Kyle? He's out on parole now, sucks that he couldn't make it.

And I throw myself into it. I flash a grin at Freddie and nudge him off towards the punch bowl. I shrug about Kyle and say maybe he shouldn't have gotten caught, then. I wink at Hiro and waggle my eyebrows when he points out his girlfriend a little way off and laugh when Tommy says he'd better keep her away from me, because Hiro won't ever find another girl that fit who's willing to put up with his bullshit.

It's like nothing's changed.

Aside from the minor, inconvenient fact that the whole exchange feels kind of routine in a way that makes me question why I thought these guys were the absolute pinnacle of hilarity when we were kids – but I'm willing to overlook that. They've all still got me on a pedestal, so. That's all that matters, really.

The group expands and a lady passes a cup of pinkish liquid into my hand. I get a whiff of gin when I lift it to take a sip, and Freddie catches my eye to wink, dead proud of himself. I look at the woman, who's got her hand on my arm and is asking how long it's been, smiling sweetly even as she fights to make eye contact with me.

Seriously? Did she miss the part where this is a 'ten-year reunion' party?

I think she might be Roisin. Roisin had thick eyebrows and one of those Marilyn Monroe beauty marks above her lip like this. Then again, Roisin wasn't honey-blonde like this woman, and I'm almost completely sure she didn't have a slight Yorkshire lilt in her accent.

So, fuck knows who she is, but I tell her, 'Thanks for the drink. Good to see you again too.'

I've always been told I'm good with people. It's why I was captain of the rugby team, and why the teachers made me Head Boy even though someone like Shaun definitely would've deserved it more than I ever did. It's why my face

47

is in the papers and on the news now, and why I've got my foot in the door at Downing Street. Butter wouldn't melt, Mum always says.

I'm not exactly surprised when everybody is too busy talking about my high-flying career and sharp rise in the world of politics and my brief stint in professional rugby to let me do the polite thing and ask them how they're all doing, what they're up to these days.

This is nothing new though. All this attention has nothing to do with that try I scored against Scotland in the Six Nations years ago, or that I could (and probably will) be running for Prime Minister one day.

Nah, it's not any of that that means I'm the star of the show tonight.

It's because I've always been the star of the show with these people. I am the jewel in Tisdale Comprehensive School's crown. Every great party, every win in a rugby match, every epic tale they remember from their school days – I'm at the centre of it all.

Well.

Mostly.

I don't even have to look around to find her, or glance her way to see that she's hyper-aware of the spectacle I'm creating and is looking right at me. I *know*, because her eyes are burning into my skin and I know the weight of that glare all too well. After a solid five years of not-so-petty rivalry, I'm finely attuned to it – even after all this time. I remember the heat of it, the fire and fury, and it makes me grin just like it used to back then, if only for the satisfaction of knowing that I've gotten under her skin. And I know exactly how she'd describe this smile: shit-eating, and unrepentant.

48

Chapter Seven

Bryony

'Most Likely to Become Famous'

For all I was worried – okay, *terrified* – about how this reunion party was going to go, I'll be the first to brag that I absolutely killed it.

People can't stop talking about the decorations, the vibes, how awesome it is to be back here with everybody. Even the cheap plastic trays of sausage rolls and sad-looking packets of crisps are going down a treat; I managed to talk Steph into ordering a bunch of pizzas, and a few other people pitched in money towards the order.

The mood took a definite lift when Ryan showed up and honestly, trust him to rock up an hour late. But he *is* the go-to party guy, even if he's a bit of a tight-laced politician these days, so I'll cut him some slack for it. It *was* a pretty epic entrance, to be fair.

But, as even Ryan Lawal knows, the spotlight in this school ultimately belongs to me.

I stride up onto the stage and use a remote control to turn the volume down on the music. I pick up the microphone from the stand and turn it on; it's temperamental at the best of times so I brace myself, but let out a sigh of relief when the screech of feedback doesn't wail through the speakers. Another sign that everything is going exactly my way tonight. *Total W, Bryony.*

And really, everything is going my way. It's exactly as I pictured in my less panicked moments in the run-up to the reunion. The flattery, the awe, the steady stream of, 'Gosh, haven't you done well for yourself!' Everybody's snooped around on social media to see what other people are up to these days, I know it – if not out of genuine curiosity, then because they're worried they *should* have been keeping up to date with their old classmates' lives all this time.

I'm no exception. I spent weeks looking people up. Although, part of that was so I could update Steph's old presentation with some more recent photos.

Well. No, actually, the presentation was just the excuse I created for myself so I could convince myself that I was being productive, instead of trying to find proof that everyone else was as miserable as me these days, trapped by the short-lived glory of their youth and long nights of marking homework in front of true crime documentaries on Netflix.

Still. We've all been trawling Instagram and Facebook and stuff, and that's why people think I spent a week on set in Sicily for the new *Knives Out* movie, when actually I just had a minor role in an indie movie of the same name on a cleverly designed set in Tenby. It's not like anything on my social media is patently *false*, but . . .

It's not exactly true, either.

On my better days, I tell myself that I'm manifesting (cue sparkle emojis). I'm putting out into the universe how I *want* my life to be; if I can create and cultivate the reality I aspire to, then it will happen. I can pretend that every local theatre production I do lifts my spirits and speaks to the performer in my soul. Or that getting cast for tiny bit-parts in productions or taking work as an extra during the school holidays scratches that itch, is a foot in the door and a step on my way to those goals of landing leading roles on the West End or in a movie.

But the sad reality is that I resent the plays and musicals I perform locally because all I can think is that I know I deserve better than this. And I cry every time I come home from set because it's not a foot in the door – it's the door slamming in my face because I was never good enough in the first place. I feel sick every time I upload something on Instagram, but it's like an addiction – corrosive and compelling all at once. That little kick of dopamine when someone comments '*wow!*' takes the edge off for a moment.

The closest I get to that pride in a job well done these days is when I see one of my kids amped up in class, because they know they nailed it, and I helped that happen.

But here – tonight – it doesn't matter what's true and what's not, and it doesn't matter what keeps me up at night.

Because the only reality here is the one they believe. The one I can make myself believe in, too, for just a little while. Long enough to numb the sting of what could have been.

Walking up on the school stage like I own it, I don't feel like a washed-up has-been whose whole life is a failure. I feel confident, comfortable, because this is exactly where I belong.

I feel like *me*. The Bryony who could have been. The 'most likely to' one.

I want to be her all the time.

The two plain white stage lights I set up here ahead of time catch perfectly on my outfit, which may or may not be (but, most definitely is) by design. My sequinned jumpsuit and I cast a sudden riot of colour throughout the room like a rainbow disco ball, even brighter and more dazzling than the coloured stage lights that are on the floor around the hall.

All eyes are on me and conversations lull instantly.

'Hello, Class of 2014!' I bellow, and a raucous cheer sounds out, amplified by the room's acoustics. Arms lift into the air to raise paper cups, and some people clap.

I give them their moment, let it settle while I soak up the atmosphere. Ryan and his mates stamp their feet in the middle of the room, but it's Steph and her girls who whoop the loudest. My eyes snag on Hayden, standing a full head above the group he's with, and he looks way more relaxed than earlier – smiling, now, with a lopsided ease in the slope of his shoulders. I see some of the spouses and other halves who've come along with flushed faces and bright eyes. If they're all having a good time, I'm considering it another win.

'God, well, it's been a while, hasn't it? I think last time I saw you lot, it was in the field behind the pub off Parsons Lane on results night. Our last hurrah before we all set off for uni and went our different ways – and one last chance to get absolutely shitfaced on Strongbow cider and vodka we nicked from our parents' liquor stash. Good times, right?'

The best of, actually.

It was all downhill from there.

'And it's so awesome to reconnect with everybody again now and see what everybody's up to! All those big dreams realised, the weddings and kids and houses and careers . . .'

I point to a few people in the crowd in turn. Roisin, who was declared 'Most Likely to Go Viral', has a fairly successful plant blog. RJ – 'Most Likely to end up on a Reality Show' – well, he was on an episode of *Watchdog* after he ended up getting his credit card stolen. Mardy Mira With The Lipliner, 'Most Likely to Change the World', has been hugely involved in protests since leaving school, and is constantly sharing petitions on Facebook to try to drum up support (and has finally stopped mismatching her lipliner to her lipstick like some ill-advised fashion statement).

'It's amazing to see where life has taken us all. Thank you everybody *so* much for making the trip here tonight and coming along. I know that the old school hall isn't where we'd picture spending an unforgettable Friday night, but . . .' A polite laugh ripples through the crowd, and I smile. 'Not to play teacher or anything and remind you about the fire exits or the no-smoking rules, but I just thought I'd pop up here and say a few words. Which, ah, now also includes a note that any designated drivers or sober people out there might want to stay away from the punch. Not that I'm naming any names, but, it looks like our future PM still has a naughty streak in him. *Ryan Lawal*.'

The rugby lads surrounding him all jeer, cuffing him around the head and shaking him with that weird brand of affectionate roughhousing that they clearly haven't grown out of. He shrugs them off and straightens up to flash me that heartbreaking grin of his. God, we used to swoon over that smile.

(Judging by the blushes I notice on more than a few cheeks, we still do.)

'Don't tempt me with a detention, Bryony,' he calls out, and winks. 'Or I'll show you just how naughty I can be.'

More jeers and laughs, but this time there are *many* high-pitched giggles from some of the women around the room. I probably would be one of them, if not for the fleeting panic that – *he knows, he knows I'm a liar and I'm just a teacher, oh, God, it's over.*

But it's just Ryan being Ryan, playing up to his adoring crowd and being a shameless flirt, and I breathe a little easier.

'Give it up for our Junior Deputy Vice . . . Assistant Minister, Associate Something of State, whatever the hell you are, for Digital, Sports and Culture, everybody.'

Someone near the stage says the correct title of his department, but I ignore them in favour of a sarcastic eye roll and clap in Ryan's direction. He gives a small bow, because we're all in on the joke.

Because I'm obligated to, I carry on by reminding everybody of the fire exits and to not smoke, vape, or anything else inside the building, and please not to go off exploring old classrooms.

'I am *not* having the headmistress phone me up on Monday and complain that some drunk ruffians defaced the whiteboards in the history rooms with drawings of penises. You're almost thirty, do better. Again, not naming names – Freddie Loughton, Greg Willis,' – God, I almost called him 'Noodles Greg' out loud, awkward – 'Hassan Khalid . . . *Ashleigh Easton.*'

Everybody turns to pin her with a look, and it's like we *are* back to being teenagers and someone getting told off in assembly, because a mocking, shocked chorus of, 'Oo-oo-ooh!'

sounds out. I'm pretty sure we *all* remember that giant, extremely detailed, flaccid dick she drew on Mr Higgins' board for us to discover one morning in Year Eleven biology.

Ashleigh, to her credit, takes a sip of her drink and raises one eyebrow, her mouth twisted up in a careless smirk. 'I just wanted to make sure they knew what they were dealing with, anatomically speaking.'

One of Shaun's mates – Two-Timing Josh – shouts, 'We knew! Ryan proved that when he returned the favour!'

As the attention swings to Ryan, Ashleigh gives a loud snort. '*Yeah*. Hardly Georgia O'Keeffe. All he did was prove that he didn't know the difference between the urethra and the clit. Small wonder he's still single.'

I choke on a laugh, glee lighting up my face as my jaw drops. Ryan is lifting his hands up in surrender and shrugging affably, not even bothering to defend himself, and all I want to do is have everybody lift Ashleigh up on their shoulders while we applaud her.

I'm so adding her on Instagram and seeing if she wants to meet up for drinks at some point after all this.

Well. If I can stomach the idea of having one person – one very judgemental and ruthless person at that – know the truth about my life. I don't know if I can stomach that; but I also know this is a lie I can't keep up in person for longer than tonight. I know not everybody has led the life we expected them to, that we've all grown up and changed and that, for all tonight's nostalgia, the reality is that we're none of us who we used to be.

But what am I supposed to do? Let go of the idea of who I could have been? As long as these people believe I'm a successful actress, that I'm making a living as a performer, doing what I love, travelling the world and leading the exciting life I always said I would . . . As long as they believe I'm that person, then part of me still *is*. These people have become strangers, but they're the ones who give life to the old dreams I'm not ready to let die just yet.

Maybe I won't try to drum up a friendship with Ashleigh beyond tonight, after all. Maybe it's – just not worth it.

Right now, all I can do is take back control of the room to say, 'Well, if in doubt – gents, ask your girlfriends, wives, whatever. Do yourself a favour and google before asking Ryan. There's a reason he's not the Health Minister. But other than that – we've got some pizzas on the way, the guest book is by the door if anybody hasn't had a chance to sign it yet . . . And have fun! Here's to the Class of 2014 – most likely to have one more truly unforgettable night together!'

Chapter Eight

Steph

'Most Likely to End Up Together'

'Sweetie, I'm just going to get another drink. Do you want anything?'

Curtis shakes his head, busy talking about some sporting scandal that's been making headlines lately with a few other guys he's made friends with. I smile at the sight; there's something that feels so inevitable about how he's getting on so well with Priya and Morgan's boyfriends. Like a jigsaw piece slotting right into place.

It really is like nothing has changed with the girls, and I can't believe we've gone ten whole years hardly speaking to one another. The friendship is so natural, so constant, and the way we giggle and talk excitedly over each other makes my heart ache; theirs is a presence I didn't even realise was missing from my life, and now I can't imagine letting them go again. We've already put brunch in our calendars for next month and Morgan has reserved a table in a cute bistro she loves, and we've been talking about another group holiday

59

as if we only just got back from the last one, and didn't drift apart for no real reason after it.

It's so nice to reconnect with the girls and to see everybody again. Ashleigh is an absolute bombshell these days, and Hayden talking excitedly about his daughters as soon as he gets the opportunity is the most adorable thing I think I've ever seen. It's even good to see people I didn't know all that well at school, nice to see them doing well and feeling like I've made some new friends.

There's just one person I haven't quite had the guts to go and catch up with properly yet, and I know I can't avoid him all night.

Shaun has stuck near the tables with the food and drink, and I have the feeling it's on purpose. He's doing it for the same reason I've stuck to the opposite side of the hall near the windows – because if we stay in the same spot and let others come to us, there's no chance of us accidentally bumping into each other.

Which is silly, because we didn't end things on bad terms, and this is a reunion – the whole *point* is to bump into people you haven't seen for ages. But it's different, because this is Shaun we're talking about.

I know, deep in my heart, that it's different, because when I caught his eye after he arrived and smiled at him, he had that look on his face. After the momentary shock, his face softened, lips curving into a sweet, subtle smile that reached his eyes and turned them to melted chocolate. It was exactly the same expression as the one on the photograph of the two of us in my handbag.

I didn't realise how nervous I was to see him again, or how much I needed that reaction from him, but the way it made my heart swell only makes me feel guilty. It's not just the two of us anymore; we aren't each other's whole world and haven't been for a long while. We've both moved on, built new lives with new people.

So . . . why does everything feel exactly the same between us?

For the last hour or so, we keep glancing towards the other at exactly the same time, or we'll look around at everyone else only to find ourselves looking at each other, and share a quick smile before going back to our conversations. We always used to be so in sync; it's astonishing that no distance or time apart could change that.

Even now, as I clutch my empty paper cup in both hands and make my way towards the table for a refill, I notice Shaun peel away from his group. His back is to me, so I know he hasn't done it on purpose, but we arrive at the punch bowl at the same time – both standing there, facing one another, unable to do anything but drink in the sight of the person we first fell in love with.

Shaun's hardly changed. His face still has that boyish quality to it that gives him a naturally approachable sort of aura, even if his jawline is a little more defined these days. There are smile lines around his brown eyes, and even if it's a little longer and thinner these days, he's still wearing his hair in that exact same style, combed into a neat quiff that accentuates his widow's peak.

I know that face so well; I have to fight every impulse to reach up and touch it.

His mouth curves into a smile, his eyes fixed so intently on mine that I wonder if he's thinking the same thing. And his voice is soft when he says my name, so quietly

61

that I shouldn't be able to hear him over all the hubbub, but I do.

'Hi, Steph.'

'Hi,' I say, and it comes out in a whisper. 'Shaun.'

He lets out a long sigh, his breath ghosting over my skin and sending a small shiver down my spine; it's as if he's been craving hearing me say his name. As ordinary and inoffensive as the exchange is, it feels so heart-wrenchingly intimate that my eyelids flutter.

Shaun gets a hold of himself first; he turns towards the punch bowl and clears his throat, sparking me into action as I mimic his movements. He fills up his own cup and then holds out a hand to do the same with mine. Some horrible, hideous part of me wants to know how it feels when his fingers brush mine, if it will still send the same thrill through me as whenever he'd hold my hand around the school corridors or on weekend trips to the cinema, but my heart is in my throat and the guilt presses down on me harder, so I hand the cup over quickly and keep my hands to myself.

It becomes so hard to look directly at Shaun as he hands my drink back to me, if only for the undeniable flutter of butterflies in my stomach and the rapid pitter-patter of my heart. It's hard to look at him and see the same tumult of old emotions resurfacing in him, too.

'This is fab, isn't it?' I say, and now my voice sounds too loud, too rushed – I've turned into a nervous fourteen-year-old talking to a boy she likes for the first time outside of class. 'The red carpet is so fun and I like the balloon arch. Have you taken pictures with it yet? We haven't had a chance, all too busy playing catch-up. It's funny, how much it feels like old times with everybody, don't you think? And I like the presentation. Such a cute touch! Bryony must've spent ages finding photos of everybody to update it.'

I have to stop to catch my breath, and find myself stealing a glance at Shaun. His mouth is split into a wide smile and it's one I recognise from way back when. He used to wear that look on his face when I'd fill him in on all the gossip and chatter about my day and the things the girls had said and the homework I'd gotten, like he can't quite keep up, but he could listen to me talk all day.

Don't do that, Shaun, please. I can't handle it.

He pauses, and his eyebrows twist upwards in the middle ever so slightly as he silently asks if I'm done. My skin is flushed hot, and I gulp down half of the punch – and promptly try (and fail) not to choke at the burn of alcohol in it.

Shaun laughs. 'Pretty strong, isn't it?'

'Mm,' I murmur. 'I don't drink much these days.' Not beyond a few mimosas once a month, or a glass of wine over dinner with Curtis every so often as a bit of a treat.

Deciding I'm finished babbling for the moment, Shaun takes a breath and says, 'Yeah, it's great, isn't it? Bryony did a brilliant job. And it's good to see all the old crowd.'

'Even RJ?'

The question slips out before I can stop it, accompanied by a tilt of my head and sceptical look. Shaun never forgave RJ for flirting with me at Morgan's New Year's Eve party in Year Twelve and even got in a bit of a fight with him during a friendly game of five-a-side one lunchtime. It was the only time Shaun ever got detention; I'd been thrilled by the idea of a boyfriend who defended my honour, even if RJ was only a harmless nuisance.

There's a beat as the memories flash in front of Shaun's

eyes, too, and he shakes his head with a warm chuckle. The sound is like treacle, sticking to me slowly, dragging me down with it. 'Well,' he says. 'Maybe not him.'

We lapse into silence. Bryony's cheesy playlist moves from Dizzee Rascal to Taylor Swift's 'Love Story', and the sound of it seems to bleed through my whole body, the lyrics suddenly the only thing I can think about. I try to count my heartbeats instead, even though I know this silence has already stretched on too long and is verging on, not awkwardness, but that old intimacy that we used to share.

That, apparently, we still do.

I say the first thing that comes to mind in an attempt to break it. 'D'you remember when I sang this to you for your birthday?'

It's the worst thing I think I could have said. It's one of those sweet but cringeworthy memories of being young and in love – doing something worthy of the movies and feeling on top of the world at the time as you set a new high bar for great romances, but also fills my adult self with horror at how I ever thought standing in front of a boy and singing a love song to him was a better idea than buying him a LYNX Africa gift set, or even a good idea at all.

It's also a terrible thing to have brought up, because it makes me think of standing in Shaun's bedroom and sitting on his lap to kiss him afterwards, and letting his hands roam underneath my school blouse for the first time.

'I learnt it on your guitar,' I add quickly. 'I – don't remember being very good. Gosh, the cringey things we used to do in the name of romance. You poor thing, having to suffer through that performance.'

Shaun's smile pulls up higher on one side. 'We have very

different memories of that birthday, in that case. I didn't exactly feel like I suffered through it, given—'

He stops abruptly and the most endearing blush steals across his cheeks. It stains the tips of his ears bright pink.

Instead of talking about my boobs and the unsure, excited fumbling around that day in his bedroom, he clears his throat and turns to face the rest of the room before asking me in a strange, rough voice, 'Is that your Curtis, then?'

My Curtis.

'My fiancé,' I say and the word tastes like ash, as if just allowing myself to entertain these memories of my relationship with Shaun, his smile, the way he says my name . . . has poisoned it. I follow Shaun's gaze across the hall. 'Yes. And – you brought Aisha with you?'

He nods.

He takes a short, sharp sip of his drink, and then another. And another.

'She's very pretty. She seems lovely.'

'She is,' he tells me, still in that strange voice.

This is wrong, it's all so wrong. When he posted online that they were engaged, I felt genuinely pleased for him when I commented to wish them both a big congratulations. We were so far in the past, and their photos together were very sweet. Likewise, Shaun congratulated me on my engagement announcement on social media, but I felt no differently over his comment than anybody else's from school or old uni friends.

But this is wrong. Talking about our partners feels wrong. *Not* talking about them feels wrong.

A man walks up to us. Or rather, he walks up to the table to get himself another drink, and we happen to be right in the way. I know he's one of the rugby lads, but his name dances right at the edge of my memory. I can remember sitting in the row behind him in French and how he'd lean his chair right back into my desk, and I know he was always acting the class clown – often only being reined in by Ryan, rather than any threats of detention from the teachers. His sense of humour tended towards bullying rather than genuine comedy, as I recall.

I can remember having to pair with him for a French oral exam and the way he laughed about the word 'oral' every time someone said it, but can't remember his name. It's funny, the things my memory has decided were worth storing in the archives, and what information it threw in the bin.

He swaggers up to us with a broad grin. 'Alright, you two?'

'Hey, Freddie,' Shaun says, and – yes! That's it! How could I have forgotten Freddie Loughton? The smell of ale clings to him, and he's clearly tipsy enough that I assume he was in the gang who went to the pub before coming here. 'How's it going, mate?'

'All good, all good, can't complain, y'know?'

We shuffle out of the way as he helps himself to the spiked punch with a sloppy pour, and drops spill onto the papery tablecloth, staining it pink. Shaun's arm bumps into mine and I have to swallow a gasp at the heat that emanates from the touch, the flutter of excitement I feel over the electricity in that simple connection. Is it still there, or is nostalgia playing tricks on me?

I peek over at Shaun, only to find him straightening up immediately and tucking his arms close into his sides. The blush is still on his cheeks, or perhaps it's a new one. I watch the motion of his throat as he clenches his jaw and swallows, hard.

Not nostalgia, I decide. *It's still there.*

Freddie stops to face the two of us. He brushes some of his heavily styled sandy hair back even though it's so full of product that not even a rainstorm could budge it. 'So what're you guys up to these days?'

I tell him that I'm a paralegal and studying part time; Shaun says he's in HR, but thinking about looking for a new job since there's not much progression available in his current company. Freddie, it turns out, works in investment banking in Manchester.

'Do you like it there?' I ask politely.

'Can't complain,' he says. 'Work with some right arseholes, but the money's good.'

I pinch my lips and notice Shaun giving me a sidelong look. He's busy trying not to laugh – probably thinking the same thing as me: that it sounds like Freddie fits right in with the other alleged arseholes in his office.

'Did you bring anyone along tonight?' I ask then, because he's still standing around with us.

'Huh? Oh, nah. The bird I'm seeing, it's just casual. This isn't her scene.'

'Oh. How long have you been with her?'

He shrugs. 'Since September.'

Shaun's tone is dry when he says, 'Only ten months or so then. Very casual.'

It goes right over Freddie's head. He grins and raises his drink. 'Exactly, mate. You get it. I mean—' A laugh bursts out of him, and his eyes dart down to the diamond sparkling on my left hand, visible where my fingers are wrapped around my cup. 'Only took you, what, ten years to put a ring on it. You get it.'

I flush. 'Oh, no, that's not—'

And Shaun is saying, 'Er, we aren't actually—'

Freddie slings his arm around my shoulder though, with a camaraderie we have never shared and which makes me stumble a little now. 'Ah, you two were always a cute pair. *Bae goals.* You've got a real keeper on your hands here, Shaun, mate. Don't let her get away. My old French buddy, huh?'

I brace myself for the inevitable 'oral' joke, a reflex honed and never quite forgotten, it seems, and note with surprise that Freddie has kept hold of those inconsequential, unremarkable memories of school, too.

He doesn't bother with the joke for once, though, and Shaun seems stunned into silence by his words. Neither of us put Freddie right when he meanders back off to where Ryan is holding court in the middle of the hall, surrounded by people eager for a piece of him. I should go and say hello, too, but I don't want to be a pest, or interrupt anything.

We both stand quietly as Freddie leaves, and then I hear the heavy rush of breath as Shaun exhales. I look over in time to see his shoulders sag, and he draws his gaze up to meet mine. There's a sadness in those eyes that hits a nerve, calls out to the ache buried deep in my heart where he used to take up so much space, and all I can do is stare back at him and think, *I know*.

The song changes; someone shrieks with laughter nearby. Reality beckons.

'Um, right,' I mumble. 'I suppose I ought to—'

At the same time, Shaun says, 'He's right.'

'Sorry?'

'Freddie. He's right. You were a real keeper, Steph.'

'I—'

68

I don't know what to say to that. I don't know what I *can* say to that, because there's a niggle of doubt about what he truly means. That he shouldn't have let me go? Or is it merely an acknowledgement that what we had was good, back when? I think I know which it is, but . . . I know that replying to it will be dangerous. The words sound like a promise; the truth is, they're a grenade.

And then Josh is calling to him, beckoning him over to go help with the pizzas that have just arrived, and Shaun gives me a small, sorry smile before he leaves me standing there with my thumb trapped on the trigger, and the potential to implode everything simmering underneath the surface.

Chapter Nine

Hayden

'Most Likely to Succeed'

I, for one, think I have been extremely successful in social-ising tonight. And, more impressively, have not screamed in anybody's face when they express sympathy for the turn my life took after school. It's also nearly an hour and a half into the evening, and I'm still here.

By those measures, I am smashing this whole reunion thing.

I busy myself with the small crowd that are arranging the pizza boxes on the trestle tables, if only for the excuse of a breather between small talk and mingling. Even if there are some people here I'm enjoying catching up with, there are so many I barely spoke to when we were spending five days a week stuck in the same building – the same classrooms – and who I'm struggling to really care about now. It feels – forced. Fake.

Everybody else is either doing a much better job of pretending than I am, or else I've reverted into my judge-mental seventeen-year-old self, assuming the worst of them. But when people like Josh or Elise or Tommy ask what I'm up to these days, when they barely bothered with me back in school in the first place, it's hard to believe they're genuinely interested in the answer.

It's entirely possible that I'm jaded by the pity parade everybody seems to be throwing me, but still.

Instead of returning to the group I just excused myself from – an odd mix of people I wouldn't have seen together outside enforced group projects – I seek out Ashleigh. I spot the back of her head and see her gesturing animatedly with one hand. Maybe I can hide in her shadow for a little while.

Funny, how I used to do that at school. We were both nerdy and conscientious, but Ashleigh never had that introverted streak I did. She was happy to stand up in front of a year-wide assembly and corral people into a fundraiser or project, and never took shit off anybody. It was hard to pay attention to me when Ashleigh was so much more noticeable, but I was always relieved when my overachievements went largely ignored by everybody else; it felt like one less thing to be bullied or teased about. She offered me a bit of breathing space in which I didn't feel forced to defend myself.

And I know, logically, that it was a case of 'wrong time, wrong place'. That, for the most part, my classmates were 'not my sort of people' – and I wasn't theirs either. I was a geek deemed just likeable enough to be included in things like orchestra trips or Shaun's house parties, but my interests were things that my peers found boring or stupid. Which was alright, because my interests were *mine*, and I didn't want anyone else to join in anyway.

I'm not quite as shy and nervous as I used to be.

Except, of course, for the indisputable fact that I apparently am, at least for the purpose of tonight. And rather than face another round of people I barely remember telling me what a shame it is that I had to quit uni and then asking why I never went back after Margot was born, or having them ask what I'm up to these days with that gleam of expectation in their eyes that dies away so quickly when they learn the truth, I would much rather lurk near Ashleigh and defer to her achievements instead.

It's . . . easier. Safer.

Any excuse to avoid thinking about the person they all expected me to become, the dreams and ambitions I used to have for myself so long ago that I'm struggling to remember the me who first conceived of them.

I grab two plates and load each with a few slices of pizza before the hordes descend, then pick my way across the room. I slip into the group at Ashleigh's side and hand her one of the plates. She tosses me a grateful smile, but is mid-flow, telling people about the first time a drug she worked on was approved and made readily available to hospitals and patients, so I fall into the lull of nodding in all the right places along with everybody else.

Bryony is with her, and snatches a slice off the plate as if the pair of them have always been so close. 'Ooh, thanks Hayden! You're a star.' Ashleigh doesn't acknowledge her either, too into her storytelling, and I wonder if it's bothering her that Bryony seems to have attached herself at her side tonight. I half expect it to be part of some childish prank – like a full *Carrie* moment is waiting just around the corner, except maybe with a bucket of glitter instead of pig's blood, knowing Bryony. But right now, she's all smiles and bubbly personality, so maybe I'm being too harsh. Maybe Ashleigh's just the shiny new thing, or, an even wilder concept, Bryony is genuinely interested in reconnecting. If Ash and I weren't good friends these days, I probably wouldn't care either way. I wonder if she cares.

'It's just so rewarding,' she says now, raising her voice to half a shout, 'to know that what I'm doing is making a *real* difference to people's lives. Saving them, even.'

My brow furrows as I give her a quizzical look. I know Ash is proud of the work she does and the moral fibre of it really grounds her, but . . . she's not the type to boast about it, make it seem so performative.

Before I can ask, though, I hear a raised voice a short distance behind us, and Ryan Lawal is saying, 'Obviously it was a *huge* compliment for the PM to call me in for the initiative when I was still relatively new to the world of politics, but that just goes to show, doesn't it? Massively successful launch, and I visited several schools *personally* to see just what a positive impact it had on the kids' lives.'

Ah.

That explains it.

I look over at him, but Ryan determinedly has his back to us. Not to us – to Ashleigh. There's a stretch of space between the two of them, a void that everybody seems to be skirting around rather than risk getting sucked into it. His posture is infused with that easy, natural confidence he's always possessed and Ashleigh makes no move to suggest she cares if he overheard her, or that she heard him – but that tether between the two of them is almost tangible.

I roll my eyes and smirk down at my plate.

'I just think,' Ashleigh says then, unprompted, 'that the government funding into this sort of research – for degenerative diseases that affect such large numbers of the population – is sadly lacking.'

73

'Well,' says a guy I vaguely recognise from A-level maths, 'the state of the NHS these days . . .'

And a woman who I *think* is someone's partner because I definitely don't recognise her, takes the position of devil's advocate to say, 'I totally agree. But I can understand why developing new medicines has to take a back seat to, say, funding nurses' salaries.'

'Mm, it's very sad when people get such tunnel vision about things and can't appreciate the big picture,' Ryan is saying to his own group, though his voice carries as if it's part of our conversation too. 'A real shame. Runs the risk of being quite selfish, though I'm sure that's not *really* the intention.'

Ashleigh bristles, lips pursing into a small, tight pucker for a brief moment, the only sign that she was paying attention to him.

She shoves a slice of pizza into her mouth and chews violently. This time, she casts me a look that lets me know *she's* the one who needs saving.

So I tell the group, 'Er, the pizza's here, if you wanted any.'

Ashleigh sighs, short and sharp, and barely audible.

But, pathetic as my attempt to steal the spotlight is, it works enough that the guy from maths (Paul? No, that can't be right, there were no Pauls in our year) says, 'Haven't seen you yet tonight, Hayden! How's things, mate? What're you up to these days, anything exciting?'

Bryony reaches her arm across Ashleigh's front and lays her hand lightly on my sleeve. Her nails are long and glitter bright pink. 'Only the most exciting adventure! You're a stay-at-home dad for the most part now, aren't you, Hayden? Now I bet *that's* rewarding.'

'Um.' I scratch the back of my neck, not sure if that's supposed to be an insult or not. A couple of people laugh; is it that laugh that you do to fill space and keep the mood up, or are they in on Bryony's joke too, if it does exist? I clear my throat and say, 'Yeah, it's quite an adventure, I suppose. I work in software development, too, but that's all remote now and the hours are flexible. I'm thinking of moving to full time now both the girls are in school, but I've been saying that for the last year and still haven't spoken to my boss about it.'

I laugh, and wait for them to join in, but this time they're all quiet. Ashleigh manages a smile, but she's still got a mouth full of pizza.

'Because the girls just take up so much of my time,' I go on, but that doesn't sound right. It's not right. It's true, but not the *truth*. I pause, floundering for the right way to phrase it, but Steph's friend Thea is nodding along and making sympathetic noises.

'I bet. And childcare is so expensive, isn't it? My sister's always banging on about that. She still hasn't gone back to work since her maternity leave, and that was four years ago, now. It must be so tricky to balance.'

Noodles Greg, who I hadn't noticed join the group, pitches in. 'No wonder you're stagnating, Hayden! You had to give everything up for those kids. Maybe soon though, eh? Now they're getting a bit older and that. Never too late to turn it all around!'

Bryony nods fiercely. 'Exactly!'

'Turn it around?'

'You know, get out there and make a name for yourself. Do all those cool things you could've done otherwise. I mean, you should *be* the boss.' Greg laughs. 'Still plenty of time to do something and make a 'thirty under thirty' list, right?'

'I, er, yes. I suppose there is.'

'And you must have something you're working on,' Thea says, with an encouraging nod. 'I always remember you shutting yourself up in the DT rooms or somewhere because you were coding something or working on those robots you used to play around with. Stuff like that. Do you still do that?'

'Not . . . so much, these days.'

'Oh, that's such a shame! You were always tinkering about! Making stuff!'

'Yeah,' not-Paul from maths says. 'It was so awesome – why'd you give it up? You could be making tons off that, I bet.'

Awesome. My attempt at a polite smile tightens into a brittle line and my teeth clench. They didn't used to think it was 'awesome' ten years ago, when it was just geeky and weird. But *now* – oh, of course, now that they recognise it could be worth money, that it might add up to something they use in their everyday lives – *now*, it's cool.

I try to think about the last time I settled into one of those projects, the sort I used to do at school. Passion projects, my parents and teachers tended to call them, and it was an apt label – I was passionate about the work. It was exciting; a novel take on something that provided just enough of a challenge to get the gears in my brain spinning. Testing it to see if it worked *this time* was the best kind of adrenaline rush.

How long has it been since I last did something like that?

I still invent things, but these days it's games for Margot and Skye or bedtime stories. I did program a mobile with

76

different settings when Skye was born – it played different songs and shone different lights depending on the setting, and what sort of mood she was in. That's the only thing I can remember making in the last ten years.

I have endless lists of notes on my phone. Scraps of ideas, or photos of diagrams scrawled haphazardly in crayon that I wanted to jot down for myself while I sat colouring with the girls – diagrams that promptly ended up scribbled over or coloured in and which I never felt any great sense of attachment to beyond a fleeting concept. Easier to get it down on paper to come back to later, rather than letting it take up space in my brain where it would fester and grow and threaten to take over when I had other – *real* – responsibilities to deal with. More important things that required that energy and focus.

Later, I think, any time that happens. *Another time.*

It's never been 'later'. That wistful 'other time' has never transpired.

I wonder what my teenage self would make of that. Not the stay-at-home dad stuff or the university drop-out status – but . . . giving up. Reprioritising. Brushing that spark and passion aside like it means so little, is so unimportant, when it used to feel more essential to me than oxygen.

I wonder what he'd think of the fact I've forgotten what it's like to let myself dream.

It's a stark realisation to discover that I've forgotten I ever even *had* those sorts of dreams, once upon a time.

My mouth drops open as I try to think up a response – *anything*, anything at all – as the others watch me expectantly. Nothing comes out.

Ashleigh finally steps in with an offhand laugh. 'Come on, guys, you really think he's about to spill all to you? Hayden's projects have *always* been top secret until they're ready to go out into the world. If he told you, he'd have to kill you.'

My smile returns and I laugh along with everybody else, but the tension remains in my shoulders. Not-Paul starts talking about some start-up he used to work for that was developing an app for home and online security for public figures and celebrities, and all the NDAs that had involved.

'Nice!' Noodles Greg says. 'Are you still there? Did you get to meet any of the celebs and that?'

'Oh, no. It . . . started coming under quite a lot of scrutiny. Data-leak risks, stuff like that, paparazzi hacking accounts. I left; it didn't seem like the sort of thing I wanted to be involved in.'

The group nods along sagely and I join in by default, but Bryony interrupts.

'I remember that app. Didn't they go bust? Lose a shed-load of money getting sued by the beta users because of violation of privacy, and some people at the company were selling the info on? And you were really all-in before that, I thought. You worked on building their partnerships, didn't you?'

He flushes a shade of puce I've never actually seen on a human. 'Well, yes, for a time, but of course I knew I had to pack it in as soon as I realised there was anything shady about it and leave before it all got, er, out of hand.'

Bryony's head tilts sideways. 'Really? You know, I'm sure I saw you post on LinkedIn about suddenly being made redundant – you were reaching out to your network to see if anybody had similar jobs going you could move on to.'

'Well. Er. You know. It . . . coincided.'

Bryony's scoff is audible. '*Riiiight*. I mean, I totally have some connections if you're still looking, though. It's got to be hard to move on after you've been sacked from a place that's been dragged for filth by the media like that.'

'Better to take the redundancy pay-out,' he says, a bit too quickly and firmly, eyes whipping around the rest of us. 'But *technically* I had already chosen to leave, so, that's . . .'

'I think I might go and get some pizza, you know,' says Thea.

'Good shout,' Greg says.

The group peel away one by one, and not-Paul (what *is* his name? Do I care enough to ask if Ashleigh knows it? Probably not) vanishes, too, looking agitated and flustered.

'What a prat,' Ashleigh mutters.

I don't know who she's talking about – it could be his careful rearranging of the truth, or even Bryony for embarrassing him. But I nod anyway.

She steals a glance over her shoulder. Ryan has moved on somewhere else; Ashleigh scowls.

Oh, right. *Him.*

Maybe he had a point about that tunnel vision. Just a minor one.

Bryony gives us both a bright smile, completely oblivious, and moves to slot herself between us and steer us to another group of people. She loops her arms through ours and I'm too taken aback to pull away.

'Come on, you two. Let's go stir up some more gossip, shall we?'

I decide I've made a dreadful mistake tonight: self-imposed success markers aside, I should have bailed when I had the chance.

Chapter Ten

Ashleigh

'Most Likely to Kill Each Other'

The glamour of being a popular girl for the night is fast wearing off.

Thanks, in no small part, to Ryan.

Bryony propels us to a spot near the pizzas, and I've done enough networking events to realise that it's very purposeful. There's so much foot traffic passing by this part of the hall now that it's a prime position to see and be seen. Which, of course, is Bryony's MO. Hayden looks a little uncomfortable, but also like figuring out a way to extricate himself is too awkward to contemplate, so he just stands quietly, his eyes tracking everyone who walks by with passive curiosity. He scratches absently at some glitter stuck to his neck.

It doesn't escape my notice that Ryan has done a similar thing. Although, actually, I think it's less a case of setting up camp where he can speak to everybody, and a bit more that he's been ambushed on his way to grab some food.

With some uncanny sixth sense, he lifts his head and turns

it precisely towards me. Not even looking around and catching sight of me. *Right at me.*

Has he been tracking me around the hall, like I have him?

I don't smile, because Ryan has rarely been worthy of my smiles, and my expression sets in stone when he smirks at me, the bright, blinding flash of his teeth showing briefly as his mouth pulls up on one side.

It's not like I've been *watching* him, but I feel like if I look away, it'll prove some kind of point in his favour, so I stare and stare until that smug expression is wiped off his face and he has to shake himself a little before turning his full attention back to his conversation.

Good.

There's a surreal quality about this whole night. A shiny gloss applied to everything – to *me* – that makes it all feel bigger, better, brighter. This is the way I dreamed of this reunion going: people fawning over how much I've achieved and how impressive they think my career is, the compliments on how I look or my clothes, the flash of envy in people's eyes as they realise that for all my bravado and braggadocio back when we were teenagers, I've *done it*. I've done the things I said I would – and more.

I was right to think that this would all be worth it for the feeling of vindication when the people who used to put me down because I was 'boring' or just 'not pretty *enough*' are forced to admit to themselves that I was always enough. That I am more than they ever expected, and the stream of snide comments and snickering behind my back all those years has only hurt them in the end.

Here, now, I'm not annoying and square and a drag. I am intimidating, impressive.

Incandescent.

It burns hot and angry in my chest, this tight ball of flame that licks at my lungs and makes my breath come fast and shallow, spiking my adrenaline and heating my skin. Barely contained, pressurised enough that I want to burst with how good it feels to come out standing on top when so many of my classmates got used to walking all over me. This must be how Bryony used to feel all the time in school.

I almost can't believe it's actually happening now. I'd think they were all in on it together as some cruel joke in one last righteous 'fuck you' to me, if not for Ryan.

As grating as his mere presence is, he is the one thing about tonight that feels – normal. Sort of . . . right. Slotting right back into place, like we never went away.

And, God, I hate him.

He's been *impossible* to avoid in the last ten years. At one point, it seemed like there was no escape from him; I'd turn on the news or open Twitter or see someone reading a newspaper on the Tube and – there he was. His quick rise to fame on the England rugby team. His brief, sterling stint there scoring tries and then the injury that knocked him out of the game for good.

I remember seeing that on the news and some horrible, nasty part of me that only reared its head when he was around thought, *that'll show him*. So it was probably karmic retribution that he started using his newfound fame and influence to get in with politicians and prominent CEOs, lending his name to projects and campaigns that mainly involved helping schools or underprivileged kids to get access to better resources and after-school programmes. He started a damned book club, for God's sake. Ryan Lawal! A *book club*! This coming from the boy who stole my course notes on *Of Mice and Men* to study for the GCSE because he 'couldn't be arsed' to read the book.

Not, of course, that he mentioned *that* in any of the interviews he did about it.

Not that I watched them. Or went looking for them. Or trawled the comments on trending Twitter threads, smirking to myself at the mean replies from trolls. Obviously not – what a colossal waste of time that would've been. How jarringly unsatisfying and agitated it would've left me feeling. So, obviously, I didn't.

Not . . . *that* often, anyway.

Bryony giggles and pushes a hand into my shoulder, and I try to scrub my head clean of any and all thoughts pertaining to Ryan Lawal. Easier said than done.

She smirks at me, a mischievous glint in her green eyes. 'It's cracking me up that you two still want to one-up each other. I thought you both would've grown out of it by now.'

'I guess not,' I mumble, then correct myself quickly to say, 'I'm not trying to one-up him.'

'Please. We *all* know what your stupid rivalry looks like. Hey, Hayden, you wanna take bets on how long it'll be before the pair of them have it out in the middle of the hall for everybody to see?'

Hayden shuffles from one foot to the other. 'That only happened a few times.'

Bryony's face lights up with a laugh that carries so well, heads turn to see what the fun's all about. 'Oh, man, do you remember when they used to get called in to the Head of Year's office because they kept 'disrupting class', or whatever, because they'd get into such an argument with each other?'

I roll my eyes. 'It's not my fault nobody else would call him out for acting like a prat, or tell him when he was wrong. I mean, trying to organise a sit-in to get them to sell pizza again at lunch? That was in *direct opposition* to how I'd got everyone signing a petition for healthier lunches. He was too impulsive and downright *silly*, and there was no reasoning with him. Not when he had his head in the clouds and didn't do an ounce of real work. Someone had to put him in his place.'

Even Hayden gives me a look over Bryony's shoulder that suggests it wasn't *always* Ryan's fault. He even pulls a face that I've seen him give Skye when she's being bloody-minded and refusing to do something like eat her vegetables or clean her teeth, and I have to look away.

Fine. So it wasn't *always* Ryan's fault. But what was I supposed to do – lie down and roll over, let him carry on unchallenged and thinking he'd won? If we hadn't both held our own so well – me at the practicalities and important things, and Ryan at being so bloody *likeable* – there's no way they would've let us carry on as Head Girl and Head Boy, and we would've been in *actual* trouble half the time, too.

But it's – it's not *fair*. Ryan wasn't supposed to be . . . *this*. Wasn't supposed to do well for himself after school. He was *supposed* to be an unthinking, laddish boy, the glory days of being the school's rugby captain long behind him, now stuck in some dry, boring job that made him grey and worn out, with the physique he boasted as a teenager turned pot-bellied and weak. He was *supposed* to fit the exact stereotype I'd crafted in my mind for him.

Oh, but that's *just* like him, isn't it? To be so damned good-looking ten years later and with the stellar career, his smug face constantly grinning out at me from the TV or my news app. *Of course* he's still flying high on that charisma that everyone else seems to find so endearing, held aloft by them, and probably all while still taking the credit for someone else's hard work.

He is the person in a group project who contributes nothing except a well-timed joke ad-libbed in the one slide he has to present, and is lauded for all his (supposed) efforts afterwards.

His A* for our chemistry project at A level can attest to that.

Yes, I bet he is *exactly* that same person now.

I just . . . I wish that this time, for once, I could have *won*. I wish that his life was a little sorrier than it is, so he has to concede that every time he tried to tear *me* down and undermine me and make me feel ashamed of myself at school, he was wrong.

He always made it so clear that it was his school. There was only room for one of us at the top, and nobody ever wanted it to be me.

It . . . would've been nice if it finally had been, that's all.

Chapter Eleven

Bryony

'Most Likely to Become Famous'

I don't know why I was so worried about saving face in front of these people I haven't seen for ten years, because honestly, some of them are doing an absolutely *terrible* job of it.

Absolute amateur hour. It's laughable. Like, genuinely, laugh-out-loud ridiculous.

Because, I'm sorry, do they *honestly* think they can straight-up contradict the things they've put on social media? I cannot be the only one who did a digital stalk of old classmates before tonight – although, admittedly, mine was probably the most in-depth, since I had the list of everyone's names and emails to send out the evite for tonight and the whole 'yearbook' presentation update project.

Do they really think they can get away with it?

I mean, I know I can't talk, but *really*. It's one thing to be – selective – with the truth, and *imply* certain things, but to tell barefaced lies? Like, we *know* you got engaged two years ago, we all congratulated you on Facebook, and we *know* you suddenly changed your profile pics to stop including them and changed your status to 'single'. Don't pretend they just couldn't make it tonight. And you're just *not* climbing the corporate ladder at an unprecedented rate, are you, we can all see that your current job title on LinkedIn includes the word 'junior'.

It's unstoppable, the urge to correct them, to point it out. Like Paul and his job at a failed start-up, or Tommy saying he runs a fitness company when he's a PT and not even *actually* working for himself (I've seen the gym branding on his polo shirt in a selfie he posted on Instagram). Or worst of all, when Morgan was showing off about her boyfriend she met at the hospital, making out he was a doctor like she is when actually he's an accountant and they met when he came into A&E with a skateboarding injury.

I don't know why she lied about it. An accountant who skateboards is arguably a *much* cooler story. And she even brought him along! Any of us could ask him and find out the truth.

I ignore the bright red flush creeping down Morgan's neck right now and smooth a hand over the leg of my jumpsuit. Some of the sequins have tilted out of place near my hip as I've been wandering around.

'Isn't he part of a group? Skateboarding, I mean.'

Josh sneers. 'What, like a hobby? God. That's a bit childish, isn't it, Morg?'

The look on her face says she thinks so too, which is a bit sad. I bet the boyfriend is definitely cooler than she is. Just because she resents having to become a doctor because that's the path her parents steered her down . . .

I arch an eyebrow at Josh, though. 'Didn't you take up rollerblading during lockdown?'

He baulks, and fidgets. Hassan starts laughing, joking around because he didn't know that, how sly of Josh to not tell him.

Well, that's what he gets for using his old MSN handle on TikTok. Like I said: *amateurs*. He mutters, 'The girl I was with at the time got into it when it started going viral and stuff.'

Hassan cracks up, gleeful. 'Mate, that's hilarious. Do you have videos of it? As *if* you took up rollerblading!'

Morgan adds in a suddenly lofty tone, 'Yes, well, Alfie's part of a local community group and participates in competitions. It's all quite serious, actually.'

'Yeah, real daredevil on the half-pipe, I bet,' Josh snipes.

'He is, actually.'

I smother my laugh and take a drink, rolling my eyes. They got themselves into this mess, really, but I fight the teacher-y urge to tell them to grow up already. Seriously, did they learn *nothing* after I had to call Elise out for her totally *not*-authentic Chanel bag she brought to school, and all the lies she tried to spin to explain why the lining didn't look the same in her cheap dupe as on the Chanel website? Clearly, everyone's gotten too comfortable without somebody around to call them on their bullshit.

I catch Hayden, on the edge of the group, frowning at me. His high forehead furrows underneath the messy spray of ginger hair, nose crinkling and pushing his wiry glasses further up. He looks at me like I'm a particularly nasty equation and he's been called up to solve it in front of the class on the whiteboard.

There's a sort of accusatory edge to it, and if Hayden wasn't the kind to keep so much to himself, I'd worry that he might have done as much research into people as I had, and knows all *my* secrets. My pulse picks up, sweat starting to slick the palms of my hands.

'What?' I ask him, careless and bold. Every bit as accusatory as the expression on his face.

Hayden's expression clears, but he ducks his head. 'Nothing. Sorry.'

I stick around for another minute or so, listening to the boys bicker and Morgan trying to pretend she's not a judgemental snob about her boyfriend's hobby, but only so that I don't let Hayden put a chink in my carefully honed armour. As if I'm going to let the most introverted, nerdiest kid in the year take *me* down. This kid used to go to Doctor Who conventions on the weekends, for crying out loud.

I count down the seconds, glad when my heart rate calms, and then move on to mingle with some other people. I notice Steph lurking near the drinks table with some of her old mates, looking unusually quiet and detached, but her fiancé, Curtis, has his arm around her and she's tucked neatly, cosily, into his side; maybe she's just tired. She *does* have a lot on, between her nine-to-five and studying part time on top of that. I scan the room for Ashleigh, who's standing with . . .

Oh, Jesus. She's with *Freddie Loughton.*

Hand on his bicep, laughing at something he's saying, standing with Freddie bloody Loughton. He tosses his heavily styled hair as I watch, looking like someone who loves himself a little *too* much. I'm pretty sure he's got a long-term girlfriend, but – then again, this is Freddie, and there was definitely a point in the last couple of years where he was dating three girls at once, if his Instagram is anything to go by. Not to mention, I know from experience that he's just not worth the effort.

Should I tell her? I'd think she needed saving if she didn't look like she was flirting right back and had him wrapped around her little finger.

Ah, it's fine. Let her have her fun. From what I hear, her

recent relationships have been pretty short-lived and her current dating life is fairly non-existent – she's too career focused, or whatever. God knows she spent long enough at school being so highly strung that she deserves to let her hair down for a night. Indulge in who teenage her could have been.

Even if it is with a prat like Freddie Loughton.

I wander towards the tables to get a refill on my drink, if only to look like I'm moving with purpose, and let my eyes skim around the room. It's funny to see old cliques re-forming: the A-level art girls have gravitated towards each other and every so often one of them will peel away to go flirt with somebody while the others watch and hide shrieks of laughter behind their hands; the rugby lads are laughing at some bawdy joke, all sprawled out on a pile of chairs near the stage, and some of the more serious kids from orchestra are in a close cluster by the balloon arch, eyes intent and gestures wide as they talk.

People call to me as I pass by, and a thrill runs through me at it.

My eyes snag on the poster of myself that's hiding my picture on the staff board and the excitement dies quickly. They wouldn't be half so excited to chat if they knew what a failure I've become. What a sad, sorry state my life is in these days. They wouldn't be so interested in hearing stories about the times I've cried myself to sleep or the heartbreak of moving home to my parents' and accepting I'd never be famous or well known or successful – a pain so deep and raw that it still confines me to the cocoon of my duvet some days even now.

Nobody wants to hear about that. Even *I* don't want to know about it.

It's better this way. Much, much better.

Standing alone at the edge of the hall with a fresh drink in hand, surveying everybody, I allow myself a little breather to wallow in the self-pity and reaffirm my plan to keep pretending. When I notice Hayden making his way towards me, I peel away and head for the group with Ryan and some of the lads, knowing he won't follow me there.

I don't think Hayden knows anything, but I *do* know he's smart enough to work it out, if I give him enough openings.

So, that's easy. I just won't do that.

Ashleigh seems to be happy to prove to people how well she's done for herself almost like it's to spite them for ever doubting her or looking down on her; I don't know if Hayden has a similar streak in him, these days, but I don't want to risk it.

I slip into the group just at the perfect moment. There's a lull in conversation and as people turn to murmur hellos at me, Ryan throws me that drop-dead lovely grin of his, which reaches his eyes and feels like its own kind of spotlight shining on me.

'There she is! Woman of the hour! Helluva party, Bryony.'

'Please.' I turn my head to flick my ponytail back over my shoulder. 'Like you'd expect anything less. Don't you know who I am?'

He laughs, and since I didn't greet him properly earlier – haven't actually so far at all, tonight – I step across the circle to give him a one-armed hug and kiss his cheek. Ryan's arm feels solid around me, his hand warm on my waist, and he draws back slowly. Purposefully. *Lingering*.

Hmm. That's interesting.

'Always a pleasure to see you, Bryony,' he says, with a wink that makes it *very* clear that he's flirting a bit.

Which, I mean, of course he is.

But still. I guess we haven't grown out of that, either.

'Miss me?' I tease, but the response is like a default setting. The slanted, closed-lipped smile I offer him is only because I'm on autopilot. This is what my character would do and say, this is the role I've taken on tonight, old habits drawn around me like a favourite dressing gown. Ryan and I were both pretty well liked and ran in the same circles together at school; we went to prom together and everything. We were never a Steph-and-Shaun kind of thing though. Beyond a few sloppy, drunk kisses at parties and casual flirting in the common room, we were only ever just friends. It was never anything *serious*.

It isn't now, either, but that doesn't mean it isn't still a bit of fun.

I couldn't have stuck having a boyfriend who wanted to share my spotlight, anyway. The whole 'power couple' thing never appealed to me – I'm too much of a one-woman show.

'Absolutely,' Ryan says, a bit loudly. A woman giggles behind him and his head ticks towards the sound, eyes darkening for a moment before he smiles again. He stands a little straighter, rearranging his limbs slightly – the roll of his shoulders, the shift of his weight from one leg to the other before a brief wince steals across his face and he thinks better of it. I remember his left leg was the injured one, and wonder if it's rude to ask about it.

Just as I'm weighing up the question, he says, like he's announcing it to the whole group, 'Hear you're doing pretty bloody well for yourself these days, babe. Still doing theatre and that?'

'I take on roles in movies and TV, sometimes, too.'

'Oh, yeah? Anything we'd have heard of?'

'Probably.' I laugh and everybody follows suit. 'I'm in a great position where I get to choose the projects that sound most interesting to me. It's totally enriching.'

And also not . . . technically a lie. Well, apart from the 'great position' part.

'I've got a few things in the works,' I add, which is also not *exactly* untrue. There's a movie coming out soon that I had a very, very tiny part in (so much so that I don't know if I'll even be in the final cut), but it was low budget and there hasn't been much fanfare about its upcoming release. And I'll be back on the circuit to pick up work as an extra soon, after term finishes in a few weeks.

'Sweet,' says Ryan. 'Reckon we all keep an eye out for you on the silver screen. Waiting to see your name in lights one day, or your face on the side of a bus.'

My smile feels rigid, and it's like the words turn my bones to lead. I'm overcome with the urge to sink into the floor and wrap my arms around my head, block out the party and disappear into the dark until sleep pulls me under. He conjures up the images from the dreams I used to cherish, which poison and plague me now.

If he weren't such a decent guy, I'd think he was laughing at me.

I fight off the melancholy that threatens to choke me – I'm playing a part. I am not that person. I am not me, I am her. My smile eases a little bit.

And, because I know this is my cue to respond, I say, 'One day. Just you wait.'

Chapter Twelve

Steph

'Most Likely to End Up Together'

'There you are, sweetie, I was just – oh! It's . . . It's you.'

Too startled to do anything but stare, I feel a blush creep over my cheeks at my mix-up. It wouldn't be so awkward if I'd mistaken anybody else here tonight for Curtis, but . . .

Shaun's hand stays where it is, his cool fingers on my bare elbow sending sparks shooting through my veins and making it all the more obvious to me how my skin seems to be burning all of a sudden. Can he tell? Surely he can feel the sprint of my pulse beneath his fingertips.

His eyes remain locked on mine; there's something agonisingly still about him, and I'm not even sure if he's breathing. His normally smiling mouth is drawn into something straighter and more serious than I'm used to, the upwards arch of his eyebrows giving his expression a plaintive quality that I know will triumph over any resistance I have. The look takes me back to the last summer before university, and his gentle, hopeful question about how we'd try long-distance, wouldn't we? And the quickness of my response – *yes, yes,*

94

of course, how could he think otherwise? This was us; we would make it work. Breaking up just because we were going to universities four hours apart was never even up for consideration, as far as I was concerned.

Now, though, Shaun says, 'I don't suppose you'd fancy . . . going somewhere for a chat?'

If my blush was starting to recede, his words bring it back with a vengeance. My entire face feels like it's on fire and Shaun's eyes widen immediately as he hears his own words. He snatches his hand from my arm, and goosebumps rise there.

Go for a chat, we always used to say, when we were among friends and wanted a few quiet minutes of privacy to share a kiss or lean into each other without everybody else's eyes on us. We both had our limits when it came to PDA.

The words conjure up memories of slipping away to deserted corridors on rainy lunchtime breaks while everybody else was huddled around the good radiator, Shaun's arms slipping around my waist and my hands sliding inside his blazer, chasing his body heat, my head tilting up to his to accept a deep, dizzying kiss.

I wonder which particular memory it brings to Shaun's mind, and take a little comfort in the simple fact he shares in my awkwardness right now. He laughs, and some of the tension in my shoulders unfurls.

'Not like *that*,' he clarifies, rolling his eyes at himself. 'I just meant – maybe we could have a proper catch-up, somewhere a bit . . . less noisy? Away from . . . all this.'

The hand that was just on my arm gestures widely around us and I instinctively follow it, glancing around the hall. Bryony is talking loudly and emphatically about a community theatre project she helped out with a little while ago, positioned in the path of one of the little light-boxes so that the pink strobe hits her sequinned outfit and casts a sparkling display. Some people have started dancing near the stage; Hayden and Ashleigh are doing some odd, coordinated dance that people are clapping along to, and Freddie Loughton is loitering nearby. The rest of the rugby lads are sprawled on some chairs by the windows; Ryan is with them, sat bent forward on his knees and nodding intently, apparently listening to something Tommy is saying, but he seems to be looking over to the dance floor instead. Morgan, Priya and the others are standing a little way off, giggling and chattering animatedly in a way that makes me itch to join them – I can see myself going over and Thea slipping an arm around my waist as I'm drawn in, and everybody pitching together to update me on whatever story I've missed, just like old times.

But the pull towards Shaun is stronger, and I keep my eyes on the hall a beat longer, even as I'm acutely aware of him sucking in a sharp breath, waiting for my response, and the way his hands begin to fidget.

On a cluster of chairs in the corner between the doors and the windows, Curtis is sat with a few people. Morgan's boyfriend is there, and Hiro from the rugby team and Shaun's friend Josh. Everybody looks relaxed, with plates of half-eaten pizza on their laps or a drink in hand, engaged even if they're less energetic (possibly simply 'less drunk') than some of the other people in the room.

I lost Curtis about fifteen minutes ago as the groups we were talking to had migrated around the hall, but didn't think very much of it. Curtis is good at getting on with people and – while I might be a bit biased – I think he's the sort of guy that's instantly likeable. He'll find common ground, listen attentively and ask thoughtful, interesting questions. It's one of the things I find most endearing about him.

And we've never been one of those couples that are completely co-dependent and only come as a package deal. Working in the same office, we set some boundaries very early on; we didn't want to make ourselves the subject of workplace gossip or drama by making it so obvious we were together, attached at the hip and never seen apart. So while I don't feel obliged to go and join him now, or that he'll worry, it seems . . . wrong, somehow, if I were to vanish altogether.

With my ex-boyfriend. The first great love of my life.

How would *I* feel, in his shoes? If he were to sneak off with his ex, away from prying eyes and ears, leaving me at a party where I know nobody?

But – no, that's not fair. I trust Curtis, and I know what kind of man he is. If he were seeing his first proper girlfriend for the first time in ten years – someone he dated as a *teenager* – then I wouldn't begrudge him a quiet catch-up. It's the natural thing to want to do, and I'd probably think it was quite sweet. I wouldn't be worried about him sneaking off to snog someone he hasn't seen in almost a decade, for goodness' sake.

He trusts me, too. And – and, well, Shaun's got a fiancée. He means it in all innocence, I know that. We're adults, now, we're going for a mature conversation, not to steal a kiss between classes.

We're not doing anything *wrong*.

I'm just being silly, that's all.

I draw a breath and turn back to Shaun with a smile I hope reaches my eyes. 'Alright then.'

There's a flicker in his eyes, and . . . I don't recognise it. Uncertainty, perhaps, or it could be resolution. It's gone before I can pinpoint it, though, and he nods before gesturing towards the doors in an 'after you' motion.

I'm too aware of each step I take; it feels like I'm running, fleeing, even as it happens in slow motion, the hall bending and warping around me and the doors looming large but never quite getting closer like in a bad dream. The music and laughter and voices become muffled, the only clear sound my heart beating in my ears and the click of my heels on the floor.

And then I'm at the doors and my eyes are focused only on Curtis. I'm directly in his eyeline and I freeze, my fingers on the cold metal handle, my entire body vibrating as I wait for him to notice me, to ask me what I'm doing.

To put a stop to this mad, selfish, innocent impulse.

But he throws his head back, laughing at something, and the spell is broken.

Nobody notices as we leave; I'm sure of it, because I brace myself for the playful jeers that I know some of our old friends and classmates haven't quite grown out of – jokes they'd make about us leaving together and the chorus of 'Oo-oo-ooh!'s.

But there's nothing, and the doors swing shut behind Shaun, and the silence of the school corridor envelops us. A fluorescent lightbulb buzzes noisily overhead, and, for a moment, we stand facing each other, and I wonder if he feels as uncomfortable in his skin as I do right now.

Because while we aren't doing anything wrong, I realise what feels so *off* about all this, and it's me – as if my body is suddenly no longer mine, should be smaller and skinnier and younger. As if there's too much in my mind, a life that doesn't belong to me and feels just out of reach now. It could belong to a character from a book I spent all day reading avidly, or a dream, instead.

It's like stepping back through the wardrobe and out of Narnia.

Looking up at Shaun, I don't feel like the paralegal with her put-together life and wedding-venue booking and council-tax bills.

I'm seventeen years old, and know these corridors and classrooms like I know my own house, and my heart is too big for my chest.

'Where should we go?' I ask, and it *is* like I'm a teenager again, because the whole world feels so big – so open.

Shaun moves as if he's about to take my hand, then thinks better of it, but the smile he gives me is warm and bright.

'I think I know just the place.'

We fall into step easily and Shaun turns into the darkened hallway that leads to the maths and geography departments. The lights flicker on as we pass, bulbs humming to life overhead. I smile at the long radiator beneath a window that looks out into the little courtyard in the centre of the school; me and the girls would sit up on the windowsill, legs dangling over it, in the winter. It was our spot, and became Shaun and his friends' spot after we started going out, too. In the window above it, I see the outline of some wooden picnic benches, which are new.

I point them out to Shaun and say, 'They must not have PE lessons out there anymore.'

'Huh. Guess not.' It's just dark enough outside that, with the lights on, our reflections are clearly visible in the window, and I see the nostalgic quality that Shaun's face takes on. It's a little bit sad. 'Bryony mentioned they've got new tennis courts and stuff, too, and the old gym has been renovated. They've got stationary bikes and stuff now, too. And rowing machines.'

'Bloody hell.'

He smirks. 'I bet they're still using the same grotty old copies of *An Inspector Calls* in English, though.'

'Probably. How did Bryony know about that? The gym and stuff, I mean.'

Shaun shrugs. 'Probably did a full tour of the building when she called up the head teacher to ask about hosting the reunion here.'

The mental picture makes me laugh, if only because it's all too easy to imagine. Given the impressive extent she's gone to with the decorations, I can absolutely see Bryony waltzing through the entire school before agreeing to use the hall – as if she were doing the school a favour, not the other way around. I wonder if it was as strange for her to come back as it is for some of us, when her reality must be so far removed.

We walk slowly, neither of us in a rush, and both too busy taking in the school to strike up conversation. There's a faint musty smell that clings to the air – old books and damp and dust and too much disinfectant; the sort of smell we'd grow used to, but notice anew every time we came back from a half-term break or summer holiday. The classroom doors are still the same shade of cobalt with the little glass pane set at an adult's eye level and covered in a black criss-cross pattern, but the nameplates on the doors are new. I don't recognise most of them, and the names that should have been there from my school years scratch at the back of my memory, too far away to recall with any real clarity.

The maths rooms wind around the corner and I think about having to queue up in the corridor and wait for the teachers to let us in, or that one time I came back from a dentist appointment late in Year Ten. Mrs Macarthur made me stand out in the hall until she was 'ready' and told me off for disrupting the class and being late and disrespectful, which had made me cry because I didn't *mean* to be late, and I had a note, and I wasn't the type of girl to get in trouble with her teachers.

Thinking about it now, I wonder if she was just having a bad day.

I say, 'Do you remember how weird it used to be to see a teacher outside of school? When you'd spot them out in the supermarket or something like that, and suddenly remember that they had whole lives outside of this place?'

Shaun's chuckle reverberates off the walls, reminding me of the awful acoustics that made it feel so noisy between classes, which in turn always made you talk louder to your friends to be heard over the noise. 'Yeah. Like they weren't quite human, somehow. It's the same way that parents never used to seem exactly like *people*, until . . .'

He trails off with a faraway look on his face and I make a soft noise of agreement. I don't know when I started to think of my parents as 'people' in that sense, either.

'It just feels strange,' I say. 'Like . . . everything used to be so insular, back then, and it's jarring to realise it wasn't ever really like that.'

'Yeah,' he says, and some of the unease and strangeness at this whole thing falls away. 'But I still feel like I'm going to get in trouble.'

My stomach plummets to the ground and I picture Curtis charging after us to have a go at Shaun, even though I know he'd never do something like that.

'What do you mean?'

101

If Shaun notices the rasp of my voice and the nerves in it, he's polite enough to ignore it. He shrugs and explains, 'Wandering around the school like this. Unsupervised, after hours. Makes me feel like I'm skiving off class or like I've snuck in on some dare and one of the teachers is going to leap out at me to tell me off and put me in detention – and remind me to tuck my shirt in properly while they're at it.'

He throws me a smile before looking down, abashed, and scuffing the toe of his shoe against the floor. I can't help but laugh, a lightness blooming through my chest to chase away the last of my unease. There's something so innocent and boyish about both the confession and the shoe-scuff that I can only see him as the boy I fell so madly in love with, not a stranger I haven't seen in ten years.

Shaun's grin widens and he shakes his head at me, then turns off to the back stairs beyond the maths rooms. There's still a strip of tape running down the centre, splitting off the 'up' and 'down' routes, and, battered and dirty and broken as it is, I know it's probably been re-laid several times since we were students.

'Where are we going?' I ask, wondering if he means to go upstairs to the RE rooms or history department, if there's some new 'secret' he's learnt from Bryony's chatter about the school, maybe some new set of benches somewhere . . . Or there's the common room up on the second floor; I wonder if it still has the large, sunken brown leather sofa that we all loved so well – even if you did need someone to give you a hand back up, because you'd sink so far into it.

As much as I'm suddenly intrigued to see what the common room is like these days (maybe they finally put some computers in there like Ashleigh petitioned for so hard), the idea of sinking into that battered sofa with Shaun, the shoddy springs and gravity forcing us to sit close together, makes me nervous.

I'm relieved when he continues up the stairs instead of making his way out to the common room. The lights in the second-floor corridor flicker to life, activated by some hidden motion sensor, and I realise only after Shaun heads for one particular door where he's leading me.

'The library?'

Fingers resting on the door handle, he glances back over his shoulder at me with a grin. 'Yeah.'

'But . . .'

Doesn't he remember all the times he'd hide in the stacks and text me to abandon my coursework or friends for a few minutes? And I'd tiptoe around looking for him like a scavenger hunt, to kiss him in front of the outdated encyclopedias?

Doesn't he remember that copy of *Wuthering Heights* I mentioned I was going to check out and read, so he hid a note inside it asking if I wanted to go to the cinema with him (the '*check yes or no*' kind), which I answered and hid inside his locker afterwards? I had to sneak into the boys' cloakroom to do it, running back to Morgan and Priya and Thea, all of us blushing and giggling over the romance of it all.

But, it's too late, because he's already opening the door and walking inside, and I'm already following, smiling to myself at the sweetness of the memory.

Chapter Thirteen

Shaun

'Most Likely to End Up Together'

The library, like the rest of the school, is exactly the same and totally different all at once.

The shelves and desks are all still exactly like I remember, but the computers are much newer models and the chairs are comfortable, upholstered ones rather than the plastic monstrosities we used to have to suffer on. The middle of the room now boasts a collection of beanbags and a low sofa all arranged around a coffee table, and there are board games on the shelves in front of the librarian's desk instead of the manky old books he was always trying to encourage us to read.

While I wander towards them for a better look, I'm half expecting Mr Fenchurch to suddenly pop out from behind the desk and try to convince me for the billionth time of the merits of reading something other than mandatory GCSE texts. Steph goes straight for the stacks. There are notices taped up about book-return rules, not eating in the library (some things have not changed at all), the study-buddy clubs available and an after-school board-game club every Thursday, which sounds way cooler than I'd ever have admitted out loud as a teenager. I imagine telling Josh and Hassan we'd go along – just for a laugh, obviously – and the three of us getting really into it. Steph would've come along, too, and brought the girls. I wonder if there's some kid like me doing just that in school now, and using it as an excuse to flirt with the girl he likes.

'They've moved it all around!' Steph exclaims suddenly, but there's an excitement to her voice and she giggles. I turn to see her darting along the rows of bookcases, exploring eagerly, and she vanishes down one.

Steph is trailing a finger along the spines of some books and turns to me with a broad, laughing smile, her eyes all lit up and cheeks flushed prettily, and I feel a tug in the pit of my stomach like I'm physically tethered to her, matching each of her steps with one of mine. Her blonde hair catches the light and the way she's looking at me . . .

It's like she hasn't changed at all.

I think about how much I miss her, missed *this*, and have visions of her reaching for my tie to tug me the rest of the way in towards her so she can kiss me, going up on her tiptoes to reach, the warmth of her arms around my neck.

'Look at all these books! Isn't it amazing? I wish we'd had a collection like this when we were here! All these YA fantasy books – Morgan would've gone crazy for these! Oh my gosh, and look, they've got all the *Angus Thongs* books! Remember Ashleigh got in a huge fight with Mr Fenchurch about them because he said they weren't appropriate for a school library, so she started like, an underground book club and we'd all sit around reading them in the yard instead?'

As she giggles at the recollection, my hand runs down the front of my chest, smoothing down a school tie I'm not wearing, trying to wipe away the mental image of Steph pulling me in for a kiss. The kind of memory she is clearly *not* thinking about right now and the kind I absolutely should not be.

She crouches down to get a better look and occasionally picking one out to read the blurb, and I stand there watching her, trying to remember any of the things I wanted to say when I suggested we go for a chat.

What comes out of my mouth is, 'Curtis won't be mad that you ditched him?'

Steph stills, and I wonder if it's on purpose that she's not looking at me. 'I hardly *ditched* him. Why would he be mad? It's not . . . Well, it's not like . . . We're just catching up, aren't we?'

That was the plan. But it seems so muddy and far away now, and this feels . . .

Steph draws a breath and asks, 'What did you tell – I mean, um . . . I didn't see Aisha just now?'

I know the question isn't an accusation, but it feels like one. Like this – stepping out to chat – is something that warrants an explanation. An excuse. Tracks that need to be covered; secrets held close to our chests.

'I think she was getting pretty pally with a few of the art girls. They were swapping Instagram handles, so.'

'Oh! That's nice. Is she quite artistic, too?'

'I mean, I wouldn't say some of those art girls were exactly masters of the craft,' I deadpan, remembering the showcase they did in Year Thirteen that me and the boys were harangued into attending after school one day, because a couple of Steph's friends were involved, and Josh had a crush

106

on one of them. Steph smiles politely, not quite laughing at their expense but not disagreeing, either. 'Aisha works in PR. She did a fine art degree, too.'

'Wow! Gosh, isn't that fab? She works for a makeup brand, doesn't she?'

'Yeah. Always coming home with freebies. She's even got me into a skincare routine, and now I don't know how I ever coped without it.'

Steph laughs. 'That's a far cry from when you used to trail around the shops with me and no matter how many times you asked, you never quite understood why I needed cleanser or how moisturiser was different from makeup remover.'

'I've received a pretty thorough education since then.'

'Does she enjoy it there, then? Is that what she wants to do? Not that she shouldn't want to, I mean, it's just that she's a couple of years older than us, isn't she? So I thought maybe this was, you know, her big plan, but that's a bit unfair of me to assume . . .'

To save Steph from herself, I say gently, 'Yeah, she likes it. She's happy there for now, but she's not especially attached to the company or the industry. If the right role came up somewhere else . . .'

'Oh, that makes sense. How did you two meet?'

It's on the tip of my tongue to say, *I don't want to talk about Aisha*, but I choke back the words and swallow them, hating myself for even thinking them. But this whole party feels so confined, so surreal, a piece of nostalgia carved out for one night and one night only, and I know that when we leave, Steph and I will default back to polite comments on the other's life updates we bother to share on Facebook, and something about that feels like it would rob us of . . .

I don't know. Maybe not *more*, but . . .

After everything we were to each other, after the way tonight has already proven that connection is still there, it feels like we owe it to our younger selves to have a proper, real conversation. We were so respectful of giving the other space after our break-up, there must be so much left unsaid.

And I know we can't hide out in the library all night long, but it feels too blunt to treat this like a meeting with a set agenda. And we're not *hiding*, per se, or anything else, so voicing the fact that it feels like there's a time limit on this will only add to the feeling that something about this is . . . seedy.

Which it isn't, so I just say, 'Dating app, actually. And here we are. How about Curtis? You guys met at work, right?'

Steph stands up straight, shoulders squared, giving off the impression that she's in a job interview. 'We didn't get to know each other properly for ages. For months it was just a case of saying hello if we walked past each other or smiling if we were in the lift at the same time, or a bit of small talk if we were both getting coffee . . .'

'Since when do you drink coffee?' I blurt, and immediately cringe. 'Sorry. Just, uh . . . You always used to say the smell made you feel sick. Gave you a headache.'

'I used to think olives were gross, too,' she says with a smile, though her eyes are downcast. 'And now I always order them for the table when I'm out with people.'

I want to ask her when she discovered that she liked coffee. If it was out of necessity for the caffeine to see her through early commutes and less a 'liking' than a habit, or if it grew on her gradually until she dared herself to try a cup and realised her tastes had changed. I want to know the ins and outs of the story, the way I used to know every scrap of arbitrary information about what made her Steph.

But it's not my place, and we don't owe each other that anymore.

Then I notice her bite the inside of her cheek and see the little wriggle she does, like it's a story and explanation she's talking herself out of telling me. I wish she wouldn't. I don't know how to tell her I want to hear it.

'Anyway,' she says, before I can prompt her about her newfound liking for coffee, 'one day the machine in the office wasn't working and he did a Starbucks run for a few people, and brought me one even though I hadn't asked. We just started talking more after that, and . . . It just . . . happened, I suppose.'

'That's nice.'

God, what a paltry bloody response. *Nice*. It sounds hollow and empty, even if I mean it sincerely. Even if it's hard to imagine Steph falling for some guy who bought her a Starbucks, because I'm so stuck on the image of her pulling a face, nauseated, from the mere mention of the brand.

We lapse into quiet and I know she must be thinking about how disingenuous I sound, what a crappy thing it was to say. I bet it's made me come across as some sort of weird, bitter ex, but if I try to address *that*, I'll probably just dig myself a deeper hole.

This was probably a bad idea all around. Maybe she doesn't have anything left unsaid, nothing she wants to talk about, and *I'm* not sure what to say now I'm faced with the opportunity, the silence and the privacy. I want to apologise but I'm not sure what for, since we're both happy and have moved on with our lives, and I worry that whatever comes out of my mouth next will sound false and shallow in the wake of '*that's nice*'.

But then she looks at me, eyes sparkling, and says, 'I got a job in the campus coffee shop in my second year, doing a few hours a week. I thought it would be a nice way to make some more friends, and . . .' Her face screws up tightly and her laugh is embarrassed and hearty. 'Oh, it was so silly. Me and my best friend I'd made from halls in first year, we both got jobs there because we thought it'd be a good way to find a boyfriend. Not that we ever had the nerve to write our number on a cup if we *did* serve a cute guy. But it seemed like a really good fantasy at the time. I think I'd gotten accustomed to the smell a bit more from generally being on campus and stuff, so it didn't seem so awful when I got the job. Anyway, I only *really* got into drinking it after a bad night out.'

'How do you mean?'

Steph winces, pulling a face at me that smacks of sticky nightclub floors and day-long hangovers. 'Too many Jägerbombs. And I mean, *way* too many. I don't even remember what we were celebrating, but I know two of my friends had to basically carry me home because I was in such a state that none of the taxis would take me. I couldn't face a Red Bull when it got to exam season and at that point, a cappuccino seemed like the lesser of two evils. It was a lot nicer than I thought; I remember being very pleasantly surprised.'

A grin splits my face. 'I can't imagine you getting into such a state. You'd barely touch a cider if we went to a party.'

'It was very much a one-time thing, believe me. I'm still not a very big drinker even now.'

I nod, remembering her reaction to the spiked punch earlier, and that fits more with the Steph I know.

And with the coffee story, the floodgates open. I have a craving to know everything, to build on the idea of Steph as I remember her against who she is now, to tell her the most inane stories of my life from the last ten years.

She's looking at me like she wants to tell me everything, and my heart thuds hard and fierce inside my chest.

Steph's free hand reaches across to settle on my arm and I realise how close to her my feet have carried me without even realising it.

'Tell me all about you,' she says. 'What've you been up to for the last ten years? Tell me everything.'

I know I should be thinking about the party and all the friends we left in the hall, and that I should be making my way back to Aisha in case her new friends split off and she's at a loose end, but . . . whatever I want to tell myself, I know, deep down, that this is exactly the way I saw this conversation going, and that this is the only place I can imagine myself being right now.

So I lean back against the bookcase opposite hers and spill every mundane detail of my life that I can think of, pausing when I know she'll laugh or adding in more information when I know she's about to ask a question, and it's like nothing else exists.

It's like I'm eighteen, and everything is exactly the way it should be.

Chapter Fourteen

Hayden

'Most Likely to Succeed'

The party seems to have turned into one giant echo chamber telling me how underwhelming my life has become, and by the twelve-hundredth time I hear that sentiment, I realise that – it's starting to ring true.

This is not some doom-scrolling that I can dip out of and immediately forget when faced with a distraction in the form of Skye spilling a cup of squash or Margot demanding to watch *Encanto* for the billionth time, and getting the words wrong no matter how patiently I try to teach her the correct Spanish. This is not out of sight, out of mind.

And how can it be, I wonder, when this is my entire *life*? It's never out of sight, nor out of mind – yet, somehow, I've been absolutely blind and ignorant to it for the last ten years.

I used to *want* things. I used to *aspire* to be more, to do something, to build things.

It's not exactly news to me that that attitude is all in the past, or that I've become a different person to the one I was supposed to be. None of my old classmates are alone in thinking that *this*, the stay-at-home dad with a part-time job he does remotely from the desk in the corner of the living room while keeping an eye on the girls, doesn't match up to the quiet, studious kid they pictured as the next Steve Jobs one day. I agree with them.

But I thought I was okay with that. I thought this life was one I've not just made my peace with and come to accept, but one that I actively *liked* having.

Somewhere between Noodles Greg smacking my shoulder and saying, 'Sucks, man,' and Thea's sympathetic smile as she told me there's still time to make it all happen, I think I started to question it, too.

The presentation is still on the projector up on the stage, circulating through the old yearbook and the new additions of 'where are they now' photos. I catch a glimpse of my own teenage face up on the screen, and . . .

I see it, too.

I think, *Sorry, kid. I'm sorry it didn't work out like we wanted it to and I messed it all up.*

Life had seemed . . . simple, then. Another equation to be balanced and solved; a problem to analyse based on previous, similar case studies and accounting for the variables of my own interests and personality. I applied for engineering degrees at top universities, had a spreadsheet balancing up the cost of halls to figure out if it would be more cost-effective to stay catered or not, applied for part-time jobs before I even officially moved to campus. I figured out which modules I wanted to take over the entire four years. I knew which graduate-scheme programmes would be top of my list to apply for. What the trajectory of my career path would look like from that first role where I'd be little more than a trainee, to the ultimate dream job where I would have freedom and authority to create and design, being challenged while experiencing the absolute exhilaration of sinking my teeth into something I loved.

It had all looked . . . so clear. Precise and straightforward and – inevitable.

I can pinpoint the exact moment it changed. I haven't thought about it much for a while, but remembering the way Lucy came to my room, ashen and tearful and too scared to go buy a pregnancy test by herself . . . God, the memory hits me with such vivid clarity it's like I'm there – fidgeting with the doorknob and watching the seconds tick down on my phone's timer, so sure that one night which we both ultimately agreed was probably a mistake and we were better off as friends anyway . . . That couldn't be *it*. This sort of thing didn't just happen like that, not to people like us.

Except it did, and all I could think was that we should make a spreadsheet to weigh up our options. The world shifted beneath my feet, but Lucy had been so close to crumbling and so I did what I do best. Lists, and logic. I was the anchor, if only because I didn't know how to get swept away.

I never gave myself a chance to mourn what I lost, or panic about how quickly everything was changing. I just made new plans. Had something else to study for and read up on.

Was it a mistake, to not have let myself feel bad about everything I was giving up? Would I be somewhere different now, if I had?

Maybe it's the effect of the echo chamber everybody has created tonight, a whirlpool made up of empty pity and thoughtless sympathies that sucks me round and under and over, scrambles my brain and leaves me struggling in the centre of it all. Maybe it's just being back here at school, and a bitter twist on the nostalgia.

Or maybe . . . It's simply that it's true, and I haven't let myself see it for a while.

Whatever conversation I'm currently part of (which is a generous term for 'standing by and pretending to listen while doing the bare minimum to actively participate') moves on, and I take the opportunity to slip quietly away, making some excuse about getting another drink. I've lost Ashleigh; she disappeared into the crowd not long after we did our routine to Taylor Swift's 'Shake It Off' (which Margot helped coordinate a couple of years ago, and is just silly enough that it borders on entertaining rather than straight-up embarrassing when performed in public like this). I can't even see Shaun anywhere, which means that I'm left alone, sinking further into my thought spiral.

Did I really do the best I could with my situation? Should I have been pushing myself more in the last few years – gotten my degree part time and not been such a pushover when it came to Lucy wanting me to have custody because it made more sense with my job? Have I skewed my entire worldview so badly that I can't even tell that I'm *not* happy, deep down?

Is everybody else right?

I mean, it'd be a turn-up for the books for people like Freddie Loughton or Morgan or even bloody Noodles Greg to know things I don't, but . . .

'You've still got that face on you, then.'

I jerk up at the voice so close beside me that I spill the Fanta I was pouring into my cup. A large hand reaches to pick up some napkins from a nearby pile, pressing them into the spill.

'Ryan. Hello,' I say, knowing that Ashleigh is going to grill me about whatever this conversation is, no end. She won't be able to help herself. 'What face?'

Ryan leaves the napkins to soak up the spilled pop, then gets himself some punch, and contorts his face in what I think is supposed to be an exaggerated mimic of my own expression. Eyebrows knotted together, mouth twisted into a diagonal line, one eye squinting.

I want to say *I don't look like that*, but then he cocks his head almost comically to one side and I have to admit, I probably do look like that.

'You used to do it at school all the time,' he says. 'We had a name for it, didn't you know? Used to say "Hayden's going haywire again", because you'd end up scribbling away some doodle about your robots or whatever, and you'd be so distracted you wouldn't notice anything. I remember I balanced six Biros on top of your head one time in the common room without you knowing, till they all fell off.'

He grins, but it's self-effacing, a bit apologetic. I wait for him to laugh at my expense, but he just hands me my forgotten cup of Fanta and leans against the table next to me as if this isn't the first exchange we've had in about ten years. I'm so taken aback by the simple amicability of this that I don't say anything at all.

'So,' he asks. 'What're you thinking so hard about?'

'N-nothing. I don't think so, anyway.'

Ryan scoffs, but even that sounds cheery. He cuts me a sidelong glance as if we're good enough buddies for me to understand what that look means. 'Counting down the minutes until you can get home? I don't remember you being one for parties very much. Didn't Ashleigh have to drag you to prom?'

'Er, not quite. My mum shoved me out of the door for that one, too. Apparently, it was a rite of passage I shouldn't miss.'

'Was it?'

'Thanks to *someone*, it was the first time I got drunk, so I suppose it was in its way.'

Ryan gives a soft chuckle and inclines his head. He takes a swig of his spiked punch. 'Everyone expected it. I didn't want to let them down.'

I don't quite know what to say to that, either. But there's such an odd vulnerability in his comment that I find myself saying, 'I was thinking about if I've let being a dad hold me back. If it's made me give up.'

'On what?'

Everything. Anything.

I shrug.

Ryan nods.

'You've got two now, haven't you? Kids, I mean.'

'Yeah.' I'm surprised he knows; I would've thought he was too busy to bother to look anybody up ahead of tonight, let alone a quiet kid he rarely spoke to at school like me. I refrain from reaching for my phone, not wanting to be the annoying parent who can't stop showing off their children and shoving photos under everybody's nose.

'Still tinkering about with things? Or is that what you've given up on?'

'Um, no, I've . . . Well . . . Sort of.' I clear my throat, rubbing the back of my neck, wishing Ryan was enough of a prat to talk solely about himself, to spare me having to say anything. 'Only a little bit – it tends to be side-projects at work, or stuff for the kids.'

'Oh, yeah?' He nods, and when I don't volunteer any more information, remembering how uninterested the last two groups I spoke to were about the Roomba I modified to be an AI-supported walking aid for Skye when she was first toddling about the house, he continues, 'You know, one of my old teammates retired not long ago, and he's gotten big into educational apps for kids, syncing them up with books and toys and stuff like that. He just got approved for some government funding, actually – nothing to do with me, before Easton asks,' he adds with a wink and a wry smile. 'It's doing pretty well, though. He's always looking for brainiacs to help build it out.'

'That's interesting. It's a great niche – huge potential.'

Ryan tosses me a grin. '*Yeah*. If you wanted, I could put you guys in touch. Sounds like it could be up your street.'

'Oh. Um . . .' Something seizes in the pit of my chest, discomfort prickling all over my skin enough to bring me out in a cold sweat. 'Er, thanks for the offer, but that's alright. I'm okay.'

'Happy with where you're at?'

It's not accusatory, like most people have sounded tonight, or even sceptical. It's – just a question, simple as that. (And I owe Ashleigh an apology for even thinking this, but Ryan might be one of the most decent conversations I've had all evening.)

Maybe that's why I give him a more honest reply than I've offered anybody so far tonight.

'It's not what I saw for myself. Being a stay-at-home dad, I mean.' But I smile a little, saying, 'I wouldn't change that. I just – I guess I started thinking that maybe there are *other* things in my life I should be changing. To be who I was supposed to be.'

'*Most likely to succeed.*'

I nod, and Ryan nods, and I think this must be the longest, oddest interaction we've ever had. I had to work with him in chemistry in Year Ten because we sat next to each other, but even then, we never had anything resembling an actual *conversation*. We stand quietly for a moment, observing the room. Or rather, I look at the crinkle in my paper cup and pick at the worn, soggy rim, and Ryan looks out at his crowd of adoring fans and friends. I wonder if he's also looking for an excuse to leave this chat without looking rude.

But then, he claps me on the shoulder – a bit too roughly, and if not for the firm clasp of his hand on my shirt, I'd stumble forward, and he says, 'Success is bullshit anyway. Make it what you want. Nobody can tell you you're not enough unless you let them, got that?'

'Uh . . .'

Is Ryan Lawal giving me a pep talk? Is this some comment he plucked from a cheesy *#motivationalmonday* post from a personal trainer or something, recycled in his public speeches? Something his rugby coaches told him once?

I expect him to drop that pearl of wisdom, down his drink and jump back into the fray, only he doesn't. Instead, he looks at me, almost insistent – staring me down. His eyes fix on mine, or would if I weren't busy looking anywhere else all of a sudden, and I squirm under the intensity of it. I've never liked being the centre of attention, and guys like Ryan are popular if only for their ability to make you feel like you've been gifted their full and complete attention.

With Margot and Skye, I am the centre of their whole world. With my friends, eye contact is easy; I am at ease.

This is so far out of my comfort zone that I'm sixteen

years old, waiting to be picked last as usual for cricket in a PE lesson while everybody watches, and wishing the ground would open up to swallow me whole.

'Got that?' he presses, and I can't work out why it matters so much to him either way.

But I say, 'Y-yes. I think so,' in the hopes it will get me out of this hellscape.

Ryan's hand gives my shoulder a friendly rattle before he lets me go. 'Nobody, Hayden. *Nobody.*'

'Learn that the hard way?' I ask.

His eyes track across the hall, distant, and that intense, overconfident demeanour slips for a moment. For just a fraction of a second, I'd say he looks as insecure as I feel, harangued by ghosts of his past and what-ifs.

It's gone in the blink of an eye, because then he's grinning at me again and accents it with a wink. 'Nah, mate. But you hang out with so-called success stories enough and you start to see the try-hard amateur behind the curtain. Try not to go haywire too hard, huh? Enjoy the party. Maybe avoid the punch.'

I nod, lifting my drink slightly in farewell as he walks away – and leaves me thinking that it's easy for someone like him to say that success is bullshit; however positively I want to look at my career and my ambitions and passions, I have nothing to show for it. Ten years of squandered opportunities and forgotten dreams, brushed so far aside they may as well no longer exist.

I abandon the cup of Fanta, and down a glass of punch instead.

Chapter Fifteen

Ashleigh

'Most Likely to Kill Each Other'

I am the centre of attention in the very best of ways, for once. I'm in the middle of the little dance floor near the stage, hips swaying and arms waving in sync with the music, enjoying when a few other people like Elise look my way and copy what I'm doing. I am the trendsetter here, *I* am the queen bee.

It's new, and novel, and glorious.

I'm enjoying this weird blend of night-out vibes and the school hall setting, surrounded by strangers I used to know and have been dying to show off to. I'm enjoying Freddie's arrhythmic thrusting and air-punches a whole lot less; he almost takes my eye out with one overly enthusiastic gesture during 'Dancing Queen'.

He's the reason the dance floor begins to lose its appeal, because he keeps putting his clammy hands on my hips rather than just letting me dance, and his hot, beery breath on the back of my neck feels anything but sexy. So much attention from one of the most popular guys in school is undeniably flattering, but when Freddie tries to slide his hand underneath my shirt for the fourth time, I peel away and excuse myself from the rest of the group and take up refuge against the wall, tucked neatly in the corner near the stage where I can survey the rest of the party.

I'm on the lookout for Hayden or Bryony when Freddie lurches into sight in front of me. I think that walk he's doing is meant to be a swagger.

And I *think* that leery expression is meant to be charming and flirty, because then he winks and says, 'Who knew you were such a good time? Where were you hiding that all this time, Ash?'

I don't bother pretending to smile or laugh at his 'joke', but Freddie, it turns out, doesn't need my encouragement to continue his attempts at flirting.

'I mean, you used to be so . . .' He pulls a grossed-out face. 'You know? But now, you're so . . .' He puffs out his cheeks, blows out a long breath, eyes me up and down and waggles his eyebrows for good measure. 'You know?'

And to think, he really believes this works.

He sweeps a hand over his hair and starts regaling me with the story of that time he scored the winning try in a school rugby match as if it wasn't twelve years ago and as if I cared even back then. Does he realise how insufferable he is? This laddish attitude might've appealed to some girls when he was a teenager, but surely it can't *actually* woo women now? The man is a child. A toddler. He's a walking advert for weaponised incompetence, I'd stake my life on it.

'But, like, obviously I hit up the gym a few times a week,' he's saying, and I don't know how we got here but also, don't care. He steps closer and places a hand behind my head against the poster of Bryony from the yearbook, taped up on the notice board. The paper crinkles as Freddie positions himself up close, side on, his torso pushing against my arm. 'Do you work out?'

It's such a line that I laugh, because, God, does this buffoon *hear himself*?

My eyes land straight ahead to the dance floor, where Ryan is dancing with Bryony and paying her no attention, because he's looking this way. Staring hard, mouth in a tense line, jaw clenched.

Is he mad that I've stolen his friend's attention, proved myself worthy of it somehow when he always deemed me so beneath them all? Good. I want him to know how wrong he was about me.

Because I'm the bigger person, I don't give him the middle finger – but I'm not above turning to Freddie with a false, flirty smile and laying my hand on his measly bicep and giving it a squeeze.

'Not much,' I finally answer him. 'Maybe you could give me some tips. Show me a proper workout, sometime.'

Eyes widening, he shifts a bit more in front of me. 'I could definitely show you a few things, Ash. Yeah. Sounds good. Do you have Snapchat?'

I weep for the women unlucky enough to swipe right on this idiot's dating profile. Truly, I do.

But I just *know* Ryan is still watching, and other people must be, too, and I don't want to lose face. I can't prove him right by chickening out – have them all know I'm still a square and boring and unsexy and drab. So what if Freddie Loughton wants to flirt with me and so what if I end up snogging him? He wouldn't be the first guy I kissed on a night out just because, even if I wasn't totally into him.

Anyway, tonight, I'm a cool girl, the it girl, the envy of everybody, and if this were ten years ago, that kind of girl would die for the chance to kiss Freddie Loughton.

I'm debating my response – I do *not* want to give this man my number, but neither am I about to download Snapchat for him – when there's a high-pitched squeal and a body slides right in between us, so close and moving so fast that my bra is knocked askew.

Bryony has sandwiched herself right in between us, her hip knocking me backwards and out of the way as she sidles up to Freddie and manoeuvres him slightly away from the wall, so she's now the one he's caging in. She blanks me completely, not so much as acknowledging my existence, as she bats her eyes up at him.

'Oh my God, Freddie, I totally missed you on the dance floor! You *have* to dance with me – you were always so good! You've still got moves, haven't you?'

I stand there, stunned by her behaviour, but Freddie doesn't seem to care that I've been replaced – is only interested in the warm female body fawning over him right now. His attention is stolen completely.

Which, really, is Bryony's MO. She always wanted to be the centre of it all.

I shouldn't be so surprised that she couldn't even stomach me having a sliver of spotlight for just one night, ten years on, but still – it stings. It's a rejection after her early display of friendship and affection, and, worse, there are even more eyes on us now. Her voice fucking carries. She makes such a spectacle of herself doing just about anything, and this is no exception.

I notice a couple of boys pointing and some girls snickering behind their hands, and I hope the heat in my cheeks isn't as obvious to all of them as it is to me. I hope they can't see it written all over my face, or the tears that threaten, prickling at the backs of my eyes.

'Come on, big boy,' Bryony is saying, her hands pressed flat to his chest as she pushes him back towards the dance floor, her body already twisting in smooth, sultry motions in time with the music. 'You don't want to waste your time over here. Show me what you've got.'

The second they're out of the way, I make a beeline for the exit.

I don't rush, don't hunch my shoulders, don't let my expression shift from the bored one I school it into on instinct.

Not that I'm running away. And not that I'm about to hide in the toilets for a quick, angry cry like I used to have to do sometimes between school council meetings and biology lessons, because I'm not seventeen fucking years old anymore. I'm an adult, and an emotionally mature one with a grip on herself at that.

But something about this reaction makes me feel so much more like myself than who I was ten minutes ago. I've spent the night peacocking for these people I don't even *think* about most of the time, and certainly won't think about much after tonight is over.

I guess I got too caught up in my new popular-girl mystique and this burning need for validation.

And I can't even blame that on Ryan. I've been parading and performing for everybody; he's bottom of the list of people to impress, because it's always been easier to think of him as someone whose shoulders I can stamp on to lift myself up.

Which is mean, and petty, and an irrefutable fact.

Am I always this bad? Or do these people – this school – just bring it out in me, now that I've grown up and moved on, left them all in the dust?

With the hall and the music and the party and all my self-centred, careless old classmates firmly behind me, I falter to a stop outside the cloakrooms and an impulse roots deep in the pit of my stomach that cries out for me to just *go*. Walk away – an Irish goodbye, how glamorously dramatic it would look, too – and call a taxi and go back to my hotel, maybe get a chippy tea on the way and then polish off that and the rest of my hip flask of tequila from the comfort of a plush hotel bed. How dreamy that sounds, rather than wringing myself out just to prove to everybody how fantastic my life is.

I know it's fantastic. I love my life. I love my career and my apartment and my sleepy Sunday lie-ins with my Kindle and the nights out at bars or comedy nights or gigs with my friends. I don't *need* anybody to tell me how great it looks; I live it, I know.

So . . . why do I care? Why do I need them to tell me?

I take my phone out, on the verge of redialling the taxi firm I used earlier. In the reflection of the screen, I see my lipstick is smudged. Should I fix it – or just wipe it off altogether and go home?

Come on, Ashleigh. Don't chicken out now, or they've won. Last woman standing. Show them all they were wrong; you'll regret it if you don't.

Yes, but counter point: chips. And battered sausage, and curry sauce.

Counter-counter point: cold pizza. Get your shit together and get back in there.

Yes, but—

126

A chuckle from somewhere in front of me startles me to attention, and my head whips up towards the sound.

Ryan is lurking in the shadows, leaning against one of the display boards with one ankle crossed over the other, and his arms folded across his chest. His eyes glint at me, his teeth like a damned toothpaste advert. How long has he been there? How long has he been watching me?

'Sorry,' he says in a low, smooth voice that suggests he is absolutely not sorry. 'Don't let me disturb you. Carry on.'

My chin jerks up of its own accord, shoulders braced. 'I wasn't doing anything.'

'Yes, you were. You were doing that thing where you get ready for a debate. Should I warn Freddie he's got his work cut out for him?'

I glower, and that prickling anger he's always instilled in me spreads from my fingertips to smother my lungs and scratch at my throat as Ryan pushes away from the wall to stride towards me. He stops about two feet away, unsettlingly close, but I bet that's exactly why he's done it, and keeps grinning down at me. I'll hand it to him, that's a feat in itself; he's hardly taller than me, with the heels I'm wearing.

'I'm not debating anybody,' I inform him. *Lie*. But I don't think it counts if I'm debating against myself, and I hate that Ryan has ever known me well enough to recognise what it looks like when I'm having a silent argument. I hate that he *still*, apparently, does. 'And as for Freddie—'

And his gross, clammy hand and stinking, boozy breath and not-even-a-little-bit-subtle cleavage ogling . . . Ugh.

Not, of course, that Ryan needs to know that. And not that I need to acknowledge that Freddie traded up for Bryony the second he had the chance . . .

'Well, I don't think it's any of your business how I spend time with Freddie, is it?'

I shouldn't say it. It's stupid – silly. Reckless, because I know I'm only saying it to try to drive a wedge between Ryan and his friend, like if Freddie picks *me*, it's some kind of insult to *him*. And it's so bloody ridiculous, because we're all grown-ups, and won't hold it against our friends if they spend a night out flirting with somebody, so it's not even like I'll achieve anything anyway.

At worst, it'll just give them all an excuse to laugh at me and say I'm a frigid bitch and that's why Freddie rejected me.

I put on my best poker face, all but daring Ryan to call my bluff.

Except it's not me with the tell.

It's him.

Because as I stare at Ryan with my sneer firmly in place, I watch as his gaze sharpens, his grin vanishing, and then – his eyes dip to my mouth. Zeroing in on the smudge of my lipstick on my lower lip. He doesn't look away for a very, very long moment.

Long enough that my heart does something funny and disturbing and quite possibly also medically concerning, and my lips part involuntarily as I swallow, my mouth bone dry, and it's only when I inhale a bit too sharply, the noise audible in the deserted corridor, and when I *don't exhale*, that Ryan's eyes tick back up to mine.

His cocksure grin slides back into place as if that never happened; the only reason I'm sure it did, and wasn't some punch-induced hallucination, is because the usual tension that charges the air between us is suddenly thick and oppressive, making me want to bolt.

128

And I've never wanted to turn my back on Ryan. Never run away from a fight. I've stayed till the bitter end every time, even when it's a losing battle.

Oh, fuck, please don't let this be a losing battle.

I'm – not prepared for this.

I don't know what to do with that look. This tension.

But Ryan just slides his hands into his trouser pockets, nonchalant as ever, and nods his head in the direction of the girls' cloakroom I'm still loitering outside. 'You know, I *thought* we weren't supposed to go sneaking off around the school. Didn't take you for such a rule breaker, Easton.'

'I don't think you know me half as well as you think you do, Lawal. And anyway – at least *I'm* not still swaggering about the school hallways like I own them.'

'Please,' Ryan scoffs, and, just like that, the tension shifts – returns to our usual back-and-forth. 'If either of us felt some sense of entitlement to this place, it was you. Or do I need to remind you of the fact that you forced the school to display your certificate for that essay competition in the trophy cabinet?'

The words – the memory – make me jerk backwards. I'd forgotten all about it. Ryan can't possibly have held some kind of grudge over that all this time? Just because I pointed out to the Head of Year how unfair it was to only display sporting accolades and not academic ones . . . Which, I totally stand by as an adult.

I cross my arms. 'I won a *national competition*. You – what, kicked a ball better than the school down the road? Whoopee. Your glory days are long behind you; it's a bit sad you're still clinging to the memory of them, when I highly doubt any evidence still exists here. That trophy probably went in the bin before long.'

'Oh, what, like they'll have kept *your* award, because it was so much *more* important?'

I doubt that, too, but I just shrug one shoulder, rather than give him the satisfaction of being right.

One of his thick, dark eyebrows arches, pulling the side of his mouth up with it. 'Want to bet?'

The tension is back with a vengeance, crackling like static before a lightning storm near my ears, and, suddenly, I cannot get back to the party soon enough. I'd take the humiliation of everybody else laughing at me for thinking I had a shot with Freddie over this. Anything but stay here and indulge him in a fight.

I'm not sure I'd win. But for now, at least, I have the last word.

'What, you want to go wandering around the school just to see if they still have your old rugby trophy? Give me a break. Isn't it time you grew up already?'

I make sure to shove him with my shoulder as I walk past, even if it doesn't make him budge or stumble in the slightest, and almost definitely leaves *me* with a bruise. Damn rugby arms. Damn him.

Until he calls after me, when I'm nearly back to the doors to the hall. '*Chicken*. I should've known you'd still be the same stick-in-the-mud you always used to be.'

There's no pretending I didn't hear that, and I can't bear to let him one-up me. I stop, turn on my heels and cross my arms. 'I am not a stick-in-the-mud.'

He takes a long, loping stride closer, head tipped back slightly and a glimmer in his eyes that just smacks of triumph, and riles me up immediately. So like him to celebrate a victory when the fight's still on.

'Yes, you are. Boring, uptight . . . Pretending you're better than everybody else.'

I move towards him. The corridor becomes a chessboard where we both only move in one direction; the difference is that he's only a pawn, and I'm a queen. He just hasn't realised that yet.

'I'm not pretending. I *am* better than everybody else.' Some of them, anyway. *Him*, specifically.

He steps closer again. 'And too much of a goody two-shoes to break the rules.'

I come up level with him. Closer than before. His face is doing a weird thing I don't usually see on Ryan, where he seems to be fighting a smile. If it's a poker face, it's a shitty one, and I elect to ignore it.

'And yet, you're the squeaky-clean politician who has to toe the line if he wants to keep his job.' *Checkmate.* 'Welcome to the stick-in-the-mud life, Ryan.'

I poke a finger into his torso to drive home the point, in the space just between his ribcage and his stomach. It's a firm wall of muscle I try not to notice. Battle won and war still not over – because it's never over, not between us – I snatch my hand back and, if I walk briskly enough, I'll be back in the hall before he can come up with a retort better than 'I know you are but what am I?'

But then . . .

Then he breaks the rules.

He catches my wrist as I move away, holding me in place. And he *winks*.

'Come on, Ash. For old times' sake.'

And, fuck. I'm suckered right back in. I tell him, 'Fine,' even as I tell myself, *Game on.*

It's . . . wholly uncomfortable. This whole thing. Him. *Me*.

This is far from the first time I've spent any time 'alone' with Ryan. There was many a time at school when we'd loiter in the corridors after the bell rang to bicker over something, usually to do with school council. One time we were so into it that it was a full hour after the buses home had all gone before we realised.

But this is *different*, and I don't like it.

I also can't admit defeat, because that would mean admitting that something has shifted beyond our usual dynamic of deep, unadulterated loathing and contempt and competition, and . . . and God, I *do not fancy him* – that's not what this is about.

It's just. Just.

It's all wilful deception on his part, I'm sure. The dynamic has only shifted because he's made it so; this is his new way of getting under my skin and trying to one-up me. He's decided to pretend to seduce me, so he can turn me down and walk away triumphant, that's all this is. And that's *such* a Ryan thing to do, the bastard.

So, I don't fancy him, and I'm not thinking about the whiff of cologne I catch as I trail after him that makes my eyes practically roll back in my head, it's so good, and I'm not admiring the tailored cut of his suit around his broad frame, or the way his butt looks . . .

Damn it.

My pace quickens and my strides lengthen so that I don't just catch up, but take the lead. This way, at least, I can make sure we don't steer off track from finding our old awards.

Like, I'm not setting foot in the common room. I can't

bear to find out if that crappy old leather sofa that sagged practically to the floor is still there. The way he'd sit on it like a fucking *throne*, holding court for his adoring subjects. The way it was *a really crappy chair*, so I organised to get it taken away, and everybody kicked up such a fuss that the school agreed to *repair it* instead, if we raised the money. Which, of course, Ryan made sure they did.

Heat flares across my face when I remember how he showed off about that damned sofa after it was fixed. Gloating at me, sprawled across it, arm flung across the back and legs wide, while I sat rigid in a plastic chair by one of the computers. *Don't you want to try it out? See what all the fuss is about?*

He meant the sofa, but it was so obvious he *didn't*, not really. The shrieks of laughter and jeers creep out of the depths of my memory, snarling around my mind like barbed wire. I can remember shutting them out, rolling my eyes, picking up my bag to leave like I was above it all, and one of the boys shoving me so I fell on Ryan's lap, his joke about my bony arse, and then everybody laughing harder when I was beet-red and half running out of the room. And even now, I'm thinking about the crude, cutting remarks I should've made, the comebacks I was too humiliated in the moment to come up with.

I glance back at him now to glower, seething at the recollection. As my head whips around, his eyes dart upwards – from looking at my arse.

Does he still think it's bony?

And, moreover, WHY DO I CARE?

'We could check out the common room on the way,' he says.

I tell him, 'No.'

Ryan's lips curve into a slight and scathing smirk, but it's – off. Wrong. It doesn't look the same without the eye roll or the tilt of his head. Feels too serious, hits a different kind of nerve, when his eyes stay fixed on mine, dark and strange and wondering.

I face away from him, and even though I know I should have just gained the upper hand, somehow the only thing I feel is lost.

Chapter Sixteen

Ryan

'Most Likely to Kill Each Other'

She won't look at me, and I ultimately decide that's probably for the best. I know what to do with Ashleigh's uppity glares and self-righteous *hah, take that* looks, but right now, I'm at a loss. A couple of times since I cornered her after she ducked out of the party, she's looked out of her depth.

I've never seen her that way before.

It's probably because Bryony told us not to go wandering around and she's worried about getting into trouble.

Probably.

A sliver of doubt, a little crack in my rationale, has me wondering if it has more to do with me than I'd like. Or maybe I *would* like it, if that coil of excitement snaking through my abdomen is anything to go by.

Or, worse, if it's nothing to do with me at all. If this is about Freddie, and how she lost her shot with him, and that she might actually be *upset* about that. That she was *into him*, and is genuinely stung by the rejection.

Impulse has me asking her, 'So, you're not seeing anybody

right now,' even though I'm pretty damn sure what the answer is.

Ashleigh doesn't even turn around, but I just *know* she rolled her eyes. She pauses until we're more in step with each other, then says, 'I'm not.'

'You're not going to ask *me*? Tsk, manners, Easton; it's only polite.'

'I'm not,' she repeats. 'Spare us both the list of B-list celebrities and socialites you've dated recently, please.'

'Who says I've been dating socialites?'

'Um, I'm pretty sure *everyone* knew you were dating that Scottish girl from *Love Island*.'

'Keeping tabs on me?'

She ignores the grin I throw her, and looks far too smug for comfort before pointing out, 'Twenty million people saw you with her in that TikTok. You know, the one of her throwing a tantrum at that nightclub and pulling some poor girl's hair? Hardly *keeping tabs* when your girlfriend goes viral.'

I hide a wince. That was two years ago – I thought everyone had pretty much forgotten about it by now. In my defence, I was trying to calm her down and smooth things over after some catfight with a frenemy, but trust Ashleigh to make me feel guilty for even being involved.

Out loud, I boast, 'Hardly newsworthy that I was even there when partying with celebs is a pretty standard night out for me. Part and parcel, when you're as notable as I am. Not that you'd understand, of course. I don't imagine *you're* chatting to Will and Kate at the polo, or grabbing drinks at a bar with the likes of Richard Ayoade or Daniel Radcliffe.'

Neither of which is exactly *normal*, even for me, but she doesn't need to know that.

Ashleigh only levels me with another self-satisfied smirk though, and says, 'No, you're right. I'm not rubbing shoulders with the rich and famous – because in *my* line of work, I'm busy helping *real* people with *real* problems.'

She waits through the beat of silence where all I can do is think, *touché.*

'Besides,' she continues, 'I don't see *you* being the face of a ground-breaking ITV documentary about the incredible breakthroughs being made to combat degenerative disease—'

I cut her off with a chuckle. 'I don't see you doing that, either.'

'Well, it's not been released yet.'

'That documentary got axed before it even made it to production. Legal issues, right? Something around risking the spread of misinformation when some drugs hadn't passed – what're they called, clinical trials, or whatever?'

Ashleigh's lips press into a fierce pout and she side-eyes me. *How's that for touché*, I think. She says, 'How would you know that?'

Maybe because she alluded to it on an Instagram Story, which led me to find the pretty impressive rant she posted about it and certain elements of the industry on LinkedIn.

I shrug. 'I heard from someone attached to the project.'

She levels me with such an accusatory look that for a second I think she sees right through me, but she only harrumphs and struts ahead.

It is *way* too much fun to one-up her like this.

I wonder what else I know about her life for the last ten years that I could throw back in her face like that? But I also wonder what she knows about *my* life in that time that she might try to levy against me, and if it's worth it when I've already won this round.

Nah, better to quit while I'm ahead.

God knows Ashleigh Easton is a force to be reckoned with. I don't want to try my luck.

Stuck walking behind her, I notice how tense her shoulders are, and try not to look too long at the smooth, creamy skin or the smattering of freckles across it. I never thought of Ashleigh as freckly.

I shake the thought away now, trying not to wonder how far those freckles go.

She reaches the door to the library before me and hesitates, gripping the handle but not opening it, and I wonder if she's going to chicken out. Maybe she's secretly hoping it's locked so she can give up on this and get back to the party – away from me. Maybe, back to Freddie.

But then she throws open the door, looking a bit surprised that it isn't locked, and storms inside. The lights flicker on as she strides past the banks of desks with computers, beyond some sad-looking beanbags and all the way past the stacks to the trophy case on the other side.

There's a thump, like a book falling, and I think I hear someone whispering, but I don't see anything when I look around. Probably just the pipes, or the door.

Either that, or someone else snuck off and was trying to hook up with their other half in the library. I smirk to myself at the thought, wondering who would be bold – or maybe just drunk – enough to do that. Didn't Steph and Shaun used to snog up here all the time? I guess someone could have taken a leaf out of their book.

I didn't, obviously. That's not why I suggested to Ashleigh we come looking for our old awards.

This is just – good old-fashioned rivalry, that's all.

I don't get a proper look at the rest of the library but, aside from being modernised, it doesn't look a whole lot different to how I remember. Not that I spent much time in here, admittedly. This wall showcasing photos of year groups or staff over time looks more or less like I remember – photos from the seventies and eighties, mainly. Relics of a tradition that hasn't been maintained.

The trophy cabinet is new, though. It's a huge glass monstrosity now, not the vintage piece with sagging shelves and nicks in the wood. It's well organised and so full that it's a little overwhelming to look at – but I find what I'm looking for quickly enough.

I jab a finger at the glass door, where there's a photo of our rugby team when I was in Year Twelve and we won the regional championship. I'm front and centre, man of the match as well as team captain. The trophy is there with everyone's names engraved, and then there's even a separate photo of me in my jersey from my days as a pro, which is a nice surprise. I always wondered if the coaches and PE teachers here would say to kids on the school team, 'You could make it, one day – like Ryan Lawal!'

'See?' I tell Ashleigh and she scowls – not at the photos, but at my finger leaving a smudge on the glass. I don't remove it. 'Told ya. So where's yours, Ash? Were your school-girl achievements worth holding onto?'

I'm pretty sure I already know the answer, but she gives me a cool smile and points at the top shelves. 'Even better,' she says, and when I look, there's a whole host of framed certificates crowded together – all from recent years, but all for essay competitions or awards for languages or science projects.

She doesn't bother to rub it in the way I did, because we both know we're looking at her legacy, a lasting change she made. How many Ashleighs are showcased here, because she demanded they should be? It's probably a better mark of success than my old trophy and a photo from a career I had to give up, as much a relic here as those class photos from the eighties.

Not, of course, that I'll ever say that out loud to her.

The two of us stand in silence, looking at the accolades on display, taking it all in, and I find my gaze drifting to Ashleigh. To the freckles on her bare shoulders. Her reflection in the glass and her mouth, parted just slightly, and that smudge of lipstick.

My mind immediately goes back to Freddie dancing with her. Flirting with her. Hands on her.

She's entitled to kiss him. Obviously. I'm not his keeper.

Ashleigh breathes in. Holds it a second or two, like she wants to say something. Breathes out.

It's fucking astonishing, that she has this way of sucking all the attention in the room and making it focus on her. I never understood how she did it back at school – when she was dorky and brash and too serious and not even very good-looking. She never cared about being popular or cool or pretty or even *nice*, half the time, and somehow everyone still listened to her.

I remember in Year Eleven, when Ms Potts was teaching us about electromagnetic fields in physics and someone made a joke that Ashleigh and I were north and south poles on a magnet because we drew people in but were so opposite.

And Ms Potts laughed and said we were more like two north poles: completely repellent of and to each other, while drawing everyone else towards us. Even our own damn teachers understood that.

It's why they made us Head Boy and Head Girl. Although I think they probably came to regret it, based on how bad we were at working *together*.

Now, though, I think maybe Ms Potts was wrong because Ashleigh is just standing there, quiet and still, and everything in me is acutely tuned towards her.

'So why'd you do it?' she asks, the question rushing out of her in a soft rush, like she's almost afraid of being overheard. She straightens up, turns towards me – and I'm closer than either of us realised. I can feel her breath, warm and sweet, against my face. Her blue eyes dart between mine. Flicker down to my mouth – once. Fleetingly. Provoking some wild, unthinking urge to run my thumb over the blush on her cheek, feel the heat of it spreading down to her neck, see if her shoulders are as soft as they look.

I shake off the urge and find her eyes still boring into mine with that new, unfamiliar twist on a look I'm so used to, and – yes, it was better when she wouldn't look at me.

This time, it's me who has to look away first. That's new and unfamiliar, too.

My fingers unfurl from the fists they bunched into at some point. I slide them into my pockets instead.

'Do what?' I ask, my voice just as quiet as hers.

'Go into politics. You could've – I don't know. Been an influencer. Become a rugby coach or managed a team. Gone on reality programmes and quiz shows and stuff. Made a living out of that chipper attitude without getting your hands dirty.'

'Ah. There she is.'

'What?'

'Little Miss Judgemental. You've got a shitty opinion of politicians, haven't you?'

'I've dealt with enough of them putting up roadblocks for our funding and research and belittling the work we're doing to know. Sometimes it's not all about the "big picture" stuff, you know. Sometimes it's all the hard work on the ground adding up to that, that matters.'

'You know, I don't think you can take the moral high ground when you're the one who's been eavesdropping.'

She huffs a sigh. 'Please. Don't act like you weren't doing it on purpose, or like you weren't listening in on my conversations, too.'

'Hard not to, when you were so loud and lording your life over everyone like you've always done. Always had to make sure everybody knew what you were doing and just *how good* you were doing it, didn't you?'

'I don't—'

'And you've always liked making sure *I* look bad in the process.' I flash her a grin, but even I know it must look stiff and bitter. Even though this isn't new for us – we've always bickered and tried to one-up each other – it feels twisted now; it's something I don't want to be saying, but can't seem to stop myself. This woman brings out the worst in me; she always has. Ashleigh pales a little bit, just as the smile drops off my face and I shake my head. 'Good to see you haven't changed a bit, Easton.'

'Excuse me?' she exclaims, and the words bounce off the walls, the ceilings, fill the space so much that I have to grit my teeth.

'Forget it,' I mutter. I move away from the trophy cabinet. Maybe we are the same pole of a magnet after all, because suddenly, I can't get far enough away from her – from this conversation, from who I am around her. 'Let's just go back to the party.'

'No! Answer me. What do you mean, *I* always made sure *you* looked bad? Don't you dare try to act like I was some petty, nasty little bully when you swanned around like you ruled this place, and when you did the *exact same thing to me*. I had to put up with *you* putting me down for years. You're not better than me, Ryan, you're—'

'Yeah, and don't I know it. Didn't you make *sure* I knew it, every damned day?'

I stop, but only to turn on her so she can feel the full brunt of my words like I had to feel hers. Ashleigh collides with me and I snatch her arm to haul her back upright. I don't let it go.

'You want to know why I'm in politics? Why I'm gunning for PM? So that you'll have to suck it up and realise once and for all that *you're not better than me.*'

Ashleigh recoils, flinching, and stares with wide eyes for a moment before wrenching her arm out of my grip. A muscle ticks in her jaw, eyebrows furrowing, and . . .

Fuck. She's about to *cry*.

I've never seen Ashleigh Easton cry. Not once. I didn't think she was capable of it.

She shoves me away with both hands, the clasp on her clutch bag digging into my shoulder. I fall back, still trying to wrap my head around the fact that she's on the verge of tears. The stony, ruthless bitch, flesh and blood after all.

'Go to hell, Ryan,' she spits, and storms out of the library before I can register what just happened.

And – that's it, I think. Fucking checkmate. I've finally won. Not just the battle, but the entire damn war between the two of us. It's over, she's conceded, and I can emerge victorious.

I forgot, though, that both sides suffer casualties in a rivalry as bitter as this.

Chapter Seventeen

Bryony

'Most Likely to Become Famous'

The party's really kicked off now and if I do say so myself, it's a bloody good party. Everyone's got full bellies from the pizza, most people are a bit tipsy off the spiked punch but nobody's verging into messy drunk to make it a problem, and spirits are high. They're all mingling and dancing and laughing and everybody is having the absolute best time of their lives.

Which, like, they're totally welcome for.

I kind of want to brag about it to Steph because she always used to arrange get-togethers and have a hand in organising house parties or prom, but I can't see her anywhere. Her fiancé is still hanging about though, so she must be here somewhere.

Pride simmers through me, bubbling up around the tips of my ears and threatening to spill over in joyful peals of laughter and smug smiles. It feels like those nights on stage where everything just goes *right* – no issues with lighting cues or people flubbing lines or costume mishaps, performing to a sold-out theatre that ends in a standing ovation. That's a high I can ride for days; this will be, too. I wonder if I can get away with making some sort of closing speech and take a bow, or if too many people will try to leave before the end of the night and make the whole thing not worth it.

Not to mention, nobody suspected *a thing* when I had to wrangle Freddie away from the staff photos in a totally non-subtle way. I haven't seen Ashleigh since, thinking about it, but she'll get over it. I mean, this is *Freddie*, it's not like she actually fancied him. I think.

Anyway, all that matters is that his hand is no longer crumpling up my yearbook print-out covering up the damning evidence of my current reality, threatening to reveal it to the world at any moment, so I'm chalking that up as another win. Gone are the mental images of the gasps all around the hall, the stunned faces of my old classmates as my façade is ripped from me before their very eyes, leaving me to flee in tears, humiliated beyond belief.

Still . . . if Freddie could almost accidentally unveil my photo on the staff board, so could someone else. I keep glancing over at that corner of the room every few seconds, *just in case* some other idiot decides to stand too close for comfort over there. The adrenaline rush I'm experiencing is all to do with how great the party is, though, and *definitely* not almost being outed as a liar and #*cancelled*.

I'm too busy watching a couple of women almost drift in the direction of the staff photos that I'm not really listening to whatever Mardy Mara With The Lipliner is saying until Elise nudges me in the arm.

'Huh?'

'I said' – gosh, she really does look so much better for having figured out how to wear lipliner, kudos to whatever YouTube or TikTok tutorial finally got through to her – 'I thought you were in that Hugh Grant movie? You know, the one on Prime? The guy from *Game of Thrones* was in it . . . You posted all about it on your Instagram. There was that selfie of you and Hugh Grant from the cast party?'

I mean, they don't need to know the selfie was from set, and I got cussed out by one of the producers for it and made to delete the photo, which obviously I resurrected from my deleted folder immediately afterwards.

'Mm-hmm. Oh my gosh, it was *so* lit, you would not believe.'

'Is he really cool? I can't believe you met him.' Elise's eyes light up and everybody else in our little circle leans in, intrigued, hanging off my every word before I can even speak, and I bask in their attention. 'He seems so awesome; I think I'd die!'

'Did you film much with him?' someone else asks. I think she was one of the geeky kids Ashleigh and Hayden were friendly with. I think we maybe did a history project together in Year Eight.

'We had a *really* great scene together, actually. Hardly took any takes, but of course, he's a pro, and he told me I take direction really well—'

Or, you know. He *would've*, if I'd been able to show off my acting talents properly. I'd stake money on it.

'You were in a scene with him?' Mara says, frowning. 'But you weren't in the movie.'

'What?'

'I watched it. I even rewound the credits to look for your name, I told my girlfriend you were in it and we were looking out for you. I didn't see you in it?'

Oh, fuck. Fuckity fuck.

'Well, you know, it was a very small role' – I was an extra

147

for one scene and my only job was to stand in the background at a party, so even that's stretching the truth – 'and a lot of things end up on the cutting-room floor. It's just Hollywood, you know how it is.'

'Wait,' says someone else, and bloody hell, when did Hayden get here? When did he decide to slink into the group all silent and stealthy like that, and butt in? He barely even used to speak up in class, but *now* – what, now, all of a sudden, he's Mr Chatterbox? His eyes are glassy, too; trust *Hayden* to have such an accurate memory even when he's a little bit drunk. 'I thought you said earlier you were an extra on that movie? You told Thea and Priya—'

'I said *I might as well have been*,' I snap, and, shit, can they all hear my heart thundering at a hundred miles an hour? I try to compose myself, but not even that *don't be suspicious* soundbite from *Parks and Rec* can save me now. I force my snarl at Hayden into more of a smile, and the laugh I attempt sounds too high-pitched to be passably realistic. I toss my ponytail over my shoulder and jut a hip out to the side, then roll my eyes at Elise. 'As if this guy here knows anything about cinema, am I right? No, it was totally just one of those things. But it was *such* a good experience . . .'

Mara doesn't look totally convinced, though, and I dare not look at everybody else to see if they've got similar responses. I can't afford to. I *have* to maintain this façade, I'm in too deep. Thankfully, I'm saved by whatever probing question Mardy Mara has started to ask when I notice Freddie Loughton, Hiro, Tommy, and two or three other people making for the doors, all of them shoving at each other and laughing.

You will *not* convince me those boys are taking a trip to the toilets together. No chance.

I'm almost tempted to let them go. They'll just muck around in the hallways a bit, maybe go visit the old common room and see what it looks like now, but . . . What if they stumble off towards the drama department? What if they see the posters from the last orchestra trip when I was a chaperone, or find my classroom? They're never going to let that lie, and everyone will know in a few seconds, and – *no*. I can't let that happen.

Plus, I don't think I can afford to stay here acting sus for another second.

I dart away from the group and make a beeline for the boys just as they get through the doors. I pick up the pace and bellow, 'Freddie Loughton! Hiro Tanaka! You lot get back in here *now*.'

The boys, to their credit, stop joking around and fall quiet.

Unfortunately for me, so does half of the rest of the hall. I feel eyes on me, see heads swivel in my direction, but stand my ground, arms crossed and one hip out, eyebrows raised. The lads all exchange uncertain looks, but shuffle back into the hall.

'I *said*, no gallivanting around the school. Didn't I say that? Tommy?'

'Yeah – um, yes, Bryony.'

'Yeah, I thought I did. So where are you all off to?'

Two of them are smart enough to say 'bathroom'. Hiro mutters something about a smoke break, which I'm not buying after all the stuff I saw he retweeted about how there should be more regulations around vapes and how bad he thinks they are.

'Aw, come on, Bryony,' Freddie says, lurching towards me with a smile. If he's trying to emulate Ryan, it's not

149

working – and if Ryan cared to get them out of this, he doesn't step forward from wherever he is to try. 'We were just having a laugh. Swear down we won't mess anything up.'

'Mm-hmm. Back inside, boys. I said no wandering around, and I *meant it*. This is my reputation on the line if you lot screw things up, okay?'

The other guys behind Freddie mumble apologies, filtering back into the hall. A few people are laughing and Tommy gives a melodramatic shrug and sheepish roll of his eyes, playing up to the attention. He claps Freddie on the back as he passes, but Freddie only scowls and stays put.

'So much for the hostess with the mostest,' he says, none too quietly. 'That was *so* anti-dank of you.'

'What's *anti-dank* is you thinking you can pull off saying that.'

'I thought you were always up for some *fun*, Bryony. Like at Morgan's New Year's party in Year Twelve, remember?'

'Oh, sweetie.' Poor kid really *hasn't* grown up in the last ten years if he thinks he can slut-shame me. I walk up and pat his shoulder, giving him my best patronising-teacher smile I use when kids act up in my classes and I need them to understand I'm not buying their bullshit. 'Sadly, all I remember about that is that it lasted about thirty seconds. I've had smear tests more intimate.'

Freddie flushes. I give his shoulder another gentle pat before turning around to a sea of grinning, scandalised, delighted faces, relishing the gossip and drama. A couple of girls raise their drinks to me; I notice Morgan almost doubled over laughing, wiping tears from her eyes.

It's tonight's equivalent of a standing ovation, and I'll take it.

Chapter Eighteen

Steph

'Most Likely to End Up Together'

I hold my breath – and my shoes – until we're safely out of the library, the volume of Ryan and Ashleigh's voices increasing behind us. They're so busy bickering that they don't notice the too-loud clunk of the door closing behind us.

My fingers tighten around the heels I took off so I could make a run for it more quietly, and it's only now that I register that my other hand is linked with Shaun's, our fingers intertwined, his palm warm and smooth against mine. Did I not notice because of the adrenaline of almost being caught, or because it's such a natural fit?

As I stare at it, Shaun's fingers tighten around mine, and he tugs me along the corridor.

'Come on!' he urges in a whisper, and we both bolt back towards the stairs, still hand in hand. I sprint to keep up with his longer strides, the laminate flooring cold beneath my bare feet, and something about this whole thing – running through a near-abandoned school after hours with the boy I used to love – feels so surreal and absurd that I start laughing.

Shaun shushes me, which only makes me giggle harder, and it's not long before he joins in. The two of us careen down the stairwell, breathless from the run and our laughter, and I have to pull him to a stop. I finally take my hand from his and try not to think about how empty it feels as I press that same hand into my side, bending over to ease the stitch in my side.

'Think we're safe?' he jokes, grinning at me. Shaun's cheeks are flushed, his eyes bright, and the whole look gives his face a boyish quality that strips the last ten years from him. It's enough to make me feel seventeen again, my outfit feeling more like a prom dress than a staple in my wardrobe for cocktail parties and wedding receptions.

'Probably.' I'm still panting, still catching my breath. The rush of sneaking about has winded me more than the activity, but the thought makes me wince. Shaun either doesn't notice or assumes it's a reaction to my stitch.

We're not, I have to remind myself, *sneaking around*. The idea feels sordid – dirty – and I know that if Ashleigh or Ryan *had* noticed us in the library, they would have jumped to conclusions. If they'd seen us hiding in the stacks, standing close and sharing stories about ourselves and our lives, smiling and laughing and teasing . . . It wouldn't have looked very innocent.

Neither, I suppose, does running away.

None of it is very innocent, except . . .

Well, of course it is. We're only talking, catching up with one another . . . how is it any different to the conversations I've had with Priya or Morgan or Thea tonight, really? It's hardly as if Shaun or I left the hall to find some peace and quiet with any sort of ulterior motive, and it's not as though either of us made a move in the library.

152

Sure, there might have been a few lingering looks, a couple of playful touches on the arm, but . . .

We were being friendly, that's all. Even after all the years and the distance and the history, it's so easy to just *be* around Shaun; he feels familiar and safe and comfortable. It's so impossible to imagine that we're anything but those teenagers who knew each other better than we knew ourselves.

Standing on the step below him now, the silence expanding around us and pressing against me like some tangible thing, swollen and soft, I study Shaun's profile. The straight, short bridge of his nose and the way his left ear sticks out a little bit more than the right one. Those thick, long eyelashes I always envied because mine were so fair you could hardly see them, which would always rest so sweetly against his cheek when he dozed next to me on the sofa while we watched a movie at one of our houses. That one bit of hair right on the crown of his head that stubbornly sticks out in the wrong direction; I would always try to put it into place, but it would never go.

I catalogue the ways he's changed, too. The fact his hair is *styled*, now, the cut purposeful. His body is a little bit taller, softer instead of bony elbows and gangly shoulders, his jaw more defined even though his face has still kept that charming boyishness. The clothes, which are more mature, though he always dressed well – a bit trendy, too. The heavy watch around his wrist even though he always swore he never liked watches, and the deeper, more confident cadence of his voice.

I search for more, but all I can think of are things I noticed while we were talking inside the library, habits and quirks that haven't changed. How he talks with his hands, how expressive his face is, the way the tone of his voice alters when he's building to a punchline, the little pauses in his storytelling when he anticipates I'm about to react somehow. He's still my Shaun, and I know him in my marrow. In every beat of my heart and every breath I take.

I've no idea how long I stand there staring at Shaun, aware that he's looking at me in exactly the same sort of way and something about that feels entirely not innocent, yet entirely expected, but finally he opens his mouth and draws breath . . .

But the words that fill the stairwell and echo off the walls aren't his.

'What's the matter, Ashleigh? Can dish it out, but can't take it?'

I glance up in the direction of the voice before my gaze darts back towards Shaun, and I watch his eyes widen in recognition. It's Ryan, and judging by the clack of heeled shoes stomping downstairs, Ashleigh is there, too.

Heading right for us.

'This is really how you want to spend your night – yelling at me? Get a life, why don't you. Go back to the party,' Ashleigh yells at him, 'I'm sure your adoring fans will be missing you. Don't worry, nobody has to know what a dickhead you still are, I'm not going to tell everyone and ruin your *perfect* reputation.'

I don't even need to say anything or gesture to Shaun; he's already read my mind. The two of us hurry down the stairs as a furious-sounding Ryan and Ashleigh draw ever closer. I'm sure I heard her voice wobble a bit there and if it were anybody but them, I'd be a bit worried – but the two of them used to have such blazing rows and were always horrible to each other, so nothing about this interaction raises alarm bells. It was always better to leave them to hash it out rather than be caught in their crossfire.

Well, no alarm bells except how bad it might look for Shaun and I to be found lurking alone together like this. Ashleigh's been terribly pally with Bryony tonight, and if she mentioned it to her, well, who knows what Bryony might say? She's always loved gossip.

I'm not hiding anything, I'm just . . . aware of the optics, is all.

I trip down the last couple of stairs and bump right into Shaun, who's come to a stop at a set of double doors elevated just above the ground floor. They lead out to the art block and the back field where they used to do rugby and football matches, and I freeze at what awaits us on the other side of them: the little set of stone steps where the two of us used to sit during free periods when the weather was nice. There was never any footfall this way while lessons were on, so it was as private as it got. The door rattles loudly and Shaun mutters a curse under his breath before reaching up for the deadbolt at the top.

It whines as it slides out of place, making us both flinch.

On the next floor up, and much too close for comfort, Ryan and Ashleigh don't seem to have noticed at all. They're completely wrapped up in their argument, which isn't unusual. Ten years ago, the school could have caught fire and burnt down around them before either of them stopped bickering long enough to notice.

Ryan huffs, exasperated. 'I'm not worried about my reputation, Ash, for God's sake—'

'*Right*, sure, you're worried about me. People change, Ryan,

155

but not that much. Go back to the fucking party already, and *leave me alone.*'

'Why are you always acting like *I'm* the villain here? What, like you're the model of perfection the rest of us should set our standards by? Newsflash, Easton, but *you're not.*'

'What part of "piss off" can you not understand?' she yells back and her voice definitely cracks this time. I swear I hear her stomp her foot, and part of me is gripped by the entire argument as if it's a soap opera on the telly.

'Steph!' Shaun hisses, gesturing through the open door.

But my heart is in my throat. For all I laughed at him earlier for saying it, now I really *do* expect someone to come and tell us off. What if the caretaker is still around, or one of the teachers has stayed behind to do some marking, and they heard?

I crowd closer like I can vanish into the shadows, or even behind him. 'We can't! Bryony said—'

'She said not to go off exploring the school and graffitiing the whiteboards. *Technically*, we'll be outside the school, so . . .'

'That's – yes, but . . .' I squirm, arms wrapping around my waist as if I can hold this new wave of nerves back before they spill out everywhere. 'It's locked for a reason! We can't just . . . We *can't*. What if somebody breaks in?'

'It's fine. We'll put the deadbolt back on when we go back in. And besides, we'll be right outside the door – it's not as if a burglar will just stroll past us, is it?'

I chew my lower lip, only stopping when Shaun's eyes flit down to catch the gesture. I know it's instinctive rather than a conscious look on his part, but I don't want him to think I'm trying to flirt. I'm not. That's not what this is.

He gives me that perpetual easy smile, the one that's so wholly him and which everybody has always loved, and his eyebrows tick up mischievously.

'Come on, Steph. When was the last time you broke the rules?'

He knows the answer to that: never.

It's not changed in ten years.

A sense of daring, unfamiliar and intoxicating, dances through me, egged on by the adrenaline of almost being caught by Ashleigh and Ryan. It fizzes in my stomach and tickles at the tips of my fingers, making me uncross my arms from around myself and stand up a little bit straighter.

I ascend the two steps to be next to Shaun and reach past him to push open the door, a rush of cool air pouring in. The corners of his mouth stretch wider, and my body grazes against his as I take the first step outside.

Chapter Nineteen

Hayden

'Most Likely to Succeed'

Backstage is dark enough that I need to navigate by the torchlight off my phone. The stark white beam falls on stacks of battered wooden chairs and an old projector set, some tables, a couple of wonky metal music stands. I stumble around them, all those glasses of punch leaving me tipsy and uncoordinated – I'm more buzzed than I thought. There's a box of props, some random pieces of costume I guess must be from the last school play. There are some folded print-outs of a programme on top, a bit crumpled and written in a basic Times New Roman font – *Tisdale Comprehensive presents* MARY POPPINS. I take a spot on one particularly wobbly chair that's off alone to one side, then click to FaceTime my ex, Lucy.

She answers on the fourth ring.

'Hayden! I think your camera's off, love, it's all dark. Everything's *fine* here, you worry wart, if you were calling to check in. Where are you? I thought you were at the reunion for another couple of hours yet?'

'Oh, um, no. I'm still at the party.' If only because every time I try to leave, someone accosts me with a gleeful friend-liness I can't wiggle out of and drags me back into the fold. I squirm, wondering if I could wait out the rest of the night here instead. It's probably a good thing that she can't see me – Lucy has always been able to read me like a book. 'I thought I'd just call and say goodnight to the girls, if that's okay? I mean, if you haven't put them to bed yet.'

Lucy laughs. 'If you didn't let these girls walk all over you, I'd worry about you being *such* a helicopter dad. Hang on, I'm just in the kitchen . . .'

The camera angle shifts sharply to an unflattering shot underneath her chin as she starts walking, and the spotlights of the kitchen ceiling vanish as she goes into the living room to call, 'Girls! Girls, your dad's on the phone. Skye, darling, come say goodnight to Daddy.'

Lucy's phone judders and the image on the screen blurs, and I'm met with the sound of toys being thrown down and a Disney film being put on mute just as Gaston starts singing to rile up a mob to go kill Beast. My gaze drifts to the lost-property box next to me and I absently pick through a tie, a single trainer, a couple of books and a shiny silver pencil case while I wait. The chair wobbles violently underneath me and I fight to regain my balance.

Then everything jerks to a halt and Margot's face appears on screen. She's scowling, huffy, and makes a dramatic gesture throwing her butterfly-clipped hair out of her face. 'Dad, you're spoiling girls' night. We've been playing hairdresser with Mum.'

'I can see that.'

'I did Go's hair!' Skye shouts, butting her face into view.

Margot shoves her aside and Lucy moves into view just behind the sofa, pulling the girls gently apart before they start fighting. 'Dad, I've decided, I'm going to be a boot-shun.'

'Beautician,' Lucy translates.

'*And* Mum did my nails, look.' Margot waves a purple-tipped hand in front of the camera, then admires it. Her scowl sets back in. 'This hand's a bit smudged. Skye helped with that one,' she mutters with a long-suffering air of martyrdom she perfected about five minutes after Skye was born.

'I did! And we did mine! Look. They're blue!'

'Wow, nice! Your favourite colour. Can you do mine for me when I get home, d'you think?'

Skye thinks about it hard for a moment, then ultimately decides, 'I don't think blue suits you very well, Daddy.'

I fight not to smile, trying to match her serious energy. 'Oh. Alright, fair enough.' It doesn't help that Lucy is in the background smothering a laugh and doing a terrible job of it.

'Is your party fun?' Margot asks, just as Skye says, 'Mummy said you're not home till after *breakfast*. You're going to have an angry tummy, like Margot when she gets hungry.'

'I'll find something to eat for breakfast,' I reassure her. 'And the party's great, thank you, Go. That was very nice of you to ask.'

'Are you playing hide-and-seek?'

'No. Why?'

'Oh. Well, why are you in the dark?'

Uh-oh, rumbled.

Skye tells me, 'I don't think you'll win – you're making too much noise talking to us. They'll find you easy.'

'That's a good point. I'd better get off the phone then,

160

hadn't I? I just wanted to call and say behave for Mum, and night-night.'

'We *are* behaving. *You're* spoiling it,' Margot tells me, but they both say goodnight (whispering, so my hiding place doesn't get found out) and let Lucy take the phone back. She puts the film back on and returns to the kitchen with me still on the line, and closes the door before frowning at the screen. It's a sweet look, mouth puckered and twisted up on the left-hand side, that same eyebrow contorting into a wavy line. Skye pulls the same face when she's thinking too hard about something.

'You *are* still at the party, aren't you?'

'Yeah. I'm, er, just . . .'

Lucy sighs, propping the phone against the counter while she fills the kettle and sets it on to boil, getting things ready to make herself a cup of tea. Her nails are messy blobs of pink nail varnish and there are little braids and butterfly clips through her dark blonde hair, obviously the work of the girls. She looks tired, when I get a proper view of her face again as she waits for the kettle, but then she says, 'Hayden . . .' and I'm not sure it's to do with the fact she's been watching Margot and Skye all evening.

'It's fine,' I tell her. 'I just wanted to say goodnight, that's all.'

'I know you love being a dad, but you know it's okay to switch off sometimes, too, don't you? Have some time for yourself? Just because you have custody . . .' She hesitates, and I can feel her guilt even through the screen. She loves the girls and enjoys spending time with them, but she's always found it hard to be a hands-on mum day to day, even when we were still trying to make a real go of it between having Margot and Skye. I've never blamed her for that, but I know plenty of other people have. Lucy finally settles on saying, 'That doesn't mean you have to go overboard to make up for it. They've got me, too, you know.'

'I know, but . . .'

But Lucy has a career she loves and is passionate about, and a thriving social life, and I hate intruding on that when I'm happy with my remote working and quiet hang-outs with people like Ashleigh – takeout and a couple of beers on the sofa. *But*, as everybody has made so abundantly clear tonight, I sacrificed everything about myself to be a dad and I'm not sure how much of me is left, if I were to look.

Certainly, there's nothing to find at the bottom of a cup of spiked punch, but that hasn't stopped me trying.

'But nothing,' Lucy says definitively, looking far more authoritative than she has any right to with that hairstyle. She only stops glaring down the camera at me to concentrate on pouring water into her mug, and I think it's uncanny that she can read me so well when she can't even *see* me. 'Go have fun, Hayden. Have a couple more drinks, huh? You deserve it.'

'I want to. I do. But everybody is making it so hard . . . You should see them, Luce. You'd hate it. It's all "best foot forward", all smug and fake, even Ashleigh's been . . .' I grimace, remembering the sight of her grinding up against Freddie Loughton on the dance floor, something she'd *never* normally do. 'It makes me feel like I'm on the back foot because I was just coming here to say hello to some old familiar faces and try to enjoy a night off, instead of *showing off* to everyone.'

162

'That sounds like a them problem, not a you problem. I bet you're overthinking it, anyway, and nobody's judging you.'

I bite my tongue, not wanting to get into it all now. Maybe tomorrow over a coffee in the kitchen, when I'm back. I settle for saying, 'Sure, maybe. I'll text you tomorrow when I'm on the way home, won't be too long. Thanks for minding them overnight.'

'You don't have to thank me, you daft thing. They're my daughters, too.'

'I know, but—'

'*But nothing*,' she says, and where this kind of loop would've sent us into a frustrated argument before, she only laughs about it now. It's as if all the tension slipped out of the relationship when we agreed to be friends rather than partners, and we're both better off for it. Lucy flaps a badly manicured hand at me. 'If you don't come home with a hangover and a fun story, we'll be having words. Talk tomorrow!'

We hang up and for a moment I cradle my phone between my hands. There's a lightness in my chest, though whether it's from the chat with Lucy or speaking to the girls, I can't tell. It makes the burden of everybody else's pity tonight weigh a little less, rallies me, gives me a second wind ready to tackle the next few hours.

I'm just about to stand when footsteps rush past and a figure bursts across the stage behind the heavy curtain that separates us from the party. The shadows bend and glimmer, faint fragments of light catching on an array of sequins.

Bryony starts pacing back and forth and muttering to herself. 'Stupid, bloody . . . Ugh! How could you be such an

163

idiot? And bloody Mardy Mara, thinking she knows everything, and *Hayden* . . .'

I sit up straighter at the sound of my name, but also hold my breath like it will help her not to notice me. I'm not exactly sure what I've done but Bryony sounds furious, and I'd really not rather have to deal with her mean-girl attitude and endure her carefully crafted put-downs.

Then she takes a deep breath – several, in fact, in such a deliberate manner it must be some kind of exercise she learnt in drama lessons or something.

More calmly this time, she tells herself, 'It's fine. *It's fine*, okay? You've got this. Nobody knows anything, not *really*, and they're not going to find out. Why would they? Why would they know?' She lets out a shrill laugh that sounds – not drunk, but worryingly hysterical. 'You'll be fine. Just a few more hours, then you're home free. *You can do this*. Those posers and pretentious little shits out there don't need to know a thing . . .'

She takes a few deep breaths and I see her silhouette as she shakes herself from head to toe, arms waggling out wildly at her sides. She throws her head back and makes a few weird noises that must be some kind of vocal warm-up, then rights herself, smooths out her sparkly jumpsuit, and strides back out like that didn't just happen.

Not that I'm sure exactly what just happened, but I give her a couple of minutes before I emerge from backstage, too. I guess maybe I'm not the only one who needs to rally themselves to make it through tonight.

When I get up to slip back into the party, though, I see Bryony hasn't gone too far. She's standing next to the poster of her teenage self from the yearbook, looking out across the room as if assessing – she's probably trying to decide which group to go and talk to next. But then I see a little crease appear between her eyebrows and she glances around quickly before turning her attention to the poster, which has slipped slightly, hanging a little crooked where the corner of the tape has peeled off. She smooths a finger gently over the tape, checking it's firmly in place before stepping back to assess her handiwork.

And then she dives back into the party, a smile plastered on her face as she shouts across to someone.

Weird.

I mean, it's not weird that she'd be obsessed with her own poster, but . . . *everything* that just happened was kind of weird.

The box of costumes and props catches my eye, and the gears in my brain are whirring before I fully process why, and my hands pick up the programme on the top of the box seemingly of their own accord.

And something finally slides into place when I open up the folded sheet of A4 and see, below the cast list, a line that reads: *Produced by Ms B Adams – Head of Drama.*

Chapter Twenty

Ashleigh

'Most Likely to Kill Each Other'

Stalking through empty halls and past closed classroom doors gives me the weirdest feeling of being late for class. The fact that it's dark, with motion sensors making lights flicker to life one by one as I storm ahead, gives the whole place the creepy aura of a nightmare.

Not that I still get nightmares about showing up to an exam I haven't revised for, or being shouted at in class for not knowing something basic. Obviously I don't. I'm almost thirty. I'm in my Charlotte Lucas era. I'm totally over it.

I escape down the corridors, past the maths classrooms, and Ryan is still chasing after me. I don't know why he didn't just leave me alone after I left him in the library, or why he hasn't gone back to the party now.

No, that's a lie. I do know – it's because his overinflated ego can't bear to concede defeat and let me win this fight. But to think he has the audacity to try to sound like my reaction to his cutting words has truly, genuinely, *bothered him* . . . I'm not falling for it.

I finally reach the science block – an extended wing of the school built decades after the original building, which has apparently had a complete revamp since we all left. The ceilings are smooth and white, free from damp spots and flaky paint. The laminate floors are still shiny with only a few dark shoe-scuffs worn in, and the nameplates on the doors declaring which teacher's classroom it is, are embossed metal ones rather than worn-out sticky labels defaced with Sharpies.

The musty, papery smell that lurks in the other corridors is replaced by plastic and disinfectant here. It's enough to make me gag.

Also enough to make me gag: Ryan calling out, 'Ashleigh, *please*, can you slow down? I can't . . .' *Can't keep up*, because he can't bloody run with that knee injury, and now *I* feel like the arsehole. Again. 'Can we talk about this?'

I grit my teeth and pick up the pace.

He doesn't want to talk; this isn't about being nice or civil or mending bridges we burnt long, long ago. I don't want him to be the bigger person here, to have *grown up* or *changed* or any of that bollocks. It's too little, too late.

As if he's got any right to act like I was the one in the wrong, when all I did was stick up for myself and retaliate when *he* started it. God knows everybody else, our teachers included, spent enough time glorifying Ryan, making him out to be some godlike figure among us mere mortals. I was the only person who ever called him out. As if he cared what I thought enough to let it bother him – never mind *still* let it bother him. And he's got no right to stand there pretending he didn't dish it out, too. Like he didn't go out of his way to belittle me and humiliate me at every turn.

I shouldn't be so shocked that he acts so untouchable, so

167

above it all, after all this time. I bet it works wonders for him in the world of politics. Butter wouldn't melt.

Except he's not special. He's not godlike or glorious or anything else. He's flawed and human like the rest of us, even if I'm the only one who sees it.

He calls out, and I spin around to face him. The heavy door behind him slides shut, the whisper of it across the floor timid and gentle. A green light blinks to life on a little keypad beside it.

Ryan stops in his tracks, mouth agape, and for once . . .

For once, he looks like he doesn't know what to say or do. *Good*.

But I can't take any pleasure in seeing him floundering and unsure like this, not when it's taking all my willpower not to cry. My mouth stays firmly shut and I blink again, but a couple of tears spill over. I brush them away quickly with the back of my hand, although I know it's futile; there's no way he didn't notice.

I can't let him see me cry. I won't.

I hate that I'm letting him get to me this much. That I was stupid enough to participate in our old rivalry just to learn that he still labours under the delusion that I was the bitch and he was the victim who never put a foot wrong. I hate that it feels like maybe he *has* changed, but suddenly I'm stuck as the same person I was ten years ago.

I hate all of this, and I can't bear to stay here and look at him for another second.

I've spent the last ten years perpetually trying to put distance between me and any mention of Ryan Lawal. I don't need to start from point zero again tonight. I don't need to put myself through this.

Ryan's standing in front of the only door out of the science block, apart from the staircase at the other end of the corridor, leading upstairs. I rack my brain for where the other fire exit was, or if there was another way back to the main building upstairs, but the memories have turned fuzzy under the stress of the moment. There are keypads next to all the classroom doors like the one next to the main door. Most of them are lit up in red, and I realise it's a snazzy security system. Some school governor must have been *really* invested in how good this was going to make them look. I wonder if they've put as much funding into the actual school equipment and resources for the students, but, at the same time, know I would've loved having a science block that looked like this when I was here.

So I head to the nearest room with a green light, leaving him in the hallway. As I step through the door, I realise it's my old A-level chemistry classroom. There are five shiny new computers on the bench that runs alongside the windows and the wood-topped stools we used to sit on have been replaced by tall chairs in dark grey plastic. The sturdy, chipped wooden benches with sinks and gas taps have been upgraded, too, although they're in exactly the same arrangement as the old ones I remember. There's a pile of textbooks at the back of the room just like there used to be when I was a student, and the chemicals cabinet is a fancy new one with a more sophisticated lock on it. It's so achingly familiar and foreign all at once.

I gravitate to my usual seat near the front. I just need a few minutes to clear my head and then I'll head back to the party. I'll scroll TikTok for a bit or check in on the group chat or something, and then I'll go back in there, if only to prove to Ryan – and Bryony and Freddie, too – that they can't spoil my entire night.

Except then, the door opens. I should have thought to lock it. I haven't even made it to my seat yet, but stop where I am, eyes closing with a sigh. Why can't he take a hint already? Ryan's footsteps are solid on the laminate flooring, so heavy they echo off the walls. He comes to a stop behind me and my skin prickles, goosebumps rising along my bare shoulders and making me itch to turn around and face him. He's so close I'm sure if I took half a step back, I'd bump into him.

The hand he lifts to place on my arm makes me flinch, the heat of his skin searing mine even through the fabric of my sleeve.

'I know that fighting is like, our thing—'

'We don't have a *thing*,' I protest, but it's a whisper, and he pretends not to hear.

'—but you think we could try something new? Like, maybe, have a fucking *conversation* for a change?'

'I don't think there's anything for us to talk about.' We've never had things to *talk* about, not really. It was always – peripheral. Stuff about school, or to do with being Head Girl and Boy, or about other people. The only time we talked to each other was to brag about ourselves or make digs at each other. 'Unless you're going to apologise, in which case, don't bother. I'm not interested.'

'What have *I* got to—' Ryan cuts himself off abruptly with a weary sigh, the sound so raw and vulnerable that I do almost turn around, if only to make sure it's actually him and not some imposter. Somehow, that idea seems more likely than Ryan having *feelings*. He reaches for my arm again and this time his touch is lighter, tentative, a brush of his fingertips against my elbow, inviting me to face him. Pleading, even.

When I don't, he moves so close that I can feel the warmth of him at my back; it tugs on the same primal, unreasonable part of me that revelled in the scent of his cologne earlier and responded to the way he looked at my smudged lipstick. I stand stock still, hardly even able to breathe, as Ryan's exhale fans over the sensitive skin where my neck and shoulder connect, and his fingers slide more firmly around my arm to anchor me in place, as if I'd even be capable of moving away right now.

Whatever hold he has on me, whatever this shift in our usual dynamic is tonight . . .

It's not because this is another game he's trying to one-up me in, I realise. It's because he must feel this insatiable pull, this magnetism between us, and I decide I hate him for giving in to it. For making me want to, too.

'It's because of you,' he says, his voice a low, gravelly rumble. It might sound seductive, if not for the trace of anger that curls the edges of his words. 'You wanted to know why I went into politics, but I didn't explain it right. It's because of you.'

My head tilts slightly, lips parting even though the question never makes it out of my mouth. Ryan must notice, because he carries on.

'You always used to say I'd never amount to anything. Peak in high school, that kind of thing. That I'd leave and my glory days would be behind me, and I'd find out that here, I was a big fish in a small pond, but out in the real world I'd just be another has-been.'

Well, yeah, I want to say. Because that was the exact

171

stereotype he fitted. Because he was such an arrogant little shit that in what world would that *not* be the case?

'And I always knew you were wrong about me, but . . . I don't know, I guess it gave – *gives* – me an extra push, when I need it. Your voice would be there in the back of my mind and I'd remember there was always gonna be *someone* out there – not necessarily you, I guess, just someone – who I'd need to prove wrong about me. People who'd think I couldn't do it or wasn't good enough. And I—' He cuts off with a short chuckle; his breath on the back of my neck sends a shiver down my spine. I imagine him scrubbing his hand over his face, running it back through his hair. 'You know me. I always liked proving people wrong.'

I know you liked proving you were the best. But again, the words don't quite make it out of my mouth. I still don't turn around, almost afraid that if I do, it'll shatter whatever this is, and I don't know that I'm ready for that to happen.

Ryan shifts slightly behind me, not exactly coming closer, but making me horribly, acutely aware of how he's almost flush at my back, and the fact he still hasn't let go of my arm.

But he doesn't say anything else. The breath I take trembles and his fingers tighten slightly at my elbow, making me sure he heard it.

'So it's all just . . . to prove me wrong?' I manage. 'You built your entire career off a petty teenage grudge?'

He doesn't deny it, but the hand finally slips away from my arm and it feels like confirmation enough. Instead of some kind of righteous sense of triumph because I could mock him mercilessly over this, there's only a pang in my heart, something sad and heavy and . . . achingly familiar.

'I never thought you weren't good enough,' I murmur,

172

and turn my head slightly until I can make out the very edge of him in my peripheral vision. I feel his eyes burning into me, the way he's hanging off my every word. 'I just . . . You were Icarus. Someone had to tell you that one day you'd fly too close to the sun. I only tore you down because you did it to me constantly. *You* were the popular one; the guy everyone wanted to be like, or be with, or be *around*, and you never had a problem reminding me that I – wasn't like that. That I wasn't pretty or fuckable or fun.'

I almost expect him to object, but he doesn't.

'And even when it wasn't you saying that stuff, you made sure to laugh loud enough when someone else said it. Made sure everybody heard and laughed as well. And as I recall, you told me plenty of times that *I* had an over-inflated sense of self and would crash and burn and not amount to anything, too.'

'But you just . . .' He trails off and has to clear his throat. 'You never *cared*. You always acted like you were better than – everyone. Couldn't wait to get out of here, like . . . Like school was just holding you back from the rest of your life.'

A laugh trips off my tongue and now, finally, I turn to face him. The confused frown on Ryan's face is set so deep that I wonder the lines in his forehead aren't permanently etched there. There's not a trace of his usual grin in the downward slant of his mouth, and his eyes search my face almost desperately.

'Why do you think I couldn't wait to get out of here? Because you and your friends and half our fucking year group did *nothing* but let me know how boring and uncool I was. You think I didn't learn that *not* responding and giving you all the satisfaction of knowing you'd upset me was the best way to make it through that? You think I was mean to you, I hurt your ego? I only gave as good as I got, Ryan.'

Impossibly, his frown deepens. His gaze lowers to our feet, but it doesn't feel like a win; it just tightens in my throat, makes fresh tears blur my eyes until I blink them away.

He doesn't apologise; neither do I. It's been ten years and I don't think it would matter at this stage anyway, neither to clear our own consciences nor soothe old wounds.

His eyes are still downcast, but one of his hands moves, as if of its own accord. It skims up the backs of my fingers, to my wrist, winding its way back down like he thought better of it, finally settling by wrapping around my hand, squeezing it softly. I don't know if it's supposed to be an apology or some sign of solidarity because maybe we were both bull-headed pricks back then, but I decide I don't care. I'm already squeezing it back, and trying to ignore the way his head is tilted towards me and the calluses on his palm and the way my pulse has suddenly started to skitter wildly.

'Ashleigh,' he murmurs, and he's so close that his chest brushes against mine and I don't know how we got *this* near to each other, and I can't do anything except breathe in and stare at him and lose count of my racing heartbeats. 'You're—'

I'm plunged into darkness, right along with Ryan, as the lights cut and the power goes out.

Chapter Twenty-One

Bryony

'*Most Likely to Become Famous*'

Okay! Okay, this is fine. This is totally, absolutely, completely *fine*.

Except, it's fucking *not*, because the music stops right in the middle of the Macarena and the lights cut out and a few people shriek and some of them yell out and there's a power cut and *shit, shit, shit*.

I lunge out of my spot on the dance floor where I've been front and centre wiggling away, and hoist myself up onto the stage. It's a clumsy manoeuvre because I misjudge just how high the stage is, so I flop onto my belly with one leg dangling down, but I make a quick recovery, bouncing up onto my feet.

My little battery-powered strobe lights carry on flashing, and, honestly, thank God for me and my party supplies, I truly am the real MVP here. Steph O'Connell could never. The colourful beams cast the school hall into an eerie glow, bouncing off people's faces in blues and pinks. Without the overhead lights on, it looks like some kind of retro nightclub

175

from up here. If the music had carried on, I think I could've convinced them it was all part of my master plan to give them the most epic, lit reunion they ever dreamed of.

Except, you know, *it's a fucking power cut*.

The exact opposite of 'lit', damn it.

Faced with a hall full of shouty voices and the tang of panic and disarray in the air, a sea of shocked and concerned faces swimming before me, something steady and calm settles in the pit of my stomach. This feels – familiar. Instinct takes over from years of wrangling rowdy teenagers into line.

I clap my hands three times and shout, 'Hands down, eyes up, everyone!'

And they do. They listen. My old classmates turn almost as one, silence descending as I become the sole focus of their attention.

'Alright, no reason to panic! It's just a little power cut. We probably tripped a fuse with too much fun, huh? I'll get this sorted ASAP. Maybe someone can set their phone up to carry on playing some music . . .' I look around, squinting against the flashes of rainbow lights and, damn it, where's Shaun when you need him? He was always great at being DJ at house parties, always picked up on the mood perfectly. I jab a finger at Hiro, since he's one of the more tame rugby lads, and he salutes me.

'No problem, Bryony, I've got you.'

'So long as you promise to do us your best rendition of "Bet On It", you wannabe Troy Bolton,' I say, and there's a peal of laughter as everyone remembers his old YouTube video he posted, recreating the moment on the rugby field one time. I shout to a few other people – including Roisin, Morgan and, damn it, where's Ryan? He'd better *not* be drawing a penis on a whiteboard somewhere. 'You guys are in charge while I fix this, okay? Make sure nobody goes wandering off. That's the last thing we need right now, especially if I can't get the power back up.'

They agree, and I see them slip into their old roles as prefects, ready to monitor their peers and lay down the law if required. Hiro starts playing some music; it sounds kind of tinny and pathetic coming from his phone, but people cheer and I feel their spirits lift, shaking off the jolt of panic that hit when the lights went out.

I clap my hands once more, then strike a pose to set the mood. 'Party's still raging on, folks! Don't have too much fun without me!'

I climb back down from the stage – much more gracefully, this time – and smooth my jumpsuit out. Then I turn on my phone torch, leave everybody singing along to 'Never Gonna Give You Up' and make my way towards the doors at the other end of the hall.

The corridor is pitch black, but for the spooky shadows thrown out by stray beams of colour coming from the lights in the hall, and a shiver rolls down my spine. I clutch my phone a bit tighter. Without the buzzing of lights overhead and the noise of the music, or the general hubbub of a school day, I can hear the floorboards groaning as they settle and pipes creaking inside the walls, and it's straight out of a horror movie. The hairs on the back of my neck prickle and my heart begins to race.

What if it's not an accident? I suddenly wonder. *What if this was sabotage? Someone cut the power; they're out to get us all. Or . . . maybe just me? They knew I'd go out on my own because I'm the only one who knows where the fuse box is, and . . .*

177

Which, like, *maybe*, I watch too many true crime documentaries. But these things happen, right?

Oh, God, is this it? Is this my penance for lying so spectacularly? Someone has found me out and decided to make me pay – decided that I will live on forever in infamy, when I am plastered all over the front page of the papers having been brutally murdered at a school reunion? Someone is going to jump out from one of those black, empty hallways and slash my throat, or—

A hand closes on my shoulder and I shriek. *Shriek*. Loud enough to shatter glass. A high G I never could hit on the stage.

My right arm swings out and someone ducks away from the hand I've fisted around my phone. It clatters to the floor and I think I black out for a second, but it's hard to tell when everything is already pitch black. My heart seizes. It feels like I've just been kicked in the chest and I'm going to be the world's easiest target for the School Reunion Slasher, because all I do is double over and clutch my knees, trying to get my breath back.

My would-be attacker bends to pick up my phone and it illuminates a tall, skinny frame, a spray of ginger hair and a pale, awkward face.

'Sorry,' Hayden says gently, and holds my phone back towards me. He sways a little, his eyes still that glassy drunk from the last time I saw him. 'I didn't mean to startle you, B. Just thought you might want some help. I . . . er – well, you know me. I know my way around a soldering iron, ha-ha.'

I shove weakly at Hayden's stomach, all I can reach of him where I'm keeled over, and my legs turn into jelly as the adrenaline rush of almost being murdered recedes.

'You dick,' I gasp out, but can't quite find it in me to scowl at him as I right myself. 'I thought you were some creeper lurking around the corridors with a hatchet or something.'

'A hatchet? Really? That's what you're going with?'

I ignore him and finally snatch my phone back. I notice his own is out, the torch on too, casting some extra light around the hallway.

'I don't need your help,' I tell him.

'Well, then, consider me a buffer from the hatchet-wielding menace you're sure is after you.' He gives me a wide, sloppy sort of grin that's so unlike him, and salutes.

'Hilarious,' I mutter, but – honestly, was Hayden always this funny? Did he always have that dry, deadpan kind of humour, or did we just never notice it?

He gives me a patient look, undeterred and unoffended. 'Look, there's not a lot I can really contribute to the party atmosphere, but I can probably help with this. Least I can do. Plus, you'd be doing me a favour, letting me tag along.'

'Oh yeah?'

He nods and doesn't expand, so I narrow my eyes at him in the most melodramatically haughty and suspicious way I can, then toss my hair. Slipping back into my role, shaking off the heebie-jeebies. If this is a spooky episode in my life, then I am Daphne. Fabulous and unfaltering. Hayden can be Scooby-Doo if he wants, I guess.

'Alright,' I tell him, very magnanimously. 'You can come along.'

He falls into step beside me with long, loping strides to match my brisk pace. The sooner I get this sorted, the less of a shitshow it threatens to become. I will *not* have this party fail on my watch, and God, how humiliating if I had to call it a night early. How quickly will the appeal of sing-alongs to a few cheesy hits from one guy's phone wear off? Everyone will get bored sooner or later, the vibe will be well and truly killed, and everybody will leave, and it will ruin the whole thing.

That's not how I want people to remember tonight.

Or me. Mostly me.

We get to the caretaker's office where I know the fuse box will be, but when Hayden jiggles the handle, it's locked. He looks at me like I have the answers.

Which I do, and before I can second-guess myself, I'm blurting, 'There's a spare key in the staffroom.'

He blinks, which feels like a question.

He says, 'Won't that be locked, too?' Only I know that's not the question he was really just about to ask and my adrenaline spikes all over again. Goddamn Scooby-Doo over here, solving mysteries. *And I would've gotten away with it, too . . .*

I wonder if, without the music leaking down the corridors from the hall, he can hear how ferociously my heart is pounding. It roars in my ears like applause and my chest tightens the way it does when my cue is approaching. *Time for the performance of a lifetime, Bryony.* My bracelet snags on a loose thread on my jumpsuit and I yank it free to gesture widely, emphatically, casually.

'You know what? Why don't you head back to the hall. I think there might be a fuse box behind the stage; you could look at that. I'll take care of this. It's no big.'

Hayden's brow furrows and he bumps his glasses up his nose a little. He's got that look brewing, the haywire one. It used to be funny; now, it just spells trouble. Capital *T*.

He's going to figure it out, he's going to know and he's going to tell people, and he'll tell Ashleigh and she'll tell Steph and Steph will tell Shaun and all their friends will know and then everyone will know and . . .

'Seriously.' I start pushing him away, chivvying him back towards the hall. 'You look backstage, okay? I'll – I'll break in! They'll *totally* understand; it's all good. I wouldn't want to get you in trouble, though. I've got this. Promise.'

'But—'

'You know what, I bet the staffroom's not even locked! And it's just going to be a tripped fuse anyway, right? So it's an easy fix! If it's not, we better not mess with it anyway, in case we break it even worse. You go on back, Hayden – it's fine.'

Even in the wake of my delusions of grandeur I've played into so much tonight – for *years* – even I can tell how try-hard and fake I sound. I could not be making it more obvious I'm hiding something. Even I wouldn't give me a callback for this role.

Hayden doesn't budge, but just says very gently, 'Which way is your classroom, B? Drama department?'

And, shit.

There goes the lie. The beautiful dream of who I used to be.

It's too late to mourn it, when that dream died almost a decade ago, but it snuffs out some flicker of hope in the pit of my chest I've been clinging to all this time, and I suddenly feel so cold and weary. My shoulders slump, the gusto and gumption vanishing from my bones in one long, heavy exhale, and I can't meet Hayden's eyes.

How many times did I pooh-pooh his dorky interests, or

giggle when someone made a joke at his expense? How many times did I overlook him because he was too quiet, too uncool? I bet he's *loving* seeing me laid low like this. I would, in his shoes.

'Yeah,' I mumble, folding my arms around myself. 'Drama department.'

Hayden nods once, and leads the way. And I don't know what else to do except trudge after him, the fragments of my glory days falling away from me in a trail of sequins, left glittering and crushed on the floor behind me.

Chapter Twenty-Two

Steph

'Most Likely to End Up Together'

The lights tick off in the stairwell behind us, apparently having been left too long without the motion sensor being activated. It should, I think, be a sign that Shaun and I have spent too long out here alone; Ashleigh and Ryan must be long gone by now. It tells me that it's time to wrap this up and go back inside – back to my fiancé, and leave our past behind us for good.

But I can't, not when this feels so right. Shaun and I have hardly stopped for breath between our conversation in the library and now out here, catching up on everything we missed in each other's lives.

Sitting next to Shaun like this, listening to him talk about how he had to brush up on his old Year Nine-level French when his parents decided to emigrate to live in the French countryside . . . It's so easy to remember all the ways I once loved him. It's painless when all those old emotions rise back up; more like sinking into a warm bath than dredging up a decade-old heartbreak.

I realise that he's just wrapped up the story he was telling – something that involved accidentally buying a bag full of cabbages instead of a bread knife – and that I've missed my cue to laugh, too wrapped up in enjoying the moment. Shaun's wide smile eases, softening, and he looks down at his feet. His inhale is like the electrical surge before a lightning strike; I can taste the charge of anticipation in the air, know instinctively that something else is about to break any moment.

And it does, when he asks me, 'Do you ever wonder what would've happened if we hadn't agreed to end things?'

Yes. Always.

And also – *not really.*

Shaun's voice is low, the question gentle in its vulnerability, steady in his ever-present lack of fear of judgement. The words carry through the air around us, like the fluff off a dandelion, delicate and mesmerising before settling around me.

As much as I want to gather them up in my hands and cherish them . . . *Make a wish, maybe, too . . .*

I swallow the lump in my throat, finding it very hard to look at him all of a sudden.

'You shouldn't be asking things like that.'

'Why not?'

'Because . . .'

Because of course I wonder. It's impossible not to let my mind drift occasionally, but up until this reunion party, Shaun was always so firmly in my past. Put away carefully and lovingly, like an old family photo album you put on the shelf and rarely bring out. We were so sure of ourselves; but that's also part of the reason I *don't* wonder, because I've always known what our life would have looked like if we'd stayed together.

184

Shaun goes on, undeterred. 'We broke up because it was the right thing for both of us, at the time. We were both overwhelmed at being away from home and when you switched your degree . . . It just got to be too much. It wasn't . . .' He sits up a little straighter and his gaze returns to me. I keep looking determinedly off at the rugby fields. 'It wasn't our time, Steph. But don't you wonder what would've happened if we'd reached out to each other *after* we graduated? If we'd ever given it another shot?'

'We shouldn't be talking about this.'

'I'm not—'

'I *know*. I know you're not.' Instinctively, I reach for his hand, squeezing his fingers in mine. This isn't Shaun trying to make a move or anything like that – he's just reaching out, speaking aloud the same things I'm too nervous to voice myself. He doesn't turn his palm to hold my hand back; he doesn't seem to know what to do about the gesture at all, in fact. 'But we still shouldn't . . . It's not . . . What about Aisha, and Curtis? We aren't being fair to them, talking about things like this.'

Speaking their names is jarring, a reminder that we might already be missed and how suspicious this might look if we were found like this. We should go back, especially before we get any further down this path. It's dangerous, if only for how simple and easy it would be.

I stand up so quickly that my handbag goes flying to the bottom of the steps. Shaun is on his feet in a moment to fetch it for me; I remember he used to help his parents put away the shopping, jumping up to help as soon as he heard the car pulling up. He was always happy to step in.

But now I wish he hadn't, because I can only stand and

watch helplessly, wordlessly, as he smoothly shuffles lipstick and my phone and keys back into my bag, and his hands linger over the photos of the orchestra trip, and the one of the pair of us has slid out from the pile, our happy, enamoured faces staring up from the floor.

He picks it up slowly.

And I was wrong – *this* is the moment the storm breaks. This is the lightning strike.

I blurt out, 'Of course I wonder about us, Shaun. I loved you.'

I stop just before I can admit, *I think part of me always will.*

It's such a simple statement, that I loved him. That he loved me. It's a piece of our history, together and alone, a truth woven into the fabric of our hearts. A story, from a long time ago.

Except it . . . it feels like so much *more* than that. The air between us is too still, too charged. The muted, distant sound of voices raised as they sing along to what sounds like Smash Mouth's 'All Star' feels like something from another world. Even the breeze seems to skirt around us, leaving us alone in this moment, afraid to intrude. There is only me, and Shaun, and the weight of the engagement ring on my left hand.

He takes a step forward, coming to a stop at the foot of the little stone staircase we've been sitting on. My bag is still in his right hand, the photos in his left. All of his attention is on me, and it swallows me whole. I don't know if it's real or only a memory, because this is exactly how it used to feel when we were alone – like an out-of-body experience, but also like every inch of my body is hyperaware and hyper-

186

sensitive, attuned to his every breath and blink, two halves of a whole. Like, without him, I stop existing.

Shaun braces his wrist against the railing, his body leaning closer to me even though his feet stay planted exactly where they are. His fingers hold the photos so delicately. Afraid that creasing or smudging them will tarnish the memories that went along with them. That it'll fracture whatever is going on *here*, *now*.

'You never got in touch,' he says, voice as soft and warm as the summer night air that cocoons us. 'After uni. When we were home for the summers. You didn't . . .'

'Neither did you.'

He shakes his head, a faraway, dazed look in his eyes. It's distant, as if he's just woken up from a dream. Or maybe like he's still in one. I imagine I must look much the same way. It takes everything in me not to reach out and cup his cheek, turn his gaze back towards me. *I know*, I want to say, *I feel that way too.*

This whole night is a dream. A nightmare. Both, neither, I don't know anymore. It's too surreal and unexpected to really wrap my head around, but at the same time . . . Did I really think it would go any differently? Did I really expect to see Shaun and *not* have all those old feelings resurface, not feel that undeniable connection with him? It would all be so much easier to suppress and ignore if I knew he didn't feel it, too.

Coming here was a mistake.

Wasn't it?

Shaun takes a deep breath. He tells me, 'It didn't feel fair. Pushing back into your life, if you weren't interested in . . .'

187

'Me, too. And you were seeing that girl during your third year—'

'It only lasted a couple of months. You were going on dates—'

'They were never anything serious.'

He shakes his head and again, I understand. This isn't things left unsaid, loose ends we might have liked to tie up all these years later, a nice, neat seal on the ending of our story – this is entire lifetimes of *what if*, that could have led us back to where we used to be. Where we thought we were supposed to end up.

Where, maybe, we should be now. Most likely to end up together.

I remain frozen, fragile, watching his chest rise and fall with each shallow, ragged breath. Every inch between us feels like a chasm and too short a space all at once. He looks down at the photos in his hand, the one of us on the top of the pile, nostalgia in his smile.

'We had it good, didn't we?'

I nod, not trusting my voice. Even if Shaun isn't quite looking at me, I know he sees.

'You were always the one who got away, you know? I'd just . . . Sometimes, I'd wonder, think about reaching out, seeing if you wanted to grab a drink or maybe just have a phone call and catch up. Maybe . . . maybe rekindle things. Maybe not. I don't know. I – missed you. I know it was the right thing, us breaking up like we did, but . . .'

'I missed you, too.'

It's not fair of me to say it. It's not fair of Shaun to say it, either. We're not being kind to each other by bringing any of this up, and it feels disrespectful and dirty when we're both engaged to other people, but . . .

But.

There are so many what-ifs, when it comes to me and Shaun.

And that tiny, incessant voice in the back of my mind asking me all night long: what if I got it wrong, with Curtis? What if . . . this *was* the path I was supposed to be on, but not because it led me to him – but back to Shaun, instead?

Chapter Twenty-Three

Shaun

'Most Likely to End Up Together'

It's sickening, dizzying, and I can't walk away. Can't be anywhere else but here, with Steph.

It shouldn't be. I shouldn't have asked if she ever thought about us. I should've just said it was good to see her and gone back inside to Aisha, and, God, *Aisha*. I never meant anything by a catch-up with Steph, but – I know, this isn't right. It's become something it shouldn't, and I . . . can't tear myself away.

It was so easy when we sat together talking earlier. Spilling our life stories from the past ten years, leaning into each other and with the occasional bump of shoulders and knees and brush of hands. It was simple, and friendly. Innocent.

This . . . does not feel innocent.

We're just stood facing each other, not even touching, and yet it feels so wildly intimate that my heart rate picks up a few notches. My skin feels hot, my shirt suddenly too tight around my throat. I fidget with it, but Steph's eyes flicker towards where my finger hooks underneath

190

the collar, and a flush creeps up her cheeks, pink and pretty and –

Is she thinking about when she used to fidget with my school tie when we snuck off together to steal a kiss away from our friends, an act that went from cute and distracted to something more purposeful, that mischievous glint in her eyes, when she'd do it after we started to be more physical?

Not that I'm thinking about it, either. It's not appropriate. It's not . . .

Not anything, except it's everything, because she was my whole world, and I thought she always would be.

And, God, but I want to kiss her. If I'm being honest with myself, I think I've been dying to kiss her all night. My gaze is on her gently parted lips, my body leaning in and I wonder – is she going to stop me?

I never find out, because I hardly even get close enough to bend my head towards hers or make a move; we're interrupted by the crunch of gravel as someone walks over, muttering to themselves and then saying loudly, 'What are you guys *doing* out here?'

Falling back a step to create some distance between us, I turn away from Steph, squinting through the darkness. It's Priya, rubbing her bare arms. She's scowling, but the look shifts from irritable to something more calculating and suspicious as her eyes dart between us.

'Alright, Shaun,' Priya says, with a bored sort of nonchalance that makes me think the greeting is an old habit rather than anything else, then turns her attention fully on Steph. 'This is where you snuck off to? We lost you ages ago. You missed "Bohemian Rhapsody" and you know Morgan's rubbish at the high parts.'

'We were just,' Steph says, and I feel her looking at me before she finally says, 'er, catching up.'

'Is *that* so?'

'Not like that!'

Steph blushes, her cheeks so bright pink they're practically glowing, and when I grin at her, trying not to laugh at her expense, she shoves my arm playfully to shut me up, which *does* make me laugh.

'We're just *talking*,' Steph reiterates.

'Okay . . .' Priya cuts me a look before turning a more neutral expression on Steph. I turn to face sideways so that I can look between them, watching them have some silent conversation through raised eyebrows and shrugs and sideways twists of the mouth, a language they both learnt as best friends in school and, I guess, haven't forgotten.

Does Steph look worried? Is Priya going to go back and tell everyone what she saw – and what even did she see? Is she going to ruin everything and drag Steph away, back inside to her fiancé, before we have the chance to . . . to finish talking, or whatever?

Would it be the worst thing, if she did go back inside and tell everyone she caught us together?

I mean, it's not like it's bloody *Bridgerton* (Aisha made me watch the first season with her – three times) and merely being caught alone in a 'compromising position' will ruin Steph's honour and I'll have to duel Curtis with pistols at dawn.

But still. People talk, gossip.

Would they believe nothing happened?

I feel bad for thinking it, but there's a vicious part of me that suddenly hopes Priya *will* go blab. Wouldn't it fix everything? And wouldn't we be just as well to *actually* kiss, then, because what difference would it make?

Aisha's face flashes up in my mind and I cringe, acutely aware of our plans and dreams for the future and our life together that I'm so dangerously close to throwing away.

Do I want to?

Is Steph worth that risk?

It's a little unnerving, how quickly and surely I can answer that question. How easy it is to imagine that life – the wedding, the house, the kids, the family holidays and Christmases and everything else – with Steph in that picture, instead of Aisha.

Interrupting their silent exchange, I ask Priya, 'What're you doing out here anyway?'

She waggles a lighter I hadn't noticed her holding. 'Nipped out for a quick cig. But I left my phone inside and the fire door out of the hall shut behind me. Sod's law, isn't it? Lucky for me to find you two out here, really.'

The words feel weighted, and I don't know if they're a threat or a warning or if I'm just making it all up. Steph's friends would always go to bat for her; I'm really hoping that's not changed.

'We'll be back inside soon,' Steph promises, and I feel some of the tension in my shoulders unfurl. *She doesn't want to leave yet, doesn't want this to end too soon either.*

Priya nods and squeezes Steph's arm on the way past.

I breathe a sigh of relief as Priya pulls the door to the stairwell closed behind her, muttering to herself, 'These bloody lights, ugh. Why's it so dark in here? Of all the times to not have my phone . . .'

The previous tension between us now well and truly

193

broken, Steph tosses me an easy smile before taking a seat at the top of the steps again.

The scent that teases my nostrils as she moves is one I can't put my finger on. Floral, I think? It's not the vanilla-y, sweet scent I'm used to Aisha wearing, and I've never learnt enough about flowers or perfume to know now – all I can say with any certainty is that it's not the smell I'd associate with Steph. Not the British Rose perfume from The Body Shop I used to buy her gift sets of at Christmastime – something lighter, more . . . dainty.

Not that I would've expected her, at twenty-eight, to still be wearing the perfume she picked out as a teenager. Steph is an adult with sophisticated taste (judging by the home décor photos she posts online every so often), so of course she'd have found a new perfume to match that.

Still, it's jarring enough that when I look at her, I don't see the girl I used to know better than anybody else. Just for that split second, she's a stranger, as new and unfamiliar to me as that building that replaced the old language demountables out the front of the school. Like, if I walked past her in the street, I wouldn't look or think twice, because – well, why would I? She's just . . . somebody. She's nothing to me, and in no way mine.

But I blink, and the moment's gone.

And not for the first time tonight, I find myself longing for things to be just the way they were ten years ago.

Chapter Twenty-Four

Hayden

'Most Likely to Succeed'

MS ADAMS, the handwritten label on the door declares in a chunky, swishy script in a bright fuchsia Sharpie. The colour matches Bryony's nails, and I wonder if it's her signature. Having a signature colour feels like a very Bryony thing to do.

I pause in front of the door and she lets out a noisy, terse sigh to let me know just *how much* she hates this whole thing before slapping a flat palm against the door and pushing her way in, bumping me roughly with her elbow as she goes past. I almost laugh, because the huff reminds me so much of Margot when she's in a mood, but I don't think Bryony would appreciate that right now. In fact, I think she might shout at me.

I watch as she flips the light switch on – muscle memory – then grumbles to herself because, of course, the power is out. Her phone hangs at her side and she makes her way across the room to her desk with the ease of someone who has walked that exact path a thousand times or more, and

195

roots around in her desk in the darkness with sure hands. Keys jangle as she yanks a lanyard out of a drawer, and I see her glower at me when she comes back to the door.

'Come on, then,' Bryony snaps, and pushes past me again. This grumpy, sullen creature is a far cry from the exuberant personality she was showing off earlier – the one we all remember from school. Is she really that angry I figured it out?

'It's not anything to be ashamed about, you know,' I tell her, following as she storms towards the staircase to go up to the staffroom on the second floor. A couple of stray sequins flutter to the floor in her wake. 'Being a teacher.'

'Shut up, Hayden.'

'It's not, though. I had to deal with Margot being home-schooled during lockdown, and that was a bit of a peek behind the curtain. It's a lot of hard work, and I imagine it can be a bit of a thankless job sometimes. You really don't—'

'I said, shut up.' She whips around, ponytail almost smacking me in the face. 'If you tell anyone—'

Bryony cuts herself off because, of course, it's an empty threat, but the fury emanates off her in waves and she is practically vibrating with it. Her hands bunch into trembling fists at her sides and I don't think it's just the glare of the phone torch making her look so pale beneath her makeup all of a sudden.

I didn't think it was possible to ever feel sorry for Bryony, but yet here I am.

When we were teenagers, she was always so melodramatic and shallow; I didn't really stop to consider that might have been a front, a bit like when Ashleigh used to hold her head high whenever people (mainly Ryan and his cronies) said something cutting. Bryony was all crocodile tears and dramatics, but this anger doesn't feel like any of that. It's not for show or attention, and I feel bad for her being so genuinely upset. My brain and body still feel a little sluggish, and now I fight through the haze to try to shake it off, sober up a bit in order to actually deal with whatever this is. It feels wrong to give up and walk away, and leave her like this.

I reach for her arm on instinct and she jerks away from me, continuing to stomp up the stairs.

'You know what, Hayden?' Bryony barks, her voice bouncing off the stairwell. 'You can't talk. *You're* a failure, too. You were meant to go off and do all those impressive things and make shedloads of money and be some successful genius, but you're *not*. All that potential, *wasted*. Now you're just a sad, stay-at-home dad, who threw his life away. So you don't get to talk to me like that, okay?'

'I . . .'

'You think everyone here tonight doesn't see how resentful you are over how your life turned out? I've seen you tonight, avoiding having to talk about your ex, your job, all the things everybody thought you were going to achieve – you look like someone pissed in your coffee, and it's so obvious that you're miserable. It's actually hilarious, how pathetic you're being. And it's not my fault, so don't take it out on me. I don't . . . I don't need you projecting your sad, sorry little life onto me, alright? So just *shut up*.'

That's not what I was doing. Was it? Is that how it sounded?

As a teenager, I was never very good at connecting with my peers. I felt like I could never quite say the right thing. But I don't think Bryony's saying the right thing now, either, and – and in all honesty, I'm starting to get a little bit sick of being the butt of everybody's joke. Maybe *they're* the ones always saying the wrong thing, did they think about that?

And – and for *fuck's sake*, I'm not sixteen anymore. I'm a grown-up. I'm twenty-eight years old, I have two daughters . . . and I don't have to retreat into the shadows and put up with this bullshit from people I haven't even thought about in *years*.

Especially not from her.

My shoulders square and I stare at Bryony's sparkling back, her swishing purple ponytail, and resolve settles in my bones. I take a step after her and it feels like throwing off a helmet, discarding the shield and armour I've been clinging to since I stepped through those front doors earlier tonight, trading them for a sword and spear instead.

'Maybe it's time you shut up.'

'What?' she snaps.

'I said, maybe it's time that *you* shut up instead,' I repeat. I chase her up a few stairs until I overtake her and stand in front of her, making her stop in her tracks. She scoffs, but I press on before she can interrupt me. I'd put this outburst down to a little liquid courage, but I know it runs deeper than that. 'Did you ever stop to consider I don't want to talk about it because everyone else assumes they already know how I must feel? Of course you didn't. Because you don't stop to think about anybody else, B – you *never have*. You haven't changed a bit, have you? Still acting like the entire world revolves around you. I'm sure this 'main character energy' schtick you pull makes you feel better about yourself, but are you that much of a narcissist that you don't consider the rest of us have thoughts and feelings, too? I'm not a fucking NPC.'

'A what?'

'A non-player character – you know what, it doesn't even matter. The point is, maybe you need to stop trying so hard to be the centre of attention and consider other people for once.'

'Who do you think you are, talking to me like this? How dare you—'

'I think I'm someone who's sick and tired of being walked all over by people like you. I had enough of it when we were at school and I don't need a repeat of it now.'

'Please.' Bryony snorts and tosses her hair, but I'm almost sure that there's something defensive about this façade now. 'I never *walked all over you*; don't be so salty just because you were such a shy little dork.'

'What aren't you getting here?' Exasperated, I drag my hand through my hair and try again, deciding to break it down for her like I would if it were Margot or Skye. I speak slowly, enunciate. 'Your actions impact other people, and that has consequences. You always wanted to be the centre of attention and even if that meant you hurt people, you did it anyway. You gossiped, you teased people, you spread rumours, you laughed at your friends behind their backs. You hooked up with Josh when he was dating Thea – you *pursued him*, that whole time, Snapchatting him and stuff even though you knew he had a girlfriend. You were – are – self-centred, inconsiderate, and rude.'

Bryony recoils, her face blank and eyes wide, mouth hanging slack and open. She stares right through me, and I wonder if she's replaying the 'highlights' of her school years through this new lens I've just offered. For once, she's speechless.

I don't feel so sorry for her now, but something swells in my chest in its place: a puffed-up feeling I only usually get when I crack a difficult piece of coding at work or help the girls learn something new. I'm not used to feeling it in this context of confrontation. (Although I'm not used to confrontation, period.)

'You think you know me,' I tell Bryony, running with this high of finally standing up for myself, 'but you don't. Whatever you found out online, or from seeing me out of my comfort zone here tonight, or whatever you've assumed . . . You don't know me. You said I'm pathetic and resentful, but you're wrong. I'm a stay-at-home dad, yes, but I didn't throw my life away, and I'm not sad. I'm quite happy, actually.'

Bryony blinks, as if she wasn't expecting that, and for a moment I see it all sink in; then she averts her eyes and her scowl returns and she pushes around me again.

'Yeah, well, you ever think maybe you could be *happier*? That, maybe, if you'd lived up to your potential, things would be *better*, huh? Then you'd really have it all, and you wouldn't be – wouldn't be slumming it, and crying yourself to sleep, and never having moved on because you're a teacher at your own goddamn school?'

I don't think this is about me anymore.

'That sounds . . . difficult.'

She snorts, and it's a wet sound. I take a tissue out of my pocket and hand it to her. Bryony snatches it off me and we exit out onto the second-floor corridor, making our way along to the staffroom. Her keys jangle at her side.

'I don't want your pity, alright? I want you to keep your mouth shut.'

'Did I say I was going to tell anybody?'

Instead of answering, she shoves a key into the lock on the door. I hold my torch up to give her some more light, and catch sight of Bryony's face. Now it's not directed at me, her anger has dissipated into something far more fragile. I've never seen her look like this unless it was on stage and the role she was performing called for such vulnerability. There's something so infinitely *broken* – so defeated – and I'm surprised to realise that I recognise it, because it's the exact feeling I've been carrying around for the last hour after being worn down by my old classmates.

The mourning for wasted potential, the grief of what if.

I understand that, far more than I ever expected to.

'Is that why you've been tearing people down all night? Picking holes in their stories, undermining them? Kicking their legs out from under them to bring them down to your level doesn't build you up any higher, you know.'

I'm still talking to her like she's a child – I don't mean for it to be patronising, and half expect Bryony to shout at me again, but her bunched-up shoulders relax a little and she hangs her head as my words sink in. I wait, try not to push her too hard, and instead we both step into the staffroom.

Well – Bryony steps in. Walks confidently through the room by the light of her phone, to a filing cabinet where she searches for the spare key to the caretaker's office. I stand against the door, not quite inside the room; even at this age, it feels like crossing a boundary I shouldn't, to go into the staffroom. Somewhere I should knock and stay respectfully on the other side of the door, only ever able to peer in from a safe distance.

Bryony collects the key, but doesn't push the drawer of

the filing cabinet shut. Instead, she leans heavily against it, brow furrowed and eyes squeezed tightly shut. I'm not sure whether to go put an arm around her, or if I should leave her with her thoughts for a moment. She's clearly going through . . . well, a lot.

And honestly? I don't think I blame her for hiding the truth, for keeping up this pretence that she's living her dreams as an actress. I faced more pity and sympathy and second-hand regret tonight than I'd care to think about; if I had the chance to do it all over again, maybe I'd have put a spin on a few things, too.

Chapter Twenty-Five

Ashleigh

'Most Likely to Kill Each Other'

This cannot be happening. Not even in my wildest nightmares would I be stuck in the science lab with Ryan Lawal during a power cut in the middle of our school reunion. And yet somehow, here we are, trapped by a government-funded, high-tech security door I was so bloody jealous of earlier.

This cannot be happening.

But Ryan wrestles with the door handle and I punch random numbers into the keypad that don't even make a little *beep* of recognition that they're being pushed at all, and the light isn't red or green or anything else, it's completely non-existent, and the door won't budge, and –

And I am actually fucking stuck in the science lab with Ryan Lawal during a power cut in the middle of our fucking school reunion.

A frustrated sigh rips from my mouth and I fall back a couple of steps, at the same moment as Ryan takes a stride back, and then throws himself shoulder-first into the door, like he can break it down by physical force.

I fold my arms across my chest and let him try, biting back a snarky comment about how he's only going to hurt himself. Not because I want him to, but – well, if anybody can do it, I bet it'd be Ryan Lawal. He'd be lauded as a hero afterwards, too.

But after the third attempt at throwing his weight (which, I imagine, is not inconsiderable, given how broad and muscular he is, which is not me *looking* but just a factual observation), Ryan gives up. He winces when he moves back on his left leg and bends slightly to knead his knuckles into his lower thigh.

'Finished?' I ask him dryly, raising my eyebrows and nodding towards the door.

He narrows his eyes at me, but he's not looking at me exactly, rather he's looking above me, at . . . 'Give me some of your hair clips.'

'Excuse me?'

'The clips, or whatever. In your hair. We could try to pick the lock.'

I examine the door handle, but that takes all of two seconds. It's literally just a handle. Aloud, I point out, 'There's no actual, physical lock to *pick*, Ryan. It's just that stupid security system, genius.'

He scowls at me. 'I don't see *you* coming up with a better plan.'

If it's a power cut, then that door will remain locked until the power is back up. I suppose there's a chance that Bryony might be able to help; if she organised tonight, maybe she has some contact information for the headmaster or caretaker – but when I check my phone, I have hardly any signal, and when I fire off a quick text to Hayden, the angry little red exclamation mark pops up beside it as it fails to send.

Shit. That's just what we need.

Our only other option is the windows, but when I cross the room and lean over the counter to flip one open, it only opens a couple of inches out from the bottom, like you get in hotels and high-rise office blocks. No good for climbing out of, which, considering we're on the ground floor, would've been no trouble at all.

'What's your next great idea, *genius*?' Ryan quips, and I shoot him a glare I'm not sure he can see anyway. There's only a little light coming in through the windows, that deep blue of a summer night that puts everything in greyscale.

'At least I'm *trying* something—'

'Oh, and I wasn't?'

'Nothing useful! So unless you want to dislocate your shoulder or use that thick head of yours as a battering ram—'

'Right. Here we go again.'

'What now? What—'

'I'm not *stupid*, you know. We were in the same top-set classes, or did you conveniently forget that? I got pretty good grades and I studied hard, too. Whatever you think of me, I'm not—'

'I don't think you're stupid, Ryan, I just think you're severely lacking in logic and common sense. Act first, think later. Which may have served you well in school, and maybe it works for you in the world of politics now, but it's not going to open that door. God, I cannot believe I'm stuck in here with *you*, of all people . . .'

'It's not exactly peachy for me being stuck with *you* either, you know.'

I huff, stalking back to the door. I know it's futile, but I try the handle again – as if it might magically give way for me, when it didn't for Ryan. Which, of course, it doesn't. I press my forehead to the door, leaning my body flat against it, eyes sliding closed, forcing my breathing to become slow and measured and even.

Maybe it's a good thing the power went out. Ryan was getting . . . *I* was getting . . .

Things got weird. Intense.

I'm not sure what would've happened next if the lights hadn't cut, and my heart gives a sickening little somersault at the possibility of what *might* have . . .

No, I'm not going down that road. Definitely not with – because of – *him*. It was just biology, that's all. My body reacting to his body, to proximity and heat and touch. Not the way he said my name, or the light caress of his fingers against mine, or the vulnerability in the things he said . . .

'I guess we've just gotta wait it out, then,' Ryan says, somewhere off to my left. I hear the scrape of a stool as he drags it out, takes a seat. The soft wince and thump as he props his leg – the left, I'm sure – up on another stool, most likely to stretch it out. I wonder if he still has physiotherapy appointments for that old rugby injury, or if he did half a dozen and thought that was fine; he was Ryan Lawal, untouchable. Achilles.

Not that I spent any amount of time looking up the wound when they reported on it, or read any medical journals online about the surgery and healing process and the recovery statistics.

Not . . . any considerable amount of time, anyway.

Scientific curiosity, that was all.

My head makes a quiet *thud* against the door, and I lean further into it, like it might swallow me whole.

'C'mon, Easton, it's not that bad being stuck in a room with me, is it? It's hardly the first time the two of us were here by ourselves after hours.'

'That was different.'

'Why? We were arguing pretty much all the time back then, too. Seems just like old times, if you ask me.'

'This is *not*—'

'Isn't it? You're still incapable of holding a friendly conversation, still putting me down at every opportunity—'

'*You're* still winding me up at every opportunity,' I bite back. 'And don't pretend like you ever so much as *tried* to have a "friendly conversation" with me.' I spit the words like the poison they are. 'All you ever did was taunt me, act like you were better than me because you were so popular, like every mean, nasty little joke out of your mouth was *soooo* innocent.'

'I never—'

'Don't. Just . . . *don't*.'

I don't want to hear it. I can't stomach listening to Ryan defend all the immature crap he said to me when we were teenagers. The flirty lines that would make other girls blush, but always had a cruel, teasing edge whenever he used them on me, with that look like he wanted to make sure I knew I was the butt of a joke, not the subject of flattery. The whip-smart remarks about me being boring and a square and uptight and frigid and haughty that made everybody else laugh, and which I had to learn to let roll off me, water off a duck's back.

He thinks *I* was mean to *him*? He doesn't know the half of it.

'You know,' he says, 'it's not my fault you thought you were too good to give me the time of day whenever I tried to talk to you. I tried to include you. I, at least, *tried* to be nice, which is more than you ever did. I invited you to parties—'

I scoff, teeth bared in a snarl, and I sway slightly against the door, fighting every impulse not to turn around and fly at him in a rage. If I want to keep the high ground, I have to keep my cool. This is just another one of his games.

'Please. Like you *wanted* me there. The one time I did show up, you dragged me into the middle of a drinking game and I was humiliated playing Never Have I Ever, and nobody ever let me live down that I'd never done *anything*, and then you "accidentally" spilled a can of beer all over me.'

'It was an accident! RJ fell into me.'

'Yeah, okay.'

'Never Have I Ever didn't start till after you showed up anyway, so I didn't do that to you on purpose, either. *And*, from what I remember, I offered to give you my T-shirt so you had something dry to wear—'

'And from what *I* remember' – my hands curl into claws against the door, body shaking – 'your mates had a good laugh after Elise made fun of my bra, because you could see it through my wet top, and then you were busy showing off your washboard abs and winking at me, telling me to get a good look while I had the chance.'

'I . . .'

But Ryan falters, because he knows I'm right. Because I *am* right. Whatever he thinks he remembers, it's warped by popularity and everybody fawning all over him, and the glossy sheen of a good time.

'I was just making a joke.'

'It wasn't very funny from where I was standing.'

He falls quiet again and I can't even relish the win; I just feel angry, and sad, and sick to my stomach. Some of the fight leaves me and I sag against the locked door, which is the only thing holding me upright.

I forgot how much it used to hurt. How much I buried that so deep down it stopped existing anymore.

'Ashleigh,' he starts. 'I'm—'

'Save it. Don't . . . It doesn't matter anymore, alright? But don't act like such a martyr, like *I* was the only villain in this story, okay? I'm not saying the way I acted or responded was right, but – we were both shitty people. Are, both shitty people. Even if I'm the only person who'll acknowledge that about you.'

For a second, I think he's going to argue. Reflexively, if for no other reason, because this is what we do. The only way we've ever been able to talk to each other. Sniping back and forth.

But Ryan breaks our rules again. He lets out a quiet breath of laughter and mutters, as if to himself, 'Only around you, Easton. Only you.'

Chapter Twenty-Six

Ryan

'Most Likely to Kill Each Other'

She doesn't move for a long time, just keeps huddling against the damn door. I liked it better when she was arguing with me. I liked it better when she was saying anything *at all*, because this quiet – this silence, this stillness – it's unnerving, coming from her.

I'd almost think she was busy plotting her next move, and my demise, if she weren't all hunched up and sad-looking like that.

Which . . . I guess, I can't really blame her for, if that's how she remembers things from school. It's not like I *set out* to embarrass her, but she'd act so high and mighty and so goddamn annoying all the time, I was constantly itching to take her down a peg or two.

I don't know how I ever thought it didn't *get* to her. It got to me badly enough that she's still nagging in the back of my mind ten years later, my career shaped around the things I think she'd have to say about it – so why did I ever think she was above such normal things as caring what I said to her?

Because she was. She did a good job at pretending to be, anyway. Ashleigh Easton wasn't *human*, in the way other people were. She was – above all that. Beyond it. We used to say she was such a square, a real bitch, because she was too mature for our childish bullshit. Sure, you'd know when she was pissed off or feeling especially self-righteous or exasperated, but she never got *sad*.

Right now, I don't know what she is. The emptiness of it seems to roar in the space between us, and the chemistry classroom feels suddenly claustrophobic – something that has nothing to do with the locked door, and everything to do with her. Like she's sucked all the air out of the room and hugged it tight to her, because my chest feels tight and my mouth is dry and my breathing is too hard, too loud.

I swing my leg back down from the stool my ankle is propped up on, standing cautiously back onto it and relieved when there's no twinge of pain.

Ashleigh doesn't so much as twitch as I make my way slowly towards her. And, in the absolute silence that surrounds us now, I know she hears me coming. My hand is reaching for her shoulder and, at the last second, I change course to set it against one of those ridiculous puffy sleeves instead of her bare skin. As if she might burn if I get too close.

Her breath sounds like a car stalling, all sharp, uneven judders as she inhales.

'I know you don't want to hear it, but – I'm sorry, anyway. I never, sort of . . . I never realised how it looked from your side. Stuff like that – with the party, I mean – I didn't do it to pick on you, or whatever. I spent a lot of time at school trying to get you to *like* me, you know?' I admit, and it's punctuated with a self-deprecating laugh. I take my hand

211

from her shoulder to run it through my hair agitatedly, the confession making me feel weirdly nervous.

I can go on national TV, debate over bills and laws and campaigns, tell my superiors when they're making reckless decisions, collaborate in the shadows with my so-called rivals on the other side of the bench, and I don't bat an eye.

But when it comes to Ashleigh Easton . . .

She's something else.

And now, she peels herself slightly away from the locked door she's been treating as some kind of sanctuary and stands a little straighter as she turns around to face me. Her arms cross and her chin ticks up in challenge, but the frown that twists her dark eyebrows is quizzical and sceptical, not scathing.

I cut off whatever she's about to say. 'What, you don't believe me? Hand on heart.' I hold it up to demonstrate. 'It drove me nuts that you didn't like me. Everybody liked me. Everybody *still* likes me, but I knew – fuck, I knew that coming here tonight, nothing would've changed, you still wouldn't like me, and it *still* bugs me.'

A smirk flits across her face, making her look more like herself. More like the version I know, anyway, and it ignites something in my chest that makes me push on.

'I've always been good with people. Connecting with them. Winning them round to my side. Getting them to like me. But you . . . You *never* liked me. You fought me tooth and nail every step of the way, and it fucking killed me. I just couldn't get my head around the fact that you *didn't*, so of course I tried to get you to like me. That's why I used to invite you to parties. I flirted with you like I did with all the other girls, but that just used to piss you off. I tried to banter with you like the guys, but you never responded to that either.'

Probably, because to her, it seemed like I was only ever taking the piss. I'm starting to understand that now.

But Ashleigh laughs, and it's a full, warm sound that makes me lean in a little closer as she tosses her head in disbelief, and grins at me like it's the greatest joke she's ever heard. The scepticism is rooted deep in her pale blue eyes, one eyebrow arching upwards. Her lips pull wide across her cheeks and I glance, again, at that lipstick smudge.

'You didn't flirt with me.'

'I absolutely did. I flirted with everybody.'

'Yeah, because you were a notorious flirt. It was practically hardwired into your DNA. I remember you flirting with Mrs Macarthur when you forgot your maths homework, one time. But you didn't flirt with *me*.'

'I told you how cute you looked that time on non-uniform day, when you wore that blue T-shirt.' It was the same colour as her eyes. The first time I noticed her eyes at all, actually.

'You also told me I was flat-chested, had a bony arse, looked – and I quote you directly here – like a sickly Victorian ghost child. Not even just a sick child, a sick *ghost child*.'

'I mean.' I don't remember that time specifically, but I don't doubt that I would've said it. I rub the back of my neck and give her a self-effacing smile I'm not sure she can even make out in the darkness. 'You're pretty bloody pale, Ashleigh.'

She rolls her eyes, but her smile creeps back out again.

'And you did have a really bony arse. I swear I got a bruise that time you fell on me in the common room.'

'Hilarious. Look, tell yourself what you want about . . . whatever you think you remember about school, but I can

213

categorically tell you, you never flirted with me. You used to take the piss' – *yup, called it* – 'and you know how I know that? Because of that one time I heard your mates dare you to kiss me at the leavers' party, and you said you wouldn't even want to hold my hand if I was the last girl in the world, and couldn't even be interested in me if you were so shit-faced you forgot your own name and I threw myself at you. You called me "decidedly unfuckable".'

'What—?' I cut off as the memory of that hits with vivid clarity, playing out in my mind like a scene from a movie. I haven't thought twice about that since it happened, but her words bring it back like it was just yesterday. Ashleigh gives me a triumphant look, so confident she's just proved me wrong, but I'm too busy trying to formulate a response that the expression doesn't bug me the way it usually would.

Finally, I manage, 'Yeah, of course I said that! What did you expect me to say? You wouldn't have wanted me to come up and snog you on our last night out with everybody after results. Or *ever*, actually, let's face it. And I didn't even fancy you to *want* to snog you, either.'

'You didn't just *not fancy* me. You didn't even want to kiss me for a dare, and I'll remind you that you ran a lap stark bollock naked around the rugby pitch one lunchtime because some of the lads egged you on, and you didn't even think twice about it.'

My mouth falls open and my eyebrows scrunch together as I try to figure out how we're seeing this so differently. The rest of our interactions at school, I can maybe under-stand, but this one seemed so cut and dried, I don't know how she's not getting it. My hands gesture awkwardly, stiffly, between us, palm up.

'Weirdly enough, Ash, I didn't want to snog you when I knew you weren't going to be into it, whatever the boys had to say about it, even for a laugh. So, yeah, I said I wouldn't touch you with a bargepole or whatever, because then they dropped it. They'd have just kept on about it all night otherwise, and that would've annoyed the both of us. Plus, I really fancied Thea at the time and she'd just broken things off with Shaun's mate, so I was planning to finally get a kiss off her at the leavers' party, and if I'd been off snogging you instead, I don't think she would've appreciated that too much.'

The smug, exasperated look finally slides off Ashleigh's face, replaced by something slack as she digests that.

Her voice is quiet and all she has to say is, 'Oh.'

Yeah, *oh*. God. This girl.

'I know you're kind of up your own arse sometimes – bony as it is – but you do realise I'm not a complete dick, don't you?'

The face she pulls this time is on instinct, I know, because it's the same withering look I remember so well from school, but even that vanishes quickly, into something that seems to say, *I'm starting to.*

Better late than never, I guess.

I don't know when it started to matter so much to me that Ashleigh *see* me, but . . . She always has, in her own annoying, holier-than-thou way. That laser focus of hers cut right through me when I played up to my own act in school and even if everybody else thought I was always so upbeat and untouchable, she didn't.

It'd just be nice if she'd see that wasn't always an act, I think.

Not so I could finally win her over and revel in the victory of saying, after all this time, even Ashleigh Easton isn't immune to the infamous Lawal charm, but just . . . because.

But, at the same time, this is us, and I can't help but slip into old habits as I smirk at her.

I brace a hand against the doorframe above her head, so that when I shift closer, I'm leaning over her, despite the fact she's almost of a height with me in those heels, and she has to move back into the door again and tilt her head to look at me properly.

'Don't tell me you were *upset* because I didn't kiss you that night.'

She scoffs, but won't quite meet my eye. I've cast her in shadow too much to tell if she's blushing, but I'm not curious enough to move away. She doesn't shove me aside, either.

'*No.*'

She sounds pretty sure about that.

'Are you sure about that?' I tease.

'*Yes.* I'm sure.'

'So . . . it didn't get to you, that I didn't want to kiss you, even for a dare? Didn't disappoint you, that I said I wasn't attracted to you?'

'*Correct.* Believe me, Ryan, when I say I could not care less that you didn't find me attractive. If anything' – her shoulders drop and her body arches towards mine, eyes glinting – 'it sounds like *you're* the one who's annoyed I never responded to your pathetic attempts to flirt with me. What did you say? It . . . drove you nuts.'

I swallow a laugh. 'Thinking about my nuts, Easton?'

'God, you're insufferable, d'you know that?'

This time, I do chuckle. And I lean in a little closer, testing

216

it – her – this tension that clings to the sliver of air between our bodies. She doesn't move this time, so I brush up against her, and the heat of her makes my jaw clench.

I didn't fancy Ashleigh at school. She was – fine. Not pretty in the way girls like Steph or Thea or Roisin were, didn't make an effort and have that allure like Bryony or Elise. She just . . . was. And she was too much of a prick to be fanciable, even if she had been especially pretty.

But the Ashleigh in front of me, right now, tonight . . .

Hell, not even just *tonight*. The one I've seen in snatches, glimpses, on social media, too. It's not like she grew into her body – more like it grew into her, shaped itself around that confidence, the way she carried herself, her absolute sureness of who she was.

But, also, it looks so damn good on her.

The wispy fringe that doesn't look fashionable so much as sexy, the cut of her outfit comfortable and decisive instead of try-hard or trendy. Even that attitude that drove me crazy when we were teenagers . . . Now, it's driving me a very different kind of crazy. The kind that makes me want to slip my tongue inside her mouth to taste her, feel the soft lines of her body pressing flush against mine.

Ashleigh draws a quiet, slow breath, and my gaze is fixed on her face as I watch her blink slowly, her whole body angled towards me, her lips parting as she moves them closer to mine . . .

'Oh, Ryan,' she breathes, barely an inch from my mouth – and just as I lean in, she draws back, challenge and triumph sparkling in her eyes as her mouth curves into a closed-lipped smile. 'You couldn't handle it.'

217

Chapter Twenty-Seven

Bryony

'Most Likely to Become Famous'

It's probably for the best that it's pitch dark and that it's Hayden who's calling me out, because something about all that makes this a little bit easier – the surrealness of it all makes it feel like a fever dream rather than anything actually real – but that doesn't make it easy.

I just keep thinking – *he knows, he figured it out, he knows and everybody else will know soon, too.* If I'm the narcissistic bully he says I was, why *wouldn't* he go and blab to everybody? I would.

I don't know how to get out of this. I can't call him a liar; even a little drunk, Hayden's smarter than that. Maybe if he was still the shy, quiet kid I remember, I'd be able to scare him into silence, but he's not. This guy loitering in the doorway is someone who's come into his own. He's also apparently got more spine than I gave him credit for, because he didn't bow out and leave me alone after I yelled at him and went for the jugular, calling him a sad failure or whatever. I can't hide behind a clever photo and carefully

218

worded caption, or dazzle my way out with a mostly true, only somewhat-exaggerated-for-dramatic-retelling-purposes, story.

And . . . part of me kind of doesn't want to, I think?

Part of me – and it is a bloody big part, I have to say – is *exhausted*.

I lean on the filing cabinet in the staffroom, letting the cold metal anchor me, and the creepy, weird noises of the old building that spooked me earlier feel homely and comforting now. This school is still standing, even after all the crap it's seen. I can come out the other side too, right?

Okay. Okay, now I'm officially losing it, comparing myself to *the school*.

If it were anybody else who put two and two together and found out I'm a teacher, I'd stand a chance at making sure nobody believed them.

If it were anybody else confronting me just now . . . I probably wouldn't have believed them, for calling me mean and self-centred. The girl Hayden described sounded like a grade-A bitch, and I'm horrified at how easy it is to see that now.

Unless I've always known it and just refused to see it? Like, I *know* it was wrong to be flirting with Josh when he was dating Thea; I knew it at the time, too, but it was fun and thrilling and – Hayden's right, I never considered anybody else's feelings in that. Josh took the fall for it all when Thea found out he'd cheated, and we all rallied behind her like 'men are trash, you deserve better, he played us both', but I knew what I was doing. I just didn't care.

How many people did I hurt, because I only ever worried about myself?

Am I still doing that? I don't *think* so, but . . .

But, I guess it doesn't matter what I think, because the reality is that I did hurt at least one person tonight, and I should take some responsibility for that. So I take a deep breath and I tell Hayden, 'I'm sorry. I shouldn't have said those things to you.'

'It's okay.'

'No, really. I'm . . . I am sorry. You're right, I was out of line. And – I'm sorry for being such a bitch when we were at school, too. I—' A bitter little laugh cuts out of me. 'I must've been so self-centred, like you said, that I never realised I came off as such a mean girl. So, I'm sorry for . . . you know, everything I did when we were kids that affected you badly. I didn't set out to bully you, or anything . . .'

'I know.' His mouth curves in an almost-smile. 'It's okay.'

I think he means it, too. He was never the type to hold a grudge or get angry though, I suppose; I must've just pushed him to breaking point for him to go off like that. He was always a nice kid. I feel bad that we never gave him more credit for that, back in the day.

'You don't have to lurk over there in the doorway, you know.'

Hayden shuffles, but doesn't come inside, and I snort. I think I mutter, 'Square,' out loud, but I only half mean it.

And since he's apparently so willing to hear me out, and he hasn't gone anywhere even after calling me on my bullshit, I find myself being as upfront with him as he just was with me.

'I shouldn't have said you were projecting your shit onto me. You might think I'm as delulu as they come, but believe me when I say I'm self-aware enough to know I only said it because that's exactly what *I* was doing to *you*. It's just . . . Everything was supposed to work out, you know? I had plans. Dreams. I was making them happen. Going to drama school, auditions . . . I was *doing it*. And none of it was working. My teachers kept pushing me to work harder, do better, which – now I'm on the other side, that's, like, *their whole job*, but at the time it was just tearing me down. Then none of my auditions were working out – I couldn't even get a bit-part on a chorus line or whatever – and that sapped all my confidence. I just cried. All the time. It was horrible, so – I came home.'

Walking into my childhood bedroom like it was some kind of shrine, remnants of who I used to be and who I thought I was supposed to be scattered everywhere in signed playbills and an old flute and a case of stage makeup. It was the Act Three conflict in the movie of my life, I told myself at the time, watching the whole thing as if it was some out-of-body experience. I'd bounce back. I had to. This was the dark before the dawn – all great heroes had to pass through this moment and so would I.

I just never thought the moment would . . . last. Forever.

I carry on monologuing at Hayden, who provides a patient and attentive audience.

'I didn't *quit*, though, I just – had to change tack. I tried again. Kept going to auditions. Started getting work as an extra. I thought that was my foot in the door, but that never really paid off. Like the director would pick me out of the crowd in a random nightclub scene for some BBC drama and say, "You! You're our leading lady!" or something. I got a few minor roles, and that was all. Half of them I had to turn down because I got this job, because – what else was

I going to do? I was living at home, sponging off my parents, and they never *said* anything, but I could tell. You know? They felt sorry for me and I hated that. It . . . I'm not someone people feel sorry for. I'm someone they look up to. And – nobody was, anymore.

'So I was like, "Great, okay, I'll fix this – I'll get a job, be a productive member of society, stand on my own two feet until it happens!" And, spoiler alert, it *still hasn't happened*. I do a few local theatre bits. Some work as an extra in the summer. I send in audition tapes and hear back about maybe one in two hundred. I'm still doing everything right, and I'm still failing, and it's like – at what point do I have to admit that? And when I do . . . Once that door closes . . . That's it. I'm not an aspiring actress anymore. I'm a failed one.'

I already am, really. But as long as I keep submitting audition tapes, or showing up to rehearsals for some shoddy local production I only half care about . . . Then it's still around the corner. My big break, just waiting for me.

I'm not ready to let that go.

I don't know how much longer I can keep holding out for it; it's already taken so much from me, I have nothing left to give.

Hayden is quiet, so I shut the filing-cabinet drawer and head over to him. We don't talk on the way back downstairs – and once we are on the ground floor, my teacher-Spidey senses start tingling. Something is *off*, trouble is *afoot*, and I must put a stop to it.

I swing my phone torch around and see the music room door down the other end of the hall is ajar. Someone steps out, a shadow shaped like a man holding a shadow shaped like a blob. His torchlight is aimed behind him and there are voices in the other shadows that move, and I decide that whatever he's holding isn't hatchet-shaped enough for him to be the School Reunion Slasher of my imagination.

'Oi!' I shout in his direction. 'What're you up to? I *said*, no wandering!'

'Sorry, miss – uh, Bryony.' It's Hassan, Shaun's friend. A couple of other people join behind him and in the added torchlight as their phones join the fray, I see them all holding instrument cases. Hassan's got a guitar. He holds it up, looking guilty. 'Thought we'd get the old band back together.'

'What?'

'The band. You know, the school orchestra.'

Thea appears over his shoulder, saying, 'Yeah, we found some instruments and there's a bunch of sheet music out, so we thought we'd give it a go until you get the power back up. I think I can still remember "Never Gonna Give You Up" on the clarinet.'

That is the dorkiest shit I have ever heard in my life.

I *love it*.

Kind of wish I could abandon my responsibilities and go join in. I bet I could still kill that flute solo in our old *Swan Lake* arrangement.

'You break it, you pay for it,' I warn them, and the gaggle of half-lit people nod and promise me they'll be careful before scurrying off to the school hall again. As they disappear down the other end of the corridor, Hayden gives a snort of laughter.

'What?'

'Nothing. Just . . .' He scratches his eyebrow, trying hard not to grin and failing miserably. (Happily?) 'You play the part of "teacher" a bit too well, that's all. I'm surprised you've flown under the radar this long.'

'Yeah, yeah, I get it. The irony of my greatest performance yet being my boring, rubbish job.'

'If you don't like being a teacher, why—'

'I love being a teacher,' I interrupt, rounding on him, catching myself before I get too shouty. Not because I'm worried about my voice travelling, although, yeah, that too, but because Hayden probably doesn't deserve me yelling at him again when he's just being nice. 'I love my job. I mean, yes, it's draining, and some of the kids can be right little shits, and the pay could be a *lot* better for the hours I put in . . . but I love what I'm doing here. It's what lifts me back up after I get rejected from a role, or if we have a lacklustre night in whatever local bit of theatre we're putting on. And seeing the way those kids shine when we do the end-of-term play, or a concert? It's like a drug. It's such a high, it's addictive.'

Hayden's head tilts sideways and his glasses skew slightly. He looks like a puppy dog – the cute-as-a-button kind that makes me wonder how this man has any sex appeal at all, never mind enough of it to have two children. 'But you seem very down on yourself about being a teacher. I assumed you must not like it.'

'It's not that, it's . . . not what I was supposed to be doing, that's all. Not to mention, it sounds extra pathetic for being at my own school. Literally like I never moved on at all. Like my whole life stalled when I was eighteen. But you—' I bite my tongue, but ask it anyway, just . . . mildly rephrased, to try to sound a bit less rude or blunt. 'Do you ever feel like that? You know, with . . .'

'Not before tonight, I don't think.' Hayden starts walking and we fall into step beside each other. 'I just accepted it for what it was. I'm – I *thought* I was happy with how my life turned out. Tonight, though, with the way everybody else reacted . . . Between us, B, it's got me wondering if I settled and gave up too much of myself when I became a dad. I always threw myself wholeheartedly into things and maybe I did that a bit when Margot was born. They've got me thinking I should've done something different, some-where along the way. For myself, I mean. With my career.'

'But – you're happy? Genuinely, really happy?'

He shrugs. His face is impassive. It makes me annoyed I didn't pay more attention to him in school to read him better now; he always kept a lot to himself, and his only *real* tell was that look when he was thinking too hard, too much in his head about something. He doesn't have that look on his face now.

We come to a stop back outside the caretaker's office. Discordant strains of instruments tuning up belt from the hall.

'And you?' he asks me. 'You're not?'

'I'm . . .'

Of course not. I hate my sucky, sucky life, that's why I gloss over everything and present it so spectacularly online, show off the existence I'm not truly living. I hate that I'm stuck here, hate that my name isn't up in lights, hate that it feels like my whole life is held together by duct tape and blind hope, and even that's fading fast.

But I . . . do love my job. Mostly. Most of the time. Overall. I love it more than enough that I wouldn't want to give it up, or try something else. I like that it's one of the few parts of my life where I feel so wholly myself, as if it's exactly where I'm meant to be.

The things I hate so desperately about my life are the same things I hold to so fast, and refuse to let go.

Who knew I had such a penchant for suffering?

I can't quite form any of that into an answer, though, so I just say to Hayden, 'Hold my phone, will you? I'll need to check the labels to see which is the right key.'

Chapter Twenty-Eight

Steph

'Most Likely to End Up Together'

Once upon a time, I used to fantasise about my life with Shaun. I had a secret Tumblr account where I'd save things like the songs I thought might work for our first dance because they felt special to 'us', or pictures of wedding décor, quotes from books about great loves, and gifsets of my favourite couples from romance movies. I used to collect fragments of the ways I loved him, the life I pictured us having together, so sure that it was forever.

It was silly and naive and . . .

Sat here on the steps at the back of the school, night drawing in around us, I miss it.

Now isn't so different, I suppose. I have Pinterest boards where I save inspo of interior design or ideas for anniversary gifts. I have several more dedicated to wedding dresses, food, venues, playlists, gift bags, name tags, cakes – all bar the dress board are shared directly with Curtis, as well as my mum, aunties, some of his side of the family, and my bridal party. They're organised, precise, but no less meaningful. We *do* have a wedding to arrange, after all.

But I don't have anything quite like that old Tumblr account. I don't think I've even got so much of a shoebox of keepsakes; the history of mine and Curtis's relationship is scattered around our flat in the form of photos and vases and coffee-table books.

I miss the hope and reckless abandon of that blog. And I *know*, deep down, it's not just the memories, but what they represent: such a strong, all-consuming kind of love.

Doesn't it mean something, that I don't have anything like that now?

Which is not, of course, to say that I don't love Curtis; I do, very much. But remembering the sort of love I used to have – the first, great one – it makes me wonder if it's . . . enough.

I don't want to think like that. I don't, because it's an awful, painful, wretched thought to have, but it slinks into my mind and takes root, and I'm forced to confront it.

I thought I was all-in with Curtis – but I was all-in with Shaun, once, too.

Shaun is watching me closely; a deep crease has formed between his eyebrows, and the weight and intensity of that look should feel like too much – but it doesn't. It just makes me think he already knows all of the thoughts spiralling through my head, and like it's safe to confide in him.

My legs feel wobbly and when I take a seat on the top step in front of the doors, Shaun doesn't hesitate to join me. I tuck my hands between my knees, but my whole body is already angled towards him. One of his hands rests flat on the ground just behind my back. Neither of us are touching, but I still feel so impossibly, dangerously close to him.

'Do you remember all the dreams we used to have about what our future would look like?' I ask him quietly. I haven't thought about them in so long . . .

Shaun smiles, and it lights up his whole face. He's so bright, it's dazzling. He looks every bit like the boy I fell in love with in that moment, and it does something terrible and wonderful to my heart.

'Remember?' He laughs, head tipping back and eyes scanning the night sky, the growing dark above us. 'How we'd move in together right out of uni and get a dog so it'd be good practice for when we had kids – three of them, wasn't it? You'd help with school fetes and I'd help coach the football team on weekends, and we'd have great big family trips to caravan parks in Devon like when *we* were little . . . And we'd move once we'd saved up enough – somewhere close to both our parents, with a big garden and one of those big driveways where we'd teach the kids to ride bikes . . . There was that old house on the corner – always had a pretty garden, with the blue fence, do you remember?'

I nod. I snuck a photo of it one day, to add to my Tumblr. I used to point at it whenever Shaun walked me home from school and say that would be our house one day; there was something so homely and classic about it, so picture-perfect for family life in the suburbs. I forgot I used to long for a life like that; it feels so alien to me now. It's hard to picture craving that remote, almost rural, lifestyle. Harder still to picture myself with a swollen belly and children running about my feet and worrying about things like nursery and reading levels and bedtime. The memory of it feels like finding a dress in the back of the wardrobe I'd forgotten all about, not even remembering buying it, and trying it on only to discover it doesn't fit and feels all kinds of wrong. A relic of another style, another version of me.

Shaun is still smiling, looking up at the sky wistfully.

It was, I concede, a very nice dream at the time.

Is that what my life would have turned out like if we hadn't split up? Would I have still wanted it, if it was a life shared with Shaun, or would we want different things anyway now that we're grown up?

I confess to him, 'I think I used to believe we weren't *really* in love, you know? Everybody thinks they fall in love when they're a teenager, but it's – different. Amped up, somehow? Not real *enough*, maybe? I think I convinced myself it was hormones and peer pressure and heightened emotions and that I'd built it all up in my head to be more than it really was, and that when I grew up and I dated more, I'd – I'd learn that really was the case. That it was just puppy love and I'd find the real deal. Fall in love *for true*.'

'And did you . . . do that? With . . .' It's like Shaun can't quite bring himself to say Curtis's name. I'm a little bit glad when he doesn't; it feels like a betrayal, somehow.

'Yes. Well, I – I did, or I . . . I thought . . .'

This time, it's my turn to trail off, and I'm not at all surprised to realise that my cheeks are wet, or feel a sob hitching in my throat.

Until tonight, I was so sure. Everything seemed so straightforward, so natural. I hate that I'm questioning it, and worse that I'm questioning *Curtis* when he's done nothing to deserve it, but – what if this is all meant to be in the end? If everything Shaun and I had *was* real after all, and it must be for us to both still feel so strongly for each other after all this time . . .

The very moment he came into the party, the second our eyes met across the room . . . It was so clear to both of us that those feelings were still there, lying dormant beneath the surface and just waiting to have each other breathe life back into them, so why, *why*, did either of us ever indulge that by coming out here to talk, to reconnect? We should have shut it down, not entertained it.

What is it about him that makes me feel seventeen again, when my whole world began and ended with us?

Shaun has wrapped an arm around me, sidling closer, and even that feels so familiar and natural that I hardly noticed it happening. Is that a sign, too? He rummages through my handbag to pass me a tissue – one stained with lipstick prints – and I dab my eyes dry. When I look at him, his face seems to reflect everything I'm feeling: the anguish and confusion and heartbreak.

Our bodies are flush from hip to knee, and he doesn't remove his arm from around my back. If anything, it curls a little further around my body, so that his hand can squeeze the top of my arm gently.

He'd do that all the time when we were dating, when we were hanging out with other people. His arm would be slung around my shoulders, and we'd be chatting and laughing as part of the group, but then he'd give my arm a little squeeze that would make me look at him. A brief few seconds of eye contact, a small shared smile as we anchored ourselves back against each other in the midst of everybody else . . . *Still here*, that gesture seemed to say. *Always here.*

My brain starts rattling at a hundred miles an hour: is he

trying to say that again, now, that he's still here – *with* me, not just next to me? That he's still mine, I'm still his?

A pang twists in my chest, so sharp that I nearly wince. I almost think that, if I could take my heart and carve out the bits that belonged to Shaun, all the parts where fond memories of him took root . . . If I could take it all away and avoid this, now, I might do it.

I wonder if he feels the same way.

It's not regret, so much as . . . as . . .

As the fact that, maybe, those parts of my heart that belonged to Shaun, still *do* belong to him, and always will, and I don't know how I am supposed to say goodbye to him later tonight and leave and live with that.

All of my emotions are in hyperdrive – the heartache and heartbreak, the longing and sorrow and joy and guilt, all muddled together and vibrating hard and fast beneath the surface of my skin, like any second I might burst into hysterical laughter or throw myself at Shaun or *away* from him, or . . .

Or blurt in a shaky voice, 'What if we got it all wrong, Shaun? Letting ourselves drift apart, never reaching back out . . .'

It's the biggest *what if* of all.

And then it's cold, and he's moved away – but only, I see when my head snaps up to look, so that he can angle himself towards me. And then I understand: he's put some physical space between us to compensate for the fact that he reaches for my hand. His palm is warm and soft as it encompasses the back of mine.

It feels – strange. Different. It's a man's hand, not the boy's I used to hold all the time. For a moment, I just stare at his hand on mine, the few dark hairs that dust the back of it, like I can't make sense of what I'm seeing.

'Did you really mean that?' Shaun asks, and his voice, too, is raw and cracked, as if he's the one who's been crying. His eyes search mine, and there's nothing desperate or plaintive or even wildly hopeful in them this time. He looks – so sure of himself, so certain. An inner gravity that centres him and helps his gaze not to falter, even as emotion bleeds into his voice.

I swallow the lump in my throat, push away the sound of Curtis's laugh and the smell of his cologne as they swim at the forefront of my memory, and give Shaun the only honest answer I can.

'I don't know. I don't suppose it . . . it matters, really, if we did.'

But I hear the lie in the second half of that statement even as the words leave my lips; I see the way Shaun's expression becomes something fierce and how his eyes seem to burn as he looks at me in such earnestness, and I realise it does matter.

It is, maybe, the only thing that matters.

The noise from the school hall falls away – a cacophony of sound that makes a distant part of my brain wonder if that really is an amateur band playing our old Pixar medley, or if it's only another memory dredged up along with those photos Shaun found in my bag, messing with my senses. I blink, realising how dark it's gotten in the time we've been out here, especially with the light off in the stairwell behind us. The darkness becomes a blanket, a curtain that separates us from everything and everyone else, like the time we snuck backstage to steal a kiss during one of the school plays, before

Mr Dougherty caught us and shooed us away so we didn't get in the way of the next scene change.

There is no Mr Dougherty to come chivvy us along now, though. No old schoolmates or even new loves. There's only us, and the only sound I can hear is the ragged inhale Shaun takes. I think it would match my own if I stopped holding my breath.

I look at his lovely brown eyes and the line of his nose, his widow's peak and the softness of his hair, sure it would feel exactly like I remember if I were to run my fingers through it, and unsure how the line of his jaw, accented by adulthood, would feel beneath my palm if I were to cup his face in my hand.

I wonder how he would taste. Like fruit punch, maybe. If he would kiss differently, or if I do, or if, even if we do, we would still kiss each other exactly the same way as we used to.

Shaun's eyes blaze a path along the outline of my mouth, as he considers it, too.

His hand on mine shifts, minutely, hardly at all, and I gasp. Something like anticipation sends a shiver down my spine, and I wonder if Shaun's eyes have grown darker in the last few seconds or if it's only a trick of the light.

The whole world falls apart around us and I'm left with only one very clear, inescapable thought: *I am about to kiss Shaun Michaels*.

And, I don't think I am going to do anything to stop it from happening.

Chapter Twenty-Nine

Hayden

'*Most Likely to Succeed*'

Bryony is far from justified in the way she's acted tonight, and part of me wants to recommend she see a therapist to work through some of these frustrations that are making her lash out like that but, admittedly, there is a part of me that understands *exactly* where she is coming from.

If nobody else believes in this other, better, more successful version of her life anymore, how is she supposed to believe in it?

Can I really blame her for being so *angry*?

I had forgotten what I used to want from my life. What it used to be like to *want* for myself, full stop. Everybody else tonight, as much as it's annoyed me, has breathed life back into that. Their reminders of my old dreams make something spark in my brain like a flint against stone, a push to get wheels turning that have ground to a halt so gradually I never noticed they stopped moving at all.

The spark of want, the reminder of all my old ambitions, does nothing except ignite an anger I can't seem to shake, though, and it's for that reason I can't blame Bryony for taking her own failure out on everybody else. Her fury and indignation, however misplaced at me and our old classmates, has become infectious. It burns my stomach like acid, makes my body feel tight and heavy and frantic; I understand why little kids throw themselves to the ground in a tantrum, and wish I could, too. I understand why Freddie Loughton punched a wall in English one time, his fist going right through the plaster, even when he looked a little bit like he was about to cry before he stormed out of the classroom.

I want to *rage*. Scream, throw things, howl at the sky and pound my fists against the ground until they bleed.

I've done this to myself. I have nobody to blame except myself.

I could've done so much – done *everything* – differently. Could've stayed at uni, or gone back, or even tried to do it part time when Margot was first born. Could've studied by my own volition and gained some other qualifications, figured out some kind of shared custody arrangement with Lucy instead of putting what we thought was best for her and the girls first. Until now I, naively, thought it was what *I* wanted, too – I thought I'd always be happy, choosing to be a stay-at-home dad and focusing on that first and foremost. But I could have set up a studio or computer lab in the box room and made the girls share a bedroom, or put it in the garage, so I could work on my own projects, delve back into the research I loved so much. Could've gotten childcare during the daytime, and gotten a job where I was on track to pursue the dreams that once meant so much to me.

I could've done *so much more*.

So I don't call Bryony out any further as she flips through

keys and reads their labels and eventually finds the one she needs for the caretaker's office. I don't push her about why she hasn't done more, or interrogate her about what's next, because her answers won't help me to figure out what *I* should be doing differently. And I don't judge her for hiding her actual job, even if it's made her vindictive, because, in this moment, with ire searing through my bones and nerves, I want to snap and snarl at anybody who threatens the delicate balance of my warped, wrong life, too.

She finally opens the door, and, once again, automatically goes to flip the light switch, and huffs when they don't come on.

I never had cause to go into the caretaker's office when I was at school, so it doesn't seem to hold that same forbidden nature the staffroom did. It's a small, square room with a cupboard that's open and stuffed with miscellaneous cleaning supplies. A spray bottle and rag are on a desk alongside some paperwork and a computer. An old floor buffer takes up the area next to the door, eating up most of the available space in the room.

Bryony promptly trips over it.

I catch her arm and haul her upright before she can face-plant onto the floor.

'Thanks.'

'No problem.'

She squints at me through the semi-darkness. 'You used to have the *worst* reflexes. D'you remember that time Mr Carey was off sick for a while so they put the boys' and girls' PE classes together, and we ended up playing dodgeball for weeks? I swear you got worse each time.'

I push my glasses up my nose, remembering the pair

that broke clean in half when one dodgeball hit me square in the face. (Ryan, to his credit, had apologised profusely, and had honestly believed I would've moved out of the way. Ashleigh tried to make me send him the bill for the replacement pair.)

'Do you do a lot of sport now?' Bryony asks, then smirks at her own joke as she teases me. 'Hone those shitty reflexes with some Wii Tennis, maybe?'

'No. Years of picking up Margot and Skye as they run around pell-mell, before they can fall over and scrape their knees, that's all.'

'Oh.' Her smile turns awkward, then vanishes altogether. 'Sure, right, yeah. That too, I guess.'

Bryony and I both turn our attention to flashing our phone torches around the room to search for the fuse box, rather than return to our previous conversation. I don't know if she can sense my newfound anger or if she's too wrapped up in her own world to notice it, but I decide that I don't care if she is.

I was used to flying under the radar at school. Preferred it, in fact, when I did.

I'm mad because, if it weren't so much my comfort zone, maybe I would've fucking *done something* with my life.

And I'm mad because this feral, furious thing howling inside my ribcage is not me. Or, I think, I don't want to admit that it *is*, and the idea that it *is* me is so grotesque and uncomfortable I want to wish it away. Ignore it into nonexistence like so much of the rest of me. The me I know would try to gently prompt Bryony to say more about the things upsetting her so much, encourage her to apologise to the other people she's hurt tonight and maybe, also, if she seemed to need it, encourage her to pursue her acting dreams with a bit more vigour.

The fact that I have suddenly decided to not care is as frightening as this sudden anger.

Has this me always existed? Is it one that I can pack away and squash down and leave lurking in the shadows out of harm's way, or will it refuse to go now that it's been unleashed?

And – I don't know that I *want* it to go away.

It's the closest thing I've felt to that old passion that used to drive me, in a long while. Fierce and full-on. Something to harness and put to work, to turn into something greater, pushing myself to some imagined goal in pure exhilaration.

I've already lost that once, without realising.

Is it worse for it to slip quietly away over time, or to actively decide to dispel it?

'Is that it, d'you think?' Bryony asks, pulling me out of my fury and fear for a moment. Her torch illuminates a box in the top corner of the room behind the desk. The front is clear, showing rows and rows of switches.

'Do I think that thing that looks exactly like a fuse box, is a fuse box?' I say, and it comes out in a cutting, sardonic drawl that I don't recognise. 'I don't know, Bryony, what do you think?'

She pulls a face, nose scrunching up. 'Alright, Mr Moody-Pants, I'm just *saying*.'

I sigh, nudging my glasses out of the way so I can pinch the bridge of my nose. I try to concentrate on breathing. In, out, for five. It used to be a coping mechanism for the anxiety that flared up during term-time at school; more recently, it's been a habit when Margot or Skye do something naughty or break something, so I can centre myself rather than react immediately.

But now it's me who needs the telling-off and the time-out, and it's only when I hear the rattle of a wheely chair moving along the floor that I stop berating myself for being such a dick to Bryony so needlessly, and open my eyes to find her climbing up in those ridiculous heels onto the office chair so she can reach the fuse box. She sets her phone torch-up on the caretaker's desk so she has both hands free to climb with.

As soon as she lifts her other leg off the ground, of course, the chair begins to swing wildly beneath her, and her arms flail, bracing against the wall for purchase. I lunge around the desk, and she's laughing.

'Whoo! Close one!'

'B, get down before you break your neck.'

'It's *fine*. Hold the chair still, will you?'

'This is *not*—'

I never get the rest of the words out, though, because she makes a wild, wide lean for the fuse box and the chair lurches beneath her, so of course I throw my arms out to hold it. I end up with my legs braced around the chair and hands holding the back of it to keep it in place, with the back of Bryony's thigh pressed into my shoulder.

She nudges me with her leg, and I have to fight the chair from swinging around again while she just laughs. 'Normally I'd make a guy buy me dinner before he ends up with his head between my legs.'

I grit my teeth. 'Bryony, I swear to God—'

'Oh, relax, will you?' She wobbles as she leans back to the fuse box. 'Which one d'you think it is? Can you shine your torch up a bit? I can't read the labels properly.'

'*No*, Bryony, I *can't* shine my torch up there because if I let you go, you're liable to fall off this fucking chair.'

'I don't see you coming up with a better idea. I'm *fine*. Look, just – this hand, here.' She pats the top of my right arm. 'Move around a bit so if I *do* fall, I'll end up against your left shoulder. So your arm's kind of around me, you know? Then this one's free to hold your torch.'

I grumble, but I suppose it's not a terrible plan, under the circumstances, so I rearrange myself as she suggested and check the chair is stable enough before I retract my right hand, and grab my phone from where I shoved it into my jeans pocket a moment ago.

As I make sure I'm stood in the right place to catch Bryony if she falls and simultaneously angle my torch so she can read the fuse-box labels, I notice something out of the corner of my eye and a snort of disbelief snags in my throat.

'B, get down. There's a bloody stepladder. I'll be tall enough to reach it on that, easy.'

'No, don't move! Keep the torch right there – I think I've got it . . .'

There's a heavy *click!* as Bryony flips one of the switches.

And, for a moment, nothing happens.

'Dammit,' she mutters.

I'm about to suggest she climb down (carefully) and let me get the ladder to try, and Bryony starts to say something else, too, but then we're both drowned out by a wailing siren as the fire alarm goes off.

Chapter Thirty

Ashleigh

'Most Likely to Kill Each Other'

I'm not flirting with Ryan Lawal, because that's not a thing that would happen.

Ever.

Under any circumstances.

Not if we were the last two people on Earth. Not even then, would I touch this man with a fucking bargepole. This – this entitled, pompous, *arrogant*, slimy, butter-wouldn't-melt bastard.

I am *not* flirting with him, because I am not attracted to him, obviously, because this is *Ryan* we're talking about, but – I am playing this game. This new, less juvenile one in which he tries to make eyes at me and pretend he's the good guy he always believed himself to be, and reckons he used to flirt with me and is doing that *lean*, now, the one . . .

God, that lean. Ryan or not, that lean does something to me. The hand braced near my head, the tension in the muscles of his arm as I follow that hand to his broad shoulders, the tilt of his face and the dark, wide pupils, the heat that consumes his gaze and threatens to consume me right along with it. It's like that lean is the optimal position to make me unable to do anything except smell his cologne (sandalwood base notes, a kick of something faintly peppery, something else that's lilting and softer that might be vanilla, all of which makes me want to bury my nose in the crook of his neck and inhale it deeper), or appreciate the strength and simple masculinity of his body, or . . .

Think about kissing him, which, of course, is *exactly* why he's doing it, I'm sure.

It also does something to me, that heady look he had in his eyes as they began to close when I leant in close like I was actually going to kiss him. Between that and the stupid bloody *leaning*, it's almost enough to make me wish I had.

Just to see.

An . . . experiment, of sorts. A data-gathering exercise.

To ascertain if all that cocksure swagger would vanish, and he'd be hesitant and unsure and maybe even *clumsy*, or if he really wasn't compensating and would know exactly what he was doing. Where would he have put his hands? Would he even have bothered to pretend to be a respectable gentleman, or gone straight for my hips to pull me close?

Heat flushes up my neck and I'm so glad it's too dark for him to see. I hope to hell he can't hear the way my breathing has changed in the few seconds my imagination has run a little *too* wild.

I fight to keep the smirk on my face, that lofty look of victory at screwing with him, besting him at his own game. If he thinks that *lean* and the *teasing* and the – the – the constant bloody *glances* at my smudged lipstick are going to get the better of me, well, he's got another think coming.

I'm not about to be seduced by Ryan Lawal.

So, I tell him, 'You couldn't handle it.'

It takes Ryan a second or two to recover from *my* lean-in, and I relish the dazed look in his eyes as he blinks a couple of times in rapid succession. His eyebrows arch, and his head tilts. It feels like he comes in even closer, but there's still that tiny, minuscule shard of empty space funnelling between our bodies. It feels electric, charged; dangerous.

'Someone thinks pretty highly of herself.'

I shrug, like it's nothing. Like of course, he would be the one to fold, like I regularly go around seducing men for kicks.

'What makes you so sure I couldn't handle it, Easton?' Ryan asks, his voice a low, rumbling murmur that seems to caress my skin, and it's all I can do not to shiver. The sudden gruff cadence, along with his signature arrogance and charisma, would make a lesser woman melt.

Probably has. Many times.

'Maybe I'm not as unfuckable as you think. Maybe you'd be surprised what I'd drink for, in a game of Never Have I Ever these days.'

I *am* talking a big game, in the scheme of what I imagine Ryan and his ilk would consider par for the course when it comes to sex and flirting and dating – but he doesn't need to know that.

Ryan assesses me for an interminable moment. Entire worlds begin and end in that time; stars are born and cycle through a supernova before the corner of his full lips draws up in a smirk I don't want to find attractive, but – God, I really do. He lifts a hand and I refuse to react as he traces the back of his index finger from the neckline of my blouse up to the top of my shoulder, and I have to wrestle away the urge to bite my lip as I think about his hand drifting lower again, but this time to cup my breast as he moves in closer . . .

Except, of course, he doesn't do that.

His finger does trail back down, but only to hook beneath the chain-link strap of my clutch bag, and then he pushes the bag into my hands.

'I saw you sneaking something out of a flask in the hall earlier. Put your money where your mouth is, why don't you?'

All I can do is stare, and wait, as he opens the bag in my useless hands, and takes out my little flask. He unscrews the top and the sharp, potent scent of tequila chokes the air.

He meets my gaze. 'Never have I ever had a one-night stand.'

Ryan takes a sip. He holds the flask between us. I'm careful not to let my fingers brush his as I take it, and have a sip myself.

It's my turn, so I say, 'Never have I ever had a three-way.'

Predictably, Ryan drinks. I do not.

'Never have I ever hooked up with someone I work with.'

We both drink.

'Never have I ever hooked up with someone who works *for* me,' I say, sure that there's no way some peppy, starstruck woman on his staff wouldn't have flirted with him at some stage, and no way that he wouldn't have reciprocated, no matter what his HR department would've had to say about it.

Except Ryan doesn't drink, and then gives me that shit-eating grin I hate so much, and places his mouth near my ear to say, 'Never have I ever dated someone I work *for*.'

Shit. Shit! How does he even know about that? That was *years* ago. A brief, misguided fling before I cut it off and then the guy left for another job, after he realised he couldn't embarrass me into switching to a different department or moving to another company.

That's not a lucky guess. That's . . .

'You've been keeping tabs on me,' I accuse him. 'Stalking my social media.'

There's no way he'd know unless he was keeping a *very* close eye on the guy I occasionally had in some of my Instagram Stories, and never tagged. He would've had to go *looking*, see who liked my posts and who . . .

Ryan doesn't even try to deny it. Just shrugs, keeps leaning, keeps that sliver of space between us, and gives a complacent half-smile like I just pointed out the obvious.

Maybe he really was being serious, when he said he still thought about me and that's part of what's driven his career. All this time he's been like a damn poltergeist in my life, cropping up when I least expect it, unable to get rid of him if I tried . . . And he's been lurking on my socials, following my life and my career, too.

'Drink,' is all he says, so I do.

'Never have I ever cheated,' I say next, throwing the words like a punch, but Ryan just shrugs and doesn't take the flask.

Damn it, I was so sure I would've had him there.

Ryan pretends to think over his next move, and I feel the shift in the tension between us as soon as his eyes cut back to mine. He takes the flask and is sure to let his fingers touch mine as he does so. They're rough, calloused, and the shock of it makes my breath catch – audibly, which makes me blush, and makes him . . .

I expect him to smirk because he's won this round, only he doesn't. If anything, his expression settles into something unnervingly serious, and I can't tear my eyes away from him.

I hear the scrape of metal; he's putting the cap back on the flask.

But it's not game over, apparently, because he breathes in and opens his mouth like he's about to say something, take his turn.

And his body is crowding even closer to mine yet somehow *still not touching*, and it's agonising, and my back is curving away from the door to bring me closer to him, waiting, wanting, in a way I've never wanted anybody, let alone Ryan, and – none of this feels like a *game* anymore, some petty fight.

It feels like we're about to ruin and raze the other.

And the exhilaration of that, combined with this unfiltered attraction, is too intoxicating to ignore.

Ryan bows his head and my eyelids flutter closed as his forehead grazes mine. His breath is hot against the side of my face, the scruff of his beard tickling my skin. It makes me tilt my head, and my nose bumps against his. His mouth is just out of reach.

Ryan murmurs, 'Never have I ever kissed a girl in the chemistry lab.'

It's pathetic, cheesy and almost childish in its absolute *line*-ness, but, God, if it doesn't work. If the *lean* and the *looks* and the *line* don't all work on me exactly like he probably knew they would, and I can't stand it any longer.

My bag falls and I think it lands directly on one of Ryan's feet.

My free hands fist in the front of his shirt and yank him

the rest of the way into me, our mouths colliding as the rest of our bodies follow suit.

Ryan, it turns out, kisses with all the arrogance with which he does anything else. His lips move languidly against mine, firm and unhurried and gentle, which makes me feel like he's won because here I am, wanting to throw myself at him – but for once, I don't mind. I am *more* than happy to let him win if it means this carries on. His tongue teases at my lower lip, and I feel his mouth curve into a smile when I don't give in straight away.

I angle my head to fit better against his and slide my tongue into his open mouth. He moans and it sends a rush of heat to the pit of my stomach. There's a faraway clang; he's dropped the flask. I nip his lip between my teeth, eager to hear him make that noise again. Wanting to know it's because of – *for* – me.

But the sound I pull out of Ryan is something rough and coarse, deep within the back of his throat, and this time I do melt. I actually understand what people mean when they say a man makes them weak at the knees.

I learn that Ryan is not the perfect gentleman he likes to pretend he is; his hands go straight for my arse, not just cupping but *grabbing*, and hoisting me off my feet. I'm pushed back into the door, not quite sure which of us wraps my legs around his hips, but very sure that it's me who grinds down against his erection, half because I want to tease him and half because of the delirium it sends spiralling through me.

In our usual, rational world, where everything makes complete sense and I am not stuck in a science classroom during a power cut with my arch-nemesis from my school days and perpetual bane of my life, I don't doubt that Ryan would never let me live it down if he made me orgasm without even having to do anything.

But I'm *this close*, and I really don't care.

One of his hands pinches playfully at my arse. 'Still bony,' he informs me, hardly taking his mouth away from mine long enough to say it.

I wriggle against him. 'Speak for yourself.'

He clutches me tighter, presses in closer – then stills, absolutely, and some of the lust-fuelled fog in my brain clears as he breathes hard, his fingers pressing into my skin like I'll slip away any second. My legs clench tighter around his hips before I can stop myself.

'Fuck, Ashleigh, what are you doing to me?'

'Putting my money where my mouth is, I guess.'

A ragged chuckle slips out of him. 'Don't talk to me about where your mouth is.'

'Why not? Wishing it was somewhere else?'

I kind of do, too. I really do, actually, now he mentions it.

His grip on me squeezes, trembles, releases again. 'Don't tempt me. Seriously, *don't*, or I might actually shag you in our old chemistry classroom, which is not . . . Not how I imagined doing that.'

'You've imagined shagging me?'

I mean for it to come out snide, teasing. To gloat in the fact that Ryan Lawal, who once called me unfuckable, thinks about having sex with me. But it doesn't; it comes out needy, and breathy, and the hand I push through his hair is tender enough that his eyes close when he nods, and I cradle his face in my hands, eyes wide and heart skittering as I wait for his response.

'I imagine a lot of things about you, Ashleigh. How you'd moan my name, the sound you'd make if I just . . .' He sighs, slides a hand up into my hair beneath my updo and tugs lightly, making me arch against him. 'Just a little.' Then he lets go, drags that same hand so feather-light down the back of my neck to follow a pattern in the freckles along my shoulder. His lips graze a kiss against my temple, another against my cheek, one more at the corner of my mouth, where that lipstick smudge was. I imagine it's smudged a whole lot worse now.

'How you take your coffee in the mornings,' he continues, then. 'What you put on TV when you get home after a long day of work. If you poke your tongue out when you paint your nails, like you used to do in art lessons, and if you still like eighties rock music.'

The simplicity of it all has me speechless. I've always seen through Ryan's bullshit act when he's hamming it up, and . . . this isn't it. This is so very, very far from anything I know Ryan to be capable of.

I don't know what to do with it, so I deflect. Defer to old habits. Joke, 'Wouldn't you like to know?'

He draws back just enough to look me in the eyes. 'Yeah. I would.'

And, goddammit. *Goddammit.*

He's got me, hook, line and sinker.

I crash my lips back down against his and his hand tangles in my hair, pins tumbling out and strands falling loose.

'Iced, extra shot of espresso, and caramel syrup. Lots of it.'

Ryan kisses a path down my neck, tongue and teeth scraping against the sensitive skin, making me grip his shoulders helplessly.

'I rewatch episodes of comedy shows. *Friends* and *Always Sunny*, or *Ted Lasso*.'

His hand slides beneath my top, fumbling for the hooks of my bra, and I tug his stupid old school tie loose to get to his shirt buttons.

'I never poked my tongue out.'

A laugh rumbles against my neck, and he licks a stripe up the column of my throat. I shiver. 'Yes, you did. So, yes, you still do.'

I'd argue, if he weren't thrusting his hips up against mine and pushing the hard length of his erection so deliciously between my legs. I just angle my hips better against him instead.

'I still like eighties rock, but not in that pretentious way I used to, when I liked it just because it made me feel better than people like you who listened solely to what was in the charts.'

'You wanna know a secret?' Ryan's teeth catch my earlobe. 'You got me into liking it, too, I was always just too proud to tell you.'

His hand finds its way inside my trousers, inside my underwear, while I'm still lifted up with my legs around him and my back against the door. My head sinks onto his shoulder as I rock against his fingers, and Ryan mutters curses like he's the one being made to see stars when I fall apart against him. I take his face in my hands to kiss him again, deeply, both of us fighting for dominance, and my legs drop back down, feet planting unsteadily on the floor. My hands travel the hard planes of his chest, beneath and on top of his half-unbuttoned shirt, and I sink to my knees, palms feeling the contours of his muscled thighs before I

251

undo his trousers and take him in my hands and mouth. I moan when his fingers grip my hair in desperation; my stomach swoops when he throws a hand flat against the door and gives a stuttering groan, fighting to keep his composure as he pulls away from me.

I stand back up, my body brushing the entire length of his.

'Told you,' I say, kissing the edge of his jaw. 'You couldn't handle it.'

'You wanna bet?' Ryan growls, and it's all teeth and tongues and hands and skin, and the scatter of clothes landing on furniture or the floor or being pushed aside in our haste, the tear of a condom packet taken from his wallet, and I'm laid out flat on one of the benches with Ryan over me, inside me, my arms and legs tangled around his, and it's all so fucking *good* that I don't know why we ever bothered to put up a fight and pretend like this wasn't always going to happen.

It wasn't. Obviously. And this is . . . unprecedented. Unforeseen.

And I do not want to be anywhere else, except locked in this dark classroom in the middle of the night with Ryan Lawal, while he mutters pure filth in my ear and thrusts into me, and gets that insufferably smug look on his face when he makes me shatter against him for a second time and I beg him in breathy, needy pants until I can only say his name while he's saying things like, 'Oh, God, just like that,' and, 'Fuck, yeah, let me hear you *scream*.'

I wouldn't normally give him the satisfaction.

Except, you know. Normally, I wouldn't be in this situation at all, or even contemplating a reality in which it might exist. And normally, I wouldn't be *quite* this satisfied.

It's a battle with Ryan I am more than happy to lose, if this is what losing entails.

So I arch into him, draw him in deeper and closer with my thighs and knees and feet while my fingers dig into the hard, smooth muscle of his biceps, and his lips do something to the tender skin of my neck at just the same time his fingers touch me and he angles his hips to hit just the right spot – and I do it, just for him, just because he asked. I cry out in wordless pleasure, a keening noise I've never heard myself make before as my whole body bucks against Ryan. His grip bites into my hips and his rhythm stutters and he groans my name in the most deliciously intoxicating sound I've ever heard.

I don't worry if anybody might overhear, because we're drowned out by the sudden wailing of the school fire alarm.

The sprinklers overhead immediately kick on, drenching us both.

Ryan is still inside me, has barely come down off his orgasm, and blinks, stunned, as water pounds against his back and drips off him, onto me. I stare back, biting my lip until I can't hold it in any longer. A giggle bursts out of me, and Ryan gives a short, stunned chuckle, and the fire alarm continues to blare and the sprinklers keep soaking us, and we both collapse against the bench, unable to stop laughing.

Which is, if you'd asked me, definitely not how I thought sex with Ryan Lawal was going to end.

Chapter Thirty-One

Bryony

'Most Likely to Become Famous'

This is one giant, colossal, cosmic joke. God is well and truly giving me the middle finger tonight, and I can just tell she's laughing as she does it.

I don't exactly have *time* to dwell on that, though, because after frantically flipping several more switches in the fuse box in blind panic, then finally toppling over and losing my balance on the spinny chair and, okay, *yes*, maybe Hayden was right because I totally would've broken a bone if he hadn't been there to catch me, steady me, and help me down . . .

Anyway, after all *that* mess, I don't have the capacity for anything else except racing to the school hall, where the dodgy sound of the old orchestra has abruptly stopped and people are looking around in a panic, phone torches flashing wildly. It'd look like a cool disco if it weren't a *total fucking disaster zone*.

I snatch up the guest book and holler over the noise of a hundred and fifty adults who have suddenly forgotten what they're meant to do in the event of a fire alarm, like, maybe, I don't know, get the hell out of the building.

Honestly. *Amateurs.*

Where would they be without me?

'Alright, everybody! I'm going to need all of you outside! Exit through the boys' cloakroom on the left as you leave the hall, no pushing, no shoving, *no panicking.* Orderly fashion – you got that? You're all grown-ups here; I don't want to see any messing about. Line up on the tarmac outside the new languages building. Out, out. Come on!'

I clap my hands like I'm chivvying along some puppies, and a few people nearby spring into action. I stand aside at the door to watch them go and make sure the hall is cleared out, shouting instructions to 'keep moving' and remind them that there's 'no pushing, no running'.

Talk about the icing on the cake . . . My epic reunion night is a confirmed shambles. The power cut, sure, was not ideal, but there was some wiggle room. I could've come back from that. I bet they were having a total hoot reuniting the old orchestra crowd and playing some live music; it would've been such a cool, kitsch vibe, the kind you know is going to make a great story afterwards and that kind of makes up for the fact you might not *totally* be enjoying it in the moment.

But this? A *fire drill?*

Yeah, I just don't know how I can come back from this one.

Spoiler alert: I can't. This is it. The end.

Roll credits.

The party to end all parties, just not in the way I hoped.

I let out a terse sigh, feeling like I've just aged about fifty years in the last five minutes. I should've just let Steph organise this bloody thing. *She* never had this kind of disaster happen at any of her parties.

One more failure to add to the tally.

Great job, Bryony. *Great fucking job.*

I seethe and sigh and wallow in my own self-pity while I automatically bark instructions for everybody to line up. I borrow a pen off Hayden (who, of course, just has a random pen in his pocket, like the nerd he is) and go down the line, ticking off names against the guestbook I made everybody sign. I dole out a few death-stares at the handful of people who admit to me that they did not, actually, um, maybe sign the guestbook.

'Well,' I snap, 'next time, you will.'

I'm almost down the line when Hayden taps me on the shoulder. Quite why he's taken it upon himself to trail along after me like some sad puppy or overly keen TA is beyond me. The fire alarm is still belting out its annoying two-tone melody behind us, setting my teeth on edge.

'What?' I shout at him. I am only shouting to be heard over the alarm, of course. Not because I'm feeling especially bitchy towards him in that moment. Or because I think he's about to point out that I'm doing it again, acting like the teacher I am, and everybody must be able to see it.

He jerks a thumb over his shoulder, looking harried and awkward. He looks like he wants to run very far, very fast, in the opposite direction. 'Should I go take another look at that fuse box?'

'*What?*'

Is he serious? He thinks *now* is the time to play boy genius and go mess around with some wires? What, would he like to detour via the DT rooms and collect a soldering iron and some crocodile clips, while he's at it? I decide to tell him all of this, very loudly and pointedly, because I'm so done with everybody's bullshit tonight. Everybody pretending they're more than they are, when they're just *not*. Can't he see we're in crisis mode? This is *not the time*.

'By all means!' I yell, throwing my arms out. 'Go! Have fun living out one last grand hurrah as boy genius in your final moments – *please*, don't let me stop you! Or maybe you could accept the fact that you're a washed-up failure who never made it, *pipe down*, get in line like everybody else and let me do my job so you don't all burn to death, okay?'

I am vaguely (or, you know, completely and very) aware of the fact that the chatter of the crowd dies down to listen to my tirade. I'm also mildly (aka: agonisingly) conscious that people are whispering behind my back, and Hayden's face flushes red all the way to the tips of his ears.

He pushes his glasses up his nose, then readjusts them right back to where they were.

'I just thought, you set the alarm off when you were messing with the fuse box. So, I could go back and fix that, and try to get the power back on, too. I'm sure I've retained enough of my 'boy genius' knowledge to figure that much out – however *washed up* I currently am. There must be some perks of having your life stall when you're eighteen and never move on – right, B?'

Oh, God.

@ me, next time, Hayden. I feel attacked.

I deserve it.

My own face must be burning. Probably enough to set off the fire alarm all over again, to be honest. But I swallow the lump in my throat (pride? Definitely pride, this time) and nod.

'That, um. That's. Yeah. Thank you. That'd be . . .'

257

I think, for a minute, Hayden's going to push it. He's going to drag it out, make me say it and suffer. But he just nods, ducks his head, and goes back into the school to fix what I broke.

I turn back to the crowd of people who, less than an hour ago, thought so much of me. They were hanging off my every word, looking up to me, *admiring me*, exactly as I expected them to. I was the belle of the ball; now, in a stunning plot twist, I've just undergone a magical transformation before their very eyes into the beast instead.

Which is, you know. Great. Super fantastic stuff.

Exactly the kind of gossip I want them to take away about me.

I carry on with the rest of my list from the guestbook, double-checking the pages with their little Biro ticks next to each name. I tick off Morgan and Thea and Priya and their spouses, and I tick off Steph's new beau, Curtis, and my heart stutters to a halt.

Because – she's not here. And now that I think about it, I haven't seen her in ages.

And . . .

I flip a few pages ahead in the guestbook, where I know I ticked off Josh and Hassan and whatsherface with the long legs and good makeup, Aisha. And *he's* not here either.

I look up at everybody, eyes scanning frantically, and they're all silent, waiting.

And shit, shit, shit. This is like last year's trip to the West End all over again; I've lost a kid.

Not just one, this time.

Dread thick in my throat, I call out, 'Has anybody seen Steph and Shaun?'

258

Chapter Thirty-Two

Steph

'Most Likely to End Up Together'

Sweet. I can almost taste the sweetness and warmth of his breath as the two of us lean imperceptibly ever closer, neither one of us seeming to move, and yet, inextricably drawn together, as if this is all – fate. Some greater force in the universe bringing us both together, as if we'd never been apart in the first place.

Is this a bad idea? No, that's a trick question; it's a *horrible* idea and I know that. This isn't me, I'm not a cheat, and Shaun's not a cheat, either, except – maybe he is, if he's so willing to kiss me? Maybe he is, and I don't know because I don't actually know everything he's been up to in the last ten years. Maybe he thinks *I* am the type to cheat, because he doesn't know me, either, not really.

We shouldn't be doing this.

But . . . all those what-ifs. The years of being apart, of wondering, of *knowing* where our lives would have ended up, had we stayed together. The thousand minuscule decisions that led me to picking up *that* exact memory stick so many weeks ago, only to discover our old yearbook; all the things that had to go right in order for Bryony to arrange this reunion and for tonight to pan out the way it has . . . Everything that brought us back together tonight . . .

It's too much to ignore, isn't it? Far too much to be merely *chance*, or *coincidence*.

This is all . . . it's a sign. A big, flashing neon sign that I'm wrong about everything, about myself and my feelings and Curtis, because why else would I be here now? Why else would Shaun's hand be so warm, so heavy, on mine, or my hand be on his knee, and our breaths mingling in the ever-narrowing space between our mouths?

It's Shaun. It always has been Shaun. Always will be.

Right?

I inhale sharply, quietly, and see Shaun's eyes darken in the instant before they close.

And this is it, I realise, in such a cold, stark moment of clarity that it feels as though this entire moment is an out-of-body experience, one I'm watching from the sidelines after the fact. This is the moment my life changes forever, erases the ten years of distance and heartache and puts us both right back where we were always meant to be. This is the moment I decide, Shaun Michaels is truly the one—

BEEEEEEEP!

BOOOOOOP!

BEEEEEEEP!

Shaun practically falls backwards into the railing. I hurtle to my feet and stumble down a step, covering my ears.

We stare at each other for the longest time. Another *beep-boop* sequence sounds in the span it takes us to gawp, and gape, and blink, and let it all settle in: how close we were to kissing each other, that we both *wanted* that kiss, that it would have involved both of us cheating on our partners . . .

And, that the fire alarm is currently blaring at full volume behind us, more aggressive than I ever remember it being. There's a tinny, artificial layer to the sound that I feel in my teeth, and Shaun looks visibly panicked at the noise.

'That's the fire alarm,' he shouts over it.

'Yes!' I shout back. I bend down to pick up my bag, even though you're not supposed to do that. How many fire drills did we go through at school where the teachers told us to leave all our things behind? One time, we ended up shivering in the rain without coats or umbrellas. Morgan got a cold and her mum came in to shout at the Head of Year about it.

But, still, I collect my bag and use the opportunity to turn my face away from Shaun. In fact, I angle my entire body away from him. My heart is in my throat, although I don't believe that has anything to do with the grating noise beep-booping away on the other side of our little stoop, or even worry about a potential fire somewhere in the building. I feel my usual, more pragmatic side returning, as if a layer of ice has been coating it all this time and now melts away. Most likely, one of the rugby lads has slipped out of the party and pulled it for a joke. Hiro *did* do that once, during a mock GCSE exam. And I can't hear screaming – just distant, firm shouting, that reminds me of a teacher calling a class to order as they're ushered outside.

So my racing pulse, the vice-like grip around my lungs, the acrid taste in my mouth . . . I know that's all down to what almost happened with Shaun.

And . . .

I consider it for a moment, use these few precious seconds

alone to weigh the tumult of emotions coursing through me, to see what rises to the surface above everything else. Disappointment? Guilt?

It's . . . *relief*.

Followed very quickly, of course, by a crushing wave of guilt, and a montage of memories from recent years.

'Here,' Curtis said, and handed over one of the Starbucks cups from the paper tray balanced carefully in his large, square palms, and it made me blush because I realised how much attention I accidentally paid to his hands whenever I saw him working the office coffee machine. Stunned at the coffee he brought me that I didn't ask for, I took it and said thank you, and that straightforward smile he always had looked so strange. A little bit shy, I thought, if I didn't know better. And didn't he maintain eye contact for just a beat too long, there?

'How are you so bad at this?' I laughed while a bowling ball clattered – yet again – down the length of the gutter, and all ten pins remained standing. Curtis looked equal parts infuriated and baffled, but it was all carried with a good-natured sigh and a mutter that he was just letting me win . . . and absolutely, categorically, wasn't only just used to bowling with his niece and always having the bumpers up.

'Do you like it?' he asked, and there it was again: the flicker of nervousness in a face that always looked so sure whenever I saw him around the office. In court, he could deliver closing statements like the course of entire lives didn't depend on how good he was at his job, but here he was, so hopeful and worried over the Valentine's dinner he planned for us in his apartment, with rose petals scattered and white pillar candles lit.

The tickle of a beard and moustache that one time he participated in Movember and the fit of giggles I was in when he finally let me shave it off, and we kept cutting it into funny shapes that ended with a Magnum PI look, and the so-bad-it-was-good impression he did. The warm arms wrapped around me on the sofa in an evening, and the tissue he would silently pass me when he knew I was about to cry at the movie we were watching. The pack of pastel-pink flashcards he ordered online for me when I started studying to gain more qualifications, and the wink he gave me when he produced a set of matching highlighters from his back pocket, and my all-too-childish squeal of delight over something so simple, that meant so much to me.

The giddy bliss. 'Yes!' I screamed, and he laughed, because he hadn't even finished asking me to marry him, hadn't even opened the ring box yet, but I was already launching myself at him to kiss him.

I can't smile over the flood of memories; they come hard and fast, snatching my breath, and leaving me only with the confusion and shame at the idea that just moments ago, I was about to kiss another man.

Is all of that really a mistake? Not real enough? Is it worth throwing away, for the first boy I fell in love with?

Those aren't questions I have time to answer right now, though, because my attention is stolen by Shaun shaking the door with more force than is really necessary to open it, and the sensation of something being *wrong* settles cold and heavy in the pit of my stomach.

'Shit. Shit!' He mutters under his breath and heaves on the door handle again. It jostles in the frame, but doesn't give way.

'What's happened? What's going on?'

He steps back with a sigh, tossing a hand at the offending door in exasperation. 'It's . . .' He groans, bending forward with both hands braced on his knees, and he laughs dryly.

'Remember they used to have a brick that always propped this door open? Like, *always*, even when it was freezing cold or bucketing down with rain?'

'Yes,' I say, and my eyes scan automatically over the shadows that now consume us, and I spy the outline of said brick, and . . . 'Oh. Oh, no. The deadbolt slips.'

'The deadbolt slips,' Shaun confirms, giving the door handle another half-hearted yank as if to demonstrate. The deadbolt he unlocked to get us out here has fallen back into place, firmly locking us out of the school and stopping us from going back the way we came to rejoin the others. 'Priya must've knocked it out of the way when she went back inside. We'll have to go back in around the front.'

Back . . .

Yes, a clipped voice in the back of my mind says. *Back in, to the party, because this 'catch-up' of yours is over; it's time to return to reality and stop living in the what-if.*

Is Shaun glad that we didn't kiss? Does he regret the missed opportunity and think he's lost his chance and shouldn't try again? Do I want him to?

No, I don't have time for these questions, either.

I slip my phone out of my bag, thinking that Curtis might worry if there's a fire alarm and he can't find me – I ought to at least let him know that I'm okay and will see him in a minute. But the screen has a hideous, brutal crack stretching from the top corner and won't turn on; it must have broken when I dropped my bag earlier. A flutter of panic erupts in my chest. What if Curtis has been looking for me at the party, texting me, and what if my lack of reply has made him worried?

He . . . would have been right, to worry. To be suspicious. I can't believe I ever betrayed his trust like this. I hate the idea that I might have been causing him pain all this time, while I was living in this nostalgic little daydream with Shaun.

'We should go back,' I say, as much to convince myself as anything else. 'We've been gone a while. If the fire alarm's gone off, I don't want . . . anybody to worry.'

Saying Curtis's name feels – not like a curse, but like the swing of a weapon. Something violent and bloody, something that will *hurt*. I'm not sure who I'm most worried about hurting here, though. Maybe all of us.

Shaun nods, though, and if he notices my clunky phrasing, he's polite enough to ignore it. We make our way down the rest of the steps, gravel crunching underfoot in the silence, giving away the fact that our steps are out of sync. We walk within arm's reach of each other, but with several inches separating us. Shaun's arm swings at his side and I hold my bag in front of me with both hands, just in case we wander too close together and my hand might brush his.

I know that our moment has passed; the kiss that almost was isn't something we could easily return to, and it's for the best.

I feel like I'm just waking up with a hangover. Groggy and disconcerted, recent events a messy jumble in my brain where it feels like entire patches are missing that would make it all make sense. My mouth is dry, my limbs shaky.

Does Shaun feel this way, too? What is he thinking right now? I sneak a peek and find a small frown puckered between his eyebrows, but his shoulders aren't hunched up and his posture is normal – maybe he isn't particularly bothered by it? Maybe he's busy thinking up a cover story for Aisha if she asks why he was gone for so long.

Maybe, I don't know Shaun as well as I once did.

265

I don't dare ask what's going on in his head right now, though. I cannot face that discussion.

The first time Shaun kissed my cheek after walking me home from school one day, I immediately ran inside to open up the Facebook Messenger group chat with Thea, Morgan and Priya, and the four of us dissected and analysed every moment to within an inch of our lives. I described to them in extensive detail how I had to put my schoolbag on my other shoulder so my hand next to him would be free, and how he kept brushing the back of my hand with his then gripping the strap of his cross-body satchel like he couldn't quite work up the nerve to hold my hand, and how it had been a little bit sweaty when he did. Then how romantic and sweet and perfect it had been when he gave my hand a little tug on the porch step so I'd turn into him, and he kissed my cheek so fast I blinked and he was already half racing away, but turned back to grin and wave goodbye.

Oh, we'd have a field day if we tried to debrief on the almost-kiss, now.

But I cannot, for the life of me, imagine what Shaun would have to say about it.

I'm not even sure what I *want* him to say, or what I'd say if he asked me, except the overarching sentiment that it's for the best we didn't.

BEEEEEEEP!
BOOOOOOP!
BEEEEEEEP!

I thought that tonight was leading me back to Shaun, but as the fire alarm continues its relentless screech and we walk out of step around the length of the dark school building, I wonder if fate has intervened after all.

And, if, maybe, Shaun Michaels is not the one after all.

Shaun comes to an abrupt stop, and it takes me a moment to realise why.

Our path is blocked by a very tall, very locked, gate. There's a chain on it, as well as something that looks like a digital pad with a keycode to keep it extra-secure. This never used to be here. It's guarding the narrow, cobblestone path around the side of the school, between the science block and a very thick row of bushes, and blocking our exit completely.

Bryony told us not to go wandering off. I wish we had listened to her.

'Oh, shit,' Shaun mutters, and starts laughing as he approaches the offending gate. He gives it a tug and a push and the chain rattles, but the gate doesn't budge even a little. He turns back to me with that boyish smile of his. 'Guess we're stuck – again.'

Maybe I'm imagining it, but it seems there's a sparkle in his eyes, a cheekiness to it.

I don't have it in me to debate if he's just being himself or if he's being flirtatious right now, because all I can do is think – my phone is broken so I can't call anybody, and if we use Shaun's phone to try to contact somebody to come and unlock the door by the stairs, they'll *know* we've been together, and any chance of downplaying this and slipping back into the party undetected will be done for. We especially can't call Bryony to help; she's always been such a terrible gossip that everybody would know that Shaun and I had snuck out to the back of the school within seconds.

I have to talk to Curtis about this, I know that. I owe it to him, right along with an apology he doesn't have to accept, but I can't bear to have this be the subject of gossip and ridicule; he's done nothing to deserve that. This is between *us*, not my entire cohort of old classmates.

There's only one thing for it.

We'll have to climb over.

Chapter Thirty-Three

Shaun

'Most Likely to End Up Together'

Steph's shoulders tense and when she looks over at me again, I hardly recognise the expression on her face; I've never seen her so stern and determined. But immediately, I know what she's thinking – she wants to try to climb over.

'Let's just call someone,' I say, already slipping my phone out of my pocket. The fire alarm is still blaring. Notifications fill the screen and I hide a wince at the string of texts from Aisha asking where I've gone.

Baby, where'd you go? Starting to get kind of bored without you . . .

Is everything okay? You've been gone ages, can't find you . . .

Explain to me why I'm stuck talking to YOUR friends when you're NOWHERE to be . . .

Where are you?

Did you leave???? Shaun I swear to God if you've left me at this naff little school reunion . . .

Seriously, this isn't funny, let me know you're okay at least . . .

I swipe away from them all, wondering if I have Bryony's number or if I'm just as well to call Josh or Hassan, but Steph lurches towards me like she's about to smack my phone out of my hands, eyes huge, agitation twisting her mouth.

'Are you mad? You can't do that! We can't – you'll . . .' She draws a deep breath, closing her eyes briefly. 'We don't need to involve anybody else in this; it'll just cause a scene, and you know what everybody's like when they get a whiff of drama. People thought Mara was a *drug dealer* just because *one* rollie cigarette fell out of her bag that time.'

I don't point out that that was years ago, and we were kids back then. The way tonight's going . . . Well, maybe Steph's got a point.

And again, I wonder if it would be the worst thing if rumours went around. They wouldn't be that far off the mark, even if we never *actually* kissed, would they? But I know, rationally, I'm not being fair or sensible, and we need to be adults here. We need to make grown-up choices.

Even if we were wrong to go our separate ways all those years ago and even if tonight is all about us finding our way back to each other, the first chapter in the sequel of our epic love story . . . I don't want to restart a relationship with Steph by being a cheat.

I don't want to hurt Aisha like that. And Curtis, I think, knowing as little as I do about the guy who put the ring on Steph's hand, would probably deck me, and he'd be right to. I'd deserve it.

If this is something we're going to try again . . .

We should do it right. We owe ourselves that much, I think.

And I know Steph – she'd never live with herself. She'd feel like a homewrecker. I probably would, too, but Steph's always felt things more deeply than anybody I know, and it'd eat away at her.

So I nod and she relaxes a bit, a smile reappearing on her face at last before she assesses the gate again. 'It can't be *that* difficult, can it? All we need to do is pull ourselves up and – and hop on over!'

I look at the gate, which is about six-and-a-half-feet tall, and made entirely of vertical bars as if to purposely deter anyone from thinking they could climb over it. I can reach the top and can probably haul myself up if I prop a foot against the wall of the school, but there's no room to sit at the top and pull Steph up. Even in her heels, she's too short to reach on her own.

There's nothing for it, I realise – I'm going to have to give her a boost.

I say as much out loud and Steph's cheeks turn pink, but after a moment of silence she nods, coming to the same conclusion I just did. She takes her heels off, manoeuvring them awkwardly between the bars to drop on the other side of the gate in order to climb more easily in bare feet.

I crouch in front of her and my head swims with how much this feels like a warped daydream – me on one knee

271

looking up at the woman I've always loved. Like, in another life, I should be pulling a ring out of my pocket and telling Steph how much she means to me. I always imagined the kind of life I'd have when I was an adult – the house in the suburbs, the dog and then the kids, family outings and holidays, kisses on cheeks in a busy, homey kitchen as we took turns cooking and washing up afterwards . . .

Steph hasn't forgotten that kind of life, either. What we wanted for ourselves. How we saw our future together. Does she have that sort of thing with *him*? Can he give that to her, the way I could?

What if Aisha wasn't the right woman, just the right time? What if I made a mistake with her, and in not chasing after Steph when I had the chance?

Steph steps delicately into my clasped hands, cringing awkwardly even as I assure her it's alright, I've got her. She lifts her other foot off the ground and I hoist her up so she can make a grab for the top of the gate.

It quickly becomes clear that she's not going to be able to pull herself the whole way up and over, though, so I step in to help before she has to ask, placing my hands on her waist to give her some extra support and guide her up.

'Thanks,' she puffs. 'Sorry, I'm not . . . This isn't, er . . .'

'Skipped arm day?' I joke, relieved when she giggles.

This close to her, the warmth of her body radiates into mine, the scent of her perfume and shampoo and something else so quintessentially *Steph* filling my nostrils, my mouth, making me long to draw her away from the gate, into me, so I can finally kiss her.

I don't, though. We have bigger things to worry about.

Like getting back to the party before anyone worries

where we are if there is a fire and it's not some prank or whatever. Like dealing with our fiancés.

I have to help hold her feet and push her up to the very top of the gate, but Steph finally manages to swing herself over, and then dangles by her fingertips on the other side, wincing at the strain in her muscles, eyes screwed shut and mouth twisted in an awkward, if slightly cute, grimace.

'Is it far?' she asks, not daring to look down.

'You got this. Bend your knees when you drop, okay?'

She does, but lands right on her shoes and tumbles over when she hits the ground anyway, rolling on the path with an 'Oomph!' There's the sound of fabric tearing, and she has to untangle the heel of one of her shoes from her now-ripped dress.

'Are you alright?'

'Yeah.' She winces again as she stands, though, rubbing her bum. 'Little bit of a bruise, probably, but I'm okay.'

I follow her over, wondering if she's not just watching but *looking*, and I wish I spent a little more time in the gym. I bet guys like Ryan and Freddie and Tommy could hurl themselves over this thing without even batting an eyelid. It's not as easy as it looks and I end up scrambling to get to the top and then flop over with my legs dangling behind me, winding myself in the process.

Steph hisses. This time it's her turn to ask, 'Are you okay? That looked painful!'

'Yeah, fine,' I manage, and decide to do the rest as quickly as I can to hopefully make up for the flailing, decidedly un-sexy display she just witnessed. If anything was going to give her the ick . . .

I'm just glad the boys aren't here to film it; they'd have

273

a great time taking the piss out of me, even if they'd be just as crap at trying to scale this bloody gate.

When I fling my legs over the top and drop down, though, I end up falling into the hedge. *Right* into it, too, crashing through the leaves, branches snapping under my weight, and landing with a thump on my back in the dirt.

Steph yelps and darts forward to offer me a hand and pull me up, and I'm already laughing at myself for managing to fail at that so spectacularly. I almost wish someone had caught it on film now; I couldn't have done it so badly if I tried.

I clamber out of the hedge with Steph's help. She's giggling too now that she sees I'm not hurt, and I dust some of the leaves and twigs off myself. She's in a bit of a state, too, with her hair out of place and her face pink and a bit sweaty, her dress so dishevelled.

I strike a pose. 'How bad is it?'

'Quite bad,' she says, but reaches to pull another leaf out of my hair. The fire alarm is still going off, though, so she nods in the direction of the front of the school. 'Come on, we'd better go. I'm starting to worry this isn't just some silly prank . . .'

There's a commotion as we round the school; on the other side of the new languages building that I know I'm about to see but still makes my stomach jolt with the unfamiliarity, there's a huge crowd of people, some of whom have the torches on their phones turned on, which is when I realise the floodlights that were illuminating the outside of the school earlier are turned off. Everyone looks like they've been corralled together by one very sparkly sheepdog.

Bryony is shouting at the group and I glance at Steph, trying to work out what's going on. I watch her eyes widen as she takes in the scene, the tinge of panic there – because, shit, she's right. There's no slipping back into the party undetected now, especially with the way we look after climbing over that stupid gate. Everybody must've come outside when the fire alarm went off, like an old-school (literally) fire drill. Shit, maybe it *is* a real fire.

There's something about the regular fire drills and false alarms from my schooldays that's made me immune to any kind of *real* reaction now, like deep down, I don't really believe this place could ever go up in flames.

Before I can wonder if I *should* be panicking – and, dammit, Aisha, is she okay? – Bryony's voice carries towards us.

'Has anybody,' she yells, projecting her voice like she's being Dorothy on stage again, 'seen Stephanie O'Connell or Shaun Michaels?'

There are mumbles, grumbles, shrugged shoulders.

Priya, I notice, is biting the inside of her cheek and looking supremely uncomfortable. She opens her mouth, but never gets to say anything because Steph is already running forward, heels clacking and an arm waving above her head. 'Hi! Hello! We're over here! We got locked out of the back door and had to go the long way round!'

Bryony turns and someone's phone torch illuminates her face enough for me to see the relief that floods it, and how pale she looks. I pick up my pace, jogging to catch up with Steph and join everybody else.

Then Bryony's face hardens and she tosses her ponytail over her shoulder, thrusts one hip to the side and plants a manicured hand on it, fingers drumming against her sequin jumpsuit. 'And just what were you doing at the back of the school? Look at the state of you both!'

Someone wolf-whistles and Freddie Loughton shouts, 'Yeah, Shaun, get in there!' and then him and some of the rugby lads and their lot are singing, '*Steph and Shaun, sitting in a tree . . .!*'

I'm about to laugh and join in when Steph flinches, looking horrified and humiliated.

Bryony, for once, is paying the crowd no mind, too busy scowling at us. 'I explicitly said, *no wandering around*. I expected better from you two, I really did.'

There's such a stern edge to her voice that I wouldn't recognise it as coming from Bryony if I weren't watching her speak.

'We were just catching up,' Steph says meekly, and now her shoulders hunch and it looks like she's fifteen and being berated by a teacher. *Sounds* like it, too, the way Bryony's talking.

I can't help but laugh now, and grin when Bryony levels me with a Very Disappointed In Me sort of look. 'Sorry, *miss*, I promise it won't happen again. What's going on? We heard the fire alarm go off.'

She huffs and flips open a thick book nestled in the crook of her right arm. It's the guestbook from the hall she made us all sign, I recognise. '*Yes*, and now I've been making sure everybody is alright and we haven't lost anyone – namely, you two. Maybe if you hadn't been sneaking off like love-struck teenagers wanting to cop a feel behind the bike sheds, you would've noticed we've had a power cut and it's triggered the fire alarm.'

'There's been a power cut?' Steph blurts, and suddenly the lack of lights from the building make sense.

Bryony's lips purse.

'We *weren't* copping a feel, for the record,' Steph mumbles, although I don't think anybody even hears her over the whoops and jeers, and she slinks over to the front of the crowd to where her girls are. Where Curtis is. He's laughing, though, like he can't even imagine her *thinking* about doing something like that, and when she's close enough he seems to ask with concern about her ripped dress. His arm slips around her shoulders and Steph closes her eyes as she leans into his body, her hand braced against his stomach.

It twists like a knife in my gut.

A little way off, Aisha jumps up from a gaggle of people to flap a hand at me.

She wriggles out of the crowd to come over, her arm sliding around my waist and a kiss landing on my cheek, then hisses in my ear, 'Where the hell have you been? What happened? You look like you've been dragged through a hedge backwards.'

'Something like that . . .'

Bryony is apparently not finished with her roll-call exercise and after a terse sigh in my direction and a pointed glare in Steph's, she continues ticking off names against the guest-book.

Aisha says, 'So that explains where you disappeared off to – you were hanging out with your ex.'

Now the guilt starts to well and truly kick in. Did I really almost kiss Steph back there when I'd left my fiancée waiting for me inside? Am I really hoping to sweep it all under the rug now?

'Did you guys have a good chat?' Aisha continues, but it's more polite than it is suspicious, and I fight hard not to squirm.

I shrug.

'Right. Well, it's good to know that you abandoned me at *your own* school reunion to go talk to your ex, and not even have the courtesy to let me know. I was getting worried about you, dropping off the face of the earth like that for a whole hour. I know how things were with you two – it's been like, ten years since you broke up, and you were just kids when you dated anyway. It's not that deep. What, do you think I would've bitched you out and had a problem with it? Give me some credit, Shaun. We've been together for five years. We're getting married. You're allowed to talk to some girl you knew when you were a teenager – it just would've been nice to have a little heads-up, that's all.'

'You're right,' I say, because it's all I've got. 'I'm sorry.'

Aisha nods, like she gets it, and I see in her face that she absolutely doesn't, and – there it is. The doubt that begins to creep in. It's not quite suspicion tainting the sparkle in her eyes, but something worse: worry, insecurity.

I squeeze her closer to reassure her she's got nothing to worry about, and wonder if she can feel the lie in it.

I don't even know if it is a lie. It's pure uncertainty, and somehow, I think, that's worse.

And then I hear myself blurting out, 'You're not going to ask me if anything happened? If I kissed her, or something?'

Aisha only rolls her eyes and scoffs. '*Please*. The state the two of you showed up in, but her lipstick is totally perfect? I don't need to insult us both by asking.'

But she doesn't laugh, and doesn't quite meet my eye when she brushes a few twigs and some mud off my shirt, and it feels off enough that I know she's not asking for the same reason I'm not telling her, because we both know the

278

answer to a question like 'did you kiss her' is a lot more complicated than just yes or no.

Bryony finishes up tallying names of people, and then studies the guestbook. My thumb draws arcs on Aisha's waist. A short way off, Steph and Curtis are having a hushed conversation and it looks serious – Morgan, Thea and Priya seem to have formed a protective wall in front of them and Curtis's head is bent low over hers, like a human blanket fort. His arms are around her, and Steph's hands flutter in between them in what I recognise as part of her usual emotive storytelling.

Is she telling him everything, or reassuring him?

I kiss the side of Aisha's head as I turn away, feeling sick as I wonder what I should be telling her. Feeling sick that there's anything to tell *at all*, and that I want to think of a good fucking way to spin it to spare her feelings.

She clings tightly to me, in a way that feels like a goodbye.

Chapter Thirty-Four

Hayden

'*Most Likely to Succeed*'

It isn't, really, anywhere near as much of a fuss as Bryony was making it all out to be. I set up the stepladder that's propped against the open cupboard; it's covered in flecks of paint and the metal groans before clicking into place, but it's sturdy enough when I climb up. The switches on the fuse box are all quite clearly labelled, even if the ink is a bit faded with time. I flip the master switch and lights flicker back on instantly. I hear them click and hum throughout the school; even the computer on the caretaker's desk whirs as it powers back up. I reset the fire alarm, too, finding the correct panel and switch.

It takes all of about two minutes, but when I climb down from the stepladder, I take a seat and sigh, burying my head in my hands, needing a moment.

I feel like this night has lasted for a thousand years. It feels like eons ago since I left the hall to follow Bryony. Even my phone call to say goodnight to Margot and Skye could have been whole decades ago.

I . . . really don't know if I can go back to that party. If I can face it all again.

I am exhausted.

Exhaustion is an old, familiar friend, after night feeds and the girls kicking me awake as they crawl into bed after a nightmare or just run rampant around the park while I try to keep up on a Saturday afternoon. But this isn't just weary, bog-standard, need-a-good-night's-sleep tired. This is heavy enough to make me want to slide to the floor, sink down through it, close my eyes and not open them until the world has moved on around me, because I cannot even contemplate returning to it.

What it is, I think, is not really being *fed up*, so much as anxiety. The old, familiar kind that had a hold on me when I was a teenager and creeps back in occasionally now. It tells me they're right, I'm wrong, everybody else knows something I do not and there is nothing I can do about that no matter how hard I try. They have it all figured out; I am the imposter, the fraud, and they all know it.

I suppose there is a chance that it's true – they're right; I'm wrong. I gave it all up and I shouldn't have, and they can all see that, and I'm the fool for burying my head in the sand.

Are they right?

Why do I care so badly if they are? These people I haven't even thought about for years, whose names I've mostly forgotten, faces I don't recall . . . Why do I suddenly value their opinions so highly, now?

I groan, the noise muffled against my palms, and wish I never came along tonight. It was a mistake.

Yes. *That* was the real mistake. Coming to the reunion,

thinking it would be anything like *fun* or remotely a good idea. That was a fool's errand.

The rest of my life – and God, I felt so *angry* about the rest of my life until that fire alarm went off and we had to spring into action. Some of that rumbles through my body now, but it doesn't have the same ferocity as before, and when I concentrate on it, I just feel pissed off at everybody who gave me those sad, sorry looks instead of that blazing, harrowing fury at the entirety of my life in the last ten years.

I am still angry. A bit at myself, yes, and mostly at them, and maybe that isn't very fair, either. But the one thing I'm certain of is that this anger isn't truly mine in the way I worried it would be. It's – a symptom. A side effect of the peer pressure and nostalgia. That will disappear with time, can be treated by distance, surely?

I wish I never came out tonight.

I wish they never instilled this doubt in me; I was happier living in ignorance.

School was draining enough when I *had* to be here. Why did I think it would be any different now? I owe these people nothing, and certainly no more of my emotional reserves or my time. I'm *tired*. I'm zapped. I want to sink into my hotel bed and treat this all like a bad dream, so I can leave it behind tomorrow and not take it with me.

Whatever everybody else thinks – whatever *I* started to think, earlier – I made the choices I made because they were what *I* wanted. Not just because they were best for the girls or for Lucy or even financially. I can regret not doing more for myself, but I can *also* contentedly stand by the choices I made in the last ten years. Those don't need to be mutually exclusive terms like everyone tonight seems so convinced they should be.

With the lights back on, I hear Bryony's playlist kick back on in the school hall, blaring through the speakers exactly where it left of, the final strains of the 'Macarena' bleeding into 'Stacey's Mom', and I wince. With the power back up, she'll surely corral everybody back into the hall to finish the party; even if some people make a move, I bet most will stick around to salvage their night out.

I, however, won't be one of them. I can slip away with the other people who decide they've had enough, disappear quietly, maybe message Bryony a *thanks for organising* or something after I'm gone, which is only polite under the circumstances.

But I'm *done*.

This reunion has taken enough from me already; I don't want to see what additional damage it can inflict in another hour or two. It's time to go home.

I clean my glasses on my shirt, scrub a hand through my hair and feel it sticking up on end, too unruly to bother tidying up now, and make my way back outside. I can hear shouting – no, cheering, and the volume of it only increases as I step through the entrance and some old classmates notice me.

The *whoop!* that cuts through the night is piercing, voracious enough to practically bowl me over. Someone – Shaun – lifts his fingers to his mouth to give a shrill whistle and the rugby lads start up a chant of my name, slicing it into two defined syllables in low bass notes.

'Hay-*den*! Hay-*den*! HAY-*DEN*!'

Other people join in the chant. People are applauding.

I'm the hero of the night, the party saviour, which is rich when RJ once accused me of being a party-pooper and tried to disinvite me from prom before Ashleigh verbally cut his legs out from under him.

Bryony turns to me, her whole body sagging in relief and a smile lighting up her face. It's much simpler than her usual practised, swaggering grin, and makes her look years younger. She mouths, 'Thank you,' to me. She might say it out loud, but I can't hear over the cacophony as everybody celebrates me.

So much for a quick getaway . . .

I don't know what to do with all the attention so for a couple of seconds I just stare blankly, trying to wrap my head around it.

When I was fourteen, I had a recurring nightmare that I forgot my PE kit and had to go to class dressed in my boxers and one of those vests my mum made me wear when I was little and it was cold out, and everybody would be picking teams for whatever sport my dream decided we were playing that lesson, and they'd start playing. And I'd realise, it was all of them against me. They'd all point and laugh and jeer and shout and inevitably, a ball of some description would come hurtling towards me and then I'd wake up, gasping and sweating.

So the baying crowd before me isn't . . . unfamiliar, exactly, but it still takes my brain a few seconds to catch up and make sense of it, and for the spike in my adrenaline to fade away.

I don't know what they want from me, so decide to treat it as if this was a game with Margot and Skye, and give them all my very best curtsey then a regal wave, calling, 'Thank you, thank you, so kind of you, thank you . . .'

Bryony steps up to me and grabs my arm in a frantic squeeze. 'All sorted?'

'Yup. Back up and running.'

She squeals, fingers pinching my arm, and she smacks a noisy, wet kiss on my cheek. 'You're a star! Literally, the star of the show. We owe you! Alright, gang,' she yells then, turning back to my adoring audience and making it her own once more. 'We are good to go! Party is back on!'

Everybody begins to surge forward as one, chattering and back in high spirits. I notice that nobody makes a move to leave, which feels like a kick in the teeth. They can't *all* be enjoying this reunion that much, can they? Hasn't *anybody* else had enough by now?

Fuck it. I'm still leaving. Might as well end on a high note, I suppose.

'Hey, have you seen Ash anywhere?' I ask Bryony. 'Only . . .'

She blanches, head jerking as if I had just slapped her, and she reels away from me to face the crowd once more.

'WAIT!' she bellows, making me wince, and she throws her arms out as if she can single-handedly stem the tidal wave of a hundred and fifty returning partygoers.

Which, unsurprisingly, she does. Bryony has always known how to keep people in the palm of her hand.

She cranes her neck, eyes scanning over our peers and their spouses. She consults her guestbook. She looks at everybody else again, and then swallows hard. Nobody moves, and people remain quiet, all curious and unsure.

And then Bryony asks, her voice carrying easily over everybody's heads, 'Where is Ashleigh? Ashleigh Easton? Has anybody seen her?'

There are rumblings of 'no'. Thea gets up on tiptoe and looks behind her like it's a game of *Where's Wally*. Roisin peers to her sides like Ashleigh might be there and she's only just noticing, and Josh gives a full-body shrug as he announces he hasn't seen her in a while.

I get my phone out of my pocket. There's no way Ashleigh would've left me to the wolves and bailed on me, but . . . maybe she didn't feel well? Maybe Ryan got under her skin a bit too much and she couldn't stick it anymore, or she felt embarrassed about having flirted with Freddie? But she hasn't texted me to say she wanted to leave or apologise for having left, and I know she would have done, so she must still be here somewhere.

Bryony looks at me, and I shrug.

With an exasperated sigh, she whips back to everyone else. 'You're telling me *nobody* has seen Ashleigh Easton for the last *hour*? For God's sake, people, someone must know something! She can't have just vanished into thin air!'

'Er . . .' Someone clears their throat and Bryony's gaze zeroes in on them. A few people shuffle to reveal Hiro, a violin in one hand and his other raised awkwardly. He coughs again and then says, 'Uh, I don't think Ryan ever signed the guestbook, Bryony. I haven't seen him for a while either.'

RJ whistles. 'Oh, shiiiiit . . .'

Priya squeals. 'Shut up.'

Shaun's girlfriend, Aisha, looks around. 'What? What's going on? What's the matter?'

Bryony throws her head back, hurls the guestbook to the floor and yells, 'Fuck!'

And Freddie Loughton cracks up laughing. 'I'm calling it now – those two have *definitely* murdered each other.'

286

Chapter Thirty-Five

Ashleigh

'Most Likely to Kill Each Other'

I'm not even pretending to myself anymore, not even for my own sense of self-preservation, because – really, what's the use? I just had sex with Ryan Lawal, and *it was great*. I'm almost willing to give him some leeway on what a swaggering, conceited prick he is, because he's certainly not all talk.

Almost. I've just been thoroughly fucked – I haven't completely lost my mind.

We don't bother to seek shelter from the sprinklers, both drenched in the instant they kick on, but I do eventually push Ryan off from on top of me to stand up on the bench and see if I can manually turn a couple of the sprinklers off, but it's no use. I don't see a valve anywhere to control them.

But, then again, I don't exactly *try* very hard to find one.

Not when I clamber down from the bench and Ryan catches me from behind to pull my body back against his, his hands roaming over my flesh. He starts kissing my neck, and I only put up a *slight* protest before leaning back against him to let him enjoy himself. The heat of his hands feels good, the roughness of his skin novel in its unfamiliarity, drawing all my nerve endings on edge in anticipation.

'We're getting soaked,' I tell him, in another feeble attempt to do something about the sprinklers. I even go so far as tugging my body forward slightly, even though my feet stay planted right where they are and I don't push his arms away.

I am shameless. And not the least bit sorry about it.

'Mm,' Ryan mumbles into my neck. He pushes a thick strand of hair away where it's fallen out of my updo and plastered itself, wet, to my shoulder. 'I thought it was meant to be romantic, kissing in the rain.'

I laugh again, and – God, when was the last time a man made me *laugh* like this? The last time anybody did, for that matter? Certainly, Ryan never did.

Would he have, if I didn't always assume that everything he said to me was some intentional ploy to undermine me and bully me? If I didn't search for an attack in every word, maybe he *would've* made me laugh. Maybe – we could've even had a friendly conversation.

No, let's not get too carried away.

But for right now, he's making me laugh, and I tell him, 'Ryan, this isn't romantic. This is a disaster.'

'Didn't sound like you thought that a few minutes ago.' He's smirking, I just *know* he is, and I want to wipe it off his face – except, he's not wrong, and his arms curl more firmly around my front so that I can't turn around to give him my usual *look* that would put him in his place.

'We're locked in the science lab while the fire alarm goes off. Explain to me what part of that *isn't* a disaster?'

He mumbles something that sounds like, 'I dunno,' and occupies himself kissing my neck again. I arch my head sideways to give him better access, but sigh as if this is all so terribly, awfully inconvenient.

Which it will be when we both catch pneumonia, but right now it's just a little water, and that's not the end of the world. (Actually, it's a *lot* of water. I am a little bit concerned about the puddles forming on the floor, sloshing around our feet.)

I do regain enough of a grip on my sanity to wriggle and get Ryan's attention.

'Plus,' I tell him, 'it's not romantic.'

'What?'

'Kissing in the rain. In – this.' I jerk my head at the water gushing from the ceiling. 'Us, right now, I mean, not the general trope of kissing in the rain. *We* aren't romantic, is what I mean.'

'Says who?'

'You're kidding, right?'

He shrugs, and lets go of me enough that I step forward and turn around. Ryan props an elbow on the bench to his left, crossing his legs at the ankles and leaning sideways. Considering the state of him, he should not be able to pull this off with anything *remotely* like arrogance. He should look like a drowned rat.

Except, of course, *he doesn't*. His shirt is still halfway unbuttoned, the sleeves clumsily rolled up, and the white fabric has turned see-through in all the water, sticking in patches to his taut, dark skin. That school tie he was enough of a prat to wear hangs loose around his neck. He's completely naked from the waist down, save for one sock on his right foot. I try to look pointedly at it, as if to undermine the whole thing he's got going on, but Ryan just grins at me, clearly enjoying the fact my attention has wandered south, and I give a long-suffering sigh. There's a scar on his left knee, twisted and pale, some of the skin around it puckered and warped.

I tear my eyes away from it, not wanting to make him uncomfortable. I might hate Ryan, but I'm not *that* much of an arsehole to him.

He shifts slightly, but only to get more comfortable in his thirty-degree lean, and then he raises his eyebrows at me. He used to give me that look all the damn time. *Explain. Go on, Ash, keep digging.*

I almost grit my teeth, but shake it off. We're *adults* now. Mature grown-ups who can have a mature conversation, even if we're both nearly naked and the fire alarm is still going off. I have to raise my voice to be heard over it, now he's not standing right behind me.

'This isn't the start of some epic love story, or something. This isn't the moment in the movie we declare our undying love for each other and run off into the sunset together. This was fun, yes, but it's . . . It's not *romantic.*'

'Because you don't want it to be,' he counters.

'And you do?'

I scoff, but . . . it immediately feels wrong. Not like a low blow, but simply incorrect. Didn't he stand there and tell me he wonders what kind of music I listen to and how I take my coffee? He knew about the time I dated my supervisor. He's not just been interested but *invested*, as aware of everything going on in my life as I have been with his – except with him, that's been a much more conscious, voluntary choice.

Is it so impossible that somewhere in the midst of that, he might've stopped hating me quite so vehemently?

I watch the emotions play out on Ryan's face, even as

the corner of his mouth pulls up in a self-effacing smirk and he rolls his eyes, looking off to the side. He looks totally unbothered by the water pounding down on him; I squint against it, less composed, and hold a hand over my eyes to try to shield my face a little bit.

He looks like he couldn't give two shits. Like I was a bit of fun and a good lay, but nothing special.

It's a good mask. But I've always been better at seeing through Ryan than he'd ever care to admit, so I notice the flicker of hurt in his eyes and the guarded look his face takes on, the way his features harden around the edges. When his eyes cut back to mine, they're every bit as derisive as a look I'd give him.

'Don't flatter yourself, Easton. Just trying to make a point.'

'Sure you were.'

'I said I flirted with you at school. I didn't say I wanted to go out with you now.'

'You're the one who brought up romance.'

'I brought up rain.'

I cut him a look but he just tips his head back and smiles wider, blinking only slightly against the water running down his face, and, just like that, I'm back to wanting to throttle him, sure he's only digging his heels in for the sole purpose of winding me up.

I cross my arms and hope that it looks half as cocky as his stance, when my boobs are out and my knickers are twisted all out of place, and my hair has half fallen out and is stuck to my face and back, makeup almost definitely smeared all over my face.

It doesn't escape my notice that there's a smear of my lipstick across Ryan's mouth.

Something about that makes my stomach flip, my toes curl.

But I stand my ground, pretend I'm not thinking about that, and say, 'Were you hoping I'd ask you out after this, Ryan, is that it? That you'd have finally won me round, got me onside, and now I'd be swooning at your feet begging you to take me out on a real date? Grow up.'

'*You* grow up,' he snipes, which only makes me roll my eyes because, wow, *what* an argument that is. Scowling, Ryan pushes away from the desk to stand upright, his shoulders squared and jaw clenched. 'I didn't fuck you to *win you round*, Ashleigh.'

'That's not what—'

'And what makes you think I'd want to date *you*, anyway? Just because you were a good shag, or we finally had something that halfway resembled a conversation for once? What, you think we're friends now? You . . .'

Ryan draws in a sharp breath and when he takes half a step forward, it's to level a finger accusingly at me, and the mask drops. There's no pretence of 'everybody's best friend' now, none of the charisma that got him so far in life. He is *seething*, but it's . . . warped, somehow. Wrong.

He . . . looks upset.

I don't think I've ever seen Ryan upset.

He's Mr Happy-Go-Lucky. Buoyant, and maybe a bit churlish or brooding when it suited him or he didn't get his way, but . . . God, it's disturbing to see him sad. It cuts sharp and deep right through my gut, realising I'm the one who's done that.

I've always wanted to take Ryan down a peg or two, hated how superior he acts, but I never set out to *hurt* him.

I'm not even really sure how I have.

He takes an uneven breath between gritted teeth, mouth working furiously as he thinks better of whatever he was about to say, and drops the finger he's pointing at me. His hand bunches into a fist at his side instead.

'You *still* refuse to do anything but think the worst of me. Can't you, for once in your self-righteous life, realise that maybe, I'm not the bad guy here? That, you know, maybe I'm a person, too? I can understand part of why you had such a low opinion of me at school and, believe me, you're not exactly absolved either, but – after everything, you can't just take me at face value? Tell me why you think I would ever want to ask you out when you consistently assume the worst of me, Ash. Tell me.'

I can't.

For once, I have no comeback to Ryan Lawal.

Chapter Thirty-Six

Ryan

'Most Likely to Kill Each Other'

She's driving me fucking crazy – and not in a good way anymore. But she's still sucking all the air out of the room and I'm still acutely attuned to her every breath and blink, and it's like I can *feel* the moment she crushes in on herself, when the truth hits her.

She's silent, and any other time, it'd be the greatest triumph of my life, to debate against Ashleigh Easton and leave her utterly speechless.

But this whole thing stopped being a game a long while ago and frankly, we're both too old to keep pulling this same shit ten years on.

I sigh, the fight leaving me when she doesn't try to argue or tell me I don't know my own mind, and – maybe I don't, actually, given that I even considered for a moment that things might have well and truly shifted between us. I really thought . . .

God, she's right. I am an idiot.

I sigh again, wipe some of the water off my face, only for

more droplets to take its place. The sprinklers are relentless and I wish I hadn't bothered to waste that time holding her close and kissing her and just let her go figure out how to turn them off instead.

The fire alarm keeps blaring, but I barely hear it.

Maybe Ashleigh and I are like one of those doomed, tragic couples from the books the girls all used to gush over in the common room. Linked together in a way that can't be broken, destined to ruin each other.

And I'm so fucking tired of it. Isn't she?

'Ryan . . .'

I pretend I don't hear her.

When the water around our feet splashes as she takes a step towards me, I lean back against the bench so she's side-on and she gets the message, stopping in her tracks. Her sadness is palpable, and I hate that. Like she has any kind of right to stand there, so wounded, and make *me* want to comfort her, when she's the one who keeps lashing out?

Go to hell, I almost snap at her.

Except I don't, obviously, because I don't want to prove her right. That'd be just like her – to turn this all around and win the fight without even having to say anything.

The silence that consumes us is so sudden, it feels like my brain short-circuited. There's a ringing in my ears like after a good night out, so it takes a second to realise that the fire alarm has finally stopped.

The lights suddenly flash back on, too.

Ashleigh winces as her eyes adjust. I blink a few times.

'Power's back up,' I say, and she doesn't even roll her eyes or say something like, *You think, smartass?*

In the bright overhead lighting, I see what a mess the

room is: a layer of water covers the floor, the pile of textbooks at the back of the room is drenched, and water sits in puddles on the tops of the desks.

Ashleigh and I haven't fared much better. I reckon I must look pretty shabby, soggy and half dressed with my dick hanging out like this, but – I choke down a laugh, because she's in such a state. Her makeup has partly washed off and only the faintest smudge of lipstick remains right in a line along the edge of her lower lip, right in the middle; her lips are swollen and the half of her hair that's still pinned up resembles a bird's nest more than anything else. A streak of mascara has run sideways across her right cheek, like she wiped her face and smeared it there. She sees me looking at her and briskly crosses her arms over her chest to cover herself, not looking in the least bit abashed at how the rest of her looks right now.

I turn away from Ashleigh and start the search for my clothes. I find my boxers bundled inside my trousers, in a sodden heap kicked to the front of the classroom. On my way back, I collect Ashleigh's trousers from where they dangle over a tap at one of the sinks, water dripping steadily off them, and I toss them her way. She catches them, and passes me the sock she finds. I hand her back her blouse.

Clothes bundled against her bare chest, she asks through gritted teeth, 'Can you see my bra anywhere?'

I look with her for a couple of minutes, under desks and in sinks and on tabletops, but we both come up empty. Her jaw is still clenched and she mutters, 'It's fine, never mind,' while sounding like she's screaming a string of curses in her head. Probably at me. Probably making it my fault for flinging it to some unseen place in my haste to get my hands and mouth on her.

Which, fine, it might be. This one time.

The two of us get dressed in silence.

For all of about two seconds, anyway. I start muttering curses, wrestling against the soaked fabric as I try to get my trousers on, and Ashleigh makes soft, agitated grunts as she fights to get back into her top. She gets stuck with both arms trapped upright, above her head, face half hidden and body wriggling uselessly.

I catch her eye, choking down a laugh.

She rolls her eyes, but more like it's a joke we're both in on.

'Need some help?' I offer, and her eyebrows draw together before she nods.

'Yes, please.' Her voice is muffled from where she's trapped within the fabric. I finish pulling on my boxers, grimacing at the sensation of cold, wet clothes, and then go help Ashleigh. I don't let my hands wander this time, and don't bother to enjoy the fact that she's stopped being so bloody-minded for the moment. I just concentrate on yanking her top into place and getting her unstuck, but my fingers graze her arms and sides and her skin is covered in goosebumps. She's trembling – shivering.

And damn it, damn her to the deepest, darkest circle of hell, because as mad as I am at her and as much as every word out of her mouth is a slap in the face – I rub my hand up and down her arm, and then I do her favourite fucking thing in the world and point out the obvious. 'You're freezing.'

'I'm *fine*.'

Oh, obviously she's fine, because her usual stubborn attitude has made a triumphant return.

I throw my hands up in defeat and storm away. Except,

297

I don't exactly do that, because my feet carry me over to the chemical cabinet at the back of the room and I yank open the packet on the wall containing the fire blanket, then storm *right back to her*, to shove it into her hands.

She looks at me like I've lost my mind.

Again, she may be correct on this occasion.

I push it at her and this time, she takes it. 'It's better than nothing. Keep the chill off, or something, anyway.'

She swallows thickly. 'Thanks. Thank you.'

I grunt, when what I really mean to say is 'you're welcome', but I guess I'm not used to saying those words to Ashleigh Easton, and I guess they stick in my throat or something. She wraps the fire blanket awkwardly around her shoulders like a shawl and starts trying to put her trousers back on. I follow suit, which is easier said than done, and I wonder if it would really be such a bad thing if I just gave up and walked out of here with them slung over my shoulder.

Give 'em all a show, at least.

Make sure everybody would be talking about this party for years.

I sit down, but that doesn't seem to be working, then try rolling the leg up like I saw Ashleigh do, and bring it all the way up before unrolling it, but the fabric twists and get stuck halfway up my thighs and I lose my balance and stumble, and twist my leg *again* when I misstep, and fall hard back against the nearest bench.

'Damn it!'

'Are you okay?'

'Fine,' I tell her, even though we both know I sound anything but. It's mostly frustration, though, the twinge of pain passing quickly. She must be *loving* this – I can't even

298

put my trousers on properly. She'll dine out on this for years at my expense.

I finally get them on and sort out my belt, then pick up my jacket from where it landed in a heap on the floor. I shake it out and check my phone (which seems fine, despite having been sat in my waterlogged jacket for several minutes, just low enough on battery that I turn it off to conserve the little power it has left), and then I notice Ashleigh staring at me.

Or, you know. Pretend to only just notice it.

I raise an eyebrow at her. She huddles inside the fire blanket, hands together and wrists propped on the edge of one of the benches as she watches me with a frown. She doesn't maintain eye contact very long, and I'm about to find something else to distract myself with so I don't have to keep paying her so much attention, but then she glances up again and I'm trapped, those blue eyes rendering me immobile.

And then she says, 'I'm sorry,' and I think I've hit my head and started hallucinating.

'What?'

'I'm sorry. And I know it's – it's too little, too late, and you probably aren't interested in hearing it, just like I said I wasn't either, but, I thought, I still appreciated an apology, and . . . And you deserve one. I'm sorry, Ryan.'

I don't really know what to say to that. I wasn't prepared for her to . . .

Do I say thank you? Is that how this works?

Predictably, Ashleigh takes advantage of my silence to continue talking. 'I'm sorry I was so mean to you at school and that I keep doing it now, even when you're not giving me reason to. You're right, I – I keep thinking the worst of you, and . . . "old habits die hard" is a really pathetic excuse, but it's true. And I think it's a sort of . . . self-defence mechanism? It's hard for me to believe you take me seriously even after all this time, and—'

I interrupt her with a short bark of laughter.

She scowls at me.

'You think I don't take you *seriously*?' I echo. 'Easton, you're the most serious person I know. You were fourteen going on forty, for Christ's sake. Do you even hear yourself right now?'

'That never stopped you!'

'Yeah, because we were kids! That's . . .' I shake my head. 'I already apologised. We were focusing on your apology here. But for the record, I have always taken you seriously.'

She doesn't look entirely convinced, but doesn't argue either.

'I think I'm still trying to process the fact that you ever even *tried* to be nice to me, and weren't just consistently taking the piss out of me. That you're, um . . .' She clears her throat. 'Not doing that now, either.'

I suck my teeth and pull a face. 'I probably was, to be fair. But like, only about half the time. Alright, maybe . . . Maybe like, two thirds of the time.'

Ashleigh gives me a flat look, but there's something indulgent in it, in the slight curve of her lips and the tilt of her head. She says, 'Anyway. I'm sorry – and I mean that.'

'Okay. Er, thank you, then, I guess.'

'You're welcome.' The words seem hard for her, too, and I crack a more sincere smile over that. Then Ashleigh takes a breath, stands upright, collects her shoes and bag, and makes for the door.

Which still has a little red light on the security pad next to it.

And which, just like earlier, doesn't budge when she tries to open it.

The grin stretches wide across my face when she gives me a put-upon look, and I like that she's a bit shorter than me now she's not wearing those heels. I like that she doesn't look too sorry to be stuck this time, too.

'Looks like we're still not free.'

What a shame, I think, but out loud I just say, 'Still got that flask, Easton?'

Chapter Thirty-Seven

Bryony

'Most Likely to Become Famous'

The second Freddie Loughton makes that joke about how Ashleigh and Ryan will have actually killed each other, I want to kill him. Because, you know, he's probably *right* – they've barely even looked at each other all night but everybody's noticed the tension. Those two are a goddamn inferno. There's an equal chance that Ashleigh will have either strangled Ryan with his own intestines or is currently forcing him to listen to a thirty-eight-point presentation on all the ways she thinks he is aiding and abetting a government she cannot and will not support.

(I bet if he was Green Party, she'd totally deny climate change, though. That's what the Green Party are all about, right?)

Anyway, *whatever* is going on with the two of them right now, it sends up nothing but red flags as everybody confirms that they're both missing, and have been for ages, which is just, you know, totally *great*, absolutely *fine*.

Except obviously, if they're missing, it'll be to one-up

each other. There will be annotated flaccid penises galore on the whiteboards, or they'll have broken into a DT room to try to show off some skill or other, or they'll have gone and found the old common room sort-of-but-not-really changed and be rearranging all the furniture . . .

Long story short – they'll be up to no good.

It is *totally* incidental to everything that Ashleigh is smart enough to glom onto the fact that there's a ton of proof around the school that I work here, if she bothers to look, which she absolutely will. And it is pure *coincidence* that without Ryan being the centre of attention and flirting shamelessly and cracking jokes, the party vibe might die down quicker than I'd like it to and it'll be a really boring, dry end to the night.

No, it's definitely the 'up to no good' thing that's the problem here. Absolutely.

'What's the big deal?' Noodles Greg asks, grinning and inching towards the doors like he can skirt around me, *like I won't notice*, which only pisses me off more. 'She'll be around somewhere!'

'Yeah, *somewhere*, that's my problem! Nobody's meant to be *anywhere* except the school hall!' My voice rises to a higher pitch. 'And—'

'She's an adult, mate!' Greg has the audacity to *clap me on the shoulder*, then, and I'm about ready to throw hands. I seethe as he grins at everybody else, oblivious. 'Come on, let's all get back to enjoy the rest of the party before we totally sober up!'

'No! Nobody's going anywhere until we track them down. I have to . . . Fuck. Fuck!'

It's not that I don't think they can look after themselves.

303

It's that when the two of them are together, it's a ticking timebomb, and they're both willing to take drastic measures to fuck the other one over.

And, ultimately, all they're doing is fucking *me* over. I bet they caused the power cut somehow. I bet they even pulled the fire alarm for a joke, and it had nothing to do with me and the fuse box. They've ruined my one perfect night. Just one night! With everyone believing I am who I want to be. Feeling like my old self again. Was that so much to ask? Was it really so goddamn unreasonable?

Steph comes over, cutting Greg a look to send him away, and then gives me a gentle, patient smile, like *she's* not in my bad books too, right now. But she says softly, 'Bryony, help us understand. Ashleigh and Ryan will be around somewhere, like Greg said. Why don't we just call them and tell them to come back?'

'Tried,' Hayden says, waggling his phone. 'Ashleigh's going straight to voicemail. I texted her, but no dice.'

'Yeah, I couldn't get hold of Ryan, either; I just tried him but got the same thing,' Hiro informs us.

Steph bites her lip, doing her best to give me a reassuring smile. 'I'm sure they can't have gotten into *too* much trouble.'

'Yeah,' RJ shouts over, and the rugby lads starts nodding like the Churchill dog and egging him on. Amped up by the instant support, RJ calls, 'And what's the big deal if they have, anyway? Not like they couldn't pay for any damages.'

'Or pay to get the bloodstains cleaned up,' Freddie adds, and I *hate* the laughter that follows.

And I crack.

I lose it. My composure, my last nerve, any semblance of willpower – it all goes flying out of me in an instant and I transform like the witch in *Into the Woods*, shedding this beautiful, pristine, glamorous shell to become something wretched and warped in front of their very eyes. I feel the way my face twists into an ugly snarl, hands curving into a claw-like grip on thin air at my sides, and I see the alarm in some people's faces, Steph's included, as I round on the rugby lads. They were mostly good banter when we were teenagers but now I'm on the other side of it, they are the bane of my life, and not the sexy Anthony Bridgerton kind. The annoying, want-the-skin-to-melt-off-my-face, about-to-scream kind.

Which may really, ultimately, be a me problem, but I'm about to make it a them problem.

Boy, am I about to make it their problem.

'This isn't *funny*,' I snap at them, and a little spit flies from my mouth. I decide I don't care. 'This isn't a *joke*, so you can stop laughing right now. You have no idea what I went through trying to pull this party together tonight, and all *you lot* have done is try to flout the rules I set and take advantage. It's like none of you have grown up in the last ten years! None of you!' I add, turning to the wider crowd, and they're a captive audience, and it makes my adrenaline spike just like if they were seated and I were on stage, and that makes me feel – for once – sick to my stomach.

I think I finally understand stage fright, because I'm about this close to vomiting.

But the show must go on, and my voice is still spilling out of my open mouth and I can't seem to stop it.

'None of you have any idea what it took to make tonight happen. Like it was just an email, maybe a phone call, ba-da-bing, ba-da-boom, but it's *not*. If things go tits-up

305

tonight – which, let's face it, they kind of already have – this isn't just an invoice I'll send to someone for busting a lock on a classroom door or a complaint over some scribbling on whiteboards, this is my job on the line!'

'Your job?' Steph asks, and she's not the only one.

And I'm *crying*, which is the icing on the cake. It's going to ruin my eyeliner. I sniffle and throw my head back, dabbing my fingertips at the corners of my eyes and trying to will the tears away. It doesn't work as well as I hoped it would.

'What do you mean, your job is on the line?' Roisin asks me.

'Do you, like . . .' Hiro laughs, and it's a bit nervous. 'D'you work here, or something?'

'Bryony,' says Trendy Elise, mouth agape. 'Are *you a teacher here?*'

One night.

That's all I wanted, just one night, living the lie I've crafted oh so carefully in an effort to keep my dreams alive.

For *ten years*, they've believed I was genuinely, truly making it as an actress. Living my best life. Being the main character – sort of. For ten whole years, they've liked my Insta posts and occasional Facebook updates and have all lived in awe, on tenterhooks to one day see me pop up as the leading lady in a trailer for a new movie as they're scrolling TikTok or whatever, stunned by the glitzy life they all knew I was destined to lead.

And all it's taken is one night to undo it all.

Time moves slowly in the next couple of seconds. I watch eyes bugging wide and jaws dropping, practically hear the cogs whirring as my old friends all turn to each other to whisper about how I pulled the wool over their eyes, everybody so confused and exhilarated by this plot twist like the reveal about the killer in a *Knives Out* movie.

It's my final flourish. The curtain descends. Hold the applause. Exit stage left, hand off your wig and props as you go. House lights come back on; reality resumes.

I blink, feeling cold all over, the sequins on my jumpsuit chafing nastily against my arms, threatening to leave my skin all raw and scratched-up tomorrow, and the sound of muttering and whispers hits me like a brick wall.

I can feel Hayden looking at me, but I don't want to see what the expression on his face is. If I were him, I'd be feeling pretty smug right now; I deserve this exposure, after I kept cutting people down to size all night. I'm no better than any of them. But Hayden's a good guy, and that's worse because I think he might be looking at me like he feels *sorry for me*, and I don't think I can handle that right now.

In fact, I don't want to handle *any* of this right now. The fallout belongs to Famous Bryony, and Famous Bryony can't come to the phone right now. She is . . .

She's not dead, because she never existed.

I let habit take over as I turn to Steph, and I raise my voice. Projecting, not like I would for a performance, but to be heard across the playground when I'm on duty.

'I need some people to help track down Ashleigh and Ryan. Trustworthy people – ones who know the school. Morgan, Hassan, Josh, you take the top floor; Priya, Thea and Hiro, you take the second . . . Roisin, Elise, I need you to check around the maths department. Steph and Shaun, you take the music and drama rooms. Hayden – you can come with me. Everybody else – back to the school hall. The music's still going, so enjoy the party.'

It sounds more like a threat than anything else, but they're all smart enough not to argue with me, shuffling en masse back indoors.

I trudge back to Hayden, snatching the elbow of his shirt and yanking him inside with me. We'll check some of the common areas and the gym, and I guess we'd better swing by the science department in case that's not locked up properly.

God, what a mess.

Hayden wriggles his arm and I think he's trying to shake me off, but when I do let go, he does it again and bumps me to get my attention. I can't look at him, but he says quietly, 'I'm sorry it all came out like that, B, but . . .'

'If you tell me it's "for the best", I might have to lock you in that cupboard by the English rooms.'

He gives a breath of laughter, and something in me relaxes a little. 'I was going to say, that was pretty badass.'

I snort. Yeah, not fucking likely. It was pathetic, and I tell Hayden, 'That's a pathetic attempt at cheering me up. But . . . thanks.'

'Sure. What're friends for?'

Chapter Thirty-Eight

Steph

'Most Likely to End Up Together'

'I'm sorry, sweetie,' I tell Curtis, making a beeline back to him before I follow Bryony's instructions, which I don't dare disregard right now. 'I should . . .'

Just go wandering off again with my ex-boyfriend, the one I very nearly kissed after spending an hour alone with him at the back of the school, immediately after telling my fiancé every single detail of it all. That's not a red flag in the slightest, is it?

But kind, lovely Curtis just nods, and throws a smile at Bryony as she retreats into the school. 'Seems like your friend is really going through something – go on, it's fine. I hope you find the others. We'll talk later, though?'

It's timid, edged with that nervousness I saw in him at the beginning of our relationship, spiking up again around our milestone moments. It's a request, a plea, and one I'm so grateful to have the chance for. I nod, and we kiss each other on the cheek before I peel away to join the search parties.

God, I love this man.

I hope he still loves me, after all this.

Shaun is saying something to his fiancée, who looks, understandably, pretty miffed. I hope that they manage to work things out, too; I know I'm not responsible for Shaun's mistakes, but I still feel guilty for any hurt I've caused her. Still, she smiles politely enough to me, wrapping her arms around her waist before she follows the tide of people making their way back to the hall.

The others are already on their way to start looking for Ashleigh and Ryan, and Shaun and I are left standing alone outside.

He struggles to look at me and jabs a thumb over his shoulder. 'We'd better . . .'

I nod, having to clear my throat. 'Yes. Definitely.'

For a second or two, neither of us move, and I can tell that Shaun's wondering if, as soon as we venture off alone together, we'll resurrect that feeling from the back steps and be about to kiss all over again.

My stomach flips; I can't quite tell if it's nerves or butterflies.

It feels different this time as we wander the school corridors. Lights are already turned on and there is a hubbub of voices that seems to come from all around, the other people Bryony dictated as her search parties chattering away and their voices bouncing off the ceilings, amplified. It doesn't feel like this is out of bounds or against the rules now, and the silence between Shaun and I stretches on, curdling into something tense and agitated that scratches at my skin and makes me want to run in the opposite direction.

Hoping that if I break the silence, things might find a

more normal balance, I say, 'That was a bit of a surprise, finding out . . .'

And at the exact same time, Shaun says, 'Wild about Bryony, don't you . . .'

We make eye contact again, both of us smiling now, and the horrible, nasty tension dissipates instantly.

And . . . there is nothing else rising up in its wake. It's as if a spell has been broken and the nostalgia stripped away, and this doesn't feel like reconnecting with my first love anymore, the great unanswered question in my life. It feels quiet, and *normal*, and like when I got chatting to the girls again or saw Greg or Hiro or Hayden. There's a nice, warm feeling in my heart at spending time with someone I once knew well – but now, it's not joined by attraction or heartache or anything else.

Shaun waves for me to continue, so I say, 'Yes, it is a bit wild, isn't it? I just didn't see it coming from her! Online, she always looks so . . . And she's got all those stories! It can't all be untrue; I don't believe that.'

He shrugs. 'I guess maybe it's something she does on the side and isn't as successful as we all thought. I just can't imagine her as a *teacher*. I mean – Bryony!'

I laugh, knowing what he means. She's so fierce and bright and bold, and . . . 'I don't know, she seemed quite stern when she was telling us all off. If she's half as enthusiastic about teaching as she was about pulling this party together, I bet she does a great job.'

Shaun hums thoughtfully, smiling as he pictures it. 'Yeah, to be fair. She must be a really fun teacher.'

We start with our search of the music and drama class-rooms, and I give an excited little squeal when I find Bryony's name on one of the doors. Maybe it isn't quite the same as seeing it in the credits of a movie, but even so. I do feel bad for her that she felt she had to hide it all this time, and I hope she's not embarrassed or ashamed. She doesn't deserve that. And I hope she doesn't get any flak from her bosses about the fire alarm or the state we might be leaving the school in; she has tried so hard to keep order tonight, and that was apparent even before the power cut or the fire alarm went off.

Most of the classroom doors are locked, but Shaun and I knock and call, 'Hello? Ryan? Ashleigh? Are you in there?' just in case anyway. It doesn't take long to clear through, and by then we've looped all the way around to the edge of the maths department. Roisin and Elise are nowhere to be seen, so they must already have gone back to the party; I wonder if they found them.

'Well, the coast is all clear here.' I get my phone out and, since I don't have her number, I find Bryony on Instagram, so I can send her a DM and let her know. As I'm doing that, I say, 'I suppose we should head back—'

'Wait. Wait, just . . . Please?'

I look up to find Shaun has stepped in front of me, keeping his distance but a hand raised, palm out, and a crushed expression on his face that I immediately understand, with a pang of sympathy – not for him, but for who we used to be. Once we go back to the party, that's it; both of us will have to face up to what almost happened outside on the steps and *really* speak to our partners about it, and deal with whatever happens next, but that won't involve each other. We might not ever bump into each other again after this, and simply return to liking each other's social media posts every once in a while, and occasionally commenting politely and supportively.

This is our last chance to talk.

So, I wait, and Shaun lowers his hand and takes a shaky breath.

I am prepared for the speech I know is going to come out of his mouth because I have already thought it all, too, in the last twenty minutes. It's been so good to reconnect and hopefully we can stay in touch, but we both got carried away and should never have . . .

'I think we should give us a go,' he says.

Wait, what?

I blink rapidly, not sure I heard correctly. 'Pardon?'

Shaun repeats himself, and adds, 'You and me. We both needed to go our separate ways ten years ago, but I think tonight has made us both realise that we made some mistakes, and this – *us* – isn't all in the past. We could have a real future together, Steph. We're endgame – meant to be, like everybody always said we were. Tonight's made me remember how much I love you, and I think we should give it a real chance.'

I'm stunned into speechlessness, lips parted and unable to do anything except stare at Shaun and search his face in case this is some sort of joke, but he is entirely earnest. He carries on, emboldened by his own words, and paints a picture of the life we were always supposed to have together, the one he believes we could still have.

It's a pretty picture, and so achingly familiar.

He talks about the big house we would have near good schools, the dogs and the kids and the weekend barbecues with friends and family and neighbours, the big white wedding and the holidays to France to visit his parents in the summer holidays, but not like it's an old, half-forgotten daydream this time – like it's the reality he craves. He tells me how happy and content we would be, how we'd do it all right, and would grow old together in the home we make, watching our children grow up and looking after grandkids in the school breaks.

And . . .

None of it matches up with the life I've envisaged for myself in the last few years. It's all the life I thought I wanted when I was a teenager and in love, because it's everything you're told to want.

I'm shaking my head and Shaun reaches for my hands, an urgency glittering in his eyes and edging his words.

'I know it's scary, Steph, and I'm not saying nobody would get hurt – we're both engaged to other people, and . . . I'm not saying it would be easy, but it feels so right, you know? It's like you said – we got it all wrong. *This* is how it's supposed to go, for us. We can still make that happen!'

'That isn't . . . Shaun, that's not . . .'

I stumble back, pulling my hands from his, and close my eyes for a moment as I try to concentrate on forming a clear, coherent sentence.

'I don't want that,' I finally tell him.

Now it's his turn to stare, not comprehending. 'What?'

'I'm sure it would be a lovely life, but it's not for me. I don't want any of those things. I like my flat in the city centre, even if the only green we have is some house plants, because we don't even have a balcony. I don't want pets, and I don't want children. I enjoy my career but I want to retire early, and travel. Maybe take up crafts, or cooking

314

classes, or learn another language. I don't want any of those things like you're talking about, Shaun, and, even if I did . . . I wouldn't want them with you.'

I cringe, hating how that sounds, even if it's true.

'What I mean,' I press on, 'is that I did get it all wrong, in doubting my relationship with Curtis. I wasn't expecting all those old feelings to return so strongly when I saw you tonight, but – *that* was the mistake, giving in to them, letting them blind me to what I have. What I want. *Who* I want. We'll always have a connection, Shaun, and you'll always have a place in my heart, but . . . I love Curtis and if you're going to ask me to choose, then, I choose him. Every time, I'll choose him.'

Shaun's lovely brown eyes fill with tears, but his face is slack with shock. I give him some space to digest what I've just said, not wanting to upset him or push him.

When he finally closes his mouth and nods a bit, his first question is, 'Did you tell Curtis about what happened?'

It's not a threat, I understand that; he's only confused, and I sense the guilt there, too, and realise he didn't tell Aisha anything. I'm too stunned to fully process that right now. How could he have not immediately confessed? Didn't he feel even half as guilty as I did about what almost happened?

But in answer to his question, I nod and say, 'Yes. I told him everything. And we still have some things to talk about, but I have to hope he'll understand how overwhelming it was to see you again, and that even if I thought I wanted to kiss you, I was still thinking about him and feeling horrible and guilty for it. If that's not something we can move past, then it's something I'll have to deal with, but I can't just throw that away. Not for anything. I'm sorry, Shaun, but whatever happens, I just can't picture a future that includes you in it.'

I twist my engagement ring around my finger, centring the diamond where it has slipped sideways, and I hope that my future will still include Curtis. But I know, in my bones, even as I look at Shaun's stricken face and feel I've broken his heart all over again, that whatever happens next, I've made the right decision.

Chapter Thirty-Nine

Hayden

'Most Likely to Succeed'

I try phoning Ashleigh again but it keeps dropping or else goes to voicemail, so I hang up and send her yet another text.

> Where are you??????? Starting to worry! Did you go home? Just let me know you're okay?

I realise what a helicopter dad I sound like to my best friend, a grown-ass woman who can more than take care of herself, but I *am* really starting to worry a bit now. This feels like that time Margot insisted on playing hide-and-seek at the park a few years ago, only to run off and hide behind a tree outside the playground. I almost called the police when I couldn't find her and she didn't come running when I yelled her name.

She is a fiercely competitive little monkey. I had all the parents and kids in the park looking for her before we tracked her down. It was the longest, most unbearable eight minutes of my life.

And Ashleigh has been MIA for a lot longer than eight minutes.

'Do you think she and Ryan have *actually* had it out?' I ask Bryony, who has been agitated and muttering and huffing and puffing like she's going to blow the school down for the last several minutes of our search. We clear the common areas and school gym, which I notice has had an upgrade, and pass Morgan and the boys on their way back to the party, after they've had no better luck than us.

Bryony scoffs. 'Wouldn't surprise me. They hated each other at school.'

'She still does. Any time he's on the telly, she gripes about him. Sends me articles that pop up on her newsfeed about him, so she can slate him. I . . . don't always have the heart to tell her I don't think he's such a bad guy.'

'Total vendetta,' she mumbles, and I can tell I've only got half her attention. It seems better than none, under the circumstances. 'He never shut up about her, you know. I dunno if you ever hung around him much at school—'

'We both know I didn't.'

Bryony lightens up as she leans into the gossip. 'Well, she was practically all he ever wanted to talk about. Ashleigh this, Ashleigh that, do you know what she said in class earlier, did we see the glare she gave him in assembly, did anybody else notice how put out she looked when he got top marks in the French vocab test and she didn't? Oh, Ashleigh's too stuck-up to come to a party, Ashleigh's steam-rolled over his sports-day plans and made it into a fundraiser, Ashleigh, Ashleigh, *Ashleigh*.' She rolls her eyes, and laughs. 'God, they were obsessed with each other. Guess nothing changes.'

'Guess not.'

'Can't wait to get fired for a double murder on school property,' she jokes, but then her smile slips and she huffs and puffs again. 'That's just what I need right now. And I bet my whole part in it for organising this reunion in the first place means I'd go viral, and then *definitely* nobody would want to work with me, because I'd have such a tainted reputation. I'd be, like, cursed. I'd be the new *Macbeth*.'

Something about how she says it sets my teeth on edge.

I surprise both of us when I mutter, 'Could you cut it out already?'

'*Excuse* me?'

I didn't really mean to say it. It just slipped out.

But she's not going to let it go, and maybe that's for the best. Maybe I *need* this outlet, and if I could endure Bryony's whinging for the last hour or so, she can certainly put up with a few minutes of it from my side.

So I stop in my tracks just outside the science block, and frown at her.

'This pity party you're throwing for yourself. Nobody's forcing you to continue going to auditions or anything, if you find it so miserable and it makes you cry. You told me you *like* being a teacher – and if you were scared about people finding out, well, it's happened. The world didn't end, did it? Nobody laughed at you. Nobody pointed the finger at you and told you what a failure you are, how sad your life is. Nobody would *dare* – not like how they've been doing it to me all night long. I know you like to believe you're the main character, but some of us have real lives and real feelings, too; you're not the only person feeling sorry for themselves or wishing things had turned out a bit differently,

319

you know? You don't think I'm not angry about things, that I don't want to shout and scream and throw my toys out of the pram? Well – maybe I didn't, before tonight, but still. This isn't how the world works, Bryony. You don't get to be this self-centred and claim to have all these dreams and not put in the effort – because from what you've told me, it sounds like you gave up on yourself a *long* time ago. How do you expect anybody else to root for you, in that case?'

Bryony's lower lip wobbles, and, oh, brilliant, I've made her *upset*.

'Do you really think I've given up on myself?' she whispers.

'Why else are you going around lying to everybody about what you do? Moping about it, instead of doing something to change it?'

It's only as I lay this out for her, able to see it clearly because it's not my life and I'm not caught up in the middle of it, that I realise how it reflects on myself. I've never felt bad about how my life turned out; I don't mope around every day and feel sorry for myself about it.

She asked me earlier if I was happy, and I didn't really have an answer, because the night had made me wonder if my wilful ignorance could count as happiness.

But – maybe it's not ignorance. Maybe it's just growing up. Taking responsibility. Understanding that the world is so much bigger than *just me*.

And, I think, I am happy with my life.

I tell her as much, and say, 'It'd be nice if you could let yourself be happy in your life, too, B. You've always been such a huge personality and presence; it's sad to think you've made yourself so small.'

Bryony's mouth falls open into a small O, and I see something click into place for her.

I think maybe she needs a hug, but that's the moment I notice the wet floor and all the water pooling out from the science block.

Chapter Forty

Ashleigh

'Most Likely to Kill Each Other'

I'm in a stand-off with Ryan, whose eyes glint and crinkle at the corners with barely restrained laughter, until I finally snatch the flask out of his outstretched hand and take a swig, admitting to the fact that, yes, okay, I did have a sex dream about him. *Once.* Like, *forever ago.* It was hardly intentional or anything.

He drank, too, though, so at least it's not just me being humiliated here in our second round of Never Have I Ever.

'Check your phone again,' I snap at him, before he *does* laugh at me. 'Have you got a signal yet?'

He sighs. 'Ash . . .'

I check mine for the billionth time, even though I already know what I'm going to see. A screen full of error messages letting me know about all the texts to Hayden that have failed to send. He won't just go home and not try to find me to say goodbye though, will he? So he'll notice I'm not at the party and he'll find me eventually, right? We won't have to, I don't know, smash a window and escape that way, or risk being trapped here until Monday morning . . .

Just as my brain starts to run away with itself about how bad this situation might be, there's a shriek from the other side of the locked door.

There's a muffled voice and then a shrill response of, 'Are you kidding me? It's not just *a bit of water*. The fucking sprinkler system! Oh, God, I'm *so* fired. And my shoes are going to be *ruined*.'

Ryan and I gawp at each other for a moment before springing into action. His body crowds behind mine as we both pound on the door, yelling 'hello' and 'help' and all that kind of stuff. The sound of feet splashing in our direction and the arrival of our rescuers – Bryony being one of them, from the sound of it – has adrenaline shooting through my veins.

'Ash, you in there?'

Oh, thank God, it's Hayden! I *knew* he wouldn't abandon me. Seriously, shoutout to his dad-honed instincts for trouble.

'Yes! Hi! It's me! The door's locked itself, and I—'

'Is Ryan in there with you?' he shouts through the door.

Bryony screeches, 'We all thought you two had killed each other!'

Ryan laughs, his breath hot at my ear and neck with the sound, sending a delicious little shiver down my spine. He doesn't move away and his left hand is braced against the door, near my waist, so he's completely encasing me. The proximity does things to me, just like that lean he did earlier.

I wonder how long we would've carried on enjoying each other, oblivious to the rest of the world. How long we could've hidden out here.

He's saying, 'Hayden, mate, Bryony, can confirm – Ryan here. Proof of life! Get us out of here, will you?'

'No worries! I've got the code saved somewhere in an email . . . Give me a couple of minutes, okay?' Bryony tells us. 'Try not to kill each other, LOL!'

I turn away from the door, expecting this to be the moment Ryan steps back – only he doesn't.

I don't know what's going on between us here; our latest argument and my apology didn't feel like the petty sniping we would both default to around each other. It felt heavy, *real*. I'm not sure if that shift is because we've grown up, or because we had sex, but I don't suppose it matters anyway. It's still shifted. The fragile sense of mutual understanding and sarcastic quips we exchanged in the last few minutes since I apologised feels so tentative, I'm terrified of saying the wrong thing and ruining it, even in an attempt to get closer to him again.

But Ryan lifts a hand to push some wet hair back from my face, and my eyes slide closed, and for once I'm glad to let him take the lead, grateful for his ridiculously high levels of self-confidence. He doesn't seem scared I'll push him away.

His palm stays on my face, cupping my cheek, fingers splayed back into my hair and resting against my neck. And I want to sink into him – not to kiss him, just to let myself be *held* by him.

'What are you doing to me, Ashleigh?' he asks, just like he did earlier, but that's different this time, too. This isn't hoarse and turned on; it's quiet and yearning, in a way I never would've imagined Ryan to be capable of, and I didn't know I was the kind of person to want – to *need* – to hear that.

I don't know when Ryan started being someone I *wanted*,

but I know he's always been tangled up in a mess of emotions I carry around with me. Even if he weren't such a public figure, I'm certain he would've been impossible to forget.

I also don't know how to answer him, so I just lean into his touch. I cover his hand with one of mine and hold his wrist with the other, wordlessly begging him not to move.

'It could be, you know,' he murmurs.

My eyes open to search his face. The dark intensity in his gaze, the glimmer of hopefulness there, the firm press of his lips into a straight line.

'Could be what?'

'Romantic,' Ryan tells me. 'If you wanted.'

Something beeps a few times and the door flies open. Ryan's hand slips from my cheek, but it squeezes my fingers briefly before he lets go, while I'm still clinging to him, too overwhelmed for my brain to react in real time. He's already turning, laughing and saying, 'About damn time!' while I blink and try to get my head around that word.

Bryony lets out a horrified scream. 'What did you guys *do*? Look at this place! Ohmigod. Oh my *God*, I'm so fired.'

'I swear, this wasn't our fault. The sprinklers went off with the fire alarm,' Ryan says. 'I'll cut a cheque for the textbooks, if it's a problem. Alright, Hayden? Thanks for the rescue, team. Hope we didn't put you out too much.'

Bryony is too busy staring at something across the room to answer and instead says, 'Is that a *bra* hanging off the lights?'

We all look up. The long, fluorescent bulbs are suspended by wires from the ceiling to give a snazzy industrial look, and there, draped over one in the middle of the room, is the very bra Ryan flung away earlier and which neither of us could locate afterwards.

Fuck. Fuckity fuck fuck, this is just what I need – for Bryony, my new-bestie-turned-frenemy for the night to find out what happened and go blab about it to everybody like the inexorable gossip that she is before *I've* even had chance to get my head around it all.

It could be, you know.

I tuck the fire blanket a bit tighter around myself and bite my tongue.

Next to me, Ryan snickers, and masks it with a cough.

'What's been going on?' he asks quickly, and – God, I thought I'd rue the day I ever needed him to come to my rescue, but I almost melt with relief now. 'What happened with the power and everything?'

'Blown fuse,' Bryony says absently, still staring up at my bra dangling from the ceiling in confusion. She waves a hand. 'Hayden fixed it.'

'What happened to you two?' Hayden asks us, less concerned with the rogue underwear and more the bedraggled state both of us are in. 'You guys look like . . . Like . . .'

Ryan is laughing in response. 'Like a wet T-shirt contest, I know.'

'You look like you've been *shagging*,' Hayden says accusingly.

Romantic.

'Shut up!' screams Bryony. 'Ohmigod! They so have! You so did. Didn't you? Ohmigod, Ashleigh, don't you dare try to tell me that isn't your bra now!' With a peal of laughter, she reaches to try and pull the fire blanket away from me to prove it, but Ryan steps in between us with a laugh, slinging an arm around her shoulder and steering her out of the door – like I'm not even there at all. Kind of like Bryony did to me in the hall with Freddie.

'Ah, come on, Bryony – you know me, never one to kiss and tell. Would I do a thing like that? Better question: would *Ashleigh*? C'mon, don't we have a party to get back to?'

And he's leaving. Walking out, cracking a joke about the power cut, and I'm left huddled in the fire blanket, my clothes clinging to my damp skin and dripping cold water onto the floor, still reeling as Hayden asks if I'm okay.

With the other two gone, I suck it up and climb on the desk to retrieve my wet bra from the lights, turning my back to Hayden as I wrangle it on beneath my top. My best friend gives me my privacy and doesn't say anything, but once we're following after Ryan and Bryony and their noisy chatter and laughter, he nudges my arm with his and gives me a small, reassuring smile. I try to return it, and fail miserably.

If you wanted.

I wish I had the chance to answer Ryan.

But it feels too late, now. Like those people who opened up and apologised and kissed . . . They're ghosts of our past, left behind, and we go right back to being who we were ten years ago and two hours ago.

Like, in the cold light of day, this version of me could never say yes.

Chapter Forty-One

Bryony

'Most Likely to Become Famous'

Considering the absolute state of the last couple of hours and the years it's robbed from my life, the final hour of my epic ten-year school-reunion party flies by in a blur. The ragtag comeback one-night-only performance of the school band play a couple more pieces – and I do in fact absolutely slay my old *Swan Lake* solo.

They don't need to know I occasionally practise it.

And after that, we turn the music back up, the last of the fruit punch and pizza is consumed, and everybody throws themselves wholeheartedly into making the most of the night. I even agree to lead a little tour party up to the old common room when enough people pester me that they want to go see it; nobody tries to sneak out now they know I could be fired for their fuck-ups, and I finally feel myself relax a little, only just realising how much I was on high alert at the start of the night.

Ryan regales everybody with a tale of being stuck in a chemistry classroom with the sprinklers going off, his damp shirt plastered to him and drawing a few ogling eyes, even as he stands around with his jacket slung over his shoulder like this is an intentional fashion choice. I notice that before coming back into the hall, he cleaned off the distinct red smudge around his mouth that looked *suspiciously* the same colour as Ashleigh's lipstick.

Ashleigh, for her part, looks miserable as sin any time she's not plastering on a smile to talk to somebody, pretending to be chipper and like everything is A-okay.

I am *dying* to ask her what actually happened between her and Ryan and get all the gory deets, but I can't seem to get her back on her own. Actually, I think she might be avoiding me; she and Hayden stay attached at the hip. I know he was practically hiding behind her earlier, although this time, I'm not sure exactly who's looking out for who.

Steph, however, I do manage to corner.

'So,' I say to her, sidling up as soon as a couple of the art girls she was talking to flit away to move on to mingle with other people. 'You and Shaun, huh?'

Steph's face crumples, and – I immediately feel bad. Like I just called her out for a little white lie, like I was doing to people earlier. But she attempts a smile and looks across the room to where Shaun is stood next to his fiancée and with his old mates.

And she shakes her head. 'I don't think so. But I think we both needed the closure.'

'Oh. So, you guys didn't . . .? I just mean, you were gone for a while, is all, and you both looked a bit . . .'

'No,' she says, and I don't believe her, but – in fairness to Steph, she doesn't owe me the truth. I'm still, clearly, a huge gossip and delighted by any scandal that's not of my own making, and we haven't hung out in ten years. She doesn't owe me anything. But she does say, 'We talked a lot. About a lot of things. I suppose we weren't meant to end up together, after all.'

'Guess not.'

Steph puts her hand on my arm and squeezes. 'We used to be so sure we knew everything, but none of us had any idea, did we? Some things just don't work out the way we planned, but that's okay. It's not our only path, is it? There are plenty of others to take.'

'Like Curtis,' I say.

She tilts her head and even though she agrees, 'Yeah, like Curtis,' I get the feeling she's trying to tell me something else, and wasn't actually talking about her and Shaun at all.

It's only after she walks away to find Morgan and co. that her words sink in, and I think maybe she's right about how we really didn't have a clue back then.

I don't bother trying to get Shaun's side of the story, because he doesn't really move from his little crowd and asking him how that closure with his ex went when his fiancée is right there feels like a total dick move, and I've put my foot in it more than enough tonight already.

Instead, I carry on mingling, moving from one group to the next to chatter and giggle and soak up praise about the party and answer questions about being a teacher.

Which is, like, *weird*.

I don't like that people are being nice about it – aside from Freddie Loughton and RJ, who make sure to get in a dig about how sad they think it is, but Ryan shuts them up pretty quick with a glare and announces loudly, 'I think it's totally badass. And it's a great move, Bryony – long holidays that give you time to pursue your acting career as well, like teaching's not already keeping you busy enough. Serious kudos to you.'

But even without Ryan having to call his mates to toe the line, people are nice about it, and not even like they're just pretending because they feel bad for me. They want to know how I find it and what it's like being back here, and how I find the time and energy to do all the other stuff on top of that, and why didn't I say before?

And when I say, 'It isn't what I saw myself doing, that's for sure.'

They say, 'Do you like it, though?'

And I don't hesitate to tell them, 'Yeah. I love it. I wouldn't give it up for anything.'

But – I still wonder. I think, maybe . . . Maybe if the right role came along, the right opportunity . . .

When was the last time that happened, though?

And when was the last time I really believed in its existence? The more I think about it, the more I realise that for the last few years, those auditions and rejections and roles I've begrudgingly taken and resented, have only been because I can't let go of it – not because I want them. Not because any part of me likes it anymore.

When those thoughts get too big for my brain, I take a step back from the party to hang out on the fringes, by the last vestiges of the soft drinks, like a chaperone at the Year Seven disco, and I let my brain get carried away with it all. I think about Steph closing the door on her and Shaun and talking about different paths, and what Hayden said about how I made myself so small, and how much I hated the bitter, mean version of me that reared its head earlier tonight

331

in a desperate attempt at self-protection. I think about all those nights I cried myself to sleep, and all the mornings I woke up on a weekend or in school holidays, knowing I had an audition tape to film or a rehearsal to get to and how bone-tired the mere thought of that made me, and I'd want to sink back into bed and bury myself under my duvet and hide until it was time to go to work again, rather than face it.

The clock ticks on and the party whirls by. I watch the whole thing unfolding, the vigour and enthusiasm even greater now than it was earlier with some renewed gossip spreading through the crowd and more memories resurrected. I look at people laughing and smiling and hugging and dancing, standing over phones as they compare calendars and swap contact info and make new plans to go alongside old memories, and . . .

It feels *good*.

It's the same warm glow that I get when my kids give a killer performance, or when we pull off a good show and they get to bask in the applause. Pride in a job well done. In knowing *I made that happen. This is all because of me.*

It's the same exhilarating rush as when it used to be me soaking up the spotlight.

At ten-thirty, when I get up on the stage and stop the music, it's a sense of homecoming. Something right and final, slotting into place – the last piece of a jigsaw. I stand front and centre with the microphone in hand, lights bouncing off my sparkly jumpsuit, and all eyes on me, a hush falling over the crowd as they wait with bated breath for me to deliver my line.

'Hi, everybody! Just a few last words from me and then it'll be time to say our goodbyes. So tonight wasn't quite the party I'd planned for you all, and it's safe to say it didn't exactly go off without a hitch.' A laugh ripples through the crowd and I smile. 'But hey! I wanted to give you all an event you'd be talking about for years, and I think I managed that, right?'

'Whooo!' someone shouts, and most people join in and applaud. I throw my free arm out to one side and take a little bow, then slip the microphone out of its stand to move around the stage a little, getting comfortable.

'We had a power cut . . . a fire alarm . . . a slightly pitchy performance from the old orchestra . . . You laughed and danced and gossiped and kissed people you fancied and caught up with friends and enjoyed some spiked punch, which sounds about like how prom went, right? And honestly, I don't know what more any of us could have wanted from this reunion. So all that's left for me to do is thank you all for coming out tonight and making this such an epic party, and wish you all a safe journey home!'

People burst into cheers and applause, and someone is running up on stage.

I turn, a grin ready for Ryan as I prepare to hand him the mic so he can say a few words, but – it's not him.

It's Hayden who gives me a bright smile and takes the mic and says, 'Thanks, B,' before he looks out to face the crowd, grabbing my hand.

'Hang on, hang on, just one last thing!' he calls, and the microphone screeches. A collective wince doesn't deter Hayden, though, whose hand turns a little sweaty in mine. 'I think we've got one more person to thank for pulling everything together to make this all happen, and even putting her career on the line for it. Whatever else you achieve in life, B – you're a leading lady as far as everybody here is concerned. Tonight's Master of Ceremonies and the wizard behind the curtain – folks, give it up for Bryony Adams!'

Hayden hurls our hands high above our heads and practically yanks my arm out of the socket doing so, but then he lets go, returns the mic to the stand and joins in the storm of applause that's not for the party, not for the joy of tonight, but purely for *me*.

I watch Hassan and Josh and Shaun stomp their feet, and Ryan and the rugby lads throw punches in the air as they shout my name, and Ashleigh and Trendy Elise and Roisin applaud over their heads, and Steph and the girls jump up and down as they scream for me, all linked elbows and smudged mascara.

I take a bow, but it's not with my usual dramatic flourish, and I give a watery laugh nobody except maybe Hayden overhears, looking out at my sea of admirers as the ferocity of their standing ovation threatens to bowl me over.

When it dies down, voices replace the sound of the music I stopped and people make their way out to taxis and cars, the night over, and I leave the stage.

Truly, the curtain fell on tonight when we were all out on the tarmac and I stopped lying to everybody. But this feels like the true grand finale.

It's a perfect encore.

And my very best, if last, performance.

Chapter Forty-Two

Steph

'Most Likely to End Up Together'

'Have a safe drive home, lovely!' I squeeze Priya tight and give her boyfriend a quick hug goodbye too, then do the same with Thea while Morgan says goodbye to Curtis. When the four of us girls are done with hugs and kisses on the cheek, we end up all facing each other, standing in a close circle, and it suddenly seems every bit as impossible to say goodbye to them as it did when we all met up for a farewell sleepover before we would leave for university.

I don't know how I've gone ten years without these girls in my life; I don't know how we ever let things fizzle out when it's so clear we're still so very much each other's kind of people. I wriggle, trying to restrain myself, but Priya catches sight of me and laughs, launching herself forward, and the four of us pile into one massive group hug.

'I'm crying!' Morgan exclaims. 'Why am I crying? We're going to see each other in a few weeks!'

'You daft thing.' Thea tsks, but her voice sounds thick, too.

We all pull apart, a little bit sniffly and watery-eyed.

A taxi beeps its horn and it's Priya and Morgan's signal to go, along with their partners; they're both staying at the same bed and breakfast, so sharing a lift. I wave them off and say one more last goodbye to Thea before she and her boyfriend leave, too, heading back towards their car.

Still waiting for my mum to come to collect us, knowing she'll be stuck in the queue of cars now steadily coming in and out through the school gates, I turn back around to Curtis, whose arm immediately curls around me as he rubs the chill of goosebumps from my bare arms, folding me into him to share his body warmth.

I look up at him, and the doubts I expressed to Shaun feel like they belong to somebody else. They're so far away, so silly to even think about now . . .

Maybe what we had as teenagers *was* real, but so is this.

I don't quite regret leaving to catch up with Shaun, but I do regret how much I let the nostalgia take over, and how quickly I let myself give in to it. I think, if I'd come here tonight and kept my distance, part of me would have always wondered. At least now, I suppose, I know for sure.

Curtis and I agreed we'd talk more about it later, and while I'm sure we both meant when we were back home – not even simply back at my parents', but *home*, in our apartment – I suddenly become a ball of anxiety, all frayed nerves and roiling stomach. It's the same feeling I used to get before an exam.

I tug on Curtis's arm to make sure I've got his attention and he's not distracted by people-watching.

He knows without me having to say a word, because his brow crumples and he sighs heavily, breath washing over my

336

face. He looks so tired, so disappointed, and I realise he was hoping to put this off for as long as possible. I wonder if, if I hadn't initiated this now, he would ever have bothered to bring it up at all. For all he can engage in a hearty debate at work, I know he hates confrontation in his personal and private life.

I feel extra guilty for causing any kind of confrontation.

I have so much to say: apologies I need to make, explanations to help him understand what was going on in my mind – not to excuse my actions, but so that he knows none of this was his fault; reassurances that while I was tempted by a kiss, this wasn't some torrid affair carried out behind his back for years. It's impossible to know where to start, especially when, 'But I didn't *actually* kiss him,' is no defence at all and, 'I'm sorry,' is so paltry.

As I hastily order my thoughts and start to say something, Curtis surprises me by speaking first.

'Just tell me this – do you still love him?'

'I think part of me will always love him,' I admit easily. 'But I'm not *in* love with him. It's more like a memory I know I'll cherish, instead of one I'm wishing I could relive.'

He nods, slowly, surely, but the gravity in his expression doesn't concern me. If he were to rant and rave or cry and question why, I would scream and grovel and beg his forgiveness, but we are neither of us those people. This discussion is had with all the same steady affection as we do anything else; a time and consideration that we believe the other deserves, no matter the outcome.

I love this man. So much.

It wouldn't be enough, if he were to decide this isn't something he could ever forgive. But it would still mean something, to both of us.

337

And after a very long moment and the passing of several cars and more calls of goodbyes from old classmates to one another around us, Curtis asks me, 'Do you still want to marry me?'

'Yes,' I say, and I can't believe it would even be a question – can't believe I have given him cause to think otherwise. '*Yes*, I do. I absolutely, really, truly do.'

Curtis nods, and his other arm comes up to hug me close, and I burrow into him, sure my relief is palpable. It doesn't feel like a goodbye sort of embrace or a final clinging to one another before parting for good; this is more of a mooring, anchoring ourselves to one another, a confirmation. I breathe in the smell of him, now a little musty and sweaty compared to when we left the house, and he presses his lips to my temple, his head bowed over mine and neither of us moving for the longest time.

And, when he does, it's to straighten up and take me gently by the elbows.

'Then that's all that matters, Steph. All that matters to me, anyway.'

My breath shudders out of me and I'm so elated that my answering smile is wobbly; I might cry happy tears, at how big a heart he has – how sure he is of me.

Curtis smiles back and then gestures with a nod off somewhere behind me. Somehow, I know exactly who must be over there.

'Maybe you should go and say goodbye.'

It's not a test, or anything like that. It's a kindness, a closure for both of us, and I nod before I step out of Curtis's arms to make my way across the tarmac. When I look back, he's smiling, hands in his pockets, perfectly patient, and I'm so overcome with seeing that smile and his face and this man for the rest of my life that I could skip.

The rest of my life, admittedly, suddenly feels like a very long time, when I consider just how much has changed in the past ten years. But even if we aren't *forever*, or meant to end up together . . .

We're together now, and it's all I could want and more.

Chapter Forty-Three

Shaun

'Most Likely to End Up Together'

With Hassan and Josh both gone, I have no more immediate buffer between me and Aisha, and no idle chatter to distract me from the shock and sting of Steph's earlier rejection. Her presence is like a physical wedge between me and Aisha, and with the boys gone, I find my gaze drifting around the people leaving the party. Some are saying final goodbyes before making their way to the car park, or standing around while an old friend tries to book an Uber and fails because they're all booked up by someone else here at the reunion already and saying, 'No, really, it's no trouble! Come on, I'll give you a lift back!'

I have to look at anything except Aisha, when any look will be the last.

I'm not looking for *her*, until I am.

Steph is out of earshot, doling out final hugs to her friends, and I'd be willing to bet they'll all be posting selfies together from a night out or brunch or something soon. I'm surprised they never all stayed friends like me, Josh and Hassan did.

I'm a little bit jealous that she's chosen to bring *them* back into her new life, but not me.

She's smiling, looking so bright and brilliant, in spite of the dirt streaked on the torn skirt of her dress and graze on her elbow from falling over. She looks like she couldn't bear to be anywhere else, and when her fiancé wraps his arm around her, she settles there like she belongs, and I'm reminded of how definitively she made her choice.

'Something happened between you, didn't it?'

My entire body jolts at the accusation, and my silence is too long to be anything but guilty before I force myself to face Aisha.

She's breathing hard, chest rising and falling shallowly, and her expression is taut. She looks like she's bracing herself to be smacked with a frying pan in a slapstick comedy bit.

'You didn't kiss her,' she says. 'But *something* happened.'

She looks like she already knows the answer to that question.

'No, I didn't kiss her,' I finally manage. 'But I would have done.'

Her mouth pinches into a small, tight pout, but not before I see her lower lip wobble, and I hate myself. There's a small voice wheedling in the back of my mind saying I should've done a better job of hiding it; another that says I knew exactly what I was getting myself into when I asked Steph to go for a quiet chat. But mostly, right now, I regret that I did anything to make Aisha hurt like this and throw everything away, when we were so close to having such a perfect life together.

'I'm sorry,' I say, but the words are flat and useless, and they won't change anything now.

I don't know how to make any of this painless for her. I wish I could spare her the truth, but it's too late for that, and maybe a different, deeper truth would've come out instead eventually. One that says we're not meant to be and she's not the one and I'm not her one, and maybe I'm not even ready for that kind of serious, lifelong commitment anyway, not if this is the kind of thing I do given half the chance, and . . .

Whatever else, I know she deserves better than that.

'I'm sorry,' I say again, unable to find any other words.

'You're still in love with her,' Aisha says, but it isn't even remotely a question. There's not an inkling of doubt in her eyes – or mine, I guess, because she adds more agitatedly, 'I saw the way you looked at her. All night. Like you were missing half of yourself and – she was it. You've never looked at me like that.'

I shrug, palms up, because I have no defence. There's only surrender. And I hear myself say, 'I'm in love with a memory. Or – a ghost, maybe. Someone she used to be. Someone I . . . thought she still was.'

Aisha's answering mirthless smirk and short breath of laughter are cutting, and I take the blow. She bites her tongue, turning half away.

'She *rejected* you.'

I don't deny it.

'When we get home tomorrow,' Aisha tells me, twisting the ring off her finger and pressing it into my palm, cold and heavy, the diamond digging into my skin, 'you can pack up your things and find somewhere else to live.' Her eyes dart over my shoulder. 'I'll give you two a minute, shall I?'

I hear a quiet, 'Hello,' behind me as Aisha passes by, and

turn, and – there she is. I can only gawk in surprise, trying to figure out why she's here and why her fiancé looks so okay about it all from where he's standing, and if I should even give her the chance to say anything at all when Aisha is fumbling through her bag for a tissue and already tapping furiously at her phone but probably doesn't want to talk to me right now anyway, understandably, and . . .

Steph follows my gaze and her expression crumbles. I feel her sorrow like it's my own.

Maybe it is. Too much has happened tonight to make sense of right now.

'Are you two . . .?'

I nod, because there's not much else to say.

'I'm sorry,' Steph tells me, and I know she means it.

'It's . . .' Not okay, at all, but there's no undoing it now. It just is. I can't hold her responsible for the breakdown of my relationship with Aisha, not when how I acted tonight was all my own decision. I ask, 'Are you two . . .?'

She also nods, but it's a very different kind of answer to the one I gave. Hopeful, and shy, and content, just like the smile she tries to keep from her face.

'I'm happy for you,' I tell her. 'Really. You guys . . . You seem good together. I'm glad that we – that *I* didn't . . .'

'We both made some mistakes,' Steph says quietly, and looks suddenly awkward, unsure of her limbs and words and like when she was fifteen and didn't know how to act around me once we both realised we fancied each other but weren't going out yet. She steps a little closer, looking like she dared herself to do it, and then reaches for my arm, giving it a firm but brief squeeze near my elbow. 'I'll always care about you, Shaun. I just want you to know that.

I hope – I hope one day, we can be friends again. Like we used to be, before.'

Before, but not 'before' like when we were teenagers in love, 'before' like when we were kids who just hung out together.

'Maybe by the next reunion,' I say, only half joking. If I haven't quite gotten over Steph in ten years – maybe another ten will finally put those 'what-ifs' to rest. I look over at Aisha, now disappearing into a taxi she's sharing with some of the art girls, and hope she'll get over me better than I ever got over my first love. But she doesn't even glance back.

Steph hesitates, but then closes the distance between us and wraps me into a warm hug, one that's unfamiliar and new. I hug her back, recognising this moment for what it is: the two of us finally deciding to move on.

I wish it weren't the case, but I wish a lot of things were different right now.

The moment passes, Steph's arms loosening from around me, and I let her go.

'See you around, Shaun,' she says quietly, and offers me one last tender smile before she turns to go back to her fiancé, who's waiting by a car, leaning to talk to her mum through the car window. I lift a hand to wave when both of them look over.

And I murmur, mostly to myself, 'Goodbye, Steph.'

Chapter Forty-Four

Hayden

'Most Likely to Succeed'

If things had gone differently, my life would probably be the exact picture everybody else has painted for me tonight. I would be breaking down barriers of the limits others perceive and making strides forward in technology – probably within AI or robotics, as those were always my particular areas of interest, the ones I felt some kind of affinity to. I'd be creating code and products and programmes that people could never have imagined ten years ago, changing the landscape of the future. I would have accolades listed against my name on Wikipedia, lined up on a shelf at home against which I would join Zoom meetings with the best and brightest or top-tier investors, or record interviews for news outlets. Perhaps I would even have collaborated with Ashleigh to build something for use in surgeries to complement her research.

But, I think, if things had gone differently, I wouldn't even be friends with Ashleigh anyway these days. If I hadn't dropped out of uni and wanted to live vicariously through her, we wouldn't have messaged as much as we did, and she wouldn't have made a point of visiting and hanging out any time she was home for term break, and we wouldn't have become such close friends. We would both have been too busy with our courses to do much more than exchange occasional texts about how things were going and how we 'must catch up soon', without ever actually organising anything.

Let's just say I stuck it out at uni. I'd have let Lucy go ahead and have Margot while I dedicated myself to finishing my studies, an actively absent father. I know myself – I would've been so intent on assuring our future that I'd neglect the present – and neglect Lucy and Margot right along with it. Maybe we wouldn't have gone on to have Skye.

I'd have been too focused on the next step. That wouldn't, in this alternate lifetime, have been 'sign Margot up for school' or 'arrange her birthday party at the soft play; don't forget to invite Jesse from swimming class'. It would've been graduating with my master's, deciding whether or not to pursue a PhD or take up any of the job offers I was sure I'd receive, which route would be the *best*. Not for my family. For me. For what I wanted to achieve.

For those accolades that never were, the breakthroughs that someone else would inevitably be credited for in this timeline I chose to be in now.

It's a world of what-ifs, and as I stay behind to help Bryony clean up the hall, I let my mind play out through all of them, exploring each branch in the multiverse, the versions of my life that might exist elsewhere . . .

And I know that, if I could go back and make all those decisions consciously, with the benefit of hindsight – I would do them all exactly as I have done.

Ashleigh and Ryan stick around for a while, helping us

346

clean up even after most everybody else goes home, and I wonder which of them will cave first – they've gone back to their earlier routine of dancing around each other, pretending not to acknowledge the other's existence even as they orbit like binary stars, bound by a common centre of gravity, unable to quite get away.

Which means that, somehow, Bryony and Ashleigh have buddied up in the cleaning efforts, and Ryan and I have been stuck together.

We work mainly in companionable silence, which is how I hear Bryony confront Ashleigh and ask, 'Are you mad at me?'

'Why'd you think that?' Ash bites back, sounding quite mad at her. It makes Ryan and I exchange a look; he smirks knowingly, shaking his head, and it occurs to him that he might know my best friend as well as I do, in spite of their rivalry and hatred for each other. Ashleigh, meanwhile, sighs and tells Bryony, 'You just acted like kind of a bitch, earlier. Getting in between me and Freddie like I didn't matter. Like, it's cool, it's – whatever, but . . .'

'Ohmigod, no! That's totally not what happened . . .'

As Bryony starts gushing explanations and apologies, I see Ryan's face cloud over, some emotion shuttering down that seems guarded, and when he notices me looking, he gives a small shrug.

'Think I blew it,' he says.

'Blew what?'

'It,' he repeats, as if it clarifies anything at all. Then he jerks his head towards the girls. 'With Ashleigh.'

'Oh.'

She hasn't said much about what happened in the chemistry lab, but she's been staring longingly at Ryan all night since, and looking like there's more going on than she could even begin to explain.

I take pity on him – surprised that, for all that's happened tonight, it's me offering the captain of the rugby team, Mr Popular, any amount of sympathy – and pat his shoulder awkwardly, a bit like he did to mine at the beginning of the night.

'I don't think you have,' I tell him. 'She can be a bit prickly, but . . . she wouldn't be avoiding you if it didn't matter to her.'

'You think?'

I'm not surprised that Ryan has this softer, vulnerable side, but I *am* surprised it's Ashleigh that's brought it out in him. He brightens a little as he looks in her direction again, where she's now giggling over something with Bryony, the two of them leaning on each other, the air cleared and a new friendship forming.

Something brightens in me, too, from the intense amount of self-reflection I've done tonight, and I find myself saying, 'Hey, Ryan? You, um . . . You still got that friend looking for developers for his start-up?'

He flashes me a grin and winks. 'Haven't lost him in the last couple of hours as far as I know. Here, give me your contact details – I'll put you in touch first thing Monday. I'll give you my number, too, just in case . . .'

We swap info, and something warm and comfortable settles in the pit of my stomach and spreads through me, like hot chocolate on a snow day. It feels right. A good next step. Something that doesn't need to turn my life upside down and put it 'back on track', because there's nothing *off*-track, but something to rekindle an old spark and passion.

There are things that, yes, after tonight, I wish were different about my life. Things about myself I would like to change and adjust, because I have let them fall too far by the wayside. But those fundamentals that have shaped the rest of my life . . . The girls, Lucy, my friendships, my home – I wouldn't give that up for anything.

We carry on cleaning up and after Ashleigh and Ryan leave, I end up helping Bryony to mop up the water in the science block, still cradling this feeling of being able to do something for myself – for this new version of myself, not the one I left behind ten years ago.

Bryony catches my eye, something in my own smile making her brighten, too. I expect her to try and tease me, or needle me about what's put such a spring in my step, but instead she just lets me be. Giving me breathing space I don't have to ask for, for once.

'I think I've got an answer for you, by the way,' Bryony says to me.

'Hmm?' I pause, wringing water out of the mop we borrowed from the caretaker's office. She, meanwhile, winces at the state of the textbooks, about a third of which are unsalvageable from the water damage they sustained.

'When we were talking, earlier. And I asked you if you were genuinely, really happy, and you asked if *I* was. I think I've got an answer for you now.'

'Oh?' I lean on the mop and push my glasses up my nose, waiting patiently. 'What is it?'

'Yes.' She beams and it's blinding. It's the most sincere she's looked all night, and the most like herself, too. 'I am genuinely, really happy.'

'Good,' I say.

Then I duck my head before changing my mind, and instead maintain eye contact with her as I finally offer up a proper answer of my own.

'I am, too.'

Chapter Forty-Five

Ashleigh

'Most Likely to Kill Each Other'

The night ends slowly, little by little, pieces of it falling away and being packed up until it ends suddenly and all at once.

One minute, I'm helping Bryony collect up her colourful little box-lights from the floor of the school hall, swapping numbers and blushing and shushing her as she giggles and tries to wheedle out of me all the details about what happened with me and Ryan . . .

'I need to know what went down!' she whispers, none too quietly, cheeks flushed and eyes glittering. 'Or, at least *who* went down!'

I cut her a look, but give in to some childish part of me that never got the chance to really do this. I break into a grin and wiggle my eyebrows, then glance at Ryan and pull a face with a small shrug, and Bryony's squeal is loud enough to make both him and Hayden look over from putting empty plastic drinks bottles into a bin bag.

And then I'm hugging her goodbye and promising Hayden to come visit him and the girls in two weeks but that, yes,

I'll text him when I get back to the hotel safe and we'll talk more tomorrow, and I'm leaving from the main entrance with Ryan just half a step behind me.

I'm not sure if this means we're leaving *together*, or if we just happen to leave at the same time.

Ryan breaks the silence. 'I reckon she fancies him.'

'What?'

'Bryony. Fancies Hayden.'

I laugh, because it's a laughable concept, but mostly only because of how different they were at school. Still, I'm not wholly convinced there's any attraction between them as adults.

'As if,' I say. 'There's no way. They're just friends, I'm telling you. There's nothing going on between them.'

Ryan's face splits into a smug grin, eyebrows twisting almost in sympathy for how wrong he thinks I am. It's an insufferable look and one I know well, one that makes me want to drag him back inside to spy on Hayden and Bryony and the rest of their clean-up just so I can point out all the ways *he's* wrong.

'I don't know, they looked pretty pally to me all of a sudden.'

'They look like two people who got stuck spending time together tonight, and bonded over it a little.'

'Oh, yeah? And that's why Hayden's stayed behind to help clean, is it?'

'That's because he's a nice guy and he can't help himself. It's the dad in him. He likes helping people. He's always doing stuff like that; it's not because he *likes*-likes her.'

And, God, did this man really make me say '*like*-like', like that?

'*Right*,' he drawls, and steps closer, readjusting his hold on his still-damp suit jacket over his shoulder. His school tie still hangs loose, undone, around his neck, and my attention is drawn momentarily to it, and then to the triangle of smooth brown skin bared by the few open buttons of his shirt . . . 'And that's why they both insisted they would finish up and couldn't get rid of us quickly enough? *Please*.'

'You've completely misread the signals. It's actually making me feel sorry for you, Ryan, how wrong you are about this.'

'And your need to constantly be right all the time is incorrigible, Easton.'

'Incorrigible? That's a mighty big word, coming from you.'

Somehow, somewhere within this petty argument, Ryan's gotten up close, or I've stepped into him, because now our bodies are flush and my insult doesn't pack a punch the way it usually would have. It comes out light and teasing, a shadow of what it used to be, and it makes Ryan smirk in genuine amusement. His hand slips to catch my waist, yanking me just a little closer so that I lose my balance and my hands catch his chest to keep me from stumbling.

Neither of us speaks, but there's some sort of understanding that passes between us in the moment before I close my eyes and his hand shifts to splay across my lower back.

And, as simply and suddenly as that, I'm kissing Ryan Lawal again.

I'm not kissing the guy who used to make my life a misery and needle at me every chance he got, while I practically made it my life's mission to tear him down whenever I thought he got too big for his boots. I'm not kissing the guy

353

whose smug face makes some angry, feral thing claw inside my chest in a mix of jealousy or resentment or plain old irritation.

I'm kissing someone who knows me maybe better than I know myself, someone surprisingly funny and devastatingly good-looking, who thinks about how I take my coffee in the mornings and isn't, underneath it all, anything but the person he's always shown himself to be.

I'm kissing Ryan Lawal and I never want to stop.

But the crunch of tyres and grumble of an engine comes towards me and – that's one of our taxis. It means our time is up. Tonight is, at last, over.

It could be, you know. Romantic. If you wanted.

I ignore the approaching car and slide my fingers through Ryan's short hair, deepening the kiss rather than ending it.

Tonight might be over, but that doesn't mean this has to be.

Chapter Forty-Six

Ryan

'Most Likely to Kill Each Other'

The car idles for a solid four or five minutes before Ashleigh and I finally peel ourselves apart, and I catch a glimpse of the driver's unimpressed face. He probably thinks we're acting like randy teenagers.

He's not wrong, really.

I look long enough to see that it's Ashleigh's Uber, not mine.

Part of me wants to pull her back in for another kiss and ask if I can come with her – we can continue this back at her hotel; I'll cancel my ride. We can fuck and kiss and stay up talking and anything, *everything*, to mean this night doesn't have to end.

Because tomorrow, I know what will happen. She'll wake up and think of me with all the usual revulsion and condescension, wonder just what the hell she must've been thinking to hook up with me, laugh at how stupid I was to suggest this could ever be anything even remotely romantic, and she'll go right back to hating me.

And then I'll go right back to hating her, too, and we'll replace the memories of tonight with excuses about booze and nostalgia and happenstance, and erase them in favour of the bitter ones we both still carry around from school.

We'll both make our own way back to London, moving in different circles and always conveniently missing each other, and I'll go back to work and think to myself, *What would wind her up the most? What would be so outrageously successful, such a complete win for me, that it'll drive her crazy when she sees me talking about it on the news or finds an article about it on her phone?*

Even as I think it, I cringe. I sound like some kind of reverse stalker.

I walk her to the car, opening the door for her, and I watch Ashleigh physically bite back a comment about how she can get her own doors thank you very much. Her lips fuse into a tight line, but there's a glint in her eyes that makes her mouth soften into more of a smile as she gets in. Her face is pale and freckly, her ruined makeup washed off at some point earlier tonight, likely with a rough blue paper towel in the bathrooms. Her hair is in limp, damp waves around her shoulders and I want to run my fingers through it.

I brace one hand against the door and the other against the car roof, and lean down towards her.

But, I know Ashleigh, and I know myself, and I think it's better if – I don't.

We'll just keep tonight contained, a one-off. A lapse in judgement on both our parts.

It's better that way.

What do I think is going to happen here exactly? She laughed in my face at the idea of anything *romantic* between us, and I don't know what I was thinking even saying it in the first place. I don't need to see the regret on her face tomorrow morning, and I don't need to experience just how much of a gut-punch her rejection will be when it inevitably comes.

I really don't need to think about whatever feelings I have for Ashleigh, and just how deep they run.

So, I don't ask to go home with her.

Instead I wink and say, 'Been fun, Easton. Look me up if you fancy doing it again sometime, yeah? Maybe on *my* desk next time.'

And at the same time her hand lands feather-light on my arm and she says, 'Do you want to get breakfast tomorrow?'

We both stop, and stare, and pull back.

'What?' I say.

'*Excuse me?*' she snaps.

'What did *you* say?'

'Breakfast, tomorrow. But if you're only looking for a booty call, then you can forget about it, and you can shove your—'

'You want to get breakfast?'

She sniffs, angry, like she no longer deigns to care for the notion. But she does, and we both know it, and I grin widely, which only makes her scowl at me.

'I'd really like to get breakfast with you, Ash.'

She blinks, giving me a sidelong look. Searching for the piss-take and the joke that aren't there, just like I've been telling her.

For once, she decides to take me at face value, and it's a weight off my shoulders.

'Okay.' A smile steals over her face, blue eyes brightening. 'Breakfast. I – I don't have your number.'

'I have your Insta. I'll DM you.'

She laughs. 'Of course you will.'

I duck down into the car just as she leans up out of it, each of us stealing one last kiss.

One last, but only as far as tonight is concerned.

I close the door and wave her off, and as soon as the car is out of sight, mine arrives. I climb in, say hello and exchange some polite small talk with my driver, even as I'm busy opening up Instagram on my phone and finding Ashleigh's profile to message her.

Easton, it's me, I say. *Sliding into your DMs as promised.*

Now who's being incorrigible? x comes her reply, and that kiss makes my heart squeeze.

Breakfast, I think, settling back more comfortably in the car, as three dots appear on the screen and Ashleigh types another message. Breakfast, and then everything else.

'School reunion, huh?' the driver says to me, and whistles. 'Dropped off some people earlier coming from here. You stayed pretty late.'

'Yeah. Stayed behind to help tidy up.'

'Good of you. So, how was it? Memorable night? Ready to do it all again in another ten years?'

My phone buzzes in my hand as Ashleigh sends me her number, and a suggestion of where to meet tomorrow morning that, obviously, I'll have to disagree with and come up with an alternative, just for old time's sake.

'Yeah,' I say out loud, and grin down at my phone. 'Ready to do it all again.'

Acknowledgements

Most likely to . . . plan a get-together! First up, the physics gang. I'm glad our little reunions aren't half as chaotic as this one, even if it sometimes involves a mad dash for the train . . . or a jumper flung up onto the lights in the library that someone can't find. Love you guys. P.S. Emily – hope you think this one is totally 'pro-dank'.

Most likely to . . . get brunch! The Gobble Gals (see, nary a 'straddle' to be found in this one!) Can't wait for our next mimosa.

Most likely to . . . listen to my rambling voice notes as I suddenly discover what a softie my male main character is! Lauren, you are SO patient and always a huge help in my very messy writing process. Hope you appreciate Ryan doing The Lean.

Most likely to . . . make me laugh! Amy, you're always so uplifting, and Aimee – I don't know anybody who is always so glam and fabulous.

Most likely to . . . be long-distance friends! The Cluster – love you guys and all your support from across the pond! Love the late-night chats I get to catch up on in the morning, and hopefully we can arrange a (very non-dramatic, non-chaotic) reunion of our own soon!

Most likely to . . . joke that they don't like my book but actually love it! Kat, hopefully this one's another hit for you! Thanks to all my family for your support, even if I make it tricky to keep up with which 'new book' I'm talking about working on sometimes!

Most likely to . . . be the wizard behind the curtain! As ever, thank you to my absolutely incredible publishing team: my brilliant agent Clare and editors for this one: Ruth, Molly, and Bec; and Bryony and Lucie on the P&M side! I'm so lucky to have you all on side and bringing this book to shelves. Thanks for all you do.

Also by Beth Reekles from Sphere...

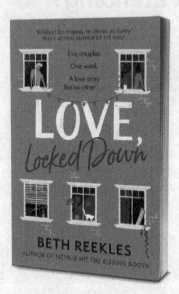

> 'Truly wonderful and brilliant ... Beth is officially the new queen of hilarious rom-coms'
>
> LUCY VINE

> 'Brilliant! So original, so clever, so funny'
>
> HELLY ACTION,
> author of *The Shelf*

Five couples. One week. A love story like no other...

When an apartment block is put on lockdown, its residents are in for a whirlwind week. In Flat 14, wild and reckless **Imogen** is stuck living with a one-night-stand whose name she can't remember.

Upstairs, **Isla** and **Danny** are still in the honeymoon period, but a warts-and-all week together so early in the relationship could make or break their romance. Meanwhile, **Zach** and **Serena's** steady relationship is on tenterhooks, and pineapple on pizza might actually be the last straw.

In Flat 22, **Olivia's** Maid of Honour duties are pushing her to the edge as a wedding-planning weekend has turned into an entire (nightmarish) week... And speaking of weddings, this whole thing has made Ethan realise he wants to spend the rest of his life with **Charlotte**, if only he can surprise her with the perfect proposal – and find a way to sneak her into the building...

OUT NOW